‘This is the [illegible] s to be both fascinating and destined for the bestsellers’
Independent on Sunday

‘Peter James’s superior thriller . . . gripping . . . nail-biting . . . a satisfyingly complex puzzle’
The Times

‘Ingenious plotting, high suspense and tight writing should guarantee instant lift-off for this new series’
Daily Mail

‘A terrific tale of greed, seduction and betrayal’
Daily Telegraph

‘Peter James is a very gifted writer and he kept me guessing with his relentless pacing and suspense. I would be reading what I thought was a lead to the climax, only to notice I was only halfway through the book. This book is a gem’
Crimespree

‘At a time when more than ever we feel beholden to be seen with pretentious novels which, in the privacy of our own homes, we find hard to pick up, what a relief to finally find a book which is well nigh literally impossible to put down’
Julie Burchill

'With memorable characters and nail-biting tension, *Looking Good Dead* is a terrifying "it could happen to you" thriller'

Kathy Reichs

'I couldn't put it down . . . even better than the first'

Independent

'Full of gripping twists and turns'

Guardian

'Will have you glued to your deckchair'

Observer

DEAD MAN'S FOOTSTEPS

Peter James was educated at Charterhouse then at film school. He lived in North America for a number of years, working as a screenwriter and film producer before returning to England. His novels, many of which have been *Sunday Times* Top 10 bestsellers, have been translated into thirty languages and three have been filmed. All his novels reflect his deep interest in the world of the police, with whom he does in-depth research, as well as science, medicine and the paranormal. He has produced numerous films, including *The Merchant of Venice*, starring Al Pacino, Jeremy Irons and Joseph Fiennes. He divides his time between his homes in Notting Hill in London and near Brighton in Sussex.

Also by Peter James

DEAD LETTER DROP
ATOM BOMB ANGEL
BILLIONAIRE
POSSESSION
DREAMER
SWEET HEART
TWILIGHT
PROPHECY
ALCHEMIST
HOST
THE TRUTH
DENIAL
FAITH
PERFECT PEOPLE

Children's novel

GETTING WIRED!

The Roy Grace series

DEAD SIMPLE
LOOKING GOOD DEAD
NOT DEAD ENOUGH
DEAD TOMORROW
DEAD LIKE YOU
DEAD MAN'S GRIP

DEAD MAN'S FOOTSTEPS

PETER JAMES

PAN BOOKS

First published 2008 by Macmillan

This edition published 2011 by Pan Books
an imprint of Pan Macmillan, a division of Macmillan Publishers Limited
Pan Macmillan, 20 New Wharf Road, London N1 9RR
Basingstoke and Oxford
Associated companies throughout the world
www.panmacmillan.com

ISBN 978-1-4472-2295-8

1 3 5 7 9 8 6 4 2

A CIP catalogue record for this book is available from
the British Library.

Typeset by SetSystems Ltd, Saffron Walden, Essex
Printed and bound by CPI Group (UK) Ltd, Croydon, CR0 4YY

TO DAVE GAYLOR

Some of this story takes place on the days surrounding the terrible events of 9/11. With deepest respect to the victims and all who lost loved ones.

1

If Ronnie Wilson had known, as he woke up, that in just a couple of hours he would be dead, he would have planned his day somewhat differently.

For a start he might not have bothered to shave. Or wasted so many of those last precious minutes gelling his hair, then messing around with it until he was satisfied. Nor would he have spent quite so long polishing his shoes, or getting the knot of his expensive silk tie absolutely right. And he sure as hell would not have paid an exorbitant eighteen dollars – which he really could not afford – for the one-hour service to have his suit pressed.

To say that he was blissfully unaware of the fate awaiting him would be an exaggeration. All forms of joy had been absent from his canon of emotions for so long, he no longer had any idea what *bliss* was. He didn't even experience bliss any more in those fleeting final seconds of orgasm, on the rare occasions when he and Lorraine still made love. It was as if his balls had become as numb as the rest of him.

In fact recently – and somewhat to Lorraine's embarrassment – when people asked him how he was, he had taken to replying with a brief shrug of his shoulders and the words, 'My life is shit.'

The hotel room was shit too. It was so small that if you fell over you wouldn't even hit the floor. It was the cheapest room the W had, but at least the address helped him to maintain appearances. If you stayed at a W in Manhattan, you were a *somebody*. Even if you were sleeping in the broom closet.

Ronnie knew he needed to get himself into a more positive mode – and mood. People responded to the vibes you gave out, particularly when you were asking for money. Nobody would give money to a loser, not even an old friend – at least, not the kind of money he needed at this moment. And certainly not this particular old friend.

Checking out the weather, he peered through the window, craning his neck up the sheer grey cliff of the building facing him across 39th Street until he could see the narrow slit of sky. The realization that it was a fine morning did nothing to lift his spirits. It merely felt as if all the clouds had drained out of that blue void and were now in his heart.

His fake Bulgari watch told him it was 7.43 a.m. He had bought it on the internet for forty pounds, but hey – who could tell it wasn't real? He had learned a long time ago that expensive watches gave off an important message to people you were trying to impress: if you cared enough about a detail like time to buy one of the best watches in the world, then you would probably care just as much about the money they were going to entrust you with. Appearances weren't everything, but they mattered a lot.

So, 7.43. Time to rock and roll.

He picked up his Louis Vuitton briefcase – also fake – placed it on top of his packed overnight bag and left the room, wheeling his luggage behind him. Emerging from the elevator on the ground floor, he skulked past the front desk. His credit cards were so maxed out he probably didn't even have enough to settle the hotel bill, but he would have to worry about that later. His BMW – the swanky blue convertible that Lorraine liked to drive around in, posing to her friends, was about to be repossessed, and the mortgage company was about to foreclose on his home. Today's meeting, he thought grimly, was the last-chance saloon. A promise he was calling in. A ten-year-old promise.

He just hoped it had not been forgotten.

*

Sitting on the subway, cradling his bags between his knees, Ronnie was aware that something had gone wrong in his life, but he couldn't really put a finger on what it was exactly. Plenty of his contemporaries from school had gone on to have big successes in their fields, leaving him floundering in their wake, getting increasingly desperate. Financial advisers, property developers, accountants, lawyers. They had their big-swinging-dick houses, their trophy wives, their kids-to-die-for. What did he have?

Neurotic Lorraine, who spent the money he didn't have on endless beauty treatments she seriously did not need, on designer clothes they seriously could not afford, and on picking up the tabs of absurdly expensive lunches of lettuce leaves and mineral water with her anorexic friends, who were all far richer than they were, in whatever happened to be the latest hip restaurant-of-the-week. And despite a fortune spent on infertility treatment, she had still been unable to produce the child he so badly wanted. The only expenditure of which he had really approved had been her boob job.

But of course Ronnie was too proud to admit to her the mess he was in. And, ever the optimist, he always believed there was a solution just around the corner. A chameleon, he blended perfectly into his environment. As a used-car dealer, then an antiques dealer and an estate agent, he used to look pin-sharp, with a gift of the gab that was, unfortunately, better than his financial acumen. After the estate agency business went down the toilet, he had rapidly segued into property developing, where he used to look convincing in jeans and a blazer. Then, as the banks foreclosed on his twenty-home development that ran aground over planning issues, he reinvented himself yet again as a financial adviser to the rich. That business hit the buffers too.

Now he was here in the hope of convincing his old friend Donald Hatcook that he knew the secret of making money out of the next golden goose – biodiesel. Donald was rumoured to have made north of a billion in derivatives – whatever they were – and had lost only a paltry couple of hundred thousand investing in Ronnie's failed estate agency business ten years ago. Claiming to accept all his friend's reasons for the failed enterprise, he had assured Ronnie he would back him again one day.

Sure, Bill Gates and all the other entrepreneurs on the planet were looking for the way forward in the new, environmentally friendly biofuel market – and had the money to throw at it to make it happen – but Ronnie reckoned he had identified a niche. All he had to do this morning was convince Donald. Donald was sharp, he'd see it. He'd get it. It ought to be – in New York parlance – a slam dunk.

In fact, the further the train headed downtown, while he mentally rehearsed his pitch to Donald, the more confident Ronnie became. He felt himself turning into the Michael Douglas character in *Wall Street*: Gordon Gekko. And he sure looked the part. Just like the dozen other sharply dressed Wall Street players sitting in this swaying carriage with him. If any of them had just half of his troubles, they were keeping it well hidden. They all looked so damned confident. And if they bothered to glance at him, they would have seen a tall guy with lean good looks and slicked-back hair who looked equally confident.

People said that if you hadn't made it by the time you were forty, then you were never going to make it. He was coming up to forty-three in just three weeks' time.

And he was coming up to his station. Chambers Street. He wanted to walk the last few blocks.

He emerged into the fine Manhattan morning and checked his bearings on the map the hotel concierge had given him last night. Then he looked at his watch: 8.10 a.m. From past experience of navigating New York office buildings, he reckoned he should allow himself a good fifteen minutes to get to Donald's office once he reached the man's building. And it was a good five minutes' walk from here, the concierge had told him – and that was assuming he did not get lost.

Passing a sign informing him he was now on Wall Street, he walked past a Jamba Juice shop on his right and a shop offering 'Expert Tailoring and Alteration', then entered the packed Downtown Deli.

The place smelled of stewed coffee and frying eggs. He sat on a red leather bar stool and ordered freshly squeezed orange juice, a latte, scrambled eggs with a side order of bacon and wheat toast. As he waited for his food, he flipped through the business plan once more, then, looking at his watch again, mentally calculated the time difference between New York and Brighton.

England was five hours ahead. Lorraine would be having lunch. He gave her a quick call on her mobile, told her he loved her. She wished him luck in the meeting. Women were easy to please, just a bit of lovey-dovey flannel every now and then, the occasional lines of poetry, and one or two pieces of expensive-looking jewellery – but not too often.

Twenty minutes later, as he was paying the bill, he heard a massive bang somewhere in the distance. A guy on the stool next to him said, 'Jesus, what the fuck was that?'

Ronnie collected his change and left a decent tip, then stepped out into the street to continue his journey towards Donald Hatcook's office, which, according to the information that had been emailed to him, was on the eighty-seventh floor of the South Tower of the World Trade Center.

It was 8.47 a.m. on the morning of Tuesday, September 11th, 2001.

2

OCTOBER 2007

Abby Dawson had chosen this flat because it felt secure. At least, in as much as she was ever going to feel secure *anywhere* at this moment.

Apart from the fire escape at the back, which could only be opened from inside, and a basement fire exit, there was just one entrance. It was eight floors directly below her, and the windows gave her a clear view up and down the street.

Inside, she had turned the flat into a fortress. Reinforced hinges, steel plating, three sets of deadlocks on the front door and on the fire escape door at the back of the tiny utility room, and a double safety chain. Any burglar trying to break in here was going to go home empty-handed. Unless they were driving a tank, no one was going to get in unless she invited them.

But just in case, as back-up, she had a canister of Mace pepper spray in easy reach, a hunting knife and a baseball bat.

It was ironic, she thought, that the first time in her life she was able to afford a home large and luxurious enough to entertain guests she had to live here on her own, in secrecy.

And there was so much to enjoy here. The oak flooring, the huge cream sofas with their white and chocolate-brown cushions, the sharp, modern art on the walls, the home-cinema system, the high-tech kitchen, the massive, deliciously comfortable beds, the under-floor heating in the bathroom and the smart guest shower room which she had not yet used – at least not for what it was *intended.*

It was like living in one of the designer pads she used to covet on the pages of glossy magazines. On fine days, the afternoon sun streamed in, and on blustery days, like today, when she opened a window she could taste the salt on the air and hear the cries of gulls. Just a couple of hundred yards beyond the end of the street, and the junction with Kemp Town's busy Marine Parade, was the beach. She could walk along it for miles to the west and along under the cliffs to the east, past the Marina.

She liked the neighbourhood too. Small shops close by, safer than going into a large supermarket, because she could always check who was in there first. All it needed was for one person to recognize her.

Just one.

The only negative was the lift. Extremely claustrophobic at the best of times, and more prone than ever to panic attacks recently, Abby never liked to ride in any lift alone unless she absolutely had to. And the jerky capsule the size of a vertical two-seater coffin that serviced her flat, and which had got stuck a couple of times in the last month – fortunately with someone else in it – was one of the worst she had ever experienced.

So normally, up until the past couple of weeks, when workmen renovating the flat below hers had turned the staircase into an obstacle course, she walked up and down. It was good exercise, and if she had some heavy shopping bags – well, that was easy – she would send them up in the lift on their own and climb the stairs. On the very rare occasions she encountered one of her neighbours, then she would ride up shoulder to shoulder with them. But mostly they were so old they never went out much. Some seemed as old as this mansion block itself.

The few younger residents, like Hassan, the smiling Iranian banker who lived two floors below her and sometimes threw all-night parties – the invites to which she always politely declined – seemed to be away, somewhere else, most of the time. And at weekends, unless Hassan was in residence, this whole west wing of the block was so silent it seemed to be inhabited only by ghosts.

In a way, she was a ghost too, she knew. Only leaving the safety of her lair after dark, her once long, blonde hair cropped short and dyed black, sunglasses on her face, jacket collar turned up, a stranger in this city where she had been born and grown up, where she had been a business studies student and had once worked bars, done temporary secretarial jobs, had boyfriends and, before the travel bug hit her, had even fantasized she would raise a family.

Now she was back. In hiding. A stranger in her own life. Desperate not to be recognized by anyone. Turning her face away on the rare occasions when she passed someone she knew. Or saw an old friend in a bar and immediately had to leave. God damn it, she was lonely!

And scared.

Not even her own mother knew she was back in England.

Just turned twenty-seven three days ago – and that was some birthday party, she thought ironically. Getting smashed up here on her own, with a bottle of Moët et Chandon, an erotic movie on Sky and a vibrator with a dead battery.

She used to pride herself on her natural good looks. Brimful of confidence, she could go out to any bar, any disco, any party and have the pick of the crop. She was good at chatting, good at laying on the charm, good at playing vulnerable, which long ago she had understood was what guys liked. But now she was vulnerable for real, and she was really not enjoying that.

Not enjoying being a fugitive.

Even though it would not be for ever.

The shelves, tables and floors of the flat were piled high with books, CDs and DVDs, ordered from Amazon and from Play.com. During the past two months on the run she had read more books, seen more films and watched more television than ever before in her life. She occupied much of the rest of her time by doing an online course in Spanish.

She had come back because she thought she would be safe here. Dave had agreed. That this was the one place *he* would not dare show his face. The only place on the planet. But she could not be completely sure.

She had another reason for coming to Brighton – a big part of her agenda. Her mother's condition was getting slowly worse and she needed to find her a well-run private nursing home where she could have some quality of life in the years remaining. Abby did not want to see her end up in one of those terrible National Health Service geriatric wards. She had already identified a beautiful home in the countryside nearby. It was expensive, but she could afford to keep her mother there for years now. All she had to do was lie low for just a little longer.

Her phone pinged suddenly with an incoming text. She looked down at the display and smiled when she saw who it was from. The one thing that helped sustain her was these texts, which she received every few days.

> *Absence diminishes small loves and increases great ones, as the wind blows out the candle and blows up the bonfire.*

She thought for some moments. A benefit of having so much time on her hands was that she could surf the net for hours without feeling guilty. She loved collecting quotations, and texted back one she had saved up.

> *Love is not gazing at each other. Love is staring together in the same direction.*

For the first time in her life she had met a man who stared in the same direction as herself. Right now it was at just a name on a map. Images downloaded from the web. A place she went to in her dreams. But soon they would both be going there for real. She just had to be patient for a little longer. They both needed to be.

She closed *The Latest* magazine, where she had been browsing dream houses, crushed out her cigarette, drained her glass of Sauvignon and began her pre-exit checks.

First she walked to the window and peered down through the blinds at the wide terrace of Regency houses. The sodium glow of the street lights bled orange into every shadow. It was dark enough, with a howling autumn gale blasting rain as hard as buckshot against the window-panes. As a child she used to be scared of the dark. Now, ironically, it made her feel safe.

She knew the cars that were regularly parked there on

both sides, with their residents' parking stickers. Ran her eyes over each of them. She used not to be able to tell one make from another, but now she knew them all. The grimy, bird-shit-spattered black Golf GTi. The Ford Galaxy people carrier belonging to a couple in a flat across the street who had grizzly twins and seemed to spend their lives lugging shopping and collapsible strollers up and down the stairs. The odd-looking little Toyota Yaris. An elderly Porsche Boxster belonging to a young man she had decided was a doctor – he probably worked at the nearby Royal Sussex County Hospital. The rusty white Renault van with soggy tyres and a FOR SALE notice written in red ink on a strip of brown cardboard stuck in its passenger-door window. Plus another dozen or so cars whose owners she knew by sight. Nothing new down there, nothing to be concerned about. And no one lurking in the shadows.

A couple were hurrying by, arms linked, with a bloated umbrella threatening to turn inside out at any moment.

Window locks in bedroom, spare bedroom, bathroom, living/dining room. Activate timers on lights, television and radio in each room in turn. Blu-Tack single cotton thread, knee high, across the hallway just inside the front door.

Paranoid? Moi? You'd better believe it!

She tugged her long mackintosh and umbrella from the hooks in the narrow hallway, stepped over the thread and peered through the spyhole. The dull-yellow fish-eye glow of the empty landing greeted her.

She unhooked the safety chains, opened the door cautiously and stepped out, instantly noticing the smell of sawn timber. She pulled the door shut and turned the keys in turn in each of the three deadlocks.

Then she stood listening. Somewhere downstairs, in one of the other flats, a phone was ringing, unanswered. She shivered, pulling her fleece-lined mac around her, still not used to the damp and cold after years of living in the sunshine. Still not used to spending a Friday night alone.

Her plan tonight was to catch a film, *Atonement*, at the multiplex in the Marina, then grab a bite to eat – maybe some pasta – and, if she had the courage, go to a bar for a couple of glasses of wine. That way at least she could feel the comfort of mingling with other humans.

Dressed discreetly in designer jeans, ankle-length boots and a black, knitted polo neck beneath the mac, wanting to look nice but not to draw attention to herself if she did go to a bar, she opened the fire door to the stairwell, and saw to her dismay that the workmen had left it blocked for the weekend with lengths of plasterboard and a whole stack of timber.

Cursing them, she debated whether to try to stumble her way through, then, thinking better of it, she pressed the button for the lift, staring at the scratched metal door. Seconds later she heard it clanking, jerking and bumping obediently upwards, reaching her floor with a jarring clang before the external door opened with a sound like a shovel smoothing gravel.

She stepped in and the door closed again with the same sound, along with the lift car's own double doors, enclosing her. She breathed in the smell of someone else's perfume, and lemon-scented cleaning fluid. The lift jerked upwards a few inches, so sharply she almost fell over.

And now, when it was too late to change her mind and get out, with the metal walls pressing in around her and a small, almost opaque mirror reflecting the dawning look of panic on her mostly invisible face, it lunged sharply downwards.

Abby was about to realize she had just made a bad mistake.

3

OCTOBER 2007

Detective Superintendent Roy Grace, seated at the desk in his office, put down the phone and leaned back with his arms folded, tilting the chair until it was resting against the wall. *Shit.* At 4.45 on a Friday afternoon, his weekend had just gone down the toilet – more or less literally. Down a storm drain, at any rate.

On top of a lousy run of cards at his weekly boys' poker game last night, when he'd lost nearly three hundred quid.

There was nothing like the idea of a field trip to a storm drain on a howling wet Friday afternoon, he thought, for putting you in a really foul mood. He could feel the icy draught of the wind blowing through the ill-fitting window-panes of his small office and listened to the rattle of the rain. Not a day to be outside.

He cursed the Control Room operator who had just rung him with the news. It was shooting the messenger, he realized, but he had everything planned to spend tomorrow night in London with Cleo, as a treat for her. Now that would have to be cancelled, for a case he knew instinctively he was not going to enjoy, and all because he had stepped in as duty Senior Investigating Officer to cover for a colleague who had gone down sick.

Murders were what really floated his boat in this job.

There were between fifteen and twenty every year in Sussex, with many of them in the City of Brighton and Hove and environs – more than enough to go round all the SIOs and give them a chance to show their abilities. It was a tad callous to think this way, he knew, but it was a fact that handling a brutal, high-profile murder inquiry well was a good career opportunity. You got noticed by the press and the public, by your peers and, most importantly, by your bosses. There was intense satisfaction to be had out of a successful arrest and conviction. More than just a job done, it allowed the family of the victim a chance of closure, to move on. To Grace, this was the most significant factor of all.

He liked to work on murders where there was a hot, live trail, where he could crack into action with an adrenaline rush, think on his feet, galvanize a team into working 24/7 and have a good chance of catching the perpetrator.

But from the sound of the operator's report, the findings in the storm drain indicated anything but a fresh murder. Skeletal remains. Might not even be a murder at all, could be a suicide, maybe even a natural death. There was even the remote possibility it could be a shop-window dummy – that had happened before. Remains like this could have been there for decades, so another couple of days wouldn't have made a sodding bit of difference.

Guilty at this sudden flash of anger, he looked down at the twenty or so blue boxes, stacked two and three deep, that were taking up most of the carpeted floor area of his office that wasn't already filled by the small round conference table and four chairs.

Each box contained the key files of an unsolved murder, a cold case. The rest of the case files were bulging out of cupboards elsewhere in the CID headquarters, or were locked up, going mouldy, in a damp police garage in the area where the murder happened, or were archived away in a forgotten basement room, along with all the tagged and bagged items of evidence.

And he had a feeling, born from close on twenty years of investigating murders, that what awaited him now in the storm drain was more than likely to result in another blue box on his floor.

He was so saturated with paperwork at the moment that there was barely a square inch of his desk that wasn't buried under mounds of documents. He was having to work through the time lines, evidence, statements and everything else needed by the Crown Prosecution Service for two separate murder trials next year. One concerned a scumbag internet sleaze merchant called Carl Venner, the other a psychopath called Norman Jecks.

Glancing through a document prepared by a young woman, Emily Gaylor from the Brighton Trials Unit, he picked up the phone and dialled an extension, taking only a small amount of satisfaction from the fact that he was about to ruin someone else's weekend too.

He was answered almost instantly. 'DS Branson.'

'What are you doing at the moment?'

'I'm about to go home, old-timer, thanks for asking,' said Glenn Branson.

'That's the wrong answer.'

'No, it's the right answer,' the Detective Sergeant insisted. 'Ari has a dressage lesson and I'm looking after the kids.'

'Dressage? What's that?'

'Something involving her horse that costs thirty quid an hour.'

'She'll have to take the kids with her. Meet me down in

the car park in five minutes. We need to take a look at a dead body.'

'I'd really prefer to go home.'

'So would I. And I expect the body would prefer to be at home too,' Grace replied. 'At home in front of the telly with a nice cuppa instead of decomposing in a storm drain.'

4

OCTOBER 2007

After just a few seconds the lift jerked sharply to a halt, swaying from side to side, banging against the walls with an echoing clang like two oil drums colliding. Then it rocked forward, throwing Abby against the door.

Almost instantly it plunged sharply again, in freefall. She let out a whimper. For a split second, the carpeted floor dropped away below her, as if she had become weightless. Then there was a jarring crash and the floor seemed to rise, striking her feet with such force it knocked the air out of her stomach – it felt as if her legs were being driven up into her neck.

The lift twisted, throwing her like a busted puppet against the mirror on the back wall, and lurched again before becoming almost still, swinging slightly, the floor tilted at a drunken angle.

'Oh, Jesus,' Abby whispered.

The lights in the roof flickered, went out, came on again. There was an acrid reek of burnt electrics and she saw a thin coil of smoke glide, unhurriedly, past her.

She held her breath, trapping another cry in her throat. It felt as if the whole damned thing was being suspended by one very thin and frayed thread.

Suddenly there was a rending sound above her. Metal tearing. Her eyes shot up in stark terror. She didn't know much about lifts, but it sounded as if something was shearing away. Her imagination running wild, she pictured the shackle holding the cable on to the roof breaking off.

The lift dropped a couple of inches.

She shrieked.

Then another couple of inches, the angle of the floor becoming steeper.

It lurched left with a massive metallic bang, then sagged. There was a sharp crack above her head, like something snapping.

It dropped a few more inches.

When she moved to try to balance herself, she fell over, bashing her shoulder against one wall, then her head against the doors. She lay still for a moment, with dust in her nostrils from the carpet, not daring to move, staring up at the roof. There was a central opaque glass panel, with illuminated strips on either side of it. Had to get out of this thing, she knew, had to get out fast. Lifts in movies had roof hatches. Why didn't this one?

The button panel was just out of reach. She tried to get on to her knees to reach it, but the lift started swaying so wildly, banging into the sides of the shaft again as if it really was held by a single thread, that she stopped, afraid that one movement too many could snap it.

For some moments she lay still, hyperventilating in utter blind terror, listening for any sounds of help coming. There were none. If Hassan, her neighbour two floors below, was away, and if the rest of the residents were either away too or in their flats with their televisions up loud, no one would know what was happening.

Alarm. Got to ring the alarm.

She took several deep breaths. Her head felt tight, as if her scalp was a size too small. The walls were closing in around her, suddenly, then expanding, moving away before closing in again, as if they were lungs. In towards her, then moving away again, lungs that were breathing, pulsing. She was having a panic attack.

'Hi,' she said quietly, in a croaking whisper, saying what she had been taught to say by her therapist whenever she felt a panic attack coming on. 'I am Abby Dawson. I am fine. This is just a wonky chemical reaction. I'm fine, I am in my body, I am not dead, this will pass.'

She crawled a few inches towards the alarm button. The floor rocked, spun, as if she was lying on a board that was balanced on the point of a sharp stick and would fall off at any moment. Waiting until it had stabilized, she inched forward again. Then again. Another wisp of blue, acrid-smelling smoke passed by her, silent, like a genie. She reached out her arm, stretching as far as she could, and jabbed her trembling finger hard against the grey metal button printed in red with the word ALARM.

Nothing happened.

5

OCTOBER 2007

There was a meagre amount of daylight left when, deep in thought, Roy Grace turned the unmarked grey car into Trafalgar Street. It might be proudly named after a great naval victory, but this skanky end of the street was lined on both sides with grimy, unloved buildings and shops and, at most times of the day and night, drug dealers. Although the foul weather this afternoon was keeping all but the most desperate of them indoors. Glenn Branson, sharply dressed in a brown chalk-striped suit and immaculate silk tie, was sitting in morose silence beside him.

Unusually for a pool vehicle, the almost new Hyundai had not yet begun to reek like a discarded McDonald's carton filled with old hair gel but still had that fresh, new-car smell. Grace turned right, alongside the tall hoarding wall of a construction company. Behind it, a large and run-down area of central Brighton was getting a makeover, transforming two old and largely disused railway goods yards into yet another urban chic development.

The artist's glossy impression of the architect's vision ran much of the length of the hoarding. THE NEW ENGLAND QUARTER. ASPIRATIONAL LIFESTYLE HOMES AND OFFICES. It looked, Grace thought, like every other modern development in every town and city you ever passed through. All glass and exposed steel beams, courtyards with neat little shrubs and trees dotted around, and not a mugger in sight. One day the whole of England would look the same and you wouldn't know what town or city you were in.

But does that actually matter, he wondered suddenly. Am I already an old fart at thirty-nine? Do I really want this city I love so much preserved, warts and all, in some kind of a time warp?

At this moment, however, he had something bigger on his mind than the Brighton and Hove Planning Department's policies. Bigger too than the human remains they were on their way to observe. Something that was depressing him a lot.

Cassian Pewe.

On Monday, after a long convalescence following a car accident and several false starts, Cassian Pewe would finally be commencing work at the CID headquarters, in the same role as Grace. And with one big advantage: Detective Superintendent Cassian Pewe was the blue-eyed boy of Assistant Chief Constable Alison Vosper, whereas he was pretty much her *bête noire.*

Despite what he considered to be some major successes in recent months, Roy Grace knew he was just one very minor screw-up away from being transferred from the Sussex Police Force to the back of beyond. He really did not want to be moved away from Brighton and Hove. Or, even more importantly, from his beloved Cleo.

In his view, Cassian Pewe was one of those arrogant men who were both impossibly good-looking and fully aware of it. He had golden hair, angelic blue eyes, a permanent tan and a voice as invasive as a dentist's drill. The man preened and strutted, exuding a natural air of authority, always acting as if he was in charge even when he wasn't.

Roy'd had a run-in with him over just this, when the Met had sent reinforcements to help police Brighton during the Labour Party Conference a couple of years ago. Through complete blundering arrogance, Pewe, then a Detective Inspector, had arrested two informants Roy had carefully cultivated over many years and then flatly refused to drop the charges. And to Roy's anger, when he had taken it to the top, Alison Vosper had sided with Pewe.

Quite what the hell she saw in the man he did not know, unless, as he sometimes darkly suspected, they were having an affair – however improbable that might be. The ACC's haste in bringing Pewe down from the Met and promoting him, effectively splitting Grace's duties – when in reality he was quite capable of handling everything on his own – smacked of some hidden agenda.

Normally irritatingly chatty, Glenn Branson had not said a word since leaving the CID headquarters at Sussex House. Maybe he really was hacked off because he was being dragged away from his Friday night with the family. Maybe it was because Roy hadn't offered to let him drive. Then suddenly the Detective Sergeant broke his silence.

'Ever see that movie *In the Heat of the Night*?' he asked.

'I don't think so,' Grace said. 'No. Why?'

'It was about a racist cop in the Deep South.'

'And?'

Branson shrugged.

'I'm being racist?'

'You could have ruined someone else's weekend. Why mine?'

'Because I always target black men.'

'That's what Ari thinks.'

'You can't be serious?'

A couple of months ago, Roy had taken Glenn in as a

lodger when his wife had thrown him out. After a few days of living at close quarters, it had nearly been the end of a beautiful friendship. Now Glenn was back with his wife.

'I am serious.'

'I think Ari has a problem.'

'The opening shot on the bridge is famous. It's one of the longest tracking shots in cinema history,' Glenn said.

'Great. I'll watch it some time. Listen, matey, Ari has to get real.'

Glenn offered him a piece of gum. Grace accepted and chewed, perked up by the instant hit of peppermint.

Then Glenn said, 'Did you really need to drag me out here tonight? You could have got someone else.'

They passed a street corner and Grace saw a shabby man in a shell suit talking to a youth in a hoodie. To his trained eye, they looked furtive. A local drug dealer serving up.

'I thought things were better between you and Ari.'

'So did I. I bought her the fucking horse she wanted. Now it turns out it was the wrong kind of horse.'

Finally, through the clunking wiper blades, Grace could see a cluster of digging machines, a police car, blue and white crime-scene tape across the entrance to a construction site, and a very drenched, unhappy-looking constable in a yellow high-visibility jacket, holding a clip-board wrapped in a plastic bag. The sight pleased Grace: at least today's uniformed police were getting the hang of what needed to be done to preserve crime scenes.

He pulled over, parking just in front of the police car, and turned to Glenn. 'You've got your inspector's promotion boards coming up soon, haven't you?'

'Yeah.' The DS shrugged.

'This could be just the type of inquiry that will give you

plenty to talk about during your interview. The interest factor.'

'Tell Ari that.'

Grace put an arm around his friend's shoulder. He loved this guy, who was one of the brightest detectives he had ever encountered. Glenn had all the qualities to take him a long way in the police force, but at a price. And that price was something that many couldn't accept. The insane hours destroyed too many marriages. Mostly, those who survived best were married to other police officers. Or to nurses, or others in professions where antisocial hours were par for the course.

'I chose you today because you are the best man to have beside me. But I'm not forcing you. You can come with me or you go home. It's up to you.'

'Yeah, old-timer, I go home and then what? Tomorrow I'm back in uniform, busting gays for indecent exposure down on Duke's Mound. Have I got it right?'

'More or less.'

Grace got out of the car. Branson followed.

Ducking against the rain and howling wind, they changed into their white oversuits and wellington boots, then, looking like a couple of sperm, walked up to the scene guard constable and signed themselves in.

'You're going to need torches,' the constable said.

Grace clicked his torch on, then off. Branson did the same. A second constable, also wearing a bright yellow jacket, led the way in the falling light. They squelched through sticky mud that was rutted with the tyre tread patterns of heavy plant, making their way across the vast site.

They passed a tall crane, a silent JCB digger and stacks of building materials battened down under flapping sheets of polythene. The crumbling Victorian red-brick wall, fronting the foundations of Brighton Station's car park, rose steeply in front of them. Beyond the darkness, they could see the orange glow of the city lights around them. A loose piece of hoarding clattered and somewhere two pieces of metal were clanging together.

Grace was eyeing the ground. Foundation pilings were being sunk. Heavy diggers would have been criss-crossing this area for months. Any evidence would have to be found inside the storm drain – anything outside would have long gone.

The constable stopped and pointed down into an excavated gully twenty feet below them. Grace stared at what looked like a partially buried prehistoric serpent with a jagged hole gouged out of its back. The mosaic of bricks, so old they were almost colourless, formed part of a semi-submerged tunnel just rising above the surface of the mud in places.

The storm drain from the old Brighton to Kemp Town railway line.

'Nobody knew it was there,' the constable said. 'The JCB fractured it earlier today.'

Roy Grace held back for a moment, trying to overcome his fear of heights, even for this relatively small distance. Then he took a deep breath and scrambled down the steep, slippery slope, exhaling sharply with relief when he reached the bottom upright and intact. And suddenly the serpent's body looked a whole lot bigger, and more exposed, than it had seemed from above. The rounded shape curved above him, nearly seven feet high, he guessed. The hole in the middle looked as dark as a cave.

He strode towards it, with Branson and the constable right behind him and switched on his torch. As he entered the storm drain, shadows jigged wildly back at him. He ducked his head, crinkling his nose at the strong, fetid smell of damp. It was higher in here than it had seemed from the outside; it felt like being in an ancient tube tunnel, with no platform.

'*The Third Man*,' Glenn Branson said suddenly. 'You've seen that movie. You've got that at home.'

'The one with Orson Welles and Joseph Cotten?' Grace said.

'Yeah, good memory! Sewers always remind me of it.'

Grace shone the powerful beam to the right. Darkness. Shimmering puddles of water. Ancient brickwork. Then he shone the beam to the left. And jumped.

'Shit!' Glenn Branson shouted, his voice echoing round them.

Although Grace had been expecting it, what he saw, several yards away down the tunnel, still spooked him. A skeleton, reclining against the wall, partially buried in silt. It looked like it was just lounging there, waiting for him. Long fronds of hair were still attached to the scalp in places, but otherwise it was mostly just bare bones, picked or rotted clean, with a few tiny patches of desiccated skin.

He squelched towards it, being careful not to slip on the mulch base. Twin pinpricks of red appeared for an instant and were gone. A rat. He swung the beam back on to the skull, its inane rictus grin chilling him.

And something else about it chilled him too.

The hair. Even though the lustre had long gone, it was the same length and had the same winter-wheat colouring as the hair of his long-vanished wife, Sandy.

Trying to dismiss the thought from his mind, he turned to the constable and asked, 'Have you searched the whole length?'

'No, sir, I thought we should wait for the SOCOs.'

'Good.'

Grace was relieved, glad that the young man had had the sense not to risk disturbing or destroying any evidence that might still be in here. Then he realized his hand was shaking. He shone the beam back on the skull.

On the fronds of hair.

On his thirtieth birthday, a little over nine years ago now, Sandy, the wife he adored, had vanished off the face of the earth. He had been searching for her ever since. Wondering every day, and every night, what had happened to her. Had she been kidnapped and imprisoned somewhere? Run off with a secret lover? Been murdered? Committed suicide? Was she still alive or dead? He'd even resorted to mediums, clairvoyants and just about every other kind of psychic he could find.

Most recently he had been to Munich, where there had been a possible sighting. That made some sense, as she had relatives, on her mother's side, from near there. But none of them had heard from her, and all his enquiries, as usual, had drawn a blank. Every time he encountered an unidentified dead woman who was remotely in Sandy's age bracket he wondered if perhaps this time it was her.

And the skeleton in front of him now, in this buried storm drain in the city where he had been born, grown up and fallen in love, seemed to be taunting him, as if to say, *You took your time getting here!*

6

OCTOBER 2007

Abby, on the hard carpeted floor, stared at the small sign beside the panel of buttons on the grey wall. In red capital letters on a white background it read:

WHEN BROKE DOWN

CALL 013 228 7828

OR DIAL 999

The grammar did not exactly fill her with confidence. Below the button panel was a narrow, cracked glass door. Slowly, one inch at a time, she crawled across the floor. It was only a few feet away but, with the lift rocking wildly at every movement, it might as well have been on the far side of the world.

Finally she reached it, prised it open and removed the handset, which was attached to a coiled wire.

It was dead.

She tapped the cradle and the lift swayed wildly again, but there was no sound from the handset. She dialled the numbers, just in case. Still nothing.

Great, she thought. Terrific. Then she eased her mobile from her handbag and dialled 999.

The phone beeped sharply at her. On the display the message appeared:

No network coverage.

'Jesus, no, don't do this to me.'

Breathing fast, she switched the phone off, then a few seconds later switched it back on again, watching, waiting for just one signal blob to appear. But none did.

She dialled 999 again and got the same sharp beep and message. She tried again, then again, jabbing the buttons harder each time.

'Come on, come on. Please, please.'

She stared at the display again. Sometimes signal strength came and went. Maybe if she waited . . .

Then she called out, tentatively at first, 'Hello? Help me!'

Her voice sound small, bottled.

Taking a deep lungful of air, she bellowed at the top of her voice, 'HELLO? HELP ME PLEASE! HELP ME! I'M TRAPPED IN THE LIFT!'

She waited. Silence.

Silence so loud she could hear it. The hum of one of the lights in the panel above her. The thudding of her own heart. The sound of her blood coursing through her veins. The rapid hiss-puff of her own breathing.

She could see the walls shrinking in around her.

She breathed in slowly, then out. She stared at the display of her phone again. Her hand was shaking so much it was almost impossible to read it. The figures were just a blur. She breathed in deeply again, and again. Dialled 999 once more. Nothing. Then, putting the phone down, she pounded hard on the wall.

There was a reverberating *boom* and the lift swayed alarmingly, clanging into one side of the shaft and dropping a few more inches.

'HELP ME!' she screamed.

Even that caused the lift to rock and bang again. She lay still. The lift settled.

Then, through her terror, she felt a flash of hysterical anger at her predicament. Hauling herself a few feet forward, she began pounding on the metal doors and yelling at the same time – yelling until her ears hurt from the din, and her throat was too sore to go on, and she began coughing, as if she had swallowed a whole lungful of dust.

'LET ME OUT!'

Then she felt the lift move, suddenly, as if someone had pushed down on the roof. Her eyes shot up. She held her breath, listening.

But all she could hear was the silence.

7

11 SEPTEMBER 2001

Lorraine Wilson was topless on a deckchair in her garden, soaking up the last of the summer, trying to prolong her tan. Through large oval sunglasses she looked at her watch – the gold Rolex Ronnie had bought her for her birthday, in June, and which he had insisted was genuine. But she didn't believe that. She knew Ronnie too well. He would not have spent ten thousand pounds when he could have bought something that looked the same for fifty. And certainly not at the moment, with his financial worries.

Not that he ever shared his problems with her, but she could tell from the way he had recently tightened up on everything, checking her grocery bills, complaining about the money she spent on clothes, her hair and even her lunches out with her friends. Parts of the house were looking embarrassingly shabby, but Ronnie refused to let her call in the decorators, telling her they would have to economize.

She loved him deeply, but there was a part of him that she could never reach, as if he had a secret internal compartment where he kept and fought his private demon, all alone. She knew a little of what that demon was – his determination to show the world, and in particular everyone who knew him, that he was a success.

Which was why he had bought this house, just off

Shirley Drive, that they really could not afford. It wasn't big, but it was in one of the most expensive residential districts of Brighton and Hove, a tranquil, hilly area of detached houses with sizeable gardens along tree-lined streets. And because the house was modern, on split levels, it looked different from most of the more conventional Edwardian mock-Tudor houses that were the mainstay of the area; people did not realize it was actually quite small. The teak decking and bijou outdoor pool added a touch of Beverly Hills glamour.

It was 1.50 p.m. Nice that he had just called. Time zones always confused her; strange that he was having his breakfast and she was having her cottage cheese and berries lunch. She was happy that he was flying back tonight. She always missed him when he was away – and, knowing he was a womanizer, she always wondered what he got up to when he was on his own. But this was a short trip – just three days, not too bad.

This part of the garden was completely private, shielded from their neighbours by a tall trellis interwoven with mature ivy and a huge out-of-control rhododendron bush that seemed to have ambitions to be a tree. She watched the electronic pool sweeper cruising up and down the blue water, sending out ripples. Alfie, their tabby cat, seemed to have found something interesting at the back of the rhododendron and was walking slowly past, staring, then turning, walking slowly past again and staring some more.

You never knew what cats were thinking, she thought suddenly. Alfie was a bit like Ronnie, really.

She put her plate down on the ground and picked up the *Daily Mail*. She had an hour and a half before she needed to leave for the hairdresser. She was going to have highlights put in and then go to the nail studio. She always wanted to look nice for him.

Luxuriating in the warm rays of sun, she turned the pages. In a few minutes she would get up and iron his shirts. He might buy fake watches, but he always bought the real thing in shirts, and always from Jermyn Street, in London. He was obsessive about them being ironed properly. Now that the cleaning lady had gone, as part of their economy drive, she was having to do all the housework herself.

Smiling, she thought back to those early days with Ronnie, when she had actually liked doing his washing and ironing. Ten years ago, when they'd first met, when she'd been working as a sales demonstrator in duty free at Gatwick Airport, Ronnie had been putting back together the broken pieces of his life after his beautiful but brainless wife had run off to Los Angeles, to shack up with someone she'd met on a girls' night out in London, a film director who was going to make her a star.

She remembered their first holiday, in a small rented flat outside Marbella, overlooking the yacht basin of Puerto Banus. Ronnie had drunk beer on the balcony, looking enviously down at the yachts, promising her that one day they'd own the biggest yacht in the harbour. And he knew how to romance a woman, all right. He was a master at it.

She had loved nothing better than to wash his clothes. To feel his T-shirts, swimming trunks, underwear, socks and handkerchiefs in her hands. To breathe in his manly smells on them. It was intensely satisfying to iron those beautiful shirts and then watch him wearing them, as if he was wearing part of herself.

Now it was a chore, and she found herself resenting his mcanness.

She went back to the article on HRT she had been reading. The ongoing debate about whether the reduction of menopause symptoms – and the retention of youthful looks – outweighed the extra risks of breast cancer and other nasties. A wasp buzzed around her head and she flapped it away, then paused to stare down at her own chest. Two years away from forty and everything was starting to go south, except for her expensive breasts.

Lorraine was not a flawless, striking beauty, but she had always been, in Ronnie's parlance, a *looker*. She owed her blonde hair to her Norwegian grandmother. Not that many years back, like a trillion other blondes around the globe, she had copied the now classic hairstyle of Diana, Princess of Wales, and on a couple of occasions she'd actually been asked if she was the Princess of Wales.

Now, she thought gloomily, *I'm going to have to do something about the rest of my body.*

Lying back in the chair, her stomach resembled a kangaroo's pouch. It was like the stomach of women who had had several children, where the muscles had gone or the skin had been permanently stretched. And there were cellulite dimples all over the tops of her thighs.

All that disaster happening to her body *despite* (and to Ronnie's chagrin at the cost) going to her personal trainer three times a week.

The wasp returned, buzzing around her head. 'Fuck off,' she said, flapping her hand at it again. 'Go away.'

Then her phone rang. She leaned down and picked up the cordless handset. It was her sister, Mo, and her normally calm, cheerful voice sounded strangely agitated. 'Have you got your telly on?'

'No, I'm out in the garden,' Lorraine replied.

'Ronnie's in New York, isn't he?'

'Yes – I just spoke to him. Why?'

'Something terrible's happened. It's all over the news. A plane's just crashed into the World Trade Center.'

8

OCTOBER 2007

The rain worsened, rattling down on the steel roof of the SOCO Scientific Support Branch van, sounding as hard as hailstones. The windows were opaque, to allow in light but keep out prying eyes. There was little light outside now, however, just the bleakness of wet dusk, stained the colour of rust from ten thousand city street lights.

Despite the large external dimensions of the long-wheelbase Transit, the seating area inside was cramped. Roy Grace, finishing a call on his mobile, chaired the meeting, the policy book he had retrieved from his go-bag open in front of him.

Squeezed around the table with him, in addition to Glenn Branson, were the Crime Scene Manager, a Police Search Adviser, an experienced SOCO, one of the two uniform scene guards and Joan Major, the forensic archaeologist Sussex Police regularly called in to help with identification of skeletons – and also to tell them whether the occasional bone found on building sites, or by children in woods, or dug up by gardeners, was human or animal.

It was chilly and damp inside the van and the air smelled strongly of synthetic vapours. Reels of plastic crime-scene tape were packed in one section of the fitted metal shelving, body bags in another, plus tenting materials and ground sheets, rope, flexes, hammers, saws, axes and plastic bottles of chemicals. There was something grim about these vehicles, Grace always felt. They were like caravans, but they never went to campsites, only to scenes of death or violent crimes.

It was 6.30 p.m.

'Nadiuska isn't available,' he informed the newly assembled team, putting his mobile down.

'Does that mean we've got Frazer?' Glenn responded glumly.

'Yes.'

Grace saw everyone's faces fall. Nadiuska De Sancha was the Home Office pathologist everyone in Sussex CID preferred to work with. She was quick, interesting and fun – and good-looking, as an added bonus. By contrast, Frazer Theobald was dour and slow, although his work was meticulous.

'But the real problem is that Frazer is finishing a PM up in Esher at the moment. The earliest he could get here is about 9 p.m.'

He caught Glenn's eye. They both knew what that meant – an all-nighter.

Grace headed the first page of his policy book: *PRE-SCENE BRIEFING. Friday 19 October. 6.30 p.m. On site. New England Quarter development.*

'Can I make a suggestion?' Joan Major said.

The forensic archaeologist was a pleasant-looking woman in her early forties, with long brown hair and square, modern glasses, dressed in a roll-neck black pullover, brown trousers and sturdy boots.

Grace gestured with his hand.

'I suggest we go and do a brief assessment now, but it may not be necessary to start work tonight – especially as it's dark. These things are always a lot easier in daylight. It sounds as if the skeleton has been there a while, so another day won't make much difference.'

'It's a good thought,' Grace said. 'One thing we need to consider, though, is the construction work going on here.' He looked directly at the Police Search Adviser, a tall, bearded man with an outdoors complexion, whose name was Ned Morgan. 'You'll need to liaise with the foreman, Ned. We'll have to stop the work directly around the storm drain.'

'I spoke to him on my way in. He's worried because they're on a time penalty,' Morgan explained. 'He nearly had a fit when I told him we could be here a week.'

'It's a big site,' Grace said. 'We don't need to shut the whole of it down. You'd better decide where you want work stopped as part of your search plan.' Then he turned back to the forensic archaeologist. 'But you are right, Joan, tomorrow would be better, in daylight.'

He put a call through to Steve Curry, the District Inspector responsible for coordinating uniform police in this area of the city, and advised him that a scene guard would need to be kept on until further notice, which didn't thrill the inspector. Scene guards were an expensive drain on resources.

Grace turned next to the Crime Scene Manager, Joe Tindall, who had earlier this year been promoted to the post. Tindall gave a self-satisfied smile. 'All the same to me, Roy,' he said in his Midlands accent. 'Now I'm a manager I get to go home at a decent hour. Gone are the days when you and your fellow SIOs can screw up my weekends. I ruin other people's weekends for you now.'

Secretly, Grace envied him. What's more, in reality the remains could easily wait until Monday – but now, as he again regretted, they had been discovered and reported, that was not an option.

*

Ten minutes later, clad in their protective clothing, they entered the storm drain. Grace led the way, followed by Joan Major and Ned Morgan. The Police Search Adviser had advised the other team members to stay in the vehicle, wanting to keep contamination of the scene to a minimum.

All three stopped a short distance from the skeleton, shining their beams on it. Joan Major played hers up and down, then stepped forward until she was close enough to touch it.

Roy Grace, feeling a tight knot in his gullet, stared again at the face. He knew the likelihood of this being Sandy was extremely small. And yet. The teeth were all intact; good teeth. Sandy had good teeth – they had been one of the many things that had attracted him to her. Beautiful, white, even teeth, and a smile that melted him every time.

His voice came out sounding lame, as if it was someone else speaking. 'Is it male or female, Joan?'

She was peering at the skull. 'The slope of the forehead is quite upright – men tend to have a much more sloped forehead,' she said, her voice echoing eerily. Then, holding the torch in her left hand and pointing at the rear of the skull with the forefinger of her gloved right hand, she went on, 'The nuchal crest is very rounded.' She tapped it. 'If you feel the back of your skull, Roy, it'll be much more pronounced – it normally is in males.' Then she looked at the left ear cavity. 'Again, the mastoid process would indicate female – it's more pronounced in the male.' Next, she traced the air in front of the eyes. 'See the skull brow ridges – I'd expect them to be more prominent if this was a male.'

'So you're reasonably sure she's female?' Grace asked.

'Yes, I am. When we expose the pelvis I will be able to say one hundred per cent, but I'm pretty sure. I'll also take some measurements – the male skeleton is generally more robust, the proportions are different.' She hesitated a moment. 'There is something of immediate interest – I'd like to know what Frazer thinks.'

'What's that?'

She pointed at the base of the skull. 'The hyoid bone is broken.'

'Hyoid?'

She pointed again, to a bone suspended from a tiny strip of desiccated skin. 'Do you see that U-shaped bone? It's the one that keeps the tongue in place. It's a possible indicator of the cause of death – the hyoid often gets broken during strangulation.'

Grace absorbed this. He stared at the bone for some moments, then back at those perfect teeth again, trying to remember everything from the last examination of skeletal remains he had attended, at least a couple of years ago.

'What about her age?'

'I'll be able to tell you better tomorrow,' she replied. 'On a quick assessment, she looks as if she was in her prime – twenty-five to forty.'

Sandy was twenty-eight when she disappeared, he reflected, continuing to stare at the skull. At the teeth. Out of the corner of his eye he saw Ned Morgan shining his torch beam one direction along the drain, then the other.

'We ought to get an engineer from the council along, Roy,' the Police Search Adviser said. 'An expert on the city's drainage system. Find out what other drains connect with this. Some of her clothing or belongings might have been washed along them.'

'Do you think this drain floods?' Grace asked him.

Morgan shone the beam up and down again pensively. 'Well, it's raining pretty hard and has been all day – not much water at the moment, but it's quite possible. This drain would probably have been built to stop water flooding the rail track, so yes. But . . .' He hesitated.

Joan cut in. 'It looks as if she's been here some years. If the drain flooded, it's likely she would have been moved up and down and would have broken up. She's intact. Also, the presence of the desiccated skin would indicate that it has been dry here for some while. But we can't rule out flooding from time to time altogether.'

Grace stared at the skull, all kinds of emotions raging through him. Suddenly, he did not want to wait until tomorrow – he wanted the team to start now, right away.

It was only with great reluctance that he told the scene guard to seal up the entrance and secure the whole site.

9

OCTOBER 2007

Abby could not believe it – she needed to pee. She looked at her watch. One hour and ten minutes had passed since she had stepped into this bloody lift. Why? Why? Why had she been so bloody stupid?

Because of the fucking builders downstairs, that's why.

Christ. It took thirty seconds to go down via the staircase, and that was good exercise. *Why? Why? Why?*

And now this sharp, biting urgency in her bladder. She had gone only minutes before leaving the flat, but it felt as if she had drunk ten pints of coffee and a gallon of water since.

No way, I am not peeing. I am not having the fire brigade turn up to find me lying in a puddle of urine. Not that indignity, thank you.

She clenched her insides, pressing her knees together, shaking, waiting for the moment to pass, then looked up at the roof of the lift again, at the gridded, opaque lighting panel. Listening. Listening for that footstep she was certain she had heard.

Or her imagination had heard . . .

In movies, people pulled the lift doors open or climbed out through the roof hatches. But in movies lifts did not sway like this.

The desire to urinate passed – it would be back, but

for the moment she felt OK. She tried to get to her feet, but the lift swung wildly again, banging into one of the shaft walls and then another with that deep, echoing *boooommmmmm*. She held her breath, waiting for it to stop moving. Praying the cable was still holding. Then she knelt, picked her mobile phone off the floor and dialled again. Same sharp beep, same no-signal message.

She placed her hands on the doors, tried to force her fingers into the gap down the centre between them but they were not moving. She opened her handbag, rummaging inside for something she could ease into the tiny crack. There was nothing there other than a metal nail file. She slid it in, but after a couple of inches it hit something solid and would go no further. She tried moving it to the right, then sharply to the left. The file bent.

She pressed every button on the panel in turn, then slapped the wall of the lift in frustration with the flat of her hand.

This was just great.

How long did she have?

There was another ominous creak above her. She imagined the cable of twisted wires steadily uncoiling, getting thinner and thinner. The bolts fixed to the roof shearing, bit by bit. She remembered a conversation at a party some years ago about what to do if a lift cable snapped and the lift plunged downwards. Several people said to jump just before you hit the bottom. But how would you know when you were going to hit the bottom? And if the lift was plunging at maybe a hundred miles an hour, you would be plunging at the same speed. Other people suggested lying flat, then some wit said your best chance of survival was not to be in the lift in the first place.

She was with that wit right now.

Oh, Jesus, this was so ironic. Thinking back to all she had gone through to be here in Brighton. The risks she had taken, the precautions to leave no trail.

Now this had to happen.

She thought suddenly of the way it would be reported. *Unidentified woman killed in freak lift accident.*

No. No way.

She stared up at the glass panel, stretched, prodded it with her finger. It did not move.

She pushed harder.

Nothing.

It *had* to move. She stretched as much as she could, just getting the fingertips of both hands against it, and pushed with all her strength. But her exertions only made the lift sway again. It bounced off the side of the shaft once more with the same dull *booommmmmmmm.*

And then she heard a scrape above her. A very distinct, long scrape, as if someone was up there and had come to rescue her.

She listened again. Trying to tune out the hissing roar of her breathing and the drumbeat thump of her heart. She listened for what must have been a full two minutes, her ears popping like they did sometimes on an aeroplane, although then it was altitude pressure and now it was fear.

All she could hear was the steady creaking of the cable and the occasional cracking, rending sound of metal tearing.

10

11 SEPTEMBER 2001

Clutching the cordless handset and feeling a terrible swirl of darkness deep inside her, Lorraine threw herself out of the deckchair. She ran across the decking, almost tripping over Alfie, and in through the patio doors, her feet sinking deep into the soft pile of the white carpet, her boobs and her gold ankle chain flapping.

'That's where he is,' she said into the phone to her sister, her voice a trembling whisper. 'That's where Ronnie is right now.'

She grabbed the remote and hit the button. BBC One came on. She saw, through a jerky, hand-held camera, the instantly recognizable image of the tall silver twin towers of the World Trade Center. Thick black smoke belched from the top section of one tower, almost obliterating it, the black and white mast standing erect above it, rising into the cloudless cobalt sky.

Oh, Christ. Oh, Christ. Ronnie is there. Which tower is his meeting in? Which floor?

She barely heard the agitated voice of an American newscaster saying, 'This is not a light aircraft, this was a large plane. Oh, God! Oh, my God!'

'I'll call you back, Mo,' she said. 'I'll call you right back.' She stabbed out Ronnie's mobile phone number. Seconds later she got the busy tone. She tried again. Then again. And again.

Oh, God, Ronnie, please be OK. Please, my darling, please be OK.

She heard the wail of sirens on the TV. Saw people staring upwards. Everywhere, scores of people, men and women in smart clothes and in work clothes, all standing still, frozen in a bizarre tableau, some with their hand in front of their faces, some holding cameras. Then the Twin Towers again. One belching that black smoke, soiling that beautiful blue of the sky.

A shiver ripped through her. She stood still.

Sirens getting louder.

Almost nobody moving. Just a few people now sprinting towards the building. She saw a fire truck with a long ladder, heard sirens howling, whupping, grinding the air.

She tried Ronnie's number again. The busy signal. Again. The busy signal. Always the busy signal.

She called her sister back. 'I can't reach him,' she said, crying.

'He'll be OK, Lori. Ronnie's a survivor, he'll be OK.'

'How – how could this happen?' Lorraine asked. 'How could a plane do this? I mean—'

'I'm sure he's OK. This is horrible, unbelievable. It's like one of those – you know – those disasters – like a disaster movie.'

'I'm going to hang up. He might be trying to get through. I'll try him again.'

'Call me when you get through to him?'

'Yes.'

'Promise?'

'Yes.'

'He's OK, sweetie, I promise you.'

Lorraine hung up again, transfixed by the images on the television screen. She started punching out Ronnie's number again. But she only got halfway.

11

OCTOBER 2007

'Am I the love of your life?' she asked him. 'Am I, Grace? Am I?'

'You are.'

Grinning. 'You're not lying to me, are you, Grace?'

They'd had a boozy lunch at La Coupole in St Germain, then ambled along the Seine on that glorious June afternoon before returning to their hotel.

It seemed that the weather was always fine when they were together. Like it was now. Sandy stood over him, in their pretty bedroom, blocking the sunlight that was streaming in through the shuttered windows. Her blonde tresses swung down on either side of her freckled face, brushing his cheeks. Then she flicked her hair across his face, as if dusting it.

'Hey! I have to read – this CPS report – I—'

'You're so boring, Grace. You always have to read! We're in Paris! Having a romantic weekend! Don't you fancy me any more?' She kissed his forehead. 'Read, read, read! Work, work, work!' She kissed his forehead again. 'So boring, boring, boring!'

She danced back, away from his outstretched arms, taunting him. She was wearing a skimpy sundress, her breasts almost falling out of the top. He caught a glimpse of her long, tanned legs as the hem rode up her thighs and suddenly he felt very horny.

She stood over him, moving closer, taking him in her hand. 'Is that all for me, Grace? I love it! That's what I call a real *hard*!'

The brilliance of sunlight was suddenly making her face difficult to see. Then all her features were gone completely and he was staring at a blank, black oval that was framed with flowing gold hair, like a moon eclipse of the sun. He felt a stab of panic, unable for a split second even to recall what she looked like.

Then he could see her clearly again.

He grinned. 'I love you more than anything in—'

Then it felt as if the sun had gone behind a cloud. The temperature dropped. The colour faded from her face, as if she was sick, dying.

He threw his arms around her neck, holding her tightly to him. 'Sandy!' he said urgently. 'Sandy, darling!'

She smelled strange. Her skin was hard, suddenly, not Sandy's soft skin. She smelled rancid. Of decay and soil and bitter oranges.

Then the light went completely, as if someone had pulled out a plug.

Roy heard the echo of his voice in cold, empty air.

'Sandy!' he shouted, but the sound stayed trapped in his throat.

Then the light came back on. The stark light of the post-mortem room. He stared into her eyes again. And screamed.

He was staring into the eyes of a skull. Holding a skeleton in his arms. A skull with perfect teeth that was grinning at him.

'SANDY!' he screamed. 'SANDY!'

Then the light changed. Soft yellow. A bedspring creaked. He heard a voice.

'Roy?'

Cleo's voice.

'Roy? You awake?'

He stared at the ceiling, confused, blinking, in a river of sweat.

'Roy?'

He was shaking. 'I – I—'

'You were shouting so loudly.'

'Sorry. I'm sorry.'

Cleo sat up, her long blonde hair tumbling all around her face, which was pale with sleep and shock. Leaning on one arm, she looked at him with a strange expression, as if he had hurt her. He knew what she was going to say even before she spoke again.

'Sandy.' Her voice full of reproach. 'Again.'

He stared up at her. The same hair colouring as Sandy, the same eye colour – perhaps a touch more grey in the blue than Sandy. A touch more *steel.* He'd read that people who were bereaved or divorced often fell in love with someone who looked like their wife. That thought had never struck him until now. But they didn't look the same, not at all. Sandy was pretty but softer, not classically beautiful in the way that Cleo was.

He stared at the white ceiling and white walls of Cleo's bedroom. Stared at the black lacquered-wood dressing table that was badly cracked. She didn't like coming to his house, because she felt too much of Sandy's presence there, preferring them to spend their time together here, in her place.

'I'm sorry,' he said. 'Just a bad dream. A nightmare.'

She stroked his cheek tenderly. 'Maybe you should go back to that shrink you used to see.'

He just nodded, and eventually fell back into an uneasy, restless sleep, scared that he might dream again.

12

OCTOBER 2007

The spasms were getting worse – more and more painful, and they were happening at increasingly frequent intervals. Every few minutes now. Maybe this was what giving birth was like.

Her watch said 3.08 a.m. Abby had been in this lift for nearly nine hours now. Maybe she would be here until Monday, if it didn't break free and plunge to the ground first.

Oh, fucking great. How was your weekend? I spent mine in a lift. It was cool. It had a mirror and a panel of buttons and a dirty glass roof with light bulbs and a scratch on the wall that looked like someone had started out carving a swastika but changed their mind – and a printed sign by some dumb fuckwit who couldn't spell – and clearly couldn't maintain the fucking thing properly either.

WHEN BROKE DOWN
CALL 013 228 7828
OR DIAL 999

She was shaking with anger and her throat was parched, raw from shouting, her voice gone almost completely. After a rest she hauled herself to her feet once more. She was beyond caring about shaking the thing and dislodging it – she *had* to get out, rather than just wait for the cable to snap or the shackles to shear, or whatever else might cause her to plunge to her death.

'I'm trying, you stupid bastards,' she croaked, staring at the sign, feeling the walls closing in around her again, another panic attack coming on.

The lift's phone was still dead. She held her mobile close to her face, breathing deeply, trying to calm herself down, willing a signal to appear, cursing her service provider, cursing everything. Her scalp was so tight around her skull it was blurring her vision and the damn urge to pee was coming again now. Coming like a train, hurtling through her insides.

Pressing her knees together, she sucked in air. Her thighs, locked against each other, were quivering. She felt an agonizing pain in her belly, as if a hot knife blade had been pushed deep inside her and was now being twisted. She whimpered, gulping down air, her whole body shaking, doubling up into a foetal ball against the wall. She wasn't going to be able to hold out much longer, she knew.

But she persevered, clenching – *mind over matter* – fighting her own body, determined not to succumb to anything it wanted to do that her brain did not. She thought about her mother, who had been incontinent with multiple sclerosis from her late fifties.

'I am not bloody incontinent. Just get me out of here, get me out of here, get me out of here.' She hissed it under her breath like a mantra until the urge peaked and then slowly, so damned slowly, began to recede.

Finally, blissfully, it had passed and she slid back down on to the floor exhausted, wondering how long you could stop yourself from peeing before your bladder ruptured.

People survived in the desert sometimes by drinking their urine. Maybe she could urinate into one of her boots, she thought wildly. Use it as a container. Emergency drinking supply? How long could you last without water? She seemed to remember having read somewhere that a human could last weeks without food but only a few days without water.

Steadying herself on the swaying floor, she removed her right boot, then jumped up as high as she could, striking the roof panel with the Cuban heel. But it did no good. The lift just swayed crazily, banging and booming off the shaft again, throwing her sideways. She held her breath. This time – surely this time something was going to break. The last frayed strand of wire that stood between her and oblivion . . .

There were moments now when she actually wanted it to break. To drop however many floors were left. It would be a solution to everything. An inelegant one, sure, but a solution all the same. And how ironic would that be?

As if in answer to her question, the lights went out.

13

11 SEPTEMBER 2001

A house burned down one night in the street where Ronnie Wilson grew up, in Coldean in Brighton. He remembered the smell, the noise, the pandemonium, the fire engines, standing out in the darkness in his dressing gown and slippers, watching. He remembered being fascinated and afraid at the same time. But most of all he remembered the smell.

A horrible stench of destruction and despair.

There was the same smell in the air now. Not the pleasant, sweet aroma of wood smoke, or the snug cindery smell of coal, but a sharp, pungent stench of burning paint, charring paper, singeing rubber and acrid gases from melting vinyl and plastics. A choking reek that stung his eyes, that made him want to cover his nose, back off, get away, retrace his steps to the deli he had just left.

But instead he stood still.

Like everyone else.

A surreal moment of silence in the Manhattan morning, as if someone had hit the freeze-frame button on all the people in the street. Just the cars kept moving, then a red light stopped them too.

People stared. It took him some moments to see what they were staring at. At first he looked at ground level along the street, past a fire hydrant and trestle tables outside a store that were stacked with magazines and tourist guides, past the awning of a shop where a sign advertised BUTTER AND EGGS. He looked beyond an illuminated DON'T CROSS! red hand a little further on, and the gantry supporting a stop light suspended over the junction with Warren Street, and the row of backed-up traffic and glowing tail lights.

Then he realized that they were all gazing up.

Following their line of sight, at first all he saw, rising above the skyscrapers just a few blocks ahead of him, was a dense plume of black smoke, as thick as if it was coming from the chimney of a petrochemical refinery.

A building was on fire, he realized. Then, through his shock and horror, his heart sank as he realized which building. The World Trade Center.

Shit, shit, shit.

Chilled and confused like everyone else, he stood rooted to the spot, still not able to believe his eyes or comprehend what he was seeing.

The stop light turned green and, when the cars and vans and a truck started moving forward, he wondered if maybe the drivers hadn't noticed, that perhaps they could not see up above the tops of their windscreens.

Then the plume thinned for a few moments, the smoke fanning out. Through it, standing tall and proud against the brilliant blue of the sky, was the black and white radio mast. The North Tower, he recognized, from a previous visit. He felt a flash of relief. Donald Hatcook's office was in the South Tower. Good. OK. He would still be able to have his meeting.

He heard the wail of a siren. Then a whup-whup-whup, getting louder, deafeningly louder, echoing all around in the silence. He turned and saw a blue and white NYPD patrol car with three occupants, the guy in the back leaning forward, craning his neck upwards. It hurtled urgently past on the wrong side of the road, roof spinners showering red sparks on the doors of three yellow cabs in a row. Then, braking hard, tyres squealing, its nose dipping, it wormed its way through the intersection, between a bakery delivery truck, a halted Porsche and another yellow cab.

'Oh, my God! Oh, Jesus! Oh, my God!' a woman somewhere close behind him was saying. 'Oh, my God, it hit the tower! Oh, my God!'

The siren receded into the distance, just audible above another long silence. Chambers Street had fallen quiet. It was empty, suddenly. Ronnie watched a man walk across. He was wearing a baseball cap, lightweight anorak and workman's boots, and carrying a plastic bag which might have contained his lunch. He could hear the man's footsteps. The man stared warily down the empty street, as if worried he might get run over by a second cop car.

But there was no second cop car. Just the silence. As if the one that had gone past was enough and could deal with the situation like it was some minor incident.

'Did you see it?' the woman behind him said.

Ronnie turned. 'What happened?'

She had long brown hair and eyes that were bulging. Two bags of shopping lay on the sidewalk either side of her, cartons and tins of stuff spilled out.

Her voice was quivering. 'A plane! Oh, Jesus, it was a fucking plane! It hit the fucking tower. I can't believe what I saw. It was a plane. It hit the fucking tower!'

'A plane?'

'It hit the tower. It hit the fucking tower.'

She was obviously in shock.

There was another siren now. Different from the cop car, a deep honking sound. A fire tender.

This is great! he thought. *Oh, this is just so bloody great! The morning I have my meeting with Donald, some fucking jerk crashes his plane into the fucking World Trade Center!*

He looked at his watch. Shit! It was almost 8.55! He'd left the deli just after a quarter to – giving him plenty of time. Had he really stood here for ten minutes? Donald Hatcook's snotty secretary told him he needed to be punctual, that Donald only had an hour before he needed to leave for the airport to catch a plane to somewhere – Wichita, he thought she'd said. Or maybe it was Washington. Just one hour. Just a one-hour window to pitch to him and save his business!

He heard another siren. *Shit.* There was going to be fucking chaos, for sure. The bloody emergency services might seal the whole area off. He had to get there before they did. Had to get to that meeting.

Have to.

There was no way he was letting some fucking jerk who crashed his plane bugger up his meeting!

Towing his bags behind him, Ronnie broke into a run.

14

OCTOBER 2007

There was an unpleasant smell in the storm drain that had not been here yesterday. A putrefying animal, probably a rodent. Roy had noticed it when he first arrived, shortly before 9 a.m., and now, an hour later, he wrinkled his nose as he re-entered the drain, holding two bulging carrier bags of hot drinks foraged from a nearby Costa by a young, eager-to-please Police Community Support Officer.

The rain drummed down relentlessly, turning the ground outside into more and more of a quagmire, but, Grace realized, there was still no rise in the water level here. He wondered how much rain that would take. From his memory of the body of a young man found in the Brighton sewer network some years ago, he knew that all the drains connected into a trunk sewer that flowed out into the sea at Portobello near Peacehaven. If this drain had flooded, then it was likely that much of the evidence, in particular the victim's clothes, would have been washed away long back.

Ignoring a couple of sarcastic comments about his new role as tea boy, his nerves ragged from his disturbed night and troubled thoughts about the skeleton, Roy began distributing the teas and coffees to the team, as if by way of apology – or atonement – for ruining their weekend.

The storm drain was a hive of activity. Ned Morgan, the

POLSA, several search-trained officers and SOCOs, all in white suits, were dispersed along the tunnel. They were searching inch by inch through the mulch for shoes, clothes, items of jewellery, any shred or scrap, however small, that might have been on the victim when she had been put down here. Leather and synthetics would have had the best chance of surviving in this damp environment.

On their hands and knees in the gloomy brick drain, in the chiaroscuro of shadows and brightness thrown by the lights that had been rigged up at intervals, the team made an eerie sight.

Joan Major, the forensic archaeologist, who was also encased from head to foot in a white suit, was working in silent concentration. If this ever came to trial, she would have to present to the court an accurate 3-D model of the skeleton in situ. She had just finished darting in and out, struggling with the lack of signal for the hand-held GPS device she was using to pinpoint and log the coordinates of the remains, and was now sketching the exact position of the skeleton in relation to the drain and the silt. Every few moments the flash from a SOCO photographer's camera strobed.

'Thanks, Roy,' she said almost absently, taking the large latte he handed her and setting it down on a wooden box full of her equipment that she had placed on a tripod structure to keep dry.

Grace had decided he would make do with a light team over the weekend and then gear up on Monday morning. To Glenn Branson's immense relief, Grace had given him the weekend off. They were working in 'slow time'; there wasn't the urgency that would apply if the death had been more recent – days, weeks, months or even a couple of years. Monday morning would be soon enough for the first press conference.

Maybe he and Cleo could still make their dinner reservation in London tonight and salvage something of the romantic weekend he had planned if – and it was a huge *if* – Joan got through her mapping and recovery process and the Home Office pathologist was able to do his post-mortem quickly. Some hope, he knew, with Frazer Theobald – and actually, where the hell was he? He should have been here an hour ago.

As if on cue, clad in white like everyone else in the drain, Dr Frazer Theobald made his entrance, warily, furtively, like a mouse scenting cheese. A stocky little man just under five feet two, he sported an untidy threadbare thatch of wiry hair and a thick Adolf Hitler moustache beneath a Concorde-shaped hooter of a nose. Glenn Branson had once said that all he needed was a fat cigar to be a dead ringer for Groucho Marx.

Muttering apologies about his wife's car not starting and having had to take his daughter to a clarinet lesson, the pathologist scurried around the skeleton, giving it a wide berth and a suspicious glare, as if challenging it to declare itself friend or foe.

'Yes,' he said to no one in particular. 'Ah, right.' Then he turned to Roy and pointed at the skeleton. 'This is the body?'

Grace had always found Theobald a little peculiar, but never more so than at this moment. 'Yes,' he said, somewhat dumbfounded by the question.

'You're looking brown, Roy,' the pathologist remarked, then took a step closer to the skeleton, so close he could have been asking it the question. 'Been away?'

'New Orleans,' Grace replied, levering the top off his own latte and wishing he was still there now. 'I was at the International Homicide Investigators' Association Symposium.'

'How's the rebuilding going there?' Theobald asked.

'Slow.'

'Still much damage from the flood?'

'A lot.'

'Many people playing the clarinet?'

'The clarinet? Yes. Went to a few concerts. Saw Ellis Marsalis.'

Theobald gave him a rare beam of pleasure. 'The father!' he said approvingly. 'Yes, indeed. You were lucky to hear him!' Then he turned back to the skeleton. 'So what do we have?'

Grace brought him up to speed. Then Theobald and Joan Major entered into a debate about whether the body should be removed intact, a lengthy and elaborate process, or taken away in segments. They decided that, because it had been found intact, it would be better to keep it that way.

For a moment, Grace watched the rain teeming steadily in through the broken section of the drain, a short distance away. The individual drops looked like elongated dust motes in the shaft of light. *New Orleans,* he thought, blowing steam from his coffee and sipping it tentatively, trying to avoid frizzing his tongue on the hot liquid. Cleo had come with him and they'd taken a week's holiday straight after the conference, staying on, enjoying the city and each other.

It seemed that everything had been much easier between them then, away from Brighton. From Sandy. They just chilled, enjoyed the heat, took a tour around the areas devastated by the flooding that had not yet been restored. They ate gumbo, jambalaya, crab cakes and oysters Rockefeller, drank margaritas, mojitos and Californian and Oregon wines, and listened to jazz in Snug Harbor and other clubs each night. And Grace fell even more in love with her.

He was proud of the way Cleo coped at the conference. As a beautiful woman who did a very unglamorous job, she was on the receiving end of a fair bit of ribbing, curiosity and some truly appalling chat-up lines from five hundred of the world's top, toughest and mostly male detectives in party mode. Always, she gave back as good as she got, and she made eyeballs pop out by dressing her five-feet eleven-inch leggy frame in her usual eccentric, sexy way.

'You asked me about her age last night, Roy,' the forensic archaeologist said, interrupting his thoughts.

'Yes?' Instantly, he was fully focused as he stared at the skull.

Pointing at the jaw, she said, 'The presence of the wisdom teeth tells us she is over seventeen. There is evidence of some dental work, white fillings – which tend to have been more common during the past two decades, and more expensive. Could be she went to a private dentist, which might narrow it down. And there's a cap on one maxillary incisor.' She pointed to a top-left tooth.

Grace's nerves began jangling. Sandy had chipped a front left tooth on one of their first dates, biting into a fragment of bone in a steak tartare, and had later had it capped.

'What else?' he asked.

'I would say from the general condition and colouring that the teeth indicate her age to be consistent with my estimated range yesterday – somewhere between twenty-five and forty.' She looked at Frazer Theobald, who gave her a deadpan nod, as if he was sympathetic to her findings but not necessarily in wholehearted agreement.

Then she pointed at the arm. 'The long bone grows in three parts – two epiphyses and the shaft. The process by which they join together is called epiphyseal fusion and it is usually complete by the mid-thirties. This is not quite complete yet.' She pointed at the collar bone. 'The same applies with the clavicle – you can see the fusion line on the medial clavicle. It fuses at around thirty. I should be able to give you a more accurate estimate when we get to the PM room.'

'So she was about thirty, you are fairly sure?' Grace said.

'Yes. And my hunch is not much more than that. Could even be younger.'

Roy remained silent. Sandy was two years younger than him. She had disappeared on his thirtieth birthday, when she was just twenty-eight. The same hair. A capped tooth.

'Are you OK, Roy?' Joan Major asked him suddenly.

At first, lost in thought, he heard her voice only as a distant, disembodied echo.

'Roy? Are you OK?'

He snapped his focus back to her. 'Yes, yes. Fine, thanks.'

'You look as if you've just seen a ghost.'

15

11 SEPTEMBER 2001

Ronnie hurried down West Broadway, crossing Murray Street, Park Place, then Barclay Street. The World Trade Center was right in front of him now, on the far side of Vesey Street, the two silver monoliths rising sheer into the sky. The smells from the fire were much stronger and sheets of curled, burning paper were floating in the air, while debris tumbled down and smashed to the ground.

Through the dense black smoke he could see crimson, as if the tower was bleeding. Then flashes of bright orange. Flames. *Jesus,* he thought, feeling a terrible dark fear in his gut. *This cannot be happening.*

People were staggering out of the entrance, looking dazed, staring upwards, men in sharp shirts and ties without jackets, some on their mobiles. For a second he watched an attractive young brunette in a power suit stumbling along with only one shoe on. She suddenly clamped her hands to her head, looking pained, as if a falling object had just struck her, and he saw a trickle of blood run down her cheek.

He hesitated. It didn't look safe to go any further. But he needed that meeting, needed it so desperately badly. *Just have to chance it,* he thought. *Run like hell.* He coughed, the smoke pricking his throat, and stepped off the sidewalk. The kerb was higher than he realized and, as the wheels of his case bumped down, the handle twisted in his hand and his briefcase fell off.

Shit! Don't do this to me.

Then, just as he ducked down and grabbed the handle of his briefcase, he heard the scream of a jet aircraft.

He looked up again. And could not believe his eyes. A split second later, before he had time to register intelligibly what he was seeing, came an explosion. A metallic thunderclap boom, like two cosmic dustbins colliding. A sound that seemed to echo in his brain and to go on echoing, rumbling around out of control inside his skull until he wanted to stick his fingers in his ears to stop it, to choke it. Then he felt the shockwave. Felt it shuffling every single atom in his body.

A massive ball of orange flames, showering diamanté sparks and black smoke, erupted from near the top of the South Tower. For one fleeting instant he was struck dumb by the sheer beauty of that sight: the contrast of colours – the orange, the black – stark against the rich blue of the sky.

It seemed as if a million, billion feathers were floating in the air around the flames, drifting unhurriedly towards the ground. All in slow motion.

Then the reality slammed into him.

Slabs of wood, glass, chairs, desks, phones, filing cabinets were bouncing, shattering, on the ground in front of him. A police car pulled up, just past him, doors opening before it had even stopped. A mere hundred yards or so to his right, along Vesey Street, what at first looked like a burning flying saucer dropped with a massive clanging sound, smashing a deep crater, then bounced, shedding parts of its covering and innards, spraying out flames. When it finally lay still it continued to burn fiercely.

To his utter numb horror, Ronnie realized that it was a jet aircraft engine.

That this was the South Tower.

Donald Hatcook's office was here. The eighty-seventh floor. He tried to count upwards.

Two planes.

Donald's office. By his quick estimate, Donald's office was right where it hit.

What the hell is happening? Oh, Jesus Christ, what the hell is going on?

He stared at the burning engine. Could feel the heat. Saw the cops run forward from their car.

Ronnie's brain was telling him there wasn't going to be any meeting. But he tried to ignore it. His brain was wrong. His eyes were wrong. Somehow he would still make that meeting. He needed to keep going. *Keep going. You can make the meeting. You can still make the meeting. YOU NEED THAT FUCKING MEETING!*

And another part of his brain was telling him that while one plane hitting the Twin Towers was an accident, two was something else. Two was badly not right.

Propelled by absolute desperation, he gripped his bag handle and walked forward determinedly.

Seconds later he heard a dull thud, like a sack of potatoes falling. He felt a wet slap on his face. Then he saw something white and ragged roll across the ground towards him and stop inches from his feet. It was a human arm. Something wet was sliding down his cheek. He shot his hand up to his face and his fingers touched liquid. He looked at them and saw they were smeared in blood.

His stomach heaved liked wet cement in a mixer. He turned away and threw up his breakfast where he stood, almost oblivious to another thud only a few feet away.

Sirens wailed, sirens from the pit of hell. Sirens from all around. Everywhere. Then another thud, another spatter on his face and hands.

He looked up. Flames and smoke and ant-like figures and sheet glass and a man, in shirtsleeves and trousers, tumbling in free fall from the sky. One shoe came away, flipping over and over. He watched it all the way down, end-over-end-over-end-over-end. People the size of toy soldiers and debris, indistinguishable from each other at first, were raining from the sky.

He just stood and stared. A set of postage stamps he had once traded, commemorating the Dutch painter Bosch's vision of death and hell, came into his mind. That's what this was. Hell.

The foul choking air was thick with noise now. Screams, sirens, cries, the overhead chop of helicopter blades. Police and fire officers were running towards the buildings. A fire truck bearing the words 'Ladder 12' pulled up in front of him, blocking his view. He moved around the far side of it as helmeted firemen poured out and broke into a run.

There was another thud. Ronnie saw a plump man in a suit land on his back and explode.

He threw up again, swaying giddily, then dropped to one knee, covering his face with his hands, and stayed there for some moments, shaking. He closed his eyes, as if somehow that would make everything go away. Then he turned in a sudden panic that someone had taken his bag and his briefcase. But they were there, right behind him. His smart fake Louis Vuitton briefcase. Not that anyone was going to care at this moment who the hell had made it. Or whether it was fake or real.

After some minutes, Ronnie pulled himself together and stood up. He spat several times, trying to get the taste of vomit out of his mouth. Then a flash of anger turned in seconds to a burning rage inside him. *Why today? Why not some other fucking day? Why did this have to happen today?*

He saw a stream of people, some of them covered in white dust, some bleeding, walking slowly, as if in a trance, out of the entrance of the North Tower. Then he heard the distant *honk-honk-honk* of another fire engine. Then another. And another. Someone in front of him was holding a video camera.

News, he thought. *Television.* Stupid bloody Lorraine would be panicking if she saw this. She panicked over everything. If there was a pile-up on a motorway she would instantly call to make sure he was all right, even when she must have known, if she'd only thought about it, that he couldn't have been within a hundred miles of it.

He pulled his mobile phone out of his pocket and dialled her number. There was a sharp beep, then the message on the display:

Network busy.

He tried again, twice more, then put the phone back in his pocket.

He would come to realize just a little while later, when he reflected on it, how lucky he was that his call did not get through.

16

OCTOBER 2007

You are meant to be bloody luminous! In the pitch, bitumen-black darkness, Abby brought her watch right up to her face, until she felt the cold steel and glass against her nose, and still she could not see a damned thing.

I paid money for a luminous watch, damn you!

Curled up on the hard floor, she had a feeling she might have slept, but she had no idea for how long. Was it day or night?

Her muscles felt as if they had seized and her arm was dead. She swung it through the air, trying to shake circulation back into it. It was like a lead weight. She crawled a couple of feet and swung it again, then winced in pain as it struck the side of the lift with a dull *boom*.

'Hello!' she croaked.

She banged again, then again and again.

Felt the lift swaying at her exertion.

Banged again. Again. Again.

Felt the urge to pee once more. One boot was already full. The reek of stale urine was growing stronger. Her mouth was parched. She closed her eyes, then opened them again, brought the watch up close until she could feel the coldness on her nose. But still she couldn't see it.

Squirming in sudden panic, she wondered if she could have gone blind.

What the hell time was it? When she had last looked, before the lights went out, it had been 3.08 a.m. Some time after then she had peed into her boot. Or at least as best she could in the darkness.

She had felt better then and had been able to think clearly. Now the need to pee was muzzing her thoughts again. She tried to push the desire from her mind. Some years ago she had watched a documentary on television about people who had survived disasters. A young woman her own age had been one of the few survivors from an aircraft that had crash-landed and caught fire. The woman reckoned she had lived because she kept calm when everyone else was panicking, had thought logically, figured out through the smoke and darkness which way the exit was.

The same theme had been echoed by all the other survivors. Keeping calm, thinking clearly. That was what you had to do.

Easier said than done.

They had exit doors on planes. And stewardesses with *Stepford Wives* expressions who pointed out the exits and held up orange life jackets and tugged at oxygen masks, as if they were addressing a convention of mentally retarded deaf mutes on every flight. England was a bloody nanny state now, so why hadn't they passed a law ensuring that every lift had a stewardess on board? Why didn't you find a robotic blonde standing inside each time you entered, handing you a laminated card that told you where the doors were? Giving you an orange life jacket in case the lift got flooded while you were in it? Waving oxygen masks in your face?

Suddenly she heard a sharp beep-beep.

Her phone!

She fumbled for her handbag. Light spilled out of it. Her phone was working! There was a signal! And, of course, there was a clock on the phone – she had totally forgotten about in her panic!

She pulled it out and stared at it. On the display were the words:

New message.

Barely able to contain her excitement, she clicked it open.

She did not recognize the number. The message read:

I know where you are.

17

OCTOBER 2007

Roy Grace shivered. Although he had on thick jeans, a heavy-knit pullover and lined boots under his paper suit, the damp inside the storm drain and the rain outside were getting into his bones.

The SOCOs and search officers, who had the unpleasant task of checking every inch of the drain, mostly on their hands and knees, had so far found a few rodent skeletons, but nothing of interest. Either the dead woman's clothing had been removed before she was deposited here, or it had been washed away, rotted or even taken for animals' nests. Working painstakingly slowly with trowels, Joan Major and Frazer Theobald were scraping away the silt around the pelvis, bagging and tagging each layer of dirt separately in neat cellophane bags. They would be another two or three hours at this rate, Grace estimated.

And all the time he was drawn back to the grinning skull. The sensation that Sandy's spirit was here with him. *Could it really be you?* he wondered, staring hard. Every medium he had been to in the past nine years had told him that his wife was not in the spirit world. Which meant she was still alive – if he believed them. But none had been able to say where she was.

A chill fluttered through him. This time it was not the cold, but something else. He had determined a while ago to find closure and move forward with his life. But each time he tried, something happened that sowed doubt in him, and it was happening again now.

The crackle of his radio phone startled him out of his reverie. He held it to his ear with a curt, 'Roy Grace?'

'Morning, Roy. Your career going down the drain, is it?' Then he heard Norman Potting's throaty chuckle.

'Very funny, Norman. Where are you?'

'With the scene guard. Want me to get togged up and come down?'

'No, I'll come to you – meet me in the SOCO van.'

Grace welcomed the excuse to get away for a bit. He wasn't strictly needed here and could easily have gone back to his office, but he liked his team to see him leading from the front. If they were having to spend their Saturday inside a dank, horrible drain, at least they could see his day wasn't any better.

It was a relief to shut the door on the elements and sit down on the soft upholstery at the work table in the van. Even if it meant being confined in a small area with Norman Potting – never an experience he relished. He could smell the stale pipe smoke coming off the man's clothes, mixed with a strong reminder of last night's garlic.

Detective Sergeant Norman Potting had a narrow, rather rubbery face criss-crossed with broken veins, protruding lips and a thinning comb-over, part of which at this moment was sticking bolt upright, having been blasted by the elements. He was fifty-three, although those who particularly disliked him spread rumours that he had knocked several years off his age so he could stay in the force longer, because he was terrified of retirement.

Grace had never seen Potting without a tie and this morning was no exception. The man was wearing a long, wet anorak with duffel tags over a tweed jacket, Viyella shirt and a fraying green knitted tie, grey flannel trousers and stout brogues. With a wheezing sound, he eased himself behind the table, on to the bench seat opposite Grace, then plonked down a large, dripping-wet cellophane folder, looking triumphant.

'Why do people always pick such bleedin' awful places to get murdered or dumped in?' he said, leaning forward and exhaling directly into Roy's face.

Trying not to wince as a blast furnace of hot and rancid smells enveloped him, Roy decided that this was probably what being breathed on by a dragon would be like. 'Maybe you should draw up some guidelines,' he said testily. 'A fifty-point code of practice for murder victims to abide by.'

Subtlety had never been Norman Potting's strong point and it took him a moment now to realize that the Detective Superintendent was being sarcastic. Then he broke into a grin, showing a mouthful of stained, crooked teeth, like tombstones on subsiding ground.

He raised a finger. 'I'm rather slow this morning, Roy. Had a bit of a night last night. Li was like a bloody tiger!'

Potting had recently 'acquired' a Thai bride and constantly regaled anyone in earshot with details of his newfound prowess in bed with her.

Heading off the subject rapidly, Grace pointed at the cellophane folder. 'You got the plans?'

'Four times last night, Roy! And she's a dirty cow – do anything! Phoawwww! She makes me a very happy man!'

'Good.'

For a brief moment, Grace actually felt pleased for him. Potting had never had a lot of luck in his love life. He was a veteran of three marriages, with several children he had once admitted, ruefully, that he rarely saw. The youngest was a girl with Down's syndrome whom he had tried and failed to get custody of. He wasn't a bad or a stupid person, Roy knew – he was a very competent detective – but he lacked the social skills essential to rising any higher in the force, should he want to. Still, Norman Potting was a solid and dependable workhorse, with sometimes surprising initiative, and those aspects of him were far more important in any major inquiry, in his view.

'You should consider it yourself, Roy.'

'Consider what?'

'Getting a Thai bride. Hundreds of them gagging for an English husband. I'll give you the website – they are bloody wonderful, I tell you. They cook, clean, do all your ironing, give you the best sex of your life – lovely little bodies—'

'The plans?' Grace said, ignoring the last remark.

'Ah, yes.'

Potting shook several large photocopies of street maps, grids and section drawings out of the folder and spread them over the table. Some of them dated back to the nineteenth century.

Wind rocked the van. Outside, somewhere in the distance, an emergency service siren sounded and then faded away. The rain drummed steadily on the roof.

Plans had never been something that Roy found easy to follow, so he let Potting talk him through the complexities of Brighton and Hove's drainage system, using the paperwork and briefing which had been given to him by a corporation engineer earlier this morning. The DS ran a grimy-nailed finger across, down, then up each of the drawings in turn, showing how the water ran, always downhill, eventually out into the sea.

Roy tried hard to keep up with him, but half an hour on he was little wiser than he had been before he started.

It seemed to him that it all added up to the fact that the weight of the dead woman's body had jammed her in the silt, while anything else would have been washed down the drain, into the trap and out to sea.

Potting concurred with him.

Grace's phone rang again. Excusing himself, he answered it, and his heart immediately sank as he heard the dentist's-drill voice of freshly appointed Detective Superintendent Cassian Pewe. The slimeball from the Met his boss had brought in to eat his lunch.

'Hello, Roy,' Pewe said. Even distanced by a phone connection, Grace had the impression that Pewe's smug, pretty-boy face was pressed claustrophobically up against his own. 'Alison Vosper suggested I give you a call – to see if you needed a hand.'

'Well, that's very kind of you, Cassian,' he replied. 'But no, actually, the body's intact – I've got both of her hands here.'

There was a silence. Pewe made a sound like a man who has started to urinate against an electric fence. A kind of stilted laughter. 'Oh, very funny, Roy,' he patronized. Then, after an awkward silence, he added, 'You've got all the SOCOs and search officers you need?'

Grace felt a band tighten inside him. Somehow he restrained himself from telling the man to go and find something else to do with his Saturday. 'Thank you,' he said instead.

'Good. Alison will be pleased. I'll let her know.'

'Actually, I'll let her know,' Grace said. 'If I need your help I will ask her, but at the moment we are all managing very well. And – I thought you weren't actually starting until Monday.'

'Oh, absolutely, Roy, that's correct. Alison just felt that

helping you out over the weekend might be a good way to get my eye in.'

'I appreciate her concern,' Grace managed to say before he hung up, boiling with rage.

'Detective Superintendent Pewe?' Potting asked him, with raised eyebrows.

'You've met him?'

'Aye, met him. Know his type. Give a pompous ass like him enough rope and he'll hang himself. Never fails.'

'Got any rope on you?' Grace asked.

18

11 SEPTEMBER 2001

Ronnie Wilson had lost all track of time. He just stood still, transfixed, holding the handle of his bag as if it was his crutch, watching something he could not comprehend unfolding before his eyes.

Stuff was tumbling out of the sky on to the plaza and the surrounding streets. Raining from the sky. A never-ending downpour of masonry, office partitions, desks, chairs, glass, pictures, framed photographs, sofas, computer screens, keyboards, filing cabinets, waste bins, lavatory seats, washbasins, paper like letter-sized white confetti. And bodies. Bodies falling. Men and women who were alive in the air one moment, exploding and disintegrating as they landed. He wanted to turn away, to scream, to run, but it was as if a massive leaden finger was pressing down on his head, forcing him to stand still, to observe in numb silence.

He felt that he was watching the end of the world.

It seemed that every fireman and every police officer in New York was running into the Twin Towers. An endless stream entering, barging past the endless stream of bewildered men and women leaving at half-speed, staggering out as if from some other world, covered in dust, dishevelled, some with their arms or faces tracked with blood, contorted by shock. Many of them had mobiles pressed to their ears.

Then came the earthquake. Just a gentle vibration beneath his feet to start with, then more vigorous, so that he really had to grip the handle of his bag hard for support. And suddenly the zombies emerging from the South Tower seemed to wake up and quicken their pace.

They started running.

Ronnie looked up and saw the reason why. But for a moment he thought it must be a mistake. This was not possible! It was an optical illusion. *It had to be.*

The entire building was collapsing in on itself, like a house of cards, except—

A police car a short distance in front of him was suddenly flattened.

Then a fire engine was flattened too.

A cloud of dust like a desert sandstorm rolled towards him. He heard thunder. Rolling, rumbling, surround-sound thunder.

A whole stream of people disappeared under masonry.

The dark grey cloud was rising in the air like a storm of furious insects.

The thunder was numbing his ears.

This was not possible.

The fucking tower was coming down.

People sprinting for their lives. A woman lost a shoe, continued limping along on one foot, then shed the other shoe. A terrible tearing sound in the air, drowning out the sirens, as if some giant monster was ripping the world in half with its claws.

They were running past him. One person, then another, and another, their faces etched into masks of panic. Some were sheet-white masks, some were dripping water from sprinkler systems, some dripping blood or showering slivers of glass. Bit-part players in a weird early-morning carnival.

A BMW suddenly jumped in the air, yards from where he stood, and came down on its roof minus its front end. Then he saw the black cloud rising, tumbling straight towards him like a tidal wave.

Gripping the handle of his bag, he turned and followed them. Not knowing where he was going, he just ran, putting one foot in front of the other, towing his bag, not sure, not even caring, whether his briefcase was still on top. Running to keep ahead of the black cloud, of the falling tower that he could hear, thundering, rumbling in his ears, in his heart, in his soul.

Running for his life.

19

OCTOBER 2007

By now the lift seemed alive, like some preternatural creature. When Abby breathed, it sighed, creaked, moaned. When she moved, it swayed, twisted, rocked. Her mouth and throat were parched; her tongue and the inside of her mouth felt like blotting paper, instantly absorbing any tiny drop of saliva she produced.

A cold, persistent draught was blowing on her face. She fumbled in the darkness for the cursor button on her phone, then pressed it to activate the light on the display. She did this every few minutes, to check whether there was any signal and to bring a small but desperately welcome ray of light into her unstable, swaying prison cell.

No signal.

The time on the display read 1.32 p.m.

She tried dialling 999 yet again. But the feeble signal had gone.

With a shiver, she again read the text that had come through:

I know where you are.

Despite not recognizing the number, she knew who it was; there was only one person who could have sent it. But how did he have her number? That was what really worried her at this moment. *How the hell do you know my number?*

It was a pay-as-you-go phone, which she had bought for cash. She'd seen enough cop shows on television to know that was what crooks did so their calls could not be traced. These were the phones drug dealers used. She had bought it to keep in touch with her mother, who now lived in nearby Eastbourne, to see if she was OK, while pretending to her that she was still abroad and was well. Almost as importantly, the phone was so she could keep in touch with Dave – and occasionally send pictures. It was hard being apart for this long from someone you loved.

The thought suddenly occurred to her: *had the sender gone to her mother?* But even if he had, he wouldn't have got her number. She was always careful to withhold it. Besides, when she had called yesterday, her mum had said nothing and sounded fine.

Could he have been following her, seen where she bought the phone and got the number that way? No. No chance. She had bought it from a small mobile phone shop in a side street off Preston Circus, where she had been able to make doubly sure no one was observing her. At least, as best she could.

Was he here in the building now? What if he was responsible for trapping her like this? And was using the time to break into her flat . . . ? What if he was in the flat now, searching?

What if he found—

Unlikely.

She looked at the display again.

The words scared her more and more. Coils of fear spiralled inside her. She stood up in panic, pressing the cursor again as the light went off, pushing her fingers in the crack between the doors for the hundredth time, trying to force them apart, weeping in frustration.

They wouldn't move.

Please, please open. Oh, God, please open.

The lift swayed wildly again. An image flashed in her mind of divers in a shark cage, with a Great White nosing against the bars. That's what he was like. A Great White. A numb, unfeeling predator. She must have been mad, she decided, to have agreed to this.

If ever there had been a moment in her life when her resolve to succeed faltered, and she would willingly have traded all she had just to turn the clock back, it was now.

20

OCTOBER 2007

Blowflies or bluebottles – or blue-arsed flies, as the Aussies called them – can scent a dead body from twelve miles away. Which gives them a considerable amount in common with crime reporters, Roy Grace was fond of telling members of his team. They feed on the fluid protein excretions that ooze from a decomposing cadaver. Not much different from crime reporters there either, he liked to add.

And, no surprise, there was one outside the door of the SOCO van at this very moment, the *Argus*'s most persistent – and best informed, it had to be said – crime reporter, Kevin Spinella. Sometimes *too* well informed.

Grace told the scene guard who had radioed to inform him of the reporter's presence that he would speak to Spinella, and stepped outside into the rain, relieved to get away from the rank smell of Norman Potting. As he walked towards the reporter, he noticed two photographers hanging around.

Spinella stood without an umbrella, hands in his pockets, wearing a sodden gumshoe raincoat with epaulettes and a belt, and the collar turned up. He was a slight, thin-faced man in his middle twenties with alert eyes and his mouth was busily working a piece of chewing gum. His thin black hair, brushed and gelled forward, was at this moment matted to his head by the rain.

Beneath the reporter's coat, Grace could see, he was wearing a dark business suit and a shirt that was at least one size too big for him, as if he hadn't grown into it yet. The collar was hanging slack around his neck, despite the big, clumsy knot of his crimson polyester tie pulled tight. His flashy black shoes were caked in mud.

'You're a bit late, old son,' Grace said as a greeting.

'Late?' The reporter frowned.

'The blowflies beat you by several years.'

Spinella gave him the merest hint of a smile, as if unsure to what extent Grace was taking the mickey. 'Wondered if I could ask you a few questions, Detective Superintendent.'

'I'll be holding a press conference on Monday.'

'Is there anything you can tell me in the meantime?'

'I thought maybe you might be able to tell me something – you normally appear to be better informed than I am.'

Again the reporter seemed uncertain about his attitude. With a thin smile of acknowledgement he said, 'Heard you found a skeleton, a woman, down in a storm drain just over there on the site. Is that correct?'

The casual way he asked the question, as if they were remains of no significance, angered Grace. But he needed to keep his cool. There was nothing to be gained by antagonizing Spinella; it was always better, in his experience of dealing with the press, to be guardedly helpful.

'The remains are human,' he replied. 'But so far the gender hasn't been positively ascertained.'

'I heard it is definitely a female.'

Grace smiled. 'You see, I just said you were better informed than me.'

'So – er – is it?'

'Who do you want to trust, your sources or me?'

The reporter stared at Grace for a few moments, as if trying to read him. A drip formed on the bottom of his nose, but he made no attempt to wipe it off. 'Can I ask you something else?'

'If it's quick.'

'I hear you've got a new colleague starting at Sussex House on Monday – an officer from the Met, Detective Superintendent Pewe?'

Grace felt himself tighten. One more smug remark and he was going to knock that drip off Spinella's nose with his bare fist. 'You hear correctly.'

'I understand the Met is the first police force in the UK to start cutting down on bureaucracy properly.'

'You do, do you?'

The reporter's snide grin was almost unbearable, as if he knew all kinds of secrets he was not revealing. For a wild moment Grace even thought that he might have been leaked something confidential by Alison Vosper.

'They're employing civilian clerks to book people into custody, so their arresting officers can go straight back out on patrol – instead of spending hours filling out forms,' Spinella said. 'Do you reckon Sussex CID will be learning things from Detective Superintendent Pewe?'

Fighting his anger, Grace was careful with his answer. 'I'm sure Detective Superintendent Pewe is going to be a valuable member of the Sussex CID team,' he said.

'I can quote you on that, can I?' The grin was getting even worse.

What do you know, you little shit?

Roy's radio phone crackled. He held it to his ear. 'Roy Grace?'

It was one of the SOCOs in the tunnel, Tony Monnington.

'Thought you'd like to know, Roy, we seem to have found our first possible piece of evidence.'

Grace politely excused himself from the reporter and made his way back to the storm drain, phoning Norman Potting to tell him he would be some minutes. It was strange how things in life changed on you constantly, he thought. A little while ago, he could not wait to get out of the storm drain. Now, when the alternatives were either standing in the rain and talking to Spinella or going back to being closeted in the SOCO van with Norman Potting, suddenly it seemed to have a lot going for it.

21

OCTOBER 2007

It was Abby's room-mate, Sue, who had inadvertently changed her life. The two of them had met working in a bar down on the Yarra waterfront in Melbourne and became instant friends. They were the same age and, like Abby, Sue had gone to Australia from England in search of adventure.

One evening, nearly a year ago, Sue told Abby that a couple of good-looking blokes, a bit older than them but very charming, had been in the bar, chatting to her. They said they were going to a barbie on Sunday with a fun crowd of people and to come along if she was free, to bring a girlfriend with her if she liked.

Having no better offers, they went. The barbecue was at a cool bachelor pad, a penthouse apartment in one of Melbourne's hippest districts, with fine views across the bay. But, in those heady first hours, Abby had barely taken in her surroundings because she had been instantly and totally smitten with her host, Dave Nelson.

There were a couple of dozen other people at the party. The men, ranging from about ten years older than her to north of sixty, looked like extras from the set of a gangster film, and the women, dripping with bling, all seemed to have just stepped out of beauty salons. But she barely noticed them either. In fact, she hardly spoke a word to anyone else from the moment she set foot in the door.

Dave was a tall, lean, rough diamond in his late forties with a rich tan, short gelled hair and a world-weary face that had probably been seriously handsome in his youth, but now looked comfortably lived in. And that was how she felt, instantaneously, with him. Comfortable.

He moved around the apartment with an easy, animal grace, lavishly sloshing out Krug from magnum bottles all afternoon. He was tired, he said, because he had been playing poker for three days around the clock, in an international tournament, the Aussie Millions, at the Crown Plaza casino. He'd paid an entry fee of one thousand dollars, and had survived four rounds, building up a pot of over one hundred thousand, before being knocked out. A trip of aces, he'd told Abby ruefully. How was he to know the guy had two aces in the hole? When he had three kings, two hidden, for Christ's sake!

Abby had never played poker before. But that night, after the rest of the guests had gone, he'd sat her down and taught her. She'd liked the attention, liked the way he looked at her all the time, told her how pretty she was, then how beautiful she was, then how good she made him feel just being there with him. His eyes scarcely left her face in all the hours they sat there together, as if nothing else mattered. They were good eyes, brown with a hint of green, alert but tinged with sadness, as if there was some loss hurting him deep inside. It made her want to protect him, to mother him.

She loved the stories he told her about his travels, and how he had made his fortune dealing rare stamps and playing poker, mostly on the internet. He worked a gambling system which seemed so obvious, when he explained it, and so clever.

Internet poker games took place all over the world, 24/7. He'd use the time zones, logging on to games that were being played where it was the small hours of the morning by people who were tired and often a little drunk. He'd watch for a while, then join in. Easy pickings for a man fully awake, sober and alert.

Abby had always been attracted to older men and this guy, who seemed so tough, yet was passionate about tiny, delicate, beautiful stamps and enthused to her about their links with history, fascinated her. For a girl from a staid British background, he was totally different from anyone she had ever met. And although there was that vulnerability about him, at the same time there was something intensely strong and manly that made her feel safe with him.

For the first time in her life, breaking her own rule with total abandon, she slept with him that very night. And she moved in with him just a couple of weeks later. He took her shopping, encouraging her to buy expensive clothes, and often came home with jewellery or a new watch or an insanely lavish bunch of flowers if he'd had a good poker win.

Sue had done her best to dissuade Abby, pointing out that he was a good deal older than her, that he had a somewhat uncertain past and a reputation as something of a ladies' man – or, put more crudely, as a serial shagger.

But Abby had ignored all of that, dumping her friendship first with Sue and subsequently with the other friends she had made since arriving in Melbourne. Instead, she enjoyed meeting Dave's older and – to her – much more glamorous and interesting circle. Big money had always had an allure for her and these people were all big spenders.

As a child, in her school holidays she had sometimes gone on jobs with her father, who ran a small floor and bathroom tiling business. She had loved helping him, but a stronger attraction for her was the houses – some of them really incredible – where rich people lived. Her mother worked at the public library in Hove and their little semi in Hollingbury, with its neat garden, which both her parents tended lovingly, was the extent of their horizons.

As she grew up, Abby felt increasingly constricted, and restricted, by her modest upbringing. In her teens she read the works of Danielle Steel, Jackie Collins and Barbara Taylor Bradford avidly, and of every other novelist who wrote about the lives of the rich and glamorous, as well as devouring *OK!* and *Hello!* magazines cover-to-cover every week. She secretly harboured dreams of vast wealth, and the grand houses and yachts in the sun that would come with it. She longed to travel and she knew, deep down, that one day she would get her chance. By the time she was thirty, she promised herself, she would be rich.

When a friend of Dave's was arrested on three murder charges she was appalled, but she couldn't help feeling a frisson of excitement. Then another of his circle was shot dead in his car, in front of his twins, while watching a children's football training session. She began to realize that she was now part of a very different culture from the one she had grown up in and had previously understood. But despite her shock at the man's death, she found the funeral exciting. To be there as part of all these people, to be accepted by them – it was the biggest turn-on of her life.

At the same time she began to wonder what else Dave

was really up to. She noticed him sometimes fawning over the guys he had told her were the biggest players, trying to do some kind of business with them. One morning she overheard him on the phone telling someone that trading in stamps was a great way to launder money, to move it around the globe, as if he was trying to sell the concept to them.

She didn't like that so much. It was as if she hadn't minded all the time they were on the fringe, just hanging out in bars and partying with these people. But actually doing business with them – almost begging them to let him do business – lowered Dave in her eyes. And yet, deep in her heart, she felt she might be able to help him, if she could just get through the wall he seemed to have erected around himself. Because, after several months with him, she realized she knew no more about his past than when she had first met him, other than that he'd had two previous wives and both his divorces had been painful.

Then one day he dropped a bombshell.

22

SEPTEMBER 2007

The metallic blue Holden pick-up headed west, away from Melbourne. MJ, a tall young man of twenty-eight with jet-black hair and a surfer's frame, wearing a yellow T-shirt and Bermudas, drove with one hand on the wheel, his free arm around Lisa's shoulders.

The ute sat low and squat on its shocks, on wide mags shod with fatties that clung sure-footedly to the contours of the winding road. This vehicle was his pride and joy, and he listened contentedly to the burble of the V8 5.7-litre engine through the drainpipe exhausts as they drove through big, open country. To their right, plains of scorched vegetation stretched out for miles. To their left, beyond a tired-looking barbed-wire fence, softly contoured brown hills rose in the near distance, parched and arid courtesy of six years' almost unbroken drought. A few thin ridges of trees were scattered over them randomly, like strips of facial hair missed by a razor.

It was Saturday morning and for two whole days MJ could forget about his intensive studies. In a month's time he was sitting tough stockbroking exams, which he needed to pass to secure a permanent job with his current employers, Macquarie Bank. Spring had been a long time coming this year, despite the drought, and this weekend promised to be the first truly glorious one after the dreary winter months. He was determined to make the most of it.

They were ambling along. With six points on his licence, he was being careful to drive well within the speed limits. Besides, he wasn't in any hurry. He was happy – intensely happy – just being here with the girl he loved, enjoying the drive, the scenery, the Saturday morning feeling of the whole weekend stretching out ahead of him.

Something he had once read was going around inside his head: *Happiness is not getting what you want. It is wanting what you have.*

He said it out aloud to Lisa, and she said they were beautiful words, and she agreed with them. Totally. She kissed him. 'You say so many beautiful things, MJ.' He blushed.

She pressed a button and music from the Whitlams thumped out of the madly expensive sound system he'd had installed. And their camping gear and the slab of VB beer thumped under the battened-down tarp behind the cab. And his heart thumped too. It was good to be here, good to feel so alive, to feel the warm air blowing on his face through the open window, to smell Lisa's perfume, to feel her tangle of blonde curls batting against his wrist.

'Where are we?' she said, not that she cared. She was enjoying this too. Enjoying the break from her weekly routine of visiting doctors' practices as a haemophilia drugs sales rep for the pharmaceutical giant Wyeth. Enjoying wearing just a loose white top and pink shorts, instead of the business suits she had to wear during the week. But most of all, enjoying precious time together with MJ.

'Nearly there,' he said.

They passed a yellow hexagonal road sign depicting a

black bicycle and stopped at a T-intersection, beside the skeletal trunk of a Radiata pine that was topped by a thick clump of needles, like a badly fitting toupee. Immediately ahead of them rose a steep, bald hill with isolated clusters of bushes looking as if they'd been stuck to it by Velcro.

Lisa, who was English, had only been in Australia for two years. She had moved to Melbourne from Perth a few months ago and the terrain was all new to her. 'When were you last here?' she asked.

'Not for some years – ten maybe. Used to come here camping with my parents, when I was a kid,' he said. 'It was our favourite place. You're going to love it. Yee-hah!'

With a sudden burst of exuberance, he tramped the accelerator. The ute shot forward, making a sharp left on to the highway with a squeal of its tyres and a roar of thunder from its exhausts.

After a few minutes they passed a sign on a pole that read BARWON RIVER, then MJ slowed down and started looking to his right as they passed another saying STONEHAVEN AND POLLOCKS FORD.

After a while he braked sharply and turned right on to a sandy track. 'I'm pretty sure this is it!' he said.

They bounced along for five hundred yards or so. Wide open country to their right, bushes to their left and an embankment down to a river they couldn't see. They passed a steel-girder bridge sitting on old brick buttresses to their left, then thick brush obscured the view. The track suddenly dipped sharply, then rose again on the far side. After a few minutes it widened out for some yards and ended, turning into scrub grass beyond which was dense brush.

MJ brought the ute to a halt and put on the handbrake.

A cloud of dust swirled over them. 'Welcome to paradise,' he said.

They kissed.

Then, after some moments, they climbed out. Into total warm silence. The engine pinged. There was the scent of dried grasses in the air. A bowerbird made a sound like someone whistling *yoo hoo!*, then was silent. Down below them, snaking into the distance, was shimmering water and further away, beneath the fierce late-morning sun, there were bald brown hills sporting just the occasional acacia or eucalyptus tree. The silence was so intense, for a moment they felt they could be the only people on the planet.

'God,' Lisa said, 'this is so beautiful.'

A fly buzzed around her face and she batted it away. Another one came and she batted that away too.

'Good old flies,' MJ said. 'This is the right spot!'

'Obviously they remember you!' she said, as a third one landed on her forehead.

He gave her a playful punch, before arcing his hand several times in rapid succession in front of his face, giving an Aussie salute to flap away more flies that were pestering him. Then, with his arm around her, MJ steered Lisa to a gap in the brush.

'This is where we used to launch our canoe,' he said.

She peered down a steep, sandy slope overgrown with bracken that was a natural slipway into the river, a good thirty yards below. The water, about twenty yards wide, was as still as a millpond. A few damsel flies sat on the surface, feeding off mosquito larvae or laying eggs, and more hovered just above. Reflections of the brush on the far bank appeared in sharp focus.

'Wow!' she said. 'Wowwwwwww! That is amazing.'

Then she noticed the series of white sticks planted all the way down the slipway. Each of them had precise ruled markings in black.

'When I was a kid,' MJ said, 'the water level was up to here.' He pointed at the top marker.

Lisa counted eight exposed rulers, all the way down to the water. 'It's dropped this much?'

'Good old global warming,' he replied.

Then she saw the looped hangman's rope fixed to the overhanging branch of a tree thick as an elephant's leg.

'We used to jump off that!' MJ said. 'It was just a short drop.'

Now it was a good five yards.

He peeled off his T-shirt. 'Coming in?'

'Let's put the tent up first!'

'Shit, Lisa, we've got the whole day to put the tent up! I'm hot!' He continued stripping. 'And the flies hate the water.'

'Tell me what the water's like – I'll think about it!'

'You're weak as piss!'

Lisa laughed. MJ stood naked, then disappeared for some moments into the undergrowth. Moments later, she saw him crawling along the overhanging branch. He reached the rope, which looked dangerously frayed, rolled over and clung to it.

'Be careful, MJ!' she shouted, suddenly alarmed.

Holding on with one arm, he beat his chest with the other, making a series of Tarzan whoops. Then he swung out over the river, his bare feet almost touching the surface of the water. He swung back and forward in several arcs, then he let go and dropped with a loud splash.

Lisa watched anxiously. Moments later he surfaced and

tossed his head, shaking wet hair away from his face. 'It's beautiful! Get in here, wuss!'

He struck out, doing a couple of powerful crawl strokes, then suddenly he raised his head with a pained expression.

'Fuck!' he spluttered. 'Shit! Owww! Bloody stubbed my toe on something!'

Lisa laughed.

MJ duck-dived. Moments later his head broke the surface and there was a look of panic on his face.

'Shit, Lisa!' he said. 'There's a car down here! There's a fucking car in the river!'

23

11 SEPTEMBER 2001

Lorraine stared in numb disbelief. The unlit cigarette between her fingers was quite forgotten. A young female reporter, talking urgently to the camera, seemed totally unaware that the South Tower, just a few hundred yards behind her, was collapsing.

It was dropping straight down out of the sky, disappearing inside itself, neatly, almost unbearably neatly, as if for one brief instant Lorraine was witnessing the greatest conjuring trick ever performed. The reporter talked on. Behind her, cars and people were disappearing under rubble and swirling dust. Others were running for their lives, running straight down the street towards the camera.

Oh, Jesus, doesn't she realize?

Still unaware, the reporter continued reading off her autocue or from a feed in her ear.

LOOK BEHIND YOU! she wanted to scream at the woman.

Then finally the woman did turn. And lost the plot totally. She took a startled, stumbling step sideways, followed by another. People were running past on either side, jostling her, almost knocking her off her feet. The mushrooming cloud was now as tall as the sky itself, and as wide as the city, tumbling like an avalanche towards her. In bewildered shock, she spoke a few more words, but there was no sound with them, as if the cable had been disconnected, then the image became just a grey swirl of shadowy figures and chaos as the camera was engulfed.

Lorraine, still in just her bikini bottoms, heard various shouts. The image on the screen cut to a jerky, hand-held shot of a massive slab of steel and glass and masonry crashing on to a red and white fire truck. It smashed through the ladder, then flattened the whole mid-section, as if this was a plastic toy truck a child had just stamped on.

A woman's voice was shouting, over and over, 'Oh, my God! Oh, my God! Oh, my God.'

There were cries. Darkness for a second, then another hand-held shot, a young man limping past holding a blood-drenched towel against a woman's face, helping her along, trying to pull her faster, ahead of the cloud that was gaining on them.

Then they were in a studio news set. Lorraine watched the anchor, a man in his forties in a jacket and tie. The images she had been viewing were all up on monitors behind his head. He looked grim.

'We're getting reports that the South Tower of the World Trade Center has collapsed. We are also going to bring you the latest on the situation at the Pentagon in just a few moments.'

Lorraine tried to light the cigarette, but her hand was shaking too much and the lighter fell to the floor. She waited, unable to bear taking her eyes from the screen for even one second in case she missed a glimpse of Ronnie. There was an agitated woman on the television now, shouting unintelligibly. She watched an attractive woman clutching a mike, who was standing against a background of dense black smoke flecked with orange flames, through which she could just make out the low roofline silhouettes of the Pentagon.

She dialled Ronnie's mobile number and once more got the lines-busy beep.

She tried again. Again. Again. Her heart was thrashing around inside her chest and she was shaking, desperate to hear his voice, to know that he was OK. And all the time inside her head was the knowledge that Ronnie's meeting was in the South Tower. The South Tower had collapsed.

She wanted more pictures of Manhattan, not the sodding Pentagon, Ronnie was in Manhattan, not the sodding Pentagon. She changed channels to Sky News. Saw another jerky hand-held shot, this time of three dusty firemen in helmets carrying a busted-looking grey-haired man, their yellow armbands jigging as they walked urgently along.

Then she saw a burning car. And a burning ambulance. Figures appearing out of the gloom behind them. Ronnie? She leaned forward, close up to the huge screen. Ronnie? The figures appeared from the smoke like faces on a developing photograph. No Ronnie.

Then she dialled his number again. For one fleeting moment it sounded as if it was going to ring! Then she was thwarted by the lines-busy signal once more.

Sky News cut to Washington. She grabbed the remote and hit another button. It seemed that every station was now showing the same images, the same news feeds. She watched a replay of the first plane striking, then the second. It replayed again. And again.

Her phone rang. She hit the answer button with a sudden burst of joy, almost too choked to get any words out. 'Hello?'

It was the washing-machine engineer, calling to confirm his appointment for tomorrow.

24

OCTOBER 2006

The target's name was Ricky. Abby had met him on a few occasions at parties, when he always seemed to make a beeline for her and chat her up. And in truth, she found him attractive and enjoyed the flirtation.

He was a good-looking guy in his forties, slightly mysterious and very self-assured, with the air of an ageing laid-back surfer dude. Like Dave, he knew how to talk to women, asking her more questions than he answered for her. He was also involved in stamps, in quite a big way.

Not all the stamps were his own. Four million pounds' worth, to be precise. There was some dispute over their ownership. Dave told her that he and Ricky had made a deal to split the proceeds fifty–fifty, but now Ricky was reneging and wanted ninety per cent. When she had asked Dave why he didn't simply go to the police he had smiled. Police, it seemed, were off limits for both of them.

Anyhow, he had a much better plan.

25

OCTOBER 2007

Roy Grace was still struggling, even with the help of the direct beam of a halogen light, to see the minute object Frazer Theobald was holding up in his stainless-steel tweezers. All he could make out was something blue and blurred.

He squinted, reluctant to admit to himself that he was getting to the point where he needed glasses. It was only when the pathologist placed a small square of paper behind the tweezers and handed him a magnifying glass that Roy could see it more clearly. It was a fibre of some kind, thinner than a human hair, like a gossamer strand of a spider's web. It appeared translucent one moment, then pale blue the next, and the ends were jigging from a combination of the faintest tremor in Theobald's hand and the icy breeze blowing through the storm drain.

'Whoever killed this woman did his best to leave no evidence,' the pathologist said. 'It's my guess he put her down here expecting that at some point she'd be washed along through the drainage system and then flushed out of the sewage outfall into the sea – thinking a sufficient distance from the shore for sewage would be a safe enough distance for a body.'

Grace stared again at the skeleton, unable to get the possibility that it was Sandy out of his mind.

'Perhaps her killer hadn't considered the drain not flooding,' Theobald went on. 'He hadn't reckoned on her getting embedded in the silt, and because the water table was down, there wasn't enough flow through the drain system to wash her free. Or maybe the drain went out of use.'

Grace nodded, looking again at the twitching thread.

'It's a carpet fibre, that's what I think. I could be wrong, but I think the lab analysis will show it's a carpet fibre. Too hard to be from a pullover or a skirt or a cushion cover. It's a carpet fibre.'

Joan Major nodded in agreement.

'Where did you find it?' Grace asked.

The forensic pathologist pointed at the skeleton's right hand, which was partially buried in the silt. The fingers were exposed. He pointed at the end of the middle finger. 'See that? It's an artificial nail – from one of those nail studio places.'

Grace felt a chill run through him. Sandy had bitten her nails. When they were watching television she would chew on them, making busy little clicking sounds like a hamster. It drove him nuts. And sometimes in bed as well. Often when he was trying to go to sleep, she would be gnawing away, as if fretting about something she could not or would not share with him. Then suddenly she'd look at her nails and get angry with herself, say to him that he must tell her when she was biting and help her to stop. And she would go to a nail studio to have expensive, artificial nails put over her bitten ones.

'A plastic compound, glued on, somehow the nails didn't get washed away when the skin beneath rotted,' Frazer Theobald said. 'The fibre was beneath this one. It could be that her assailant dragged her along a carpet and she dug her nails in. That's the most likely explanation of how it got there. Bit of luck that it didn't get washed away.'

'Luck, yes,' Grace said distantly. His mind was racing. *Dragged along a carpet.* A blue carpet fibre. Pale blue. Sky blue.

There was a pale blue carpet at home. In the bedroom. The bedroom he and Sandy had shared until the night she disappeared.

Into the blue.

26

11 SEPTEMBER 2001

Ronnie had been running for maybe a minute when day changed into night, as if there had been an instant, total eclipse of the sun. Suddenly he was stumbling through a choking, stinking void, with the sound of thunder in his ears, thunder that was rising from the ground.

It was as if someone had emptied a billion tons of foul-smelling, bitter-tasting black and grey flour into the sky directly above him. It stung his eyes, filled his mouth. He swallowed some of it and coughed it back up, immediately swallowing more. Grey shapes like ghosts swirled past him. He stubbed his toe painfully on something – a fire hydrant, he realized – as he tripped over the damned thing and fell forward, hard, on to the ground. Ground that was moving. It was vibrating, quaking, as if some giant monster had awakened and was breaking free from the belly of the earth itself.

Have to get out of here. Away from here.

Someone trod on his leg and crashed down on top of him. He heard a woman's voice, cursing and apologizing, and smelled a fleeting whiff of fine perfume. He wriggled free of her, tried to stand up, and immediately someone slammed into his back, hurtling him forward again.

Hyperventilating in panic, he scrambled to his feet and saw the woman, looking like a grey snowman clutching a pair of court shoes, get up. Then a huge fat man with mad hair crashed into him, cursing, punching him out of the way, and ran stumbling on to be swallowed by the fog.

Then he was knocked over again. *Got to get up. Get up. Get up!*

Memories of reading about people being crushed to death in panicking crowds swirled in his mind. He struggled to his feet again, turned, saw more snowy figures lumbering out of the gloom. One knocked him sideways. He searched through the oncoming legs, shoes, bare feet, for his bag and his briefcase, saw them, ducked down, grabbed them both, then was barged over on to his back again.

'Fuck you!' he screamed.

A stiletto heel passed over his head like a spiky shadow.

Then suddenly there was silence.

The rumbling stopped. The thunder stopped. The ground wasn't vibrating any more. The sirens stopped too.

For an instant, he felt elation. He was OK! He was alive!

People were walking past more slowly now, more orderly. Some were limping. Some were holding on to each other. Some had glass in their hair, like ice crystals. Blood was the only colour in an otherwise grey and black world.

'This is not happening,' a male voice near him said. 'This is so not happening.'

Ronnie could see the North Tower and then, to the right, a hill of twisted, lopsided wreckage, rubble, window frames, broken cars, burning vehicles, broken bodies lying motionless on the stained ground. Then he saw sky where the South Tower should have been.

Where it had been.

The Tower was gone.

It had been there minutes ago and now it wasn't there any more. He blinked, to check it wasn't some kind of trick, an optical illusion, and more of the dry stuff got caught in his eyes, making them water.

He was shaking, shaking all over. But mostly he was shaking deep inside.

Something caught his eye, drifting down, flapping, rising for a moment – caught in an updraught – then continuing its descent again. A piece of fabric. It looked like one of those felt cloths you got when you bought a new laptop, to stop the screen being scratched when you closed it.

He watched it fall all the way to the ground like a dead butterfly, landing just yards in front of him, and for an instant, amid all that was going on in his mind, he wondered if it was worth picking up, because he had long ago lost the one that had come with his laptop.

More people trudged past. An endless line, all in black and white and grey, like an old war movie or documentary showing refugees on the march. He thought he heard a phone ring. His own? In panic, he checked his pocket. His phone was still there, thank God! He pulled it out, but it wasn't ringing and there was no missed-call sign. He tried Lorraine again, but there was no signal, just a hollow beep-beep-beep, which was drowned out after a few seconds by the chop of a helicopter right above his head.

He did not know what to do. His thoughts were all jumbled. People were injured and he was OK. Maybe he should try to help people. Maybe he'd find Donald. They must have evacuated the building. They would have got everyone out before it came down, for sure. Donald was back there somewhere, maybe wandering around looking for him. If they could find each other, they could go to a café or a hotel and still have their meeting . . .

A fire truck blasted past him, almost running him down, then was gone in a blaze of red flashing lights and sirens and honking.

'Bastards!' he shouted. 'You fuckers, you almost killed—'

A group of black women caked grey, one carrying a satchel, one rubbing the back of her dreadlocked head, glided towards him.

'Excuse me?' Ronnie said, stepping into their path.

'Just keep going,' one of them replied.

'Yeah,' said another. 'Don't go that way!'

More emergency vehicles blasted past. The ground crunched. Paper snow beneath his feet, Ronnie realized. *The paperless society,* he thought cynically. *So much for the bloody paperless society.* The whole road was covered in grey paper. The sky was thick with falling sheets, zigzagging down, plain, typed, shredded, every shape and size you could imagine. Like a billion filing cabinets and waste bins had tipped their contents from a cloud.

He stopped for a moment, trying to think clearly. But the only thought that came into his head was, *Why today? Why fucking today?*

Why did this shit have to happen today?

New York was under some kind of terrorist attack, that much was blindingly obvious. A dim voice inside his head told him he should be scared, but he wasn't, he was just fucking angry.

He marched forward, crunching on paper, past one bewildered person after another coming from different directions. Then, as he approached the mayhem of the plaza, he was stopped by two NYPD cops. The first was short with cropped fair hair; his right hand was resting on the butt of his Glock, while his left was holding a radio to his ear. He was shouting a report into it one moment and then listening the next. The other, much taller cop had shoulders like a padded-up footballer player, a pockmarked face and an expression that was part apologetic, part *don't fuck with me, we're all fucked enough.*

'I'm sorry, sir,' the tall cop said. 'You can't go past here – we need the space right now.'

'I have a business meeting,' Ronnie said. 'I – I – ' he pointed – 'I have to see—'

'I think you'd better reschedule. I don't think anyone's meeting anyone right now.'

'The thing is, I have a flight to the UK tonight. I really need—'

'Sir – I think you're gonna find your meeting and your flight have been cancelled.'

Then the ground began rumbling. There was a terrible cracking sound. The two cops turned in unison and looked up, straight up the silver-grey wall of the North Tower. It was moving.

27

OCTOBER 2007

The lift was moving. Abby felt the floor pressing against her feet. It was rising, jerkily, as if someone was hauling it up by hand. Then it stopped sharply. She heard a thud, following by the sloshing of liquid.

Shit.

Her boot had fallen over. Her latrine boot.

The lift swayed suddenly, as if it had been given a massive push, and boomed into the side of the shaft, throwing her off her feet, against a wall, then slamming her on to the wet floor. *Jesus.*

There was a massive bang on the roof. Something struck it with the force of a sledgehammer. The sound echoed, hurting her ears. There was another bang. Then another. As she tried to scramble to her feet, the lift lurched violently sideways, striking the shaft with such force she could feel the shockwave running through the steel walls. Then it tilted, throwing her across the small space, thumping her into the opposite wall.

Then another bang on the roof.

Christ, no.

Was he up there? Ricky? Trying to smash his way into the lift to get her?

It rose again a few inches, then swung wildly again. She

whimpered in terror. Pulled out her phone, pressed the cursor. The light came on and she could see a small indent in the roof.

Then another bang and the indent grew larger. Dust motes swarmed crazily.

Then another bang. Another. Another. More dust.

Then silence. A long silence. A different sound now. A dull thudding. It was her heart. Pounding. *Boomf . . . boomf . . . boomf.* The roaring sound in her ears of her blood coursing. Like a wild ocean racing inside her.

The light on her phone went off. She pressed the cursor and it came back on again. She was thinking. Desperately thinking. What could she use as a weapon when he broke through? She had a canister of pepper spray in her bag, but that would only stall him for a few moments – maybe a couple of minutes if she could get it in his eyes. She needed something to knock him down.

Her boot was the only thing. She picked it up, aware of the wet, soft leather, and touched the Cuban heel. It felt reassuringly hard. She could conceal it behind her, wait until his face appeared, then swing it up. Surprise him.

Her brain was all over the place with questions. Did he know she was in here for sure? Had he been waiting for her on the staircase, then somehow stopped the lift when he realized she had taken it?

The silence continued. Just that fast thud of her heartbeat. Like a boxing glove pounding against a punchball.

Then through her fear she felt a flash of anger.

So close, so damned close!

So tantalizingly close to my dreams!

I have to get out of this. Somehow I have to get out of this!

Suddenly the lift began to rise slowly again, before stopping with another sharp jerk.

The grinding sound of metal against metal.

Then the angular tip of a crowbar screeched in through the crack between the doors.

28

SEPTEMBER 2007

The grinding whine of the winch. The rattle of the idling diesel of the R&K 24-Hour Rescue tow truck.

Lisa batted away a whole bloody cloud of flies. 'Piss off!' she shouted at them. 'Just go away, will you!'

The rattle turned into a roar as the steel hawser tightened and the guy in the cab accelerated, giving more power to the winch.

She was intrigued to know what would happen next. To find out what the car was doing there in the first place. No one drove three klicks down a dirt track and then into a river by accident, MJ said. Then he'd added, 'Not even a woman driver,' for which he had received a kick on the shin from her.

One of the local Geelong cops who had turned up, the shorter, calmer of the two, told them the car had probably been used in a crime and then dumped. Whoever had put it here hadn't reckoned on the drought causing the water level to drop so much.

A fly landed on her cheek. She slapped her face, but it was too fast for her. Time was different for flies, MJ had told her that once. One second to a human was like ten seconds to a fly. It meant that the fly saw everything as if in slow motion. It had all the time in the world to get away from your hand.

MJ knew all about flies. Not surprising, she thought, if you lived in Melbourne and liked to go out in the bush. You'd become an expert faster than you could ever have believed possible. They bred in dung, he had told her last time they went camping, which meant she would no longer eat anything once a fly had landed on it.

Lisa stared at the white cop car with its blue and white chequered band, and the white police van in the same livery, both with their racks of blue and red roof lights. There were two police divers in wet suits and flippers, masks on their heads, standing down below her in the shrubbery at the edge of the water, watching the taut steel hawser steadily rising out of the water.

But flies performed a service as well. They helped clear dead things away: birds, rabbits, kangaroos and humans too. They were some of Mother Nature's little helpers. They just happened to have lousy table manners, such as vomiting on their food before eating it. All in all, they didn't make great dinner guests, Lisa decided.

Perspiration from the heat was running down her face. MJ stood with one arm around her, the other holding a water bottle which they were sharing. Lisa had her arm around his waist, fingers tucked into his waistband, feeling the sweat in his damp T-shirt. Flies liked to drink human sweat, that was another nugget he had given her. Sweat didn't have much protein in it, but it contained minerals they needed. Human sweat was the fly world equivalent of Perrier, or Badoit, or whatever bottled water floated your particular boat.

The river just ahead of where the hawser had entered became a sudden mass of whirlpools. It looked like it was boiling. Bubbles burst on the surface, turning to foam. The taller, more panicky officer kept shouting out instructions, which seemed unnecessary to Lisa, as everyone seemed to know what they needed to do. In his early forties, she guessed, he had brush-cut hair and an aquiline nose. Both he and his younger colleague wore regulation open-throat shirts with epaulettes and a woven Victoria Police shield on one sleeve, navy blue trousers and stout shoes. The flies were enjoying them too.

Lisa watched the rear end of a dark green saloon car breaking the surface, water tumbling off it, which she could hear above the roar of the winch and the bellow of the truck engine. She read the number plate, OPH 010, and the legend that was written beneath it: VICTORIA – ON THE MOVE.

How long had it been down there?

She wasn't an expert on cars, but she knew a little about them. Enough to recognize that this was an older-model Ford Falcon, a good five or maybe even ten years old. Soon the rear windscreen appeared, then the roof. The paintwork was shiny from the water, but all the chrome had rusted. The tyres were almost flat, flapping on the arid, sandy soil as the car was hauled backwards up the steep slope. Water poured out from the empty interior through the door sills and the wheel arches.

It was an eerie sight, she thought.

After several minutes, the Falcon was finally up on the level ground, sitting motionless on its rims, tyres like black paunches. The hawser was slack now, with the tow-truck driver on his knees under the tailgate, unhooking it. The grinding sound of the winch had stopped and the tow-truck engine was silenced. There was just the steady splashing of the water pouring from the vehicle.

The two cops walked around it, peering warily in through the windows. The tall, panicky one had his gun hand on his gun butt, as if he expected someone to jump out of the car at any moment and challenge him. The shorter one saluted away some more flies. The bowerbird *yoo-hooed* again in the new silence.

Then the taller cop pressed the boot release button. Nothing happened. He tried again, exerting leverage on the lid at the same time. It lifted a few inches with a sharp screech of protest from its rusted hinges. Then he raised it all the way up.

And took a step back, in shock, as he smelled what was inside before he even saw her.

'Oh, strewth,' he said, turning away and gagging.

29

OCTOBER 2007

Grey was the default colour of death, Roy Grace thought. Grey bones. Grey ash when you were cremated. Grey tombstones. Grey X-rayed dental records. Grey mortuary walls. Whether you rotted away in a coffin or in a storm drain, all that was eventually left of you would be grey.

Grey bones lying on a grey steel post-mortem table. Being probed by grey steel instruments. Even the light in here was grey, strangely diffused ethereal light that seeped in through the large opaque windows. Ghosts were grey too. Grey ladies, grey men. There were plenty of them in the post-mortem room of the Brighton and Hove City Mortuary. The ghosts of thousands of unfortunate people whose remains had ended up here, inside this grim bungalow with its grey, pebbledash-rendered walls, residing behind one of its grey-steel freezer locker doors before their penultimate journey to an undertaker's premises, then burial or cremation.

He shuddered. He couldn't help it. Despite the fact that he minded coming here less these days because the woman he loved was in charge, it still gave him the creeps.

Gave him the creeps to see the skeleton, with its artificial fingernails and fronds of winter wheat-coloured hair still attached to the skull.

And it gave him the creeps to see all the green-gowned

figures in the room. Frazer Theobald, Joan Major, Barry Heath – the latest addition to the team of Coroner's Officers for the area, a short, neatly dressed, poker-faced man, recently retired from the police force, whose grim job it was to attend not only all murder scenes but also sudden-death scenes, such as traffic accident fatalities and suicides, and then the post-mortems. There was also the SOCO photographer, recording every step of the process. Plus Darren, Cleo's assistant, a sharp, good-looking and pleasant natured lad of twenty with fashionably spiky black hair, who had started life as a butcher's apprentice. And Christopher Ghent, the tall, studious forensic odontist, who was occupied taking soft-clay impressions of the skeleton's teeth.

And finally Cleo. She hadn't been on duty, but had decided that, as he was working, she might as well too.

Sometimes Roy found it hard to believe that he really was dating this goddess.

He watched her now, tall and leggy and almost impossibly beautiful in her green gown and white wellies, long blonde hair clipped up, moving around this room, *her* room, *her* domain, with such ease and grace, sensitive but at the same time impervious to all its horrors.

But all the time he was wondering if, in some terrible irony, he was witnessing the woman he loved laying out the remains of the woman he had once loved.

The room smelled strongly of disinfectant. It was furnished with two steel post-mortem tables, one fixed and the other, on which the remains of the woman now lay, on castors. There was a blue hydraulic hoist by a row of fridges with floor-to-ceiling doors. The walls were tiled in grey and a drainage gully ran all the way around. Along one wall was a row of sinks, with a coiled yellow hose. Along another were a wide work surface, a metal cutting board and a glass-fronted display cabinet filled with instruments, some packs of Duracell batteries and grisly souvenirs that no one else wanted – mostly pacemakers – removed from victims.

Next to the cabinet was a wall chart listing the name of the deceased, with columns for the weight of their brain, lungs, heart, liver, kidneys and spleen. All that was written on it so far was 'ANON. WOMAN'.

It was a sizeable room but it felt crowded this afternoon, as it always did during a post-mortem by a Home Office pathologist.

'There are four fillings,' Christopher Ghent said, to no one in particular. 'Three white composite and one gold inlay. An all-porcelain bridge from upper right six to four, not cheap. No amalgams. All high-quality stuff.'

Grace listened, trying to remember what dental work Sandy had had. She had been fastidious about her teeth. But the description was too technical for him.

Joan Major was unpacking, from a large case, a series of plaster of Paris models. They sat there on square black plastic plinths like broken archaeological fragments from an important dig. He had seen them before, but he always found it hard to get his head around the subtle differences they illustrated.

When Christopher Ghent finished reciting his dental analysis, Joan began to explain how each model showed the comparison of different stages of bone development. She concluded by stating that the remains were female, around thirty years old, give or take three years.

Which continued to cover the age Sandy had been when she disappeared.

He knew he should put that from his mind, that it was unprofessional to be influenced by any personal agenda. But how could he?

30

11 SEPTEMBER 2001

The floor was shaking. Key blanks, dozens of them hanging in rows on hooks along one wall of the store, were clinking. Several cans of paint fell from a shelf. The lid came off one as it hit the floor and magnolia emulsion poured out. A cardboard box tumbled, sending brass screws wriggling like maggots across the linoleum.

It was dark in the deep, narrow hardware store just a few hundred yards from the World Trade Center, where Ronnie had taken refuge, following the tall cop in here. Some minutes earlier the power had gone off. Just one battery-powered emergency light was on. A raging dust tornado twisted past the window, blacker some moments than night.

A shoeless woman in an expensive suit, who didn't look like she had been in a hardware store before in her life, was sobbing. A gaunt figure in brown overalls, grey hair bunched in a ponytail, stood behind the counter that ran the full length down one side, presiding over the gloom in grim, helpless silence.

Ronnie still held tightly on to the handle of his suitcase. Miraculously, his briefcase was still resting on top.

Outside, a police car spun past on its roof, like a top, and stopped. Its doors were open and its dome light was on. The interior was empty, a radio mike dangling from its twisted cord.

A crack suddenly appeared in the wall to his left and an entire stack of shelves, laden with boxes of different-sized paintbrushes, crashed to the floor. The sobbing woman screamed.

Ronnie took a step back, pressing against the counter, thinking. He had been in a restaurant in Los Angeles once during a minor quake. His companion then had told him the doorway was the strongest structure. If the building came down, your best chance of survival was to be in the doorway.

He moved towards the door.

The cop said, 'I wouldn't go out right now, buddy.'

Then a massive avalanche of masonry and glass and rubble came down right in front of the window, burying the cop car. The store's burglar alarm went off, a piercing banshee howl. The ponytailed guy disappeared for a moment and the sound stopped, as did the clinking of the keys.

The floor wasn't shaking any more.

There was a very long silence. Outside, quite quickly, the dust storm began to lighten. As if dawn was breaking.

Ronnie opened the door.

'I wouldn't go out there – know what I'm saying?' the cop repeated.

Ronnie looked at him, hesitating. Then he pushed the door open and stepped out, towing his bag behind him.

Stepped out into total silence. The silence of a dawn snowfall. Grey snow lay everywhere.

Grey silence.

Then he started to hear the sounds. Fire alarms. Burglar alarms. Car alarms. Human screams. Emergency vehicle sirens. Helicopters.

Grey figures stumbling silently past him. An endless

line of women and men with hollow, blank faces. Some walking, some running. Some stabbing buttons on phones. He followed them.

Stumbling blindly through the grey fog that stung his eyes and choked his mouth and nostrils.

He just followed them. Towing his bag. Following. Keeping pace. The girders of a bridge rose on either side of him. The Brooklyn Bridge, he thought it was, from his scant knowledge of New York. Running, stumbling, across the river. Across an endless bridge through an endless swirling, choking grey hell.

Ronnie lost track of time. Lost track of direction. Just followed the grey ghosts. Suddenly, for one fleeting instant, he smelled the tang of salt, then the burning smells again – aviation fuel, paint, rubber. At any moment there might be another plane.

The reality of what had happened was starting to hit him. Hopefully Donald Hatcook was OK. But what if he wasn't? The business plan he had created was awesome. They stood to make millions in the next five years. Fucking millions! But if Donald was dead, what then?

There were silhouettes in the distance. Jagged high-rise silhouettes. Brooklyn. He had never been to Brooklyn before in his life, just seen it across the river. It was getting nearer with every step forward. The air was getting better too. More prolonged patches of salty sea air. Thinning mist.

And suddenly he was going down an incline towards the far end of the bridge. He stopped and turned back. Something biblical came into his mind, some memory about Lot's wife. Turning her head. Becoming a pillar of salt. That's what the endless line of people passing him looked like. Pillars of salt.

He held on to a metal railing with one hand and stared back. Sunlight dappled the water below him. A million brilliant specks of white dancing on the ripples. Then beyond it the whole of Manhattan looked as if it was on fire. The high-rises all partially shrouded in a pall of grey, brown, white and black smoke clouds billowing up into the deep blue sky.

He was shaking uncontrollably and badly needed to collect his thoughts. Fumbling in his pockets, he pulled out his Marlboros and lit one. He took four deep puffs in quick succession, but it didn't taste good, not with all the stuff in his throat, and he dropped it into the water below, feeling giddy, his throat even drier.

He rejoined the procession of ghosts, following them on to a road where they seemed to disperse in different directions. He stopped again as a thought struck him, and as it took hold he suddenly wanted some peace and quiet. Turning off, he walked along a deserted side street, past a row of office buildings, the wheels of his bag still bump-bump-bumping along behind him.

Totally absorbed, he walked through almost empty urban streets for a long time, before finding himself at the entrance ramp to a highway. A short distance in front of him was a tall, girdered advertising hoarding rising into the sky, emblazoned with the word KENTILE in red. Then he heard the rumble of an engine and the next moment, a blue four-door pick-up truck stopped alongside him.

The window slid down and a man in a chequered shirt and a New York Yankees baseball cap peered out of the window. 'You wanna ride, buddy?'

Ronnie stopped, startled and confused by the question, and sweating like a hog. A *ride*? *Did* he want a ride? Where to?

He wasn't sure. Did he?

He could see figures inside. Ghosts huddled together.

'Got room for one more.'

'Where are you going?' he asked lamely, as if he had all kinds of options.

The man spoke in a nasal voice, as if the bass on his vocal cords was turned up to max. 'There's more planes. There's more planes any moment. Gotta get away. Ten more planes. Maybe more. Shit, man, it's just friggin' started.'

'I – ah – I have to meet—' Ronnie stopped. Stared at the open door, at the blue seats, at the man's dungarees. He was an old guy with a bobbing Adam's apple and a neck like a turkey. His face was wizened and kind.

'Jump in. I'll give you a ride.'

Ronnie walked around and climbed into the front, next to the man. The news was on, loudly. A woman was saying that the Wall Street area of Manhattan and Battery Park were impassable.

As Ronnie fumbled for his seat belt, the driver handed him a bottle of water. Ronnie, suddenly realizing how parched he was, drained it gratefully.

'I clean the windows, right? The Center, yeah?'

'Right,' Ronnie said distantly.

'All my fuggin' cleaning stuff's in the South Tower – know what I'm saying?'

Ronnie didn't, not exactly, because he was only half listening. 'Right,' he said.

'I guess I'll have to go back later.'

'Later,' Ronnie echoed, neither agreeing nor disagreeing.

'You OK?'

'Me?'

The truck moved forward. The interior smelled of dog hair and coffee.

'Gotta get away. They hit the Pentagon. There's ten fucking planes up there right now, coming at us. This is *yuge. Yuge!*'

Ronnie turned his head. Stared at the four huddled figures behind him. None of them met his eyes.

'A-rabs,' the driver said. 'A-rabs done this.'

Ronnie stared at a plastic Starbucks beaker with a coffee-stained paper towel wrapped around it in the cup holder. A bottle of water was jammed in next to it.

'This thing, it's just the beginning,' the driver said. 'Lucky we got a strong president. Lucky we got George Dubya.'

Ronnie said nothing.

'You OK? Not hurt or nothing?'

They were heading along a freeway. Only a handful of vehicles were coming in the opposite direction, on an elevated section. Ahead of them was a wide green road sign divided into two. On the left was written EXIT 24 EAST 27 PROSPECT EXPWY. On the right it said 278 WEST VERRAZANO BR, STATEN IS.

Ronnie did not reply, because he did not hear him. He was deep in thought again.

Working through the idea. It was a crazy idea. Just a product of his shaken state. But it wouldn't go away. And the more he thought about it, the more he began to wonder if it might have legs. A back-up plan to Donald Hatcook.

Maybe an even better plan.

He switched his phone off.

31

OCTOBER 2007

Abby watched the tip of the iron crowbar in terror. It was jerking sharply, blindly, left then right, levering the doors apart, just a couple of inches each time before they sprang shut again, clamping tight on the tip.

There was another huge crash on the roof and this time it really did feel as if someone had jumped on to it. The lift swayed, thumping the side of the shaft, throwing her off balance, the small canister of pepper spray dropping with a thud from her hand as she tried to stop herself smashing into the wall.

With a loud metallic screech of protest, the doors were opening.

Cold terror flooded through her.

Not just opening a couple of inches now, but wider, much wider.

She ducked down, desperately scrabbling on the floor for the spray. Light spilled in. She saw the canister and grabbed it, panic-stricken. Then, without even wasting time to look up, she launched herself forward, pressing down on the trigger, aiming straight into the widening gap between the doors.

Straight into powerful arms that grabbed her, yanking her up out of the lift and on to the landing.

She screamed, wriggling desperately, trying to break

free. When she pressed down on the trigger again, nothing came out.

'Fuck you,' she cried. 'Fuck you!'

'Darlin', it's all right. It's OK, darlin'.'

Not any voice she recognized. Not *his*.

'Lemme go!' she screamed, lashing out with her bare feet.

He was holding her in a grip like a vice. 'Darlin'? Miss? Calm down. You're safe. It's OK. You are safe!'

A face beneath a yellow helmet smiled at her. A fireman's helmet. Green overalls with fluorescent stripes. She heard the crackle of a two-way radio and what sounded like a control-room voice saying, 'Hotel 04.'

Two firemen in helmets stood on the stairs above her. Another waited a few stairs down.

The man holding her smiled again, reassuringly. 'You're all right, love. You're safe,' he said.

She was shivering. Were they real? Was this a trap?

They seemed genuine, but she continued gripping the pepper spray tightly. She would put nothing past Ricky.

Then she noticed the surly face of the elderly Polish caretaker, who was puffing up the stairs in his grubby sweatshirt and brown trousers.

'I not paid to work weekends,' he grumbled. 'It's the managing agents. I speak to them about this lift for months! Months.' He looked at Abby and frowned. Jerked a finger with a blackened nail upwards. 'Flat 82, right?'

'Yes,' she replied.

'The managing agents,' he wheezed in his guttural accent. 'They no good. I tell them, every day I tell them.'

'How long you been in there, darlin'?' her rescuer said.

He was in his thirties, good-looking in a boy-band sort of way, with black eyebrows almost too neat to be real. She looked at him warily, as if he was too handsome to be a fireman, as if he was all part of Ricky's elaborate deception. Then she found she was shaking almost too much to speak.

'Do you have any water?'

Moments later a water bottle was put in her hand. She drank in greedy gulps, spilling some so that it ran down her chin and trickled down her neck. She drained it before she spoke.

'Thank you.'

She held out the empty bottle, and an unseen hand took it.

'Last night,' she said. 'I've been – since – I think – in this sodding thing – last night. It's Saturday now?'

'Yes. It's 5.20, Saturday afternoon.'

'Since yesterday. Since just after 6.30 yesterday evening.' She looked in fury at the caretaker. 'Don't you check the bloody alarm's working? Or the bloody phone in the thing?'

'The managing agents.' He shrugged, as if every problem in the universe could be blamed on them.

'If you don't feel well you should go to A and E at the hospital for a check-up,' the good-looking fire officer said.

That panicked her. 'No – no – I'm really fine, thank you. I – I just—'

'If you're really bad, we can call you an ambulance.'

'No,' she said firmly. 'No. I don't need hospital.'

She looked at her fallen-over boots, which were still in the lift, and at the damp stain on the floor. She couldn't smell anything but she knew it must reek in there.

His radio crackled again and she heard another call sign.

'I – I thought it was going to plunge. You know? At any moment. I thought it was going to plunge – and I was going to be—'

'Na, no danger. Got a back-up centrifugal locking

mechanism, even if it did. But it wouldn't have fallen.' His voice tailed away and he seemed pensive for a moment, his eyes darting to the ceiling of the lift. 'You live here?'

She nodded.

Relaxing his grip on her, he said, 'You ought to check your service charges. Make sure the lift maintenance is on them.'

The caretaker made a comment, something else about the managing agents, but she barely heard it. Her relief at being freed was only fleeting. Great that she was out of the bloody lift. But that did not remotely mean she was out of danger.

She knelt down, trying to reach her boots without going back in the lift. But they were out of reach. The fireman bent down and hooked them out with the reverse of his axe. He clearly wasn't stupid enough to go in there himself.

'Who alerted you?' she asked.

'A lady in – ' he paused to read a note on his pad – 'flat 47. She tried to call the lift several times this afternoon, then reported she heard someone calling for help.'

Making a mental note to thank her some time, Abby looked warily up the stairs, which were covered in the workmen's dust sheets and littered with plasterboard and building materials.

'You should get plenty of fluids down you, and eat something as soon as you can,' the fireman recommended. 'Just something light. Soup or something. I'll come up to your flat with you, make sure you're all right.'

She thanked him, then looked at her Mace spray, wondering why it hadn't fired, and realized she had not flipped the safety lock. She dropped it in her bag and, holding her boots, began to climb the stairs, carefully negotiating the builders' mess. Thinking.

Had Ricky sabotaged the lift? And the phone and the bell? Was it too far-fetched to think he had done that?

All the locks were as she had left them, she was relieved to discover when she reached her front door. Even so, after thanking the fire officer again, she let herself in warily, checking the thread across the hall was intact before locking the door again behind her and securing the safety chains. Then, just to be sure, she checked each room in the flat.

Everything was fine. No one had been here.

She went to the kitchen to make herself some tea and grabbed a KitKat out of the fridge. She had just popped a piece in her mouth when the doorbell rang, followed immediately by a sharp rap.

Chewing, nerves jangling in case this was Ricky, she hurried warily to the front door and peered through the spyhole. A slight, thin-faced man in his early twenties, with short black hair brushed forward, wearing a suit, was standing there.

Who the hell was he? A salesman? A Jehovah's Witness – but didn't they normally come in pairs? Or he might be something to do with the fire brigade. Right now, dog tired, very shaken and ravenous, she just wanted to make a cup of tea, have something to eat, then down several glasses of red wine and crash out.

Knowing that the man would have had to pass the caretaker and the firemen to get here eased her fears about him a little. Checking that the two safety chains were properly engaged, she unlocked the door and pushed it open the few inches it would travel.

'Katherine Jennings?' he asked in a voice that was sharp and invasive. His breath was warm on her face and smelled of peppermint chewing gum.

Katherine Jennings was the name under which she had rented the flat.

'Yes?' she replied.

'Kevin Spinella from the *Argus* newspaper. I wonder if you could spare a couple of moments of your time?'

'I'm sorry,' she said, and immediately tried to push the door shut. But it was wedged open by his foot.

'I'd just like a quick quote I could use.'

'I'm sorry,' she said. 'I have nothing to say.'

'So you are not grateful to the fire brigade for rescuing you?'

'No, I didn't say—'

Shit. He was now writing that down on his pad.

'Look, Ms – Mrs Jennings?'

She didn't rise to the bait.

He went on. 'I understand you've just had quite an ordeal – would it be OK for me to send a photographer round?'

'No, it would not,' she said. 'I'm very tired.'

'Perhaps tomorrow morning? What time would be good for you?'

'No, thank you. And please remove your foot.'

'Did you feel your life was in jeopardy?'

'I'm very tired,' she said. 'Thank you.'

'Right, I understand, you've been through a lot. Tell you what, I'll pop back tomorrow with a photographer. About 10 tomorrow morning suit you? Not too early for you on a Sunday?'

'I'm sorry, I don't want any publicity.'

'Good, well, I'll see you in the morning then.' He removed his foot.

'No, thank you,' she said firmly, then pushed the door

shut and locked it very carefully. Shit, that was all she bloody needed, her photo in the paper.

Shaking, her mind a maelstrom of thoughts, she pulled her cigarettes from her bag and lit one. Then she walked through into the kitchen.

*

A man seated in the rear of an old white van that was parked in the street below also lit a cigarette. Then he popped the tab of a can of Foster's lager, being careful not to spray the expensive piece of electrical kit he had alongside him, and took a swig. Through the lens inserted in the tiny hole he had drilled in the roof of the van, he normally had a perfect view of her flat, although it was partly obscured at this moment by a parked fire engine blocking the street. Still, he thought, it relieved the monotony of his long vigil.

And he could see to his satisfaction, from the shadow moving back past the window, that she was in there now.

Home sweet home, he thought to himself, and grinned wryly. That was almost funny.

32

11 SEPTEMBER 2001

Lorraine, still wearing nothing but her bikini bottoms and gold ankle chain, sat on a bar stool in her kitchen, watching the small television mounted above the work surface, waiting for the kettle to boil. The butts from half a dozen cigarettes lay in the ashtray in front of her. She had just lit another and was inhaling deeply as she held the phone to her ear, talking to Sue Klinger, her best friend.

Sue and her husband, Stephen, lived in a house that Lorraine had always coveted, a stunning detached mansion in Tongdean Avenue – considered by many people to be one of the finest residences in Brighton and Hove – with views across the whole city, down to the sea. The Klingers also owned a villa in Portugal. They had four gorgeous children, and, unlike Ronnie, Stephen had the Midas touch. Ronnie had promised Lorraine that if Sue and Stephen ever sold the house, he would find a way to come up with the money to buy it. Yep, sure. *In your dreams, my love.*

They were replaying the images of the two planes striking the towers again, and then again, over and over. It was as if whoever was producing or directing this programme couldn't believe it either, and had to keep replaying them to be sure it was real. Or perhaps someone in shock thought that if they repeated these images enough times, eventually the planes would miss the towers and fly past safely, and it would be just a normal Tuesday morning in Manhattan, business as usual. She watched the sudden orange fireball, the dense black clouds, feeling sicker and sicker.

Now they were showing the towers coming down again. First the South, then the North.

The kettle came to the boil but she didn't move, not wanting to take her eyes off the screen in case she missed Ronnie. Alfie rubbed against her leg, but she ignored him. Sue was saying something to her, but Lorraine didn't hear because she was peering at the screen intently, scanning every face.

'Lorraine? Hello? You still there?'

'Yes.'

'Ronnie's a survivor. He'll be OK.'

The kettle switched itself off with a click. *Survivor.* Her sister had used that word as well.

Survivor.

Shit, Ronnie, you'd better be.

A beeping sound told her there was a call waiting. Barely able to contain herself she shouted excitedly, 'Sue, that might be him! Call you straight back!'

Oh, God, Ronnie, please be on the phone. Please. Please let this be you!

But it was her sister. 'Lori, I just heard that all flights in the US have been grounded.' Mo worked as a stewardess for British Airways long-haul.

'What – what does that mean?'

'They're not letting any planes in or out. I was meant to be flying to Washington tomorrow. Everything's grounded.'

Lorraine felt a new wave of panic. 'Until when?'

'I don't know – until further notice.'

'Does that mean Ronnie might not get back tomorrow?'

'I'm afraid so. I'll find out more later in the day, but they're making all planes that are heading to the States turn back. Which means the planes will be in the wrong places. It's going to be chaos.'

'Great,' Lorraine said glumly. 'That's just bloody great. When do you think he might get back?'

'I don't know – I'll get an update as soon as I can.'

Lorraine heard a child calling, and Mo saying, 'One minute, darling. Mummy's on the phone.'

Lorraine crushed out her cigarette. Then she jumped down from the stool, still watching the television screen, pulled out a tea bag and a mug, and poured in the water. Still without taking her eyes from the screen, she stepped back and bumped her hip, painfully, into the corner of the kitchen table.

'Shit! Fuck!'

She looked down for a moment. Saw the fresh red mark among the uneven line of bruises, some black and fresh, some yellow and almost gone. Ronnie was clever, he always hit her in the body, never her face. Always made bruises she could easily hide.

Always cried and begged forgiveness after one of his – increasingly frequent – drunken rages.

And she always forgave him.

Forgave him because of the deep inadequacy she felt. She knew how badly he wanted the one thing she had not been able, so far, to give him. The child he so desperately wanted.

And because she was terrified of losing him.

And because she loved him.

33

OCTOBER 2007

It hadn't been the best weekend of his life, Roy Grace thought to himself at 8 o'clock on Monday morning, as he sat in the tiny, cramped dentist's waiting room, flicking through the pages of *Sussex Life*. In fact, it didn't really feel as if the previous week had actually ended.

Dr Frazer Theobald's post-mortem had gone on interminably, finally finishing around 9 p.m. on Saturday. And Cleo, who had been fine during the post-mortem, had been uncharacteristically ratty with him yesterday.

Both of them knew it was no one's fault that their weekend plans had been ruined, yet somehow he felt she was blaming him, just the way Sandy used to blame him when he'd arrive home hours late, or have to cancel some long-term plan at the last minute because an emergency had come up. As if it was *his* fault a jogger had discovered a dead body in a ditch late on a Friday afternoon, instead of at a more convenient time.

Cleo knew the score. She knew the world of the police and their erratic hours better than most – her own weren't much different. She could be called out at any time of the day or night, and frequently was. So what was eating her?

She had even got annoyed with him when he'd gone back to his own house for a couple of hours to mow the badly overgrown lawn.

'You wouldn't have been able to mow it if we'd been up in London,' she'd said. 'So why now?'

It was his house that was the real problem, he knew. His house – his and *Sandy's* house – still seemed a red rag to a bull with Cleo. Although he had recently removed a lot of Sandy's possessions, Cleo still very rarely came round and always seemed uncomfortable when she did. They'd only made love there once, and it hadn't been a good experience for either of them.

Since then they always slept at Cleo's house. The nights they spent together were becoming increasingly frequent, and he now kept a set of shaving kit and washing stuff there, as well as a dark suit, fresh white shirt, plain tie and a pair of black shoes – his weekday work uniform.

It had been a good question and he didn't tell her the truth, because that would have made things worse. The truth was that the skeleton had shaken him. He wanted to be on his own for a few hours, to reflect.

To think about how he would feel if it was Sandy.

His relationship with Cleo had gone way, way further than any other he had had since Sandy, but he was conscious that, despite all his efforts to move forward, Sandy remained a constant wedge between them. A few weeks ago at dinner, when they'd both had too much to drink, Cleo had let slip her concern about her biological clock ticking away. He knew she was starting to want commitment – and sensed she felt that, with Sandy in the way, she was never going to get it from him.

That wasn't true. Roy adored her. Loved her. And had begun seriously to contemplate a life together with her.

Which was why he had been terribly hurt early yesterday evening when, having gone back to her house clutching a couple of bottles of their current favourite red Rioja wine, he had opened her front door with his key to be greeted by a tiny black puppy which sprinted towards him, put its paws around his leg and peed on his trainers.

'Humphrey, meet Roy!' she said. 'Roy, meet Humphrey!'

'Who – whose is this?' he asked, bewildered.

'Mine. I got him this afternoon. He's a five-month-old rescue puppy – a Lab and Border Collie cross.'

Roy's right foot felt uncomfortably warm as the urine seeped in. And a strange hot flush of confusion swirled through him as he knelt and felt the dog's slippery tongue lick his hand. He was totally astonished.

'You – you never told me you were getting a puppy!'

'Yep, well, there's lots you don't tell me either, Roy,' she said breezily.

*

An elderly woman came into the waiting room, gave him a suspicious look, as if to say, *I've got the first appointment, sonny boy,* then sat down.

Roy had a packed schedule. At 9 a.m. he was going to see Alison Vosper and have it out with her about Cassian Pewe. At 9.45, later than normal, he was holding the first briefing meeting of *Operation Dingo* – the random name thrown up by the Sussex House computer for the investigation into the death of the *Unknown Female,* as the skeleton in the storm drain was currently called. Then at 10.30 he was due at *morning prayers* – the jokey name given to the newly reinstated weekly management team meetings.

At midday he was scheduled to hold a press conference on the finding of the skeleton. Not a huge amount to tell at this point, but hopefully by revealing the age of the dead woman, the physical characteristics and the approximate period when she died, it might jog someone's memory about a mis-per from around that time. Supposing, of course, that it was not Sandy.

'Roy! Good to see you!'

Steve Cowling stood in the doorway in his white gown, beaming with his perfect white teeth. A tall man in his mid-fifties, with a ramrod-straight military bearing, immaculate hair becoming increasingly grey every time Roy saw him, he exuded charm and confidence in equal measure, combined always with a certain boyish enthusiasm, as if teeth really were the most exciting thing in the world.

'Come in, old chap!'

Grace gave an apologetic nod to the elderly lady, who looked distinctly miffed, and followed the dentist in to his bright, airy torture chamber.

While, like himself, Steve Cowling grew a little older with each visit, the dentist had an endless succession of assistants who grew younger and more attractive. The latest, a leggy brunette in her early twenties, holding a buff envelope, smiled at him, then removed a clutch of negatives and handed them to Cowling with a flirty glance.

He picked up the alginate cast Roy had given him twenty minutes earlier. 'Right, Roy. This is really quite interesting. The first thing I have to say is that it is definitely not Sandy.'

'It's not?' he echoed, a little flatly.

'Absolutely not.' Cowling pointed at the negatives. 'Those are Sandy's – there's no comparison at all. But the cast provides quite a lot of information that may be helpful.' He gave Grace a bright smile.

'Good.'

'This woman has had implants, which would have been

quite expensive when they were done. Screw-type titanium – made by a Swiss company, Straumann. They're basically a hollow cylinder put over a root, which then grows into them and makes a permanent fixing.'

Grace felt a conflicting surge of emotions as he listened, trying to concentrate but finding it hard suddenly.

'What is interesting, old boy, is that we can put a rough date on these – which corresponds to an estimate of how long ago this woman died. They started going out of fashion about fifteen years ago. She's had some other quite costly work done, some restorations and bridge work. If she's from this area, then I would say there are only about five or six dentists who could have done this work. A good place to start would be Chris Gebbie, who practises in Lewes. I'll write down the others for you as well. And it means that she'd have been reasonably well off.'

Grace listened, but his thoughts were elsewhere. If this skeleton had been Sandy, however grim, it would have brought some kind of closure. But now the agony of uncertainty continued.

He didn't know whether he felt disappointed or relieved.

34

SEPTEMBER 2007

The stench that erupted from the car's boot made everyone on the river bank gag. It was like a blocked drain that had suddenly been cleared and months – maybe years – of trapped gases from decomposition were freed into the air, all at once.

Lisa backed away in shock, pinching her nose shut with her fingers, and closed her eyes for a moment. The searing midday sun and the relentless flies somehow made things even worse. When she opened her eyes and took in a gulp of air just through her mouth, the smell was still as bad. She was really struggling not to vomit.

MJ didn't look like he was finding this any easier, but both of them were doing better than the panicky cop, who had turned away from the car and was now on his knees, actually throwing up. Holding her breath, ignoring the cautionary pull on her hand from MJ, Lisa took a few steps towards the rear of the car and peered in.

And wished she hadn't. The ground beneath her feet suddenly felt unsteady. She gripped MJ's hand tightly.

She saw what looked at first like a shop-window dummy that had melted in a fire, before realizing that it was the body of a woman. She was filling most of the deep boot space, lying partially submerged in slimy, glistening black water that was steadily draining away. Her shoulder-length fair hair was splayed out like matted weed. Her breasts had a soapy colour and texture, and there were large black blotches covering much of her skin.

'Has she been burned?' MJ, who was curious about everything, asked the shorter cop.

'That's – no – no, mate, that's not burning. Skin slippage.'

Lisa looked at the cadaver's face, but it was bloated and shapeless, like the half-melted head of a snowman. Her pubic hair was intact, a thick brown triangle looking so fresh it seemed unreal, as if someone had just stuck it on as a grotesque joke. She felt almost guilty looking at it. Guilty being here, staring at this body, as if death was a private thing and she was intruding.

But she could not tear her eyes away. The same questions kept going round and round in her mind. *What happened to you, you poor thing? Who did this to you?*

Eventually, the panicky cop recovered his composure and moved them back abruptly, saying this was a crime scene and he would need to tape it off.

They edged back several paces, unable to avert their eyes, as if they were watching some episode from *CSI* in real time. Shocked, gripped and numb – but curious as the circus grew. MJ produced some water and baseball caps from the car and Lisa drank gratefully, then pulled a cap on to keep the searing heat off her head.

A white crime scene van arrived first. Two men in slacks and T-shirts climbed out and began pulling on white protective suits. Then a smaller, blue van from which a crime scene photographer emerged. A short while later, a blue VW Golf arrived and a young woman climbed out. She was in her twenties, in jeans and a white blouse, with a frizz of fair hair, and stood for some moments observing the scene.

She was holding a notebook in one hand and a small tape recorder. Then she walked over to MJ and Lisa.

'You're the ones who found the car?' She had a pleasant but brisk voice.

Lisa pointed at MJ. 'He did.'

'I'm Angela Parks,' she said. 'From the *Age*. Could you tell me what happened?'

A dusty gold Holden was now pulling up. As MJ told his story, Lisa watched two men in white shirts and ties climb out. One was stocky, with a serious, boyish face, while the other looked like a bruiser: tall, powerfully built – if a little overweight – with a bald head and a narrow ginger moustache. He had an expression like thunder – probably from being called out on a weekend, Lisa thought, though she rapidly discovered otherwise.

'You bloody idiot!' he yelled at the panicky cop, by way of a greeting, standing some distance back from the crime scene tape. 'What a fuck-up! Didn't yer ever do any basic fucking training? What have you done to my crime scene? You've not just contaminated it, you've fucking desecrated it! Who the fuck told you to move the car out of the water?'

The panicky cop seemed lost for words for some moments. 'Yeah, well, sorry about that, sir. Guess we screwed up a bit.'

'You're fucking standing in the middle of it now!'

The stocky one walked over to Lisa and MJ and nodded at the reporter. 'How you doing, Angela?'

'Yeah, OK. Nice to see you, Detective Sergeant Burg,' she said.

Then his colleague, the bruiser, walked across in big sturdy strides, as if he owned the river bank and all around it. He gave a cursory nod to the journalist and then addressed Lisa and MJ. 'Detective Senior Sergeant George

Fletcher,' he said. His manner was professional and surprisingly gentle. 'You the couple that found the car?'

MJ nodded. 'Yep.'

'I'm going to need a statement from you both. Would you mind coming to Geelong Police Station?'

MJ looked at Lisa, then at the detective. 'You mean now?'

'Some time today.'

'Of course. But I don't think there's a lot we can tell you.'

'Thank you, but I'll be the judge of that. My sergeant will take your names and addresses and contact phone numbers before we leave.'

The journalist held out her recorder to the detective. 'Detective Senior Sergeant Fletcher, do you think there is any connection between the Melbourne gangs and this dead woman?'

'You've been here longer than I have, Ms Parks. I don't have any comment for you at this stage. Let's find out who she is first.'

'Was?' the journalist corrected him.

'Well, if you want to be that pedantic, let's wait for the police surgeon to turn up and make sure she is actually dead.'

He gave a challenging grin, but no one smiled.

35

11 SEPTEMBER 2001

Still nobody spoke except the driver, who talked non-stop. He was like a television in a bar, with the volume irritatingly high, that you couldn't switch off or change channels. Ronnie was trying to listen to the news that was coming out of the pick-up truck's radio and to collect his own thoughts, and the driver was preventing him from doing either.

What's more, the strong Brooklyn accent made it hard for Ronnie to decipher what he actually said. But as the man was being kind and giving him a ride, he could hardly tell him to shut up. So he sat there, half listening, nodding from time to time and occasionally saying, 'Yep,' or 'No shit,' or 'You have to be kidding,' depending on which he deemed the most appropriate.

The man had trashed most of the ethnic minorities of This Great Country and now he was talking about his ladders in the South Tower. He seemed pretty bothered about them. He was pretty bothered about the IRS too, and began trashing the US taxation system.

Then he lapsed back into a few moments of merciful silence and let the radio speak. All the ghosts behind Ronnie in the pick-up truck remained silent. Maybe they were listening to the radio, maybe they were in too much shock to absorb anything.

It was a litany. A list of all the stuff that had happened

that he already knew. And some time soon George Bush was going to be saying something. Meantime, Mayor Giuliani was on his way downtown. America was under attack. There would be more information as it came in.

Inside Ronnie's mind, his plan was coming together steadily.

They were gliding along a wide, silent street. To their right was a threadbare grass verge with trees and lamp-posts. Beyond the grass was a pathway, or a cycleway, and then a railing, and beyond that another street, running parallel, with cars and vans parked along it, and red-brick apartment buildings that were not too tall, nothing like the Manhattan monoliths. After half a mile or so they gave way to big, angular, detached dwellings that might have been single-occupancy or divided into apartments. It looked a prosperous area. Pleasant and tranquil.

They passed a road sign which said 'Ocean Parkway'.

He watched an elderly couple walking slowly on the sidewalk and wondered if they knew the drama that was unfolding just a short distance away across the river. It didn't seem like it. If they had heard, they would surely now be glued to their television set. Apart from them, there was not a soul in sight. OK, at this time of day, during the week, a lot of people would ordinarily have been in their offices. But mothers would be out pushing infants in strollers. People would be walking dogs. Youths would be loitering. There was no one. The traffic seemed light too. Much too light.

'Where are we?' he said to the driver.

'Brooklyn.'

'Ah, right,' Ronnie said. 'Still Brooklyn.'

He saw a sign on a building saying YESHIVA CENTER. It seemed like they had been driving for an age. He hadn't realized Brooklyn was so large. Large enough to get lost in, to disappear in.

Some words came into his head. It was a line from a Marlowe play, *The Jew of Malta,* that he'd gone to see recently with Lorraine and the Klingers at the Theatre Royal in Brighton.

> But that was in another country.
> And besides, the wench is dead.

The street continued dead straight ahead. They crossed an intersection, where the elegant red brick gave way to more modern pre-cast concrete blocks. Then, suddenly, they were driving along beneath the dark green steel L-Train overpass.

The driver said, 'Rushons. This whole fuggin' area is now Rushon.'

'*Rushon?*' Ronnie queried, not knowing what he meant.

The driver pointed to a row of garish store fronts. A nail studio. The Shostakovich Music, Art and Sport School. There was Russian writing everywhere. He saw a pharmacy sign in Cyrillic. Unless you spoke Russian, you wouldn't know what half these stores were. And he didn't speak a word.

Rushon. Now Ronnie understood.

'*Little Odessa,*' the driver said. 'Yuge fuggin' colony. Didn't used to be, not when I was a kid. Perestroika, glasnost, right? They let them travel, waddya know? They all come here! Whole world's changing – know what I'm saying?'

Ronnie was tempted to shut the man up by telling him that the world had changed once for the Native Americans too, but he didn't want to get thrown out of the truck.

So he just said another, 'Yep.'

They made a right turn into a residential cul-de-sac. At the far end was a row of black bollards with a boardwalk beyond, and a beach beyond that. And then the ocean.

'Brighton Beach. Good place. Be safe here. Safe from the planes,' the driver said, indicating to Ronnie that this was journey's end.

The driver turned to the ghosts behind. 'Coney Island. Brighton Beach. I gotta get back to find my ladders, my harnesses, all my stuff. Expensive stuff, you know.'

Ronnie unclipped his seat belt, thanked the man profusely and shook his big, callused hand.

'Be safe, buddy.'

'You too.'

'You bet.'

Ronnie opened the door and jumped down on to the tarmac. There was a tang of sea salt in the air. And just a faint smell of burning and aviation fuel. Faint enough to make him feel safe here. But not so faint that he felt free of what he had just been through.

Without casting a backwards glance at the ghosts, he walked on to the boardwalk, with almost a spring in his step, and pulled his mobile phone from his pocket to check that it was definitely off.

Then he stopped and stared past the sandy beach at the vast flat expanse of rippling, green-blue ocean and the hazy smudge of land miles in the distance. He took in a deep breath. Followed by another. His plan was still only very vague and needed a lot of work.

But he felt excited.

Elated.

Not many people in New York on the morning of 9/11 punched the air in glee. But Ronnie Wilson did.

36

OCTOBER 2007

Abby sat cradling a cup of tea in her trembling hands, staring through a gap in the blinds down at the street below. Her eyes were raw from three sleepless nights in a row. Fear swirled inside her.

I know where you are.

Her suitcase was by the front door, packed and zipped shut. She looked at her watch: 8.55. In five minutes she would make the call she had been planning to make all yesterday, just as soon as office hours started. It was ironic, she thought, that for most of her life she had disliked Monday mornings. But all of yesterday she had willed it to come.

She felt more scared than she had ever felt in her life.

Unless she was completely mistaken, and panicking needlessly, he was out there somewhere, waiting and watching. Her card marked. Waiting and watching and *angry*.

Had he done something to the lift? And its alarm? Would he have known what to do? She repeated the questions to herself, over and over.

Yes, he'd been a mechanic once. He could fix mechanical and electrical things. But why would he have done something to the lift?

She tried to get her head around that. If he really knew where she was, why hadn't he just lain in wait for her? What did he have to gain by getting her stuck in the lift? If he wanted time to try to break in, why hadn't he just waited until she went out?

Was she, in her panicked state, simply putting two and two together and getting five?

Maybe. Maybe not. She just didn't know. So most of the day, yesterday, instead of going out, buying the Sunday papers and lounging in front of the television, as she would ordinarily have done, she sat here, in the same spot where she was now, watching the street below, passing the time by listening to one Spanish lesson after another on her headphones, pronouncing, and repeating, words and sentences out aloud.

It had been a foul Sunday, a south-westerly twisting off the English Channel, continuing to blast the rain on the pavement, the puddles, the parked cars, the passers-by.

And it was the cars and the passers-by that she was watching, like a hawk, through the rain that was still pelting down today. She checked all the parked cars and vans first thing, when she woke up. Only a couple had changed from the night before. It was a neighbourhood where there was insufficient street parking, so once people found a space, they tended to leave their cars until they really needed to go somewhere. Otherwise, the moment they drove off, another vehicle took their place, and when they came back they might have to park several streets away.

She'd had two visitors yesterday, a photographer from the *Argus*, whom she'd told on the entryphone to go away, and the caretaker, Tomasz, who had come to apologize, maybe concerned for his job and hoping she wouldn't make a complaint about him if he was nice to her. He explained that vandals must have broken into the lift motor-room and tampered with the brake mechanism and electrics. Low-lifes, he said. He had found a couple of syringes in there. But he wasn't able to explain convincingly to her why the alarm system, which should have rung through to his flat, had failed to do so. He assured her the lift company was working on it, but the damage the firemen had done meant it would be several days before it was working again.

She got rid of him as quickly as she could, in order to return to her vigil of watching the street.

She called her mother, but she said nothing about receiving any phone calls from anyone. Abby continued the lie that she was still in Australia and having a great time.

Sometimes text messages went astray, got sent to wrong numbers by mistake. Could this have been one?

I know where you are.

Possible.

Coming on top of the lift getting stuck, was she jumping to conclusions in her paranoid state? It was comforting to think that. But complacency was the one luxury she could not afford. She had gone into this knowing the risks involved. Knowing that she would only get away with it by living on her wits, 24/7, for however long it took.

The only thing that had made her smile yesterday was another of his lovely texts. This one said:

> *You don't love a woman because she is beautiful, but she is beautiful because you love her.*

She had replied:

> *It's beauty that captures your attention –*
> *personality which captures your heart.*

She saw nothing untoward in the street all Sunday. No strangers watching her. No Ricky. Just the rain. Just people. Life going on.

Normal life.

Something she was – for just a short while longer, she promised herself – no longer a part of. But all that would be changing soon.

37

OCTOBER 2007

Rain rattled down on the roof and the van rocked in strong gusts of wind. Although he was well wrapped up, he was still cold in here, only daring to run the engine occasionally, not wanting to attract attention to himself. At least he had a comfortable mattress, books, a Starbucks nearby and music on his iPod. There was a public toilet close by on the promenade with an adequate washing facility and it was conveniently out of sight of any of the city's CCTV cameras. Very definitely a public convenience.

He had once read a line in a book someone had given him which said, *Sex is the most fun you can have without laughing.*

The book was wrong, he thought. Sometimes revenge could be fun too. Just as much fun as sex.

The van still had the FOR SALE note written in red ink on a strip of brown cardboard stuck in its passenger-door window, although he had actually bought it, for three hundred and fifty pounds cash, over two weeks ago. He knew Abby was sharp, and had observed her checking the vehicles daily. No point in removing the sign and alerting her to any change. So if the previous owner got pissed off with people phoning, wanting to buy it, tough. He hadn't bought it because he needed transport. He had bought it for the view. He could see every window of her flat from here.

It was the perfect parking spot. The van had a valid tax disc and MOT and residents' parking sticker. All of them ran out in three months' time.

By then he would be long gone.

38

OCTOBER 2007

It was the same every damn time. Whatever confidence Roy Grace felt when he set off to come to this impressive place deserted him when he actually arrived.

Malling House, the headquarters of Sussex Police, was just a fifteen-minute drive from his office. But in atmosphere, it was on a different planet. Strike that, he thought as he drove past the raised barrier of the security gate, it was in a whole different *universe.*

It sat within a ragbag complex of buildings on the outskirts of Lewes, the county town of East Sussex, housing the administration and key management for the five thousand officers and employees of the Sussex Police Force.

Two buildings stood out prominently. One, a three-storey, futuristic glass and brick structure, contained the Control Centre, the Crime Recording and Investigation Bureau, the Call Handling Centre and the Force Command Centre, as well as most of the computing hardware for the force. The other, an imposing red-brick Queen Anne mansion, once a private stately home and now a Grade 1 listed building, was what had given its name to the HQ.

Although conjoined to the ramshackle sprawl of car parks, single-storey pre-fabs, modern low-rise structures and one dark, windowless building, complete with a tall smokestack, which always reminded Grace of a Yorkshire textile mill, the mansion stood proudly aloof. Inside were housed the offices of the Chief Constable, the Deputy Chief Constable and the Assistant Chief Constables, of whom Alison Vosper was one, together with their support staff, as well as a number of other senior officers working either temporarily or permanently out of these headquarters.

Grace found a bay for his Alfa Romeo, then he made his way to Alison Vosper's office, which was on the ground floor at the front of the mansion. It had a view through a large sash window out on to a gravel driveway and a circular lawn beyond. It must be nice to work in a room like this, he thought, in this calm oasis, away from the cramped, characterless spaces of Sussex House. Sometimes he thought he might enjoy the responsibility – and the power trip that came with it – but then he would always wonder whether he could cope with the politics. Especially the damned, insidious, political correctness that the brass had to kowtow to a lot more than the ranks.

The ACC could be your new best friend one day and your worst enemy the next. It had seemed a long time since she had been anything but the latter to Grace, as he stood now in front of her desk, used to the fact that she rarely invited visitors to sit down, in order to keep meetings short and to the point.

Today he was actually rather hoping he wouldn't get invited to sit down. He wanted to deliver his angry message standing up, with the advantage of height.

She didn't disappoint him. Giving him a cold, hard stare, she said, 'Yes, Roy?'

And he felt himself trembling. As if he had been summoned to his headmaster's study at school.

In her early forties, with wispy blonde hair cut conservatively short, and framing a hard but attractive face,

Assistant Chief Constable Alison Vosper was very definitely not happy this morning. Power-dressed in a navy suit and a crisp white blouse, she was sitting behind her expansive, immaculately tidy rosewood desk with an angry expression on her face.

Grace always wondered how his superiors kept their offices – and their desks – so tidy. All his working life, his own work spaces had been tips. Repositories of sprawling files, unanswered correspondence, lost pens, travel receipts and out-trays that had long given up on the struggle to keep pace with the in-trays. To get to the very top, he had once decided, required some kind of a paperwork management skill for which he was lacking the gene.

Rumour was that Alison Vosper had had a breast cancer operation three years ago. But Grace knew that's all it would ever be, just rumour, because she kept a wall around herself. Nonetheless, behind her hard-cop carapace, there was a certain vulnerability that he connected to. In truth, she wasn't at all bad-looking, and there were occasions when those waspish brown eyes of hers twinkled with humour and he sensed she might almost be flirting with him. This morning was not one of them.

'Thanks for your time, Ma'am.'

'I've literally got five minutes.'

'OK.'

Shit. Already his confidence was crumbling.

'I wanted to talk to you about Cassian Pewe.'

'Detective Superintendent Pewe?' she said, as if delivering a subtle reminder of the man's position.

He nodded.

She opened her arms expansively. 'Yes?'

She had slender wrists and finely manicured hands, which seemed, somehow, slightly older and more mature than the rest of her. As if making a statement to show that although the police force was no longer a man-only world, there was still considerable male dominance, she wore a big, loud, man's wristwatch.

'The thing is . . .' He hesitated, the words he had planned to deliver tripping over themselves inside his head.

'Yes?' She sounded impatient.

'Well – he's a smart guy.'

'He's a very smart guy.'

'Absolutely.' Roy was struggling under her glare. 'The thing is – he rang me on Saturday. On *Operation Dingo*. He said you'd suggested that he call me – that I might need a hand.'

'Correct.' She took a dainty sip of water from a crystal tumbler on her desk.

Struggling under her laser stare, he said, 'I'm just not sure that's the best use of resources.'

'I think I should be the judge of that,' she retorted.

'Well, of course – but—'

'But?'

'This is a slow-time case. That skeleton has been there ten to fifteen years.'

'And have you identified it yet?'

'No, but I have good leads. I'm hoping for progress today from dental records.'

She screwed the top back on the bottle and set it down on to the floor. Then she placed her elbows on the shiny rosewood and interlocked her fingers. He smelled her scent. It was different from the last time he had been here, just a few weeks ago. Muskier. Sexier. In his wildest fantasies he had wondered what it might be like to make love to this woman. He imagined she would be in total control, all of the time. And that as easily as she could arouse a man, she could rapidly make his dick shrivel in terror.

'Roy, you know that the Metropolitan Police have been one of the first forces in the UK to start getting rid of bureaucracy on arrests? That they now employ civilians to process criminals so police officers don't have to spend two to four hours on paperwork on every person they arrest?'

'Yes, I had heard that.'

'They're the biggest and most innovative police force in the UK. So don't you think we can learn something from Cassian?'

He noted the use of the man's first name. 'I'm sure we can – I don't doubt that.'

'Have you thought about your personal development record this year, Roy?'

'My record?'

'Yes. What's your assessment of how you have done?'

He shrugged. 'Without blowing my own trumpet, I think I've done well. We got a life sentence on Suresh Hossain. Three serious crime cases solved, successfully. Two major criminals awaiting trial. And some real progress on several cold cases.'

She looked at him for some moments in silence, then she asked, 'How do *you* define success?'

He chose his words carefully, aware of what might come next. 'Apprehending perpetrators, securing charges against them from the Crown Prosecution Service and getting convictions.'

'Apprehending suspects regardless of cost or danger to the public or your officers?'

'All risks have to be assessed in advance – when practical. In the heat of a situation, it's not always practical. You know that. You must have been in situations where you had to make snap decisions.'

She nodded and was silent for some moments. 'Well, that's great, Roy. I'm sure that helps you to sleep at night.' Then she fell silent again, shaking her head in a way that he really did not like.

He heard a distant phone ringing, unanswered, in another office. Then Alison Vosper's mobile pinged with a text. She picked it up, glanced at it and put it back down on her desk.

'I look at it slightly differently, Roy. And so do the Independent Police Complaints Authority. OK?'

Grace shrugged. 'In what way?' He already knew some of the answers.

'Let's look at your three major operations in the past few months. *Operation Salsa.* During a chase you were handling personally, an elderly member of the public was hijacked and physically injured. Two suspects died in a car crash – and you were in the pursuit car right behind them. In *Operation Nightingale,* one of your officers was shot and another was severely injured in a pursuit – which also resulted in an accident causing serious injury to an off-duty police officer.'

That officer had been Cassian Pewe. Delaying his start here by some months.

She continued. 'You had a helicopter crash, and an entire building burned down – leaving three bodies beyond identification. And in *Operation Chameleon* you allowed your suspect to be pursued on to a railway line, where he was maimed. Are you proud of all this? You don't think there is room for improvement with your methods?'

Actually, Roy Grace thought, he was proud. Extremely proud of everything but the injuries to his officers, for which he would always blame himself. Maybe she genuinely did not know the background – or she was choosing to ignore it.

He was cautious in his reply. 'When you look at an operation after the event, you can always see ways you could have improved it.'

'Exactly,' she said. 'That's all Detective Superintendent Pewe is here to do. Bring the benefit of his experience with the best police force in the UK.'

He would have liked to have replied, *Actually, you are wrong. The guy is a total wanker.* But his earlier feeling that Alison Vosper had some other agenda with this man was even stronger now. Maybe she really was shagging him. Unlikely, for sure, but there was something between them, some hold over her that Pewe had. Whatever, it was clear that at this moment Grace was definitely not teacher's pet.

So, on one of the rare occasions in his career, he played along with the politics.

'Fine,' he said. 'Thanks for clarifying that. It's really helpful.'

'Good,' she said.

As Grace left the room, he was deep in thought. There had been four Senior Investigating Officers at Sussex House for the past five years. The system was fine. They didn't need any more. Now they had five, at a time when they were short of recruits lower down and running way over budget. It would not be long before Vosper and her colleagues started reducing the number back down to four. And no prizes for guessing who would be axed – or, rather, transferred to the back of beyond.

He needed a plan. Something that would cause Cassian Pewe to shoot himself in the foot.

And at this moment he didn't have one.

39

OCTOBER 2007

He could have murdered a Starbucks latte. Or any freshly ground coffee. But he didn't dare leave his observation post. There was only one way out of her building, regardless of whether she used the lift or the fire escape staircase, and that was through the front door he was staring at. He wasn't taking any chances. She had remained inside for too long, much longer than normal, and he had a feeling she was up to something.

Finding her had been hard enough – and *expensive* enough. With just one piece of luck on his side: an old friend in the right place.

Well, actually the wrong place, because Donny Winters was in jail for identify theft and fraud, but it was Ford Open Prison, where visiting hours were reasonable and it was under an hour's drive from here. It had been a risk going to see him, and it had cost him, for the bungs Donny said he would need.

He'd been right, of course, in his hunch. All women called their mums. And Abby's mum was sick. Abby thought she would be safe, calling from a pay-as-you-go mobile with the number withheld. Stupid cow.

Stupid, greedy cow.

He smiled at the GSM 3060 Intercept, which sat on a wooden vegetable box in front of him now. If you were in range of either the mobile handset making the call or the mobile receiving it, you could listen in and, very usefully, see the number of the caller, even if it was withheld, and the recipient, regardless of whether it was a mobile or landline. But of course she wouldn't know that.

He'd simply camped out in a rental car close to her mother's flat in Eastbourne and waited for Abby to call. He hadn't had to wait long. Then it had taken Donny just one call, to a bent mate who worked on an installation team rigging mobile phone radio masts. Within two days he had established the location of the mast which had picked up the signals from Abby's phone.

He learned that mobile phone masts in densely populated cities were rarely more than a few hundred yards apart, and often even closer together than that. And he learned from Donny that, in addition to receiving and transmitting calls, mobile phone masts act as beacons. Even on stand-by, a phone keeps in touch with its nearest beacon, constantly transmitting a greeting signal and receiving one back.

The pattern of signals from Abby's phone showed she barely went out of range of one particular beacon, a Vodafone macrocell sited at the junction of Eastern Road and Boundary Road in Kemp Town.

This was a short distance from Marine Parade, which ran from the Palace Pier to the Marina, fronted on one side by some of the finest Regency façades in the city and on the other by a railed promenade and views out across the beach and the English Channel. There was a rabbit warren of streets immediately off and behind Marine Parade, most of them residential, almost all of them containing a mix of flats, cheap hotels and B&Bs.

He remembered how much she loved the sea view from

his own flat and he figured she would be close to the sea now. And almost certainly have some kind of a view of it. Which had made it a simple measuring job to identify the group of streets in which she must be residing. All he'd had to do was patrol around them, disguised, in the hope that she would appear. And that had happened within three days. He had spotted her going into a newsagent on Eastern Road, then followed her back to her front door.

It had been tempting to grab her then and there, but too risky. There were people around. All she had to do was shout, and game over. That was the problem. That was the advantage she had over him. And she knew it.

The rain was coming down even harder now, drumming noisily, reverberating all around him. On a day like this it would have been nice to have room service, he thought. But hey, you couldn't have everything! Not, at any rate, without a little patience.

He used to go fishing with his dad when he was a kid. Like him, his dad had always been into gizmos. He'd bought one of the earliest electronic floats. The first strike from a fish, pulling the float under, would trigger a short, high-pitched beep from the little transmitter on the ground beside their folding chairs.

It was similar to the beep he heard now from his interceptor system, as he flipped through the pages of the *Daily Mail*, a distinct, sharp, high-pitched beep. Followed by another.

The bitch was making a phone call.

40

OCTOBER 2007

The automated voice said, 'Thank you for calling Global Express. Please press any key to continue. Thank you. To check the status of a delivery, please press 1. To request a collection, press 2. If you are an account customer requesting a collection, press 3. If you are a new customer requesting a collection, press 4. For all other enquiries, press 5.'

Abby pressed 4.

'For deliveries within the UK, please press 1. For overseas deliveries, press 2.'

She pressed 1.

There was a brief silence. She hated these automated systems. Then she heard a couple of clicks, followed by a young, male voice.

'Global Express. Jonathan speaking. How can I help you?'

Jonathan sounded like he'd be better suited helping young men into trousers in a gents' outfitters.

'Hi, Jonathan,' she said. 'I have a package I need delivered.'

'No problem at all. Would that be letter size? Parcel size? Larger than that?'

'An A4 envelope about an inch thick,' she said.

'No problem at all,' Jonathan assured her. 'And where would that be going?'

'To an address just outside Brighton,' she said.

'No problem at all. And where would we be picking up from?'

'From Brighton,' Abby said. 'Well, Kemp Town, actually.'

'No problem at all.'

'How soon can you collect?' she asked.

'In your area – one moment – we will collect between 4 and 7.'

'Not before?'

'No problem at all, but that would be an extra charge.'

She thought quickly. If the weather remained like this it would be fairly dark by about 5 o'clock. Would that be an advantage or a disadvantage?

'Will you be sending a bike or a van?' she asked.

'For overnight it will be a van,' Jonathan replied.

A revised plan was forming in her mind. 'Is it possible you could ask them not to come before 5.30?'

'Not to come before 5.30? Let me just check.'

There were some moments of silence. She was trying hard to think this through. So many variables. Then there was a click and Jonathan was back with her.

'No problem at all.'

41

SEPTEMBER 2007

Oh yes, what a great place to be – *not* – on a Monday morning this was, thought Detective Senior Sergeant George Fletcher. It was bad enough to have a blinding hangover on a Monday morning. But being here, in the Forensic Pathology department of the Victorian Institute of Forensic Medicine, greatly compounded it. And he hated all this bullshit newspeak. It was the *city morgue*, for God's sake. It was the place where dead bodies got even more dead. It was the last place before the cemetery where you'd ever have your name on the guest check-in register.

And at this moment he was being assaulted by a grinding, whining sound that shook every atom in his body as he stood in the cramped CT room, watching the body of *Unidentified Female* pass slowly through the doughnut-shaped hoop of the CT scanner.

She had not been touched since being removed from the boot of the car yesterday, bagged and brought here, where she had been stored in a fridge overnight. The smell was unpleasant. A cloying stink of drains and a sharp, sour odour that reminded George of pond weed. He not only had to fight the pounding noise in his brain, but the heavings inside his stomach. The woman's skin had a soapy, bloated look, with large areas of black marbling. Her hair, which had probably been blonde and was still fair, was matted and had insects, bits of paper and what looked like a small bit of felt in it. It was hard to make out the features of her face as part of it had either rotted or been nibbled away. The pathologist put her age, as a guess-timate, at mid-thirties.

George was dressed in a green gown over his white shirt, tie and suit trousers, and white rubber boots, like his colleague, DS Troy Burg, beside him. Thin, wiry-haired and with a prickly attitude, Barry Manx, the Senior Forensic Technician, operated the machine, and the pathologist stood running his eyes up and down the woman's body, reading it like the pages of a book.

It was routine that all bodies admitted here for post-mortem were scanned, checking primarily for signs of any infectious disease, before they were opened up.

Unidentified Female's flesh was missing in several places. Her lips had partially gone, as had one ear, and bones showed through the fingers of her left hand. Although she had been sealed in the boot of a car, plenty of aquatic wildlife had, nonetheless, managed to gain entry and had had a good time feasting on her remains.

George had had a good time yesterday with his wife, Janet, feasting on his cooking. A few months back he had enrolled on a cookery course at the technical college in Geelong. He'd prepared a meal last night of stir-fried Morton Bay Bugs, followed by garlic-marinated rib-eye beef, finishing with kiwi panacotta. And accompanied by—

He groaned, silently, at the memory.

Far too much Margaret River Zinfandel.

And now it was all coming back to bite him.

He could do with water now, and a strong black coffee, he thought, as he walked behind Burg down a shiny, spot-less, windowless corridor.

The post-mortem room was not his favourite place. Not at any time of any day and least of all with a hangover. It was a cavernous arena which felt like a cross between an operating theatre and a factory floor. The ceiling was aluminium with massive air ducts and recessed lights, while a forest of booms swung out from the walls, containing spotlights and electrical sockets which could be directed over any part of a body under inspection. The floor was a deep blue, as if in an attempt to bring some cheer into the place, and along each side were work surfaces, trolleys of surgical instruments, red trash cans with yellow liners, and hoses.

Five thousand cadavers were processed here each year.

He slipped a couple of paracetamol capsules into his mouth, swallowing each one with difficulty with his own saliva. A forensic photographer was taking pictures of the corpse and a retired policeman George had known for years, who was now the Coroner's Officer for this case, stood on the far side of the room, by a work table, leafing through the brief dossier that had been put together, including the photographs taken at the river yesterday.

The pathologist worked at a brisk pace, stopping every few minutes to dictate into his machine. As the morning ticked away, George, whose presence here, along with Troy's, was almost superfluous, spent most of the time in a quiet corner of the room, working on his mobile phone, assembling his inquiry team and assigning each of them duties, as well as preparing for the first press conference, which he was delaying as long as possible in the hope of getting some positive information from the pathologist that he could release.

His two priorities at this moment were the woman's identity and cause of death. Troy's sick joke that maybe she had been trying to replicate one of Harry Houdini or David Blaine's stunts might normally have raised a smile, but not today.

The pathologist pointed out to George that the hyoid bone was broken, which was an indicator of strangulation. But her eyes had deteriorated beyond the point of providing supporting evidence he might have got from petechial haemorrhaging, and her lungs were too badly decomposed to yield clues as to whether she was already dead when the car had gone into the water.

The condition of the woman's flesh wasn't good. Prolonged immersion in water caused degradation of not only all soft tissues and hair, but, most crucially, the nuclear – single-cell – DNA that could be obtained from them. If there was too much degradation, they would have to rely on the DNA from the woman's bones, which provided a much less certain match.

When he wasn't on the phone, George was propping himself quietly against a wall, badly wanting to sit down and close his eyes for a few moments. He was feeling his age. Policing was a young man's game, he had thought more than once recently. He had three years to go before collecting his pension, and although he still enjoyed his work, most of the time, he looked forward to not having to keep his phone on day and night, and worry about being dispatched to some grim discovery in the middle of his Sunday morning lie-in.

'George!'

Troy was calling him.

He walked over to the table the woman was lying on. The pathologist was holding something up with forceps. It looked like a dimpled, translucent jellyfish without tentacles.

'Breast implant,' the pathologist said. 'She's had a boob job.'

'Reconstruction from breast cancer?' George asked. A friend of Janet's had recently had a mastectomy, and he knew a little about the subject.

'No, just bigger boobs,' the pathologist said. 'Which is good news for us.'

George frowned.

'All silicone breast implants have their manufacturer's batch numbers stamped on them,' the pathologist explained. 'And each implant has a serial number that would be kept in the hospital register against the recipient's name.' He held the implant a little closer to George, until he could see a tiny row of embossed numbers. 'That'll take us to the manufacturer. Should be a shoo-in for you to find her identity.'

George returned to his phone calls. He made a quick one to Janet, to tell her he loved her. He had always called her, at least once a day from work, from almost their first date. And he meant what he said. He still loved her just as much all these years on. His mood had improved with the pathologist's discovery. The paracetamols were kicking in nicely. He was even starting to think about lunch.

Then suddenly the pathologist called out, 'George, this might be of real significance!'

He hurried back over to the table.

'The uterus wall is thick,' the pathologist said. 'With a body that's been immersed for a length of time like this, the uterus is one of the parts that degrades the slowest. And we've just got really lucky!'

'We have?' George said.

The pathologist nodded. 'We'll get our DNA now!' He

pointed down at the dissecting board that stood, on its steel legs, above the dead woman's remains.

There was a mess of body fluids on it. In the midst sat a cream, internal organ, like a U-shaped sausage that had been sliced open. George could not identify it. But it was the object that lay in the middle that instantly drew his eye. For a moment he thought it was an undigested prawn in her intestine. But then, peering closer, he realized what it actually was.

And he lost all his appetite for lunch.

42

OCTOBER 2007

The first, and most welcome, sign that there had been a regime change at Sussex House was that senior CID officers here now actually had a parking bay of their own, and in the best position, outside the front of the building. Which meant that Roy Grace no longer had to drive around trying to find a space out on the street, or furtively leave his car in the ASDA supermarket car park across the street, like most of his colleagues, and then trudge back through the pissing rain, or take the muddy short cut through the bushes, followed by a death-defying leap off a brick wall.

Situated on a hill in what had been open countryside, a safe distance from Brighton and Hove, the Art Deco-influenced low-rise had originally been built as a hospital for contagious diseases. There had been several changes of use before the CID had taken it over, and at some point in its history the urban sprawl had caught up with it. It now sat rather incongruously in an industrial estate, directly opposite the ASDA which served as the building's unofficial but handy canteen and parking overflow.

Since the very recent departure of the amiable but lax Detective Chief Superintendent Gary Weston, who had been promoted to Assistant Chief Constable in the Midlands, tough, no-nonsense, pipe-smoking Jack Skerritt was making his presence felt throughout the place. Skerritt, the former Commander of Brighton and Hove Uniform, who was fifty-two, combined old-school toughness with modern thinking, and was one of the most universally liked – and respected – police officers in the force. The return of this weekly meeting was his biggest innovation so far.

Another instantly noticeable change, Grace reflected, as he entered the front door and exchanged a cheery greeting with the two security guards, was that Skerritt had imposed a modern stamp on the entrance staircase. The displays of antique truncheons had been dispatched to a museum. The cream walls had been freshly painted and there was now a new, wide blue felt board containing photographs of all the senior personnel currently manning HQ CID.

Most prominent was the photograph of Jack Skerritt himself. He was a lean, square-jawed man, good-looking in a slightly old-fashioned Hollywood matinée-idol way. He had a stern expression, a slick of tidy brown hair, and was wearing a dark suit jacket and a muted, chequerboard tie. He exuded a commanding presence which seemed to be saying, *Don't fuck with me and I'll be fair to you.* Which was in fact the essence of the man.

Grace respected and admired him. He was the kind of policeman he would like to be. With three years to go before retirement, Skerritt didn't give a stuff for political correctness, nor was he too concerned about directives from above. He saw his role as being to make the streets and homes and businesses of Sussex safe places for law-abiding citizens, and how he did it was his business. And in his past two years as Commander of Brighton and Hove, before this new posting here, he had made a considerable impact on crime levels across the city.

At the top of the stairs was a broad, carpeted landing,

with a rubber plant that looked as if it was on growth hormones and a potted palm that looked as if it should have been in a hospice.

Grace pressed his card against the door security pad and entered the rarefied atmosphere of the command floor. This first section was a large, open-plan area, with a dark orange carpet down the centre, with clusters of desks on either side for the support staff.

Senior departmental heads had their own offices. The door to one was open and Grace exchanged a nod with his friend Brian Cook, the Scientific Support Branch Manager, who was on his feet, finishing a call. He then hurried past the large, glassed-in office of Jack Skerritt, wanting a quick word with Eleanor Hodgson, his Management Support Assistant, as his PA was called these days in this bonkers, politically correct world.

Posters were stuck up all over the walls. A big red and orange one stood out the loudest:

RAT ON A RAT
DRUG DEALERS RUIN LIVES
TELL CRIMESTOPPERS WHO THEY ARE

He hurried past his office and one marked 'Detective Superintendent Gaynor Allen, Operations and Intelligence Branch', and went over to where Eleanor was sitting.

It was a cluttered area of desks stacked with over-full red and black in-trays and littered with keypads, phones, file folders, writing pads and Post-it notes. A car 'L' plate had been stuck to the rear of one flat computer screen by some joker.

Eleanor's was the only orderly desk. A rather prim, quietly efficient if nervy middle-aged woman with neat black hair and a plain, slightly old-fashioned face, she ran much of Roy Grace's life for him. She was looking nervous now as he approached her, as if he was about to shout at her for some balls-up, although he had never once raised his voice at her in the eighteen months she had worked for him. It was just the way she was.

He asked her to check with the Thistle Hotel on the size of the tables for the Rugby Club Dinner for this December, and quickly ran through some urgent emails she drew to his attention, then, glancing at his watch and seeing it was two minutes after 10.30, he entered Skerritt's spacious, impressive domain.

Like his own new office – he had recently been moved from one side of the building to the other – it had a view over the road towards ASDA. But that was where the similarity ended. While his just had room for his desk and a small round table, Skerritt's cavernous room accommodated, as well as his large desk, a rectangular conference table.

There were changes in here too. Gone were the framed photographs of racehorses and greyhounds that had dominated the walls in Gary Weston's day, showing his priorities in life. They had been replaced by a single framed photograph of two teenage boys, and several of Labrador dogs and puppies. Skerritt's wife bred them, but they were also the police officer's own passion – on his rare moments away from work.

Skerritt exuded a faint smell of pipe tobacco smoke, just as Norman Potting usually did. On Potting, Grace found the smell noxious, but on Skerritt he liked it. It suited the senior officer, enhancing his tough-man image.

To his dismay, he saw Cassian Pewe seated at the table, along with the rest of the SIOs and other senior members of the Command Team. He did not imagine tobacco had ever crossed Cassian Pewe's lips in his life.

The new Detective Superintendent greeted him with a reptilian smile and a treacly, 'Hello, Roy, good to see you,' and held out his moist hand. Roy shook it as briefly as he could, then took the only empty seat, muttering apologies for being late to Skerritt, who was a stickler for punctuality.

'Good of you to make it, Roy,' the Detective Chief Superintendent said.

He had a strong, classless voice that always sounded sarcastic, as if he had spent so much of his life interrogating lying suspects it had rubbed off permanently on him. Roy couldn't tell now whether he was actually being sarcastic or not.

'Right,' Skerritt went on. 'The business of today.'

He sat bolt upright, with a fine, confident posture, and had an air of being physically indestructible, as if he was hewn from granite. He read from a printed agenda in front of him. Someone passed a copy to Roy, which he glanced through. The usual stuff.

Minutes of previous meeting.

Annual motor incident report.

2010 Challenge Programme – shortfall of £8–10m.

Joining forces – update on merging Sussex and Surrey Police Forces . . .

Skerritt steered the assembled group through each of the items at a brisk pace. When they reached 'Operational Updates', Roy brought them up to speed on *Operation Dingo.* He did not have a lot of news for them at this stage, but told them he was hopeful that dental records might produce the dead woman's identity quite quickly.

When he reached 'Any Other Business', Skerritt suddenly turned to Grace. 'Roy, I'm making a few changes in the team.'

For a moment, Grace's heart sank. Was the Vosper–Pewe conspiracy finally showing its colours?

'I'm giving you Major Crime,' Skerritt said.

Grace could hardly believe his ears, and indeed wondered if he had misheard, or misunderstood. 'Major Crime?'

'Yes, Roy, I've given it some thought.' He pointed at his own head. 'Up here in the old brainbox, you know. You keep your SIO roles, but I want you to head up Major Crime. You're going to be my number two – you head up CID if I'm not around.'

He was being promoted!

Out of his peripheral vision he saw Cassian Pewe looking as if he had just bitten into a lemon.

Grace knew that although his rank remained the same, covering for Jack in his absence and running HQ CID from time to time, was a big step up.

'Jack, thank you. I – I'm delighted.' Then he hesitated. 'Is Alison Vosper OK with this?'

'Leave Alison to me,' Skerritt replied dismissively. Then he turned to Pewe. 'Cassian, welcome aboard our team. Roy's going to have his hands full with his extra workload, so I'd like you to start here by taking on his cold-case files – which means you will be reporting to Roy.'

Grace was having trouble suppressing a grin. Cassian Pewe's face was a picture. Rather like one of those television weather maps dotted with rain and thunderclouds and not a ray of sunshine in sight. Even his perma-tan seemed, suddenly, to have faded.

The meeting ended on target, at exactly 11.30. As Grace was leaving, Cassian Pewe intercepted him in the doorway.

'Roy,' he said. 'Alison thought it might be a good idea if I sat in with you today – at your press conference and at your evening briefing. To sort of find my feet. Get the general gist of how you do things down here. Still OK with you – in the light of what Jack's just instructed me to do?'

No, Grace thought. *Not at all OK with me.* But he didn't say that. He said, 'Well, I think it might be a better use of your time to familiarize yourself with my caseload. I'll show you the cold-case files and you can make a start.'

And then he spent a few moments thinking how very pleasant it might be to stick hot needles into Pewe's testicles.

But from the expression on Pewe's face, it seemed that Jack Skerritt had just done that job for him.

43

OCTOBER 2007

Grace kept the press briefing short. It was party political conference season and a lot of reporters, even if not directly interested in politics, were up in Blackpool with the Tories – who at this moment seemed likely to provide richer pickings than a skeleton in a sewer, for the nationals at any rate.

But the *Unknown Female* was a good local story, particularly as the remains had been discovered beneath one of the biggest property developments ever in the city, and it had a whiff of both history in the past and history in the making. Analogies were being made to the Brighton Trunk Murders, two separate incidents in 1934 when dismembered bodies were found in trunks, earning Brighton the unwelcome sobriquet 'Crime Capital of England'.

One local television crew from the BBC had turned up, as did Southern Counties Radio, a young man with a video camera from a new Brighton internet television channel, Absolute Television, a couple of stringers from London papers whom Grace knew, a reporter from the *Sussex Express* and, of course, Kevin Spinella from the *Argus*.

Although Spinella irritated him, Grace was beginning to develop a grudging respect for the young journalist. He could see that Spinella was a hard worker, like himself, and after an encounter on a previous case, when Spinella had honoured a promise to withhold some important information, he had shown himself to be a reporter the police could do business with. Some police officers viewed all press as vermin, but Grace felt differently. Almost every major crime relied on witnesses, on members of the public coming forward, on memories being jogged. If you handled the press correctly you could get them to do quite a bit of your work for you.

With little information to give out this morning, Grace concentrated on getting a few key messages across. The age and as much description of the woman as they could give out, and an estimate of how many years she might have been down that storm drain, in the hope that a family member or friend might come forward with details of a person who had gone missing within that time frame.

Grace had added that although the cause of death was unknown, strangulation was a possibility, and that whoever had murdered her would probably have had good local knowledge of Brighton and Hove.

As he left the conference room, shortly before 12.30, he heard his name being called.

Irritatingly, Kevin Spinella had taken to waylaying Grace after press conferences, cornering him in the corridor, out of earshot of the other journalists.

'Detective Superintendent Grace, could I have a quick word?'

Roy wondered for a moment if perhaps Spinella had heard about his promotion. It should have been impossible for him to find out this quickly, but for some time now he had suspected that Spinella had an informer somewhere inside Sussex Police. He always seemed to know of any incident ahead of everyone else. At some point Roy was determined to get to the bottom of it, but that was no easy thing to do. When you started digging below the surface, you risked alienating a lot of your colleagues.

The young reporter, as ever in a suit, shirt and tie, was looking sharper and more spruce than at his rain-soaked appearance at the site on Saturday morning.

'Nothing to do with this,' Spinella said, his teeth working on a piece of gum. 'Just something I thought I ought to mention to you. On Saturday evening I got a call from a contact in the fire brigade – they were going into a flat in Kemp Town to rescue someone stuck in a lift.'

'Boy, do you have an exciting life!' Grace ribbed him.

'Yeah, all go,' Spinella replied earnestly, missing the barb, or deliberately ignoring it. 'The thing is, this woman . . .' He hesitated and tapped the side of his nose. 'You got a *copper's nose,* right?'

Grace shrugged. He was always careful what he said to Spinella. 'That's what people say about police officers.'

Spinella tapped his own nose. 'Yeah, well, I got it too. A nose for a good story – know what I mean?'

'Yes.' Grace looked at his watch. 'I'm in a rush—'

'Yeah, OK, I won't keep you. Just wanted to alert you, that's all. This woman they freed – late twenties, very pretty – I felt something wasn't right.'

'In what way?'

'She was very agitated.'

'Not surprising if she'd been stuck in a lift.'

Spinella shook his head. 'Not that kind of agitated.'

Grace looked at him for a moment. One thing he knew about local newspaper reporters was the range of stories they got sent to cover. Sudden deaths, road crashes, mugging victims, burglary victims, families of missing persons. Reporters like Spinella met agitated people all day long. Even at his relatively young age and experience, Spinella probably had learned to recognize different types of agitation. 'OK, what kind?'

'She was frightened about something. Refused to answer the door the next day when the paper sent a photographer round. If I didn't know better, I'd say she was in hiding.'

Grace nodded. A few thoughts went through his mind. 'What nationality?'

'English. White – if I'm allowed to say that.' He smirked.

Ignoring the comment, Grace decided that ruled out her being an imprisoned sex slave – they were mostly from Eastern Europe and Africa. There were all kinds of possibilities. A million things could make you agitated. But being agitated wasn't enough reason for the police to pay a call on someone.

'What's her name and address?' he asked, then dutifully wrote down *Katherine Jennings* and the flat number and address on his pad. He would get someone to run it through PNC and see if the name got flagged. Other than that, all he could do was wait to see if the name appeared again.

Then, as Roy pressed his card against the security panel to step through into the Major Incident Suite, Spinella called after him again. 'Oh – and Detective Superintendent?'

He turned, irritably now. 'Yes?'

'Congratulations on your promotion!'

44

11 SEPTEMBER 2001

Ronnie stood in the sunshine on the empty boardwalk and checked once again that his mobile phone was switched off. Very definitely switched off. He stared ahead, past the benches and the beach-front railing, beyond the deserted golden sand, out across the expanse of rippling ocean, at the distant pall of black and grey and orange smoke that was steadily staining the sky, turning it the colour of rust.

He barely took any of it in. He had just realized that he had left his passport in the room safe back at his hotel. But perhaps that could be helpful. He was thinking. Thinking. Thinking. His brain was all jammed up with thoughts. Somehow he needed to clear his head. Some exercise might do it. Or a stiff drink.

To his left the boardwalk stretched out as far as he could see. In the distance, to his right, he could see the silhouettes of the rides in the amusement park at Coney Island. Nearer, there was a messy-looking apartment building, covered in scaffolding, about six storeys high. A black dude in a leather jacket was engaged in a discussion with an Oriental-looking guy in a bomber jacket. They kept turning their heads, as if checking they weren't being watched, and they kept looking at him. Maybe they were doing a drugs deal and thought he might be a cop. Maybe they were talking about football, or baseball, or the fucking weather. Maybe they were the only people on the fucking planet who didn't know something had happened to the World Trade Center this morning.

Ronnie didn't give a shit about them. So long as they didn't mug him they could stand there all day and talk. They could stand there until the world ended, which might be pretty damned soon, judging by the events of today so far.

Shit. Fuck. What a day this was. What a fuck of a day to pick to be here. And he didn't even have Donald Hatcook's mobile phone number.

And. And. And. He tried to shut that thought out, but it kept knocking on his door until he had to open up and let it in.

Donald Hatcook might be dead.

An awful lot of people might be fucking dead.

There was a parade of shops, all with Russian signs on them, to his right, lining the boardwalk. He began walking towards them, towing his bag behind him, and then stopped when he reached a large sign in a green metal frame with an arched top, framing one of those YOU ARE HERE! maps. It was headed:

RIEGELMANN WALKWAY. BRIGHTON BEACH.
BRIGHTON 2ND STREET.

Despite all that was going through his mind, he stopped and smiled wryly. Home from home. Sort of! It would have been fun to have someone take his photograph beside it. Lorraine would be amused. On another day, under different circumstances.

He sat down on the bench beside the sign and leaned back in the seat, unfastened his tie, coiled it and put it in his pocket. Then he opened the top button of his shirt. The air felt good on his neck. He needed it. He was shaking. Palpitating. His heart was thumping. He looked at his watch. Nearly midday. He began patting dust out of his hair and clothes and felt in need of a drink. He never normally drank in the daytime, well, not until lunchtime anyhow – most days. But a stiff whisky would slip down nicely. Or a brandy. Or even, he thought, thinking about those Russian signs, a vodka.

He stood up, gripped the handle of his bag and carried on pulling it along behind him, listening to the steady bump-bump-bump of the wheels on the planks. He saw a sign on a shop ahead. The first shop in the parade. In blue, red and white were the words: MOSCOW and BAR. Beyond was a green awning on which was a name in yellow letters: TATIANA.

He went into the Moscow bar. It was almost empty and felt gloomy. There was a long wooden counter to his right, with round, red leather bar stools on chromium feet, and to the left, red leather banquette seats and metal tables. A couple of men who looked like heavies from a Bond movie sat on bar stools. Their heads were shaven, they wore black, short-sleeve T-shirts and they were silently glued to a wide-screen television on the wall. Mesmerized by it.

Shot glasses sat in front of them on the counter, along with a bottle of vodka wedged into a bed of ice in a bucket. Both held cigarettes and an ashtray filled with butts sat beside the ice bucket. The other occupants, two young hunks, both wearing expensive-looking leather jackets and sporting large rings, were seated at one banquette. They were both drinking coffee and one was smoking.

It was a good smell, Ronnie thought. Coffee and cigarettes. Strong, Russian cigarettes. There were signs around the bar written in Cyrillic, banners and flags from football clubs, mostly English. He recognized Newcastle, Manchester United and Chelsea.

On the screen was an image of hell on earth. No one in the bar spoke. Ronnie began watching as well; it was impossible not to. Two planes, one after the other, flying into the Twin Towers. Then each of the towers coming down. Didn't matter how many times he saw it, each time was different. Worse.

'Sir, yes?'

Broken English. The barman was a shrimp with a fuzz of cropped black hair brushed forward, wearing a grungy apron over a denim shirt that needed ironing.

'Do you have Kalashnikov vodka?'

He looked blank. 'Krashakov?'

'Forget it,' Ronnie said. 'Any vodka, neat, and an espresso. You have espresso?'

'Russian coffee.'

'Fine.'

The shrimp nodded. 'One Russian coffee. Vodka.' He walked with a stoop as if his back was hurting.

A man was hurting on the screen. He was a bald, black guy covered in grey powder, with a clear breathing mask over his face, attached to an inflated bag. A man in a red helmet with a visor, a red face mask and a black T-shirt was urging him forward through grey snow.

'So much shit!' the shrimp said in broken English. 'Manhattan. Unbelievable. You know about this? You know what happening?'

'I was there,' Ronnie said.

'Yes? You was there?'

'Get me a drink. I need that drink,' he snapped.

'I get you a drink. Don't worry. You was there?'

'Some part of that you don't understand?' Ronnie said.

The barman turned away huffily and produced a vodka bottle. One of the Bond heavies turned to Ronnie and raised his glass. He was drunk and slurring his speech. 'You know what? Thirty years ago I'd have said *comrade* to you. Now I say *buddy*. Know what I mean?'

Ronnie raised his glass seconds after the barman put it down. 'Not exactly, no.'

'You gay or something?' the man asked.

'No, I'm not gay.'

The man put his glass down and windmilled his arms. 'I don't have no problem with gays. Not that. No.'

'Good,' Ronnie said. 'I don't either.'

The man broke into a grin. His teeth were terrible, Ronnie thought. It looked like he had a mouthful of rubble. The man raised his glass and Ronnie clinked it. 'Cheers.'

George Bush was on the screen now. He was wearing a dark suit with an orange tie, sitting at the back of a school classroom, in front of a small blackboard, and there were pictures stuck to the wall behind them. One depicted a bear with a striped scarf riding a bicycle. A man in a suit was standing over George Bush, whispering into his ear. Then the image changed to wreckage of a plane on the ground.

'You're OK,' the man said to Ronnie. 'I like you. You're OK.' He poured more vodka into his own glass, then held the bottle over Ronnie's for a moment. He squinted, saw it was still full and set the bottle back down in the ice. 'You should drink.' He drained his glass. 'Today we need to drink.' He turned back to the screen. 'This not real. Not possible.'

Ronnie took a sip. The vodka burned his throat. Then, moments later, he tipped the glass back and drained it.

The effect was almost instant, burning deep inside him. He poured another for himself and for his new best friend.

They fell silent. Just watching the screen.

After several more vodkas, Ronnie was starting to feel rather drunk. At some point he staggered off his stool, stumbled over to one of the empty booths and fell asleep.

When he woke up, he had a blinding headache and a raging thirst. Then a sudden moment of panic.

My bags.

Shit, shit, shit.

Then, to his relief, he saw them, still standing where he had left them, by his vacated bar stool.

It was 2 o'clock.

The same people were still in the bar. The same images were still repeating on the screen. He hauled himself back on to the bar stool and nodded at his friend.

'What about the father?' the Bond heavy said.

'Yeah, why they don't mention him?' the other heavy said.

'Father?' the barman said.

'All we hear is this *Son of Bin Laden.* What about the father?'

Mayor Giuliani was now on the screen, talking earnestly. He looked calm. He looked caring. He looked like a man who had things under control.

Ronnie's new best friend turned to him. 'You know Sam Colt?'

Ronnie, who was trying to listen to Giuliani, shook his head. 'No.'

'The guy invented the revolver, right?'

'Ah, OK, him.'

'Know what this man said?'

'No.'

'Sam Colt said, *Now I've made all men equal!*' The Russian grinned, baring his revolting teeth again. 'Yeah? OK? Understand?'

Ronnie nodded and ordered sparkling mineral water and coffee. He hadn't eaten anything since breakfast, he realized, but he had no appetite.

Giuliani was replaced by stumbling grey ghosts. They looked like the grey ghosts he had seen earlier. A poem from way back at school suddenly came into his head. From one of his favourite writers, Rudyard Kipling. Yeah. He was *the Man.*

Kipling understood about power, control, empire-building.

> If you can keep your head when all about you
> Are losing theirs . . .
> If you can meet with Triumph and Disaster
> And treat those two impostors just the same . . .

On the screen he saw a fireman weeping. His helmet was covered in grey snow and he was sitting, visor up, cradling his face in his hands.

Ronnie leaned forward and tapped the shoulder of the barman. He turned from the screen. 'Uh huh?'

'Do you have rooms here? I need a room.'

His new best friend turned to him. 'No flights. Right?'

'Right.'

'Where you from anyway?'

Ronnie hesitated. 'Canada. Toronto.'

'Toronto,' the Russian repeated. 'Canada. OK. Good.' He fell silent for a moment, then he said, 'Cheap room?'

Ronnie realized he could not use any cards – even if they had any credit left on them. He had just under four hundred dollars in his wallet, which would have to tide him over until he could convert some of the other currency he had in his bag – if he could find a buyer who would pay him the right money. And not ask questions.

'Yes, a cheap room,' he replied. 'Cheaper the better.'

'You're in the right place. You want SRO. That's what you want.'

'SRO?'

'Single Room Occupancy. That's what you want. You pay cash, they no ask you questions. My cousin has SRO house. Ten minutes' walk. You want I give you the address?'

'Sounds like a plan,' Ronnie replied.

The Russian showed him his teeth again. 'Plan? You have plan? Good plan?'

'*Carpe diem!*'

'Huh?'

'It's an expression.'

'*Carpe diem?*' The Russian pronounced it slowly, clumsily.

Ronnie grinned, then bought him another drink.

45

OCTOBER 2007

Major Incident Room One was the larger of two airy rooms in the Major Incident Suite of Sussex House, which housed the inquiry teams working on serious crime investigations. Roy Grace entered it shortly before 6.30, carrying a mug of coffee.

An open, modern-feeling L-shaped room, it was divided up by three principal work stations, each comprising a long, curved, light-coloured wooden desk with space for up to eight people to sit, and massive whiteboards, most of which at the moment were blank, apart from one marked *Operation Dingo*, and another on which were several close-up photographs of the *Unknown Female* in the storm drain and some exterior shots of the New England Quarter development. On one, a red circle drawn in marker pen indicated the position of the body in the drain.

A large inquiry might have used up all the space in here, but because of the relative lack of urgency in this case – and therefore the need to budget manpower and resources accordingly – Grace's team occupied only one of the work stations. At the moment the others were vacant, but that could change at any time.

Unlike the work stations throughout the rest of the building, there were few signs of anything personal on the desks or the walls here: no pictures of families, football fixture lists, jokey cartoons. Almost every single object in this room – apart from the furniture and the business hardware – was related to the matters under investigation. There wasn't a lot of banter either. Just the silence of fierce concentration, the muted warble of phones, the clack-clack-clack of paper shuffling from printers.

Seated at the work station were the team Grace had selected for *Operation Dingo*. An ardent believer in keeping the same people together whenever possible, he had worked with all of them during the previous months. His only hesitant choice had been Norman Potting, who constantly upset people, but the man was an extremely capable detective.

Acting as his deputy SIO was Detective Inspector Lizzie Mantle. Grace liked her a lot and in truth had long had a sneaking fancy for her. In her late thirties, she was attractive, with neat, shoulder-length fair hair, and exuded a femininity that belied a surprisingly tough personality. She tended to favour trouser suits and she was wearing one today, in grey pinstripe, that wouldn't have looked out of place on a stockbroker, over a man's white shirt.

Her fair good looks were something Lizzie shared with another DI at Sussex House, Kim Murphy, and there had been some sour-grape rumblings that if you wanted to get ahead in this force, having the looks of a bimbo was your best asset. It was totally untrue, of course, Grace knew. Both women had achieved their ranks, at relatively young ages, because they thoroughly deserved it.

Roy's promotion would undoubtedly result in new demands on his time, so he was going to have to rely heavily on Lizzie's support in running this investigation.

Along with her, he had selected Detective Sergeants Glenn Branson, Norman Potting and Bella Moy. Thirty-five years old and cheery-faced beneath a tangle of hennaed brown hair, Bella was sitting, as ever, with an open box of Maltesers inches from her keyboard. Roy crossed the room, watching as she typed in deep concentration. Every so often her right hand would suddenly stray from the keyboard, like some creature with a life of its own, pluck a chocolate, deliver it to her mouth and return to the keyboard. She was a slim woman, yet she ate more chocolate than anyone Grace had ever come across.

Next to her sat gangly, tousle-haired Detective Constable Nick Nicholl, who was twenty-seven and beanpole tall. A zealous detective and once a handy centre forward, he had been encouraged by Grace to take up rugby and was now a useful member of the Sussex Police team – though not as useful at the moment as Grace had hoped, because he was a recent father and appeared to be suffering from constant sleep deprivation.

Opposite him, reading her way through a thick wodge of computer printouts, was young, feisty DC Emma-Jane Boutwood. A few months earlier she had been badly injured on a case when she was crushed against a wall by a stolen van in a pursuit. By rights she should still be convalescing, but she had begged Grace to let her come back and do light duties.

The team was completed by an analyst, an indexer, a typist and the system supervisor.

Glenn Branson, dressed in a black suit, a violent blue shirt and a scarlet tie, looked up as Grace entered. 'Yo, old-timer,' he said, but more flatly than usual. 'Any chance of a quiet chat later?'

Grace nodded at his friend. 'Of course.'

Branson's greeting prompted a few other heads to be raised as well.

'Well, here comes God!' said Norman Potting, doffing a non-existent hat. 'May I be the first to proffer my congratulations on your elevation to the brass!' he said.

'Thank you, Norman, but there's nothing very special about brass.'

'Well, that's where you are wrong, Roy,' Potting retorted. 'A lot of metals rust, you see. But brass doesn't. It corrodes.' He beamed with pride as if he had just delivered the complete, final and incontrovertible Theory of Everything.

Bella, who very much disliked Potting, rounded on him, her fingers hovering above the Maltesers like the talons of a bird of prey. 'That's just semantics, Norman. Rust, corrosion, what's the difference?'

'Quite a lot actually,' Potting said.

'Perhaps you should have been a metallurgist instead of a policeman,' she said, and popped another Malteser in her mouth.

Grace sat down in the one empty seat, at the end of the work station between Potting and Bella, and immediately crinkled his nose at the stale reek of pipe tobacco on the man.

Bella turned to Grace. 'Congratulations, Roy. Very well deserved.'

The Detective Superintendent spent some moments accepting and acknowledging congratulations from the rest of the team, then laid his policy book and agenda for the meeting out in front of him.

'Right. This is the second briefing of *Operation Dingo*, the investigation into the suspected murder of an unidentified female, conducted on day three following the discovery of her remains.'

For some minutes he summarized the report of the

forensic archaeologist. Then he read out the key points from Theobald's lengthy assessment. Death by strangulation, evidenced by the woman's broken hyoid, was a possibility. Forensic tests for toxins were being carried out from hair samples recovered. There were no other signs of injury to the skeleton, such as breakages, or cuts indicating knife wounds.

Grace paused to drink some water and noticed that Norman Potting was looking very smug.

'OK, *Resourcing*. In view of the estimated time period of the incident I am not looking to expand the inquiry team at this stage.' He went on through the various headings. *Meeting cycles*: he announced there would be the usual daily 8.30 a.m. and 6.30 p.m. briefings. He reported that the HOLMES computer team had been up and running since Friday night. He read out the list under the heading *Investigative Strategies*, which included *Communications/Media*, emphasizing the need for press coverage, and said that they were working on getting this case featured on next week's *Crimewatch* television programme, although they were struggling because it wasn't considered *newsworthy* enough. Then he handed the floor to his team, asking Emma-Jane Boutwood to report first.

The young DC produced a list of all missing persons in the county of Sussex who fell into the estimated time period of the victim's death, but without any conclusion. Grace instructed her to broaden her search to the nationwide missing-persons files for that time.

Nick Nicholl reported that DNA samples from the woman's hair had been sent to the lab at Huntingdon, along with a bone sample from her thigh for DNA extraction.

Bella Moy reported that she had met with the city's chief engineer. 'He showed me through the flow charts of the sewer system and I'm now mapping possible places of entry further up the drain network. I'll have that complete some time tomorrow.'

'Good,' Grace said.

'There's one thing that could be quite significant,' Bella added. 'The outlet from the sewer network goes far enough out to sea to ensure that all the sewage gets transported offshore by the currents, rather than towards it.'

Grace nodded, guessing where this was heading.

'So it's possible that the murderer was aware of this – he might be an engineer, for instance.'

Grace thanked her and turned to Norman Potting, curious to know what the Detective Sergeant was looking so pleased about.

Potting pulled a set of X-rays from a buff envelope and held them up triumphantly. 'I've got a dental records match!' he said.

There was a moment of total silence. Every ear in the room was tuned to him.

'I got these from one of the dentists on the list you gave me, Roy,' he said. 'The woman had extensive dental work done. Her name is – or rather was – Joanna Wilson.'

'Nice work,' Grace said. 'Was she single or married?'

'Well, I've got good and bad news,' Potting said, and fell into a smug silence, grinning like an imbecile.

'We're all ears,' Grace prompted him.

'She had a husband, yes. Stormy relationship – so far as I've been able to discover – the dentist, Mr Gebbie, knows a little of the background. I'll get more on that tomorrow. She was an actress. I don't know the full story yet, but they split up and she left. Apparently she went to Los Angeles to make her name – that's what the husband told everyone.'

'Sounds like we should have a little chat with the husband,' Grace said.

'There's a bit of a problem with that,' Norman Potting replied. Then he nodded pensively for some moments, pursing his lips, as if carrying the weight of the world on his shoulders. 'He died in the World Trade Center, on 9/11.'

46

OCTOBER 2007

At 6.45 Abby was beginning to worry that the courier company had forgotten her. She had been ready and waiting since 5.30, her suitcase by the door, coat slung over it, Jiffy bag addressed and sealed.

It was completely dark outside now and, with the rain still torrenting down, she could see very little. She was watching for a Global Express van to come down the street. For the umpteenth time she removed the Mace pepper spray canister from the hip pocket of her jeans and examined it.

The small red cylinder with its finger-grip indents, key chain and belt clip was reassuringly heavy. She repeatedly flipped open the safety lid and practised aiming the nozzle. The guy who had sold it to her in Los Angeles, on her way back to England, told her it contained ten one-second bursts and would blind a human for ten seconds. She had smuggled it into England inside her make-up bag in her suitcase.

She put it back in her pocket, stood up and took her mobile phone out of her handbag. She was about to dial Global Express when the intercom finally buzzed.

She hurried down the hall to the front door. On the small black and white monitor she could see a motorcycle helmet. Her heart sank. That twerp assistant, Jonathan, had told her it would be a van. She had been banking on a van.

Shit.

She pressed the intercom button. 'Come up, eighth floor,' she said. 'I'm afraid the lift's not working.'

Her brain was racing again, trying to do a fast rethink. She picked up the Jiffy bag. Have to revert to her original plan, she decided, thinking it through in the two long minutes that passed before the sharp rap on the door.

Vigilant as ever, she peered through the spyhole and saw a motorcyclist, clad in leather, in a black helmet, with a dark visor that was down, holding some kind of clipboard.

She unlocked the door, removed the safety chains and opened it.

'I – I thought you were coming in a van,' she said.

He dropped the clipboard, which fell to the ground with a clank, then punched Abby hard in the stomach. It caught her totally off guard, doubling her up in winded pain. She stumbled sideways into the wall.

'Nice to see you, Abby,' he said. 'Not crazy about your new look.'

Then he punched her again.

47

OCTOBER 2007

Shortly before 7 o'clock, Cassian Pewe drove his dark green Vauxhall Astra through the buffeting wind and neon-lit darkness of the cliff-top coast road. He crossed two mini-roundabouts into Peacehaven, then continued for the next mile past endless parades of shops, half of them seemingly estate agents, the rest garish fast-food places. It reminded him of the outskirts of small American towns he had seen in films.

Unfamiliar with this area a few miles east of Brighton, he was being bossed through it by the female voice of his plug-in sat nav. Now, past Peacehaven, he was following a crawling camper van down the winding hill into Newhaven. The sat-nav woman instructed him to keep straight on for half a mile. Then his mobile phone, in the hands-free cradle, rang.

He peered at the display, saw it was from Lucy, his girlfriend, and reached forward to answer it.

'Hello, darling,' he cooed. 'How is my precious angel?'

'Are you on your hands-free?' she asked. 'You sound like a Dalek.'

'I'm sorry, my precious. I'm driving.'

'You didn't call,' she said, sounding hurt and a tad angry. 'You were going to call me this morning, about tonight.'

Lucy, who lived and worked in London as a PA for a hedge-fund manager, had not been impressed by his recent move to Brighton. Most probably, he thought, because he hadn't invited her to move with him. He always kept his women at a distance, rarely rang them when he said he would and frequently cancelled dates at the last moment. Experience had taught him that was the best way to keep them where he wanted them.

'My angel, I have been soooooo busy,' he cooed again. 'I just didn't have a moment. I've been in wall-to-wall meetings all day.'

'In one hundred and fifty yards turn left,' the sat-nav lady instructed him.

'Who's that?' Lucy demanded suspiciously. 'Who's that in the car with you?'

'Only the sat nav, sweetheart.'

'So are we meeting tonight?'

'I don't think it's going to work tonight, angel. I've been dispatched on an urgent case. Could be the start of a major murder inquiry, with some rather ugly consequences within the local police here. They thought I was the right man for it, with my Met experience.'

'So what about afterwards?'

'Well – if you were to jump on a train, we could maybe have a late dinner down here. How does that sound?'

'No way, Cassian! I've got to be in the office at 6.45 in the morning.'

'Yes, well, just a thought,' he replied.

He was driving over the Newhaven bridge. A barrage of signs lay ahead: one to the cross-Channel ferry, another to Lewes. Then, to his relief, he saw a sign pointing to Seaford, his destination.

'Take the second left turn,' the sat nav dictated.

Pewe frowned. Surely the Seaford sign had indicated straight on.

'Who was that?' Lucy asked.

'The sat nav again,' he replied. 'Aren't you going to ask me how my day was? My first day at Sussex CID?'

'How was your day?' she asked grudgingly.

'Actually,' he said, 'I got a bit of a promotion!'

'Already? I thought moving from the Met was a promotion. Going from a Detective Chief Inspector to a Detective Superintendent.'

'It's even better now. They've put me in charge of all cold cases – and that includes all unaccounted-for missing persons.'

She was silent.

He made the left turn.

The sat-nav display of the road ahead disappeared from the screen. Then the voice commanded, 'Make a U-turn.'

'Fuck,' he said.

'What's going on?' Lucy asked.

'My sat nav doesn't know where the hell I am.'

'I have some sympathy with her,' Lucy said.

'I'll have to call you back, my angel.'

'Was that you or your sat nav speaking?'

'Oh, very droll!'

'I suggest you have a nice romantic dinner with her.' Lucy hung up.

*

Ten minutes later, the sat nav had found its bearings again and delivered him to the address he was seeking in Seaford, a quiet, residential coastal town a few miles on from Newhaven. Peering through the darkness at the numbers on the front doors, he pulled up outside a small, nondescript pebbledashed semi. A Nissan Micra was parked on the drive.

He switched on the interior light, checked the knot of his tie, tidied his hair, climbed out of the car and locked it. A gust of wind immediately blew his hair into disarray as he hurried up the path of the neat garden to the front door, found the bell and pressed it, cursing that there was no porch. There was a single, rather funereal chime.

After a few moments the door opened a few inches and a woman – in her early sixties, he guessed – stared out at him suspiciously from behind rather stern glasses. Twenty years ago, with a better hairdo and the thick worry creases airbrushed from her face, she might have been quite attractive, he thought. Now, with her short, iron-grey hair, a baggy orange jumper that swamped her, brown polyester trousers and plimsolls, she looked to Pewe like one of those doughty, backbone-of-England ladies you find manning stalls at the church bazaar.

'Mrs Margot Balkwill?' he asked.

'Yes?' she said hesitantly and a little suspiciously.

He showed her his warrant card. 'I'm Detective Superintendent Pewe of Sussex CID. I'm sorry to trouble you, but I wonder if I could have a word with you and your husband about your daughter, Sandy?'

Her small, round mouth fell open, revealing neat teeth that were yellow with age. 'Sandy?' she echoed, shocked.

'Is your husband in?'

She considered the question for a moment, like a schoolmistress who had just been thrown a curve by a pupil. 'Well, he is, yes.' She hesitated for a moment, then indicated for him to come in.

Pewe stepped on to a mat which said WELCOME, and

into a tiny, bare hall which smelled faintly of a roast dinner and more strongly of cats. He heard the sound of a television soap opera.

She closed the door behind him, then called out, a little timidly, 'Derek! We have a visitor. A police officer. A detective.'

Tidying his hair again, Pewe followed her through into a small, spotlessly clean living room. There was a brown velour three-piece suite with a glass-topped coffee table in front, arranged around an elderly, square-screened television on which two vaguely familiar-looking actors were arguing in a pub. On top of the set was a framed photograph of an attractive blonde girl of about seventeen, unmistakably Sandy from the pictures Pewe had studied this afternoon in the files.

At the far end of the small room, next to what Pewe considered to be a rather ugly Victorian cabinet full of blue and white willow-pattern plates, a man was sitting at a small table covered in carefully folded sheets of newspaper, in the process of assembling a model aircraft. Strips of balsa wood, wheels and pieces of undercarriage, a gun turret and other small objects Pewe could not immediately identify were laid out on either side of the plane, which rested at an angle, as if climbing after take-off, on a small raised base. The room smelled of glue and paint.

Pewe made a quick scan of the rest of the room. A fake-coal electric fire, which was on. A music centre that looked like it played vinyl rather than CDs. And photographs everywhere of Sandy at different ages, from just a few years old through to her twenties. One, in pride of place on the mantelpiece above the fire, was a wedding photograph of Roy Grace and Sandy. She was in a long white dress, holding a bouquet. Grace, younger and with much longer hair than he had now, wore a dark grey suit and a silver tie.

Mr Balkwill was a big, broad-shouldered man who looked as if he'd once had a powerful physique before he let it go to seed. He had thin grey hair swept back on either side of a bald head and a flabby double chin that disappeared in the folds of a multicoloured roll-neck sweater that was similar to his wife's – as if she had knitted both of them. He stood up, round-shouldered and stooping, like someone who had been defeated by life, and ambled to the front of the table. Below the sweater, which came almost to his knees, he wore baggy grey trousers and black sandals.

An overweight tabby cat, which looked as old as both of them, wandered out from under the table, took one look at Pewe, arched its back and stalked out of the room.

'Derek Balkwill,' he said, with a quiet, almost shy voice that seemed much smaller than his frame. He held out a big hand and gave Pewe a crushing shake that surprised and hurt him.

'Detective Superintendent Pewe,' he replied with a wince. 'I wondered if I could have a word with you and your wife about Sandy?'

The man froze. What little colour he had drained from his already pallid face and Pewe saw a slight tremor in his hands. He wondered for a horrible moment if the man was having a heart attack.

'I'll just turn the oven down,' Margot Balkwill said. 'Would you like a cup of tea?'

'Tea would be perfect,' Pewe said. 'Lemon, if you have it.'

'Working with Roy, are you?' she asked.

'Yes, absolutely.' He continued to stare, concerned, at her husband.

'How is he?'

'Fine. Busy on a murder inquiry.'

'He's always busy,' Derek Balkwill said, seeming to calm down a little. 'He's a hard worker.'

Margot Balkwill scurried out of the room.

Derek pointed at the aircraft. 'Lancaster.'

'Second World War?' Pewe responded, trying to sound knowledgeable.

'Got more upstairs.'

'Yes?'

He gave a shy smile. 'Got a Mustang P45. A Spit. A Hurricane. Mosquito. Wellington.'

There was an awkward silence. Two women were discussing a wedding dress on the television screen now. Then Derek pointed at the Lancaster. 'My dad flew 'em. Seventy-five sorties. Know about the Dambusters? Ever see the film?'

Pewe nodded.

'He was one of 'em. One of the ones that came back. One of the Few.'

'Was he a pilot?'

'Tail gunner. Tail End Charlie, they called 'im.'

'Brave guy,' Pewe said politely.

'Not really. Just did his duty. He was a bitter man after the war.' Then after some moments he added, 'War buggers you up, you know that?'

'I can imagine.'

Derek Balkwill shook his head. 'No. No one can imagine. Been a police officer long?'

'Nineteen years next January.'

'Same as Roy.'

*

When his wife returned with a tray of tea and biscuits, Derek Balkwill fumbled with the remote control, then silenced the television but left the picture on. The three of them settled down, Pewe in one armchair, the Balkwills on the settee.

Pewe picked his cup up, holding the dainty handle in his manicured fingers, blew on the tea, sipped and then set it down. 'I've very recently moved to Sussex CID from the Met, in London,' he said. 'I've been brought in to review cold cases. I don't know how to put this delicately, but I've been going through the missing-persons files and I really don't think that your daughter's disappearance has been investigated adequately.'

He sat back and opened his arms expansively. 'By that I mean – without casting any aspersions on Roy, of course . . .' He hesitated, until their joint nods gave him the assurance to continue. 'As a completely impartial outsider, it seems to me that Roy Grace is really too emotionally involved to be able to conduct an impartial review of the original investigation into his wife's disappearance.' He paused and took another sip of his tea. 'I just wondered if either of you might have any views on this?'

'Does Roy know you are here?' Derek Balkwill asked.

'I'm conducting an independent inquiry,' Pewe said evasively.

Sandy's mother frowned but said nothing.

'Can't see it would do any harm,' her husband eventually said.

48

11 SEPTEMBER 2001

Ronnie was drunk. He walked unsteadily past low-rise red-brick apartment buildings, pulling his bags behind him along the sidewalk, which was pitch-poling like the deck of a boat. His mouth was dry and his head felt as if it was clamped in a steadily tightening vice. He should have eaten something, he knew. He would get some food later, after he had checked in and stored his luggage.

In his left hand he held a crumpled bar receipt, on the back of which his new best friend – whose name he had already forgotten – had written an address and drawn a map. It was five in the afternoon. A helicopter flew low overhead. There was an unpleasant smell of burning in the air. Was there a fire somewhere?

Then he realized it was the same smell as earlier, when he had been in Manhattan. Dense and cloying, it seeped into his clothes and into the pores of his skin. He was breathing it in, deep lungfuls of it.

At the end of the road he squinted at the map. It appeared to be telling him to turn right at the next crossing. He passed several shops with signs in Cyrillic, then Federal Savings, which had a hole-in-the-wall cash machine. He stopped, tempted for a moment to draw out whatever his cards would allow, but that would not be smart, he realized. The machine would record the time of the transaction. He walked on. Past more storefronts. On the far side of the street a limp banner hung, screen-printed with the words, KEEP BRIGHTON BEACH CLEAN.

It began to dawn on him just how deserted the street was. There were cars parked on either side, but now there were no people. The shops were almost entirely empty too. It was as if the entire suburb was at a party to which he had not been invited.

But he knew they were all at home, glued to their television sets. *Waiting for the other shoe to drop*, someone in the bar had said.

He passed a dimly lit store with a sign outside, MAIL BOX CITY, and stopped.

Inside, to the left, he could see a long counter. To the right were rows and rows of metal boxes. At the far end of the store a young man with long black hair sat hunched over an internet terminal. At the counter, an elderly, grizzled man in cheap clothes was carrying out some kind of transaction.

Ronnie was starting to sober up, he realized. Thinking more clearly. Thinking that this place might be useful for his plans. He walked on, counting the streets to his left. Then, following his directions, he turned left, into a run-down residential street. The houses here looked as if they had been constructed from broken bits of Lego. They were two- and three-storey, semi-detached, no two halves the same. There were steps up to front doors, awnings and doors where there should have been garages; pantiles, crazy brickwork and shabby plasterwork facings, and mismatching windows that looked as if they had been bought in assorted job lots.

At the first intersection the map told him to turn left

into a narrow street called Brighton Path 2. He walked past two white Chevy Suburbans parked outside a double garage with both doors covered in graffiti, and a row of single-storey dwellings, then made a right into an even more run-down street of semis. He reached No. 29. Both halves of the house were the colour of pre-cast concrete. A torn poster was wrapped around a telegraph pole outside. But he barely noticed. He looked up the grimy steps and saw, in red letters on a small white board nailed to the door lintel, SRO.

He climbed the steps, hefting his bags, and rang the bell. Moments later a blurred figure appeared behind the frosted glass and the door opened. A flat-chested waif of a girl, dressed in a grubby smock dress and flip-flops, stared out at him. She had dirty, straggly fair hair like tendrils of seaweed and a wide, doll-like face with large, round, black-rimmed eyes. She said nothing.

'I'm looking for a room,' Ronnie said. 'I was told you have a room.'

He noticed a payphone on the wall beside her and a strong smell of damp and old carpet. Somewhere in the building he could hear the news on television. Today's events.

She said something that he did not understand. It sounded like Russian but he wasn't sure.

'Do you speak English?'

She raised a hand, indicating that he should wait, then disappeared back into the house. After a little while a huge shaven-headed man of about fifty appeared. He was wearing a collarless white shirt, grubby black chinos held up with braces, and trainers, and he stared at Ronnie as if he was a turd blocking a lavatory.

'Room?' he said in a guttural accent.

'Boris,' Ronnie said, suddenly remembering his new best friend's name. 'He told me to come here.'

'How long?'

Ronnie shrugged. 'A few days.'

The man stared at him. Assessing him. Maybe checking out that he wasn't some kind of terrorist.

'Thirty dollars a day. OK?'

'Fine. Grim day, today.'

'Bad day. Most bad day. Whole world crazy. From 12 o'clock to 12 o'clock. OK? Understood. You pay each day in advance. You stay after midday, you pay another day.'

'Understood.'

'Cash?'

'Yep, fine.'

The house was bigger than it had looked from the outside. Ronnie followed the man through the hall and along a corridor, past walls the colour of nicotine with a couple of cheap, framed prints of stark landscapes. The man stopped, disappeared into a room for a moment, then emerged with a key with a wooden tag. He unlocked the door opposite.

Ronnie followed him into a gloomy room which stank of stale cigarette smoke. It had a window looking on to the wall of the next house along. There was a small double bed with a pink candlewick spread that had several stains on it and two cigarette burn holes. In one corner there was a washbasin, next to a shower with a cracked plastic yellow curtain. A beat-up armchair, a chest of drawers, a couple of cheap-looking wooden tables, an old television set with an even older-looking remote and a carpet the colour of pea soup completed the furnishing.

'Perfect,' Ronnie said. And at this moment, for him, it was.

The man folded his arms and looked at him expectantly. Ronnie pulled out his wallet and paid for three days in advance. He was handed the key, then the man departed, closing the door behind him.

Ronnie checked the room out. There was a half-used bar of soap in the shower with what looked suspiciously like a brown pubic hair nestling on it. The image on the television was fuzzy. He switched on all the lights, drew the curtain and sat down on the bed, which sagged and clanked. Then he mustered a smile. He could put up with this for a few days. No worries.

Hell, this was the first day of the rest of his life!

Leaning forward, he lifted his briefcase off the top of his overnight bag. He removed all the folders containing the proposal and supporting data he had spent weeks preparing for Donald Hatcook. Finally, he reached the clear plastic wallet, closed with a pop stud, at the very bottom. He extricated the red folder that he had not risked leaving in his room at the W, not even in the safe. And opened it.

His eyes lit up.

'Hello, my beauties,' he said.

49

OCTOBER 2007

'What's wrong with liking Guinness?' Glenn Branson asked.

'Did I say there was anything wrong?'

Roy Grace set Glenn's pint and his own large Glenfiddich on the rocks down on the table, along with two packets of bacon-flavoured crisps, then sat facing his friend. Monday night at 8 o'clock and the Black Lion was almost empty. Even so they had chosen to sit in the far corner, far enough from the bar not to be overheard by anyone. The piped music also helped to mask their voices and give them privacy.

'It's the way you look at me every time I order Guinness,' Branson said. 'Like it's the wrong kind of drink or something.'

Your wife is turning you from a confident man into a paranoid one, Grace thought but didn't say. Instead he quoted, 'To the man who is afraid, everything rustles.'

Branson frowned. 'Who said that?'

'Sophocles.'

'What movie was that in?'

Grace shook his head, grinning. 'God, you're an ignoramus sometimes! Don't you know *anything* that isn't in a movie?'

'Thanks, Einstein. You really know where to hit a man when he's down.'

Grace raised his glass. 'Cheer up.'

Branson raised his, with no enthusiasm, and clinked it against Grace's.

They both took a sip, then Grace said, 'Sophocles was a playwright.'

'Dead?'

'He died in 406 BC.'

'Before I was born, old-timer. I suppose you went to his funeral?'

'Very witty.'

'I remember, when I stayed with you, all those philosophy books you had lying around.'

Grace took another pull of his whisky and smiled at him. 'You have a problem with someone trying to educate themselves?'

'Trying to keep up with their bird, you mean?'

Grace blushed. Branson was quite right, of course. Cleo was doing an Open University course in philosophy and he was trying hard in his free time to get his head around the subject.

'Hit a nerve, did I?' Branson gave him a wan smile.

Grace said nothing.

'Rhinestone Cowboy' was playing. They both listened to it for a while. Grace mouthed the words and swayed his head to the music.

'Jesus, man! Don't tell me you like Glen Campbell?'

'I do, actually, yes.'

'The more I get to know you, the more sad I realize you are!'

'He's a real musician. Better than that rap crap you like.'

Branson tapped his chest. 'That's my music, man. That's my people speaking to me.'

'Does Ari like it?'

Branson suddenly looked deflated. He peered into his beer. 'She used to. Dunno what she likes any more.'

Grace took another sip. The whisky felt good, giving him a warm buzz. 'So tell me? You wanted to talk about her?' He tore open his packet of crisps and dug his fingers in, pulled out several crisps in one go and crammed them into his mouth. He crunched as he spoke. 'You look like shit, you know that. You've looked terrible for the last two months, since you went back to her. I thought everything was better, that you bought her the horse and she was fine. No?' He ate another fistful of crisps hungrily.

Branson drank some more of his Guinness.

The pub had a pristine smell of carpet cleaner and polish. Grace missed the smell of cigarettes, the fug of cigar and pipe smoke. For him, pubs didn't have any atmosphere any more now the smoking ban had come into force. And he could have done with a cigarette right now.

Cleo hadn't invited him over later because she had a paper to write for her course. He was going to have to grab something to eat, either here or from the freezer at home.

Cookery had never been his strong point and he was getting dependent on her, he realized. These last couple of months she had cooked for him most nights, healthy food mostly, steamed or stir-fried fish and vegetables. She was appalled at the junk-food diet most police officers existed on much of the time.

'Rhinestone Cowboy' finished and they sat in silence for a while.

Glenn broke it. 'You know we haven't had sex, right?'

'Not since you went back to her?'

'Nope.'

'Not once?'

'Not once. It's like she's trying to punish me.'

'For what?'

Branson drained his pint, blinked at the empty glass and stood up. ''Nother?'

'Just a single,' he said, mindful that he had to drive.

'Usual? Glenfiddich on the rocks. Tiniest bit of water?'

'So your memory hasn't gone?'

'Fuck off, old-timer!'

Grace thought hard for a few moments, his mind back on his work. Chewing over the 6.30 briefing meeting they'd just had. Joanna Wilson. Ronnie Wilson. He knew Ronnie from a long time back. One of Brighton's rogues. So Ronnie had died in 9/11. Events like that were so random. Had Ronnie killed his wife? His team were on the case. Tomorrow they would start checking into the man's background, and his wife's.

Branson returned and sat back down.

'What do you mean, Glenn, that Ari's trying to punish you?'

'When Ari and me met, we shagged all day. You know? We'd wake up and shag. Go out somewhere, get an ice cream maybe, and we'd fool around. Shag again in the evening. Kind of like it wasn't the real world.' He drank some more of his beer, almost half the glass, straight down. 'OK, I know you can't maintain that for ever.'

'It was the real world,' Roy said. 'But the real world doesn't stay the same. My mother used to say that life is like a series of chapters in a book. Different things happen at different times. Life changes constantly. You know one of the secrets of a happy marriage?'

'What?'

'Don't be a police officer.'

'Funny. Ironic, isn't it, that's what she wanted me to

be.' He shook his head. 'What I don't get is why she's angry all the time. At me. You know what she said this morning?'

'Tell me?'

'She said that I deliberately keep her awake, right? Like, when I get up in the night to go to the toilet, you know, have a piss, that I deliberately aim into the water so it makes a splashing sound. She said that if I really loved her, I would pee on the side of the bowl.'

Grace tipped the contents of the new glass into his existing one. 'You're not serious?'

'I'm serious, man. There's nothing I can do right. She's, like, told me she needs her space, and screw my career as a policeman. She's gonna go out in the evenings, she's not prepared to be tied to the kids, and it's my responsibility. If I have to work lates, then I have to find babysitters.'

Grace sipped his drink and wondered if perhaps Ari was having an affair. But he didn't want to upset his friend further by suggesting it.

'You can't live like this,' he said.

Branson picked up his packet of crisps and turned it over and over in his hands. 'I love my kids,' he said. 'I can't go through some divorce shit and, like, see them for a few hours once a month.'

'How long has it been like this?'

'Ever since she got this bug in her head about self-improvement. Mondays she does evening classes in English literature, Thursdays she does architecture. And all kinds of other shit in between. I don't know her any more – I can't reach her.'

They sat in silence for a while before Branson mustered a cheerful smile and said, 'Anyhow my shit to deal with, right?'

'No,' Roy replied, even though he knew that if Ari threw

Glenn out again, he'd be lumbered once more with the lodger from hell. He'd had Glenn to stay a couple of months ago and the house would have been tidier if he'd had an elephant high on magic mushrooms come to stay. 'I sort of feel we are in this together.'

For the second time that evening Glenn smiled. Then he finally ripped open his packet of crisps, peering inside with a faint look of disappointment, as if he had been expecting it to be filled with something else.

'So, what's happening with Cassian Pewe – sorry, *Detective Superintendent* Cassian Pewe?'

Grace shrugged.

'Is he eating your lunch?'

Grace smiled. 'I think that was his game plan. But we've put him back in his box.'

50

OCTOBER 2007

Cassian Pewe took another tentative sip of his tea, wincing as the hot liquid touched his teeth. Last night he had slept with whitening gel on them and today they were sensitive to extremes of temperature.

Putting the cup down in the saucer, he said to Sandy's parents, 'I do want to make one thing clear. Detective Superintendent Grace is a well-respected police officer. I have no agenda other than to discover the truth about your daughter's disappearance.'

'We need to know,' Derek Balkwill said.

His wife nodded. 'That's the only thing that matters to us.'

'Good,' he said. 'It's very reassuring to know we are all on the same page.' He smiled at them. 'But,' he went on, 'without wanting to cast any aspersions, there are a number of senior officers in the Sussex CID who feel that a proper investigation has never been carried out. This is one of the main reasons I have been drafted in.'

Pausing, he was satisfied by their receptive nods, and a little emboldened. 'I've been studying the case file all day today and there are many unanswered questions. I think, if I was in your shoes, I would be feeling less than satisfied with the work of the police to date.'

They both nodded again.

'I really don't understand why Roy was allowed to review the investigation himself, when he was so personally involved.'

'We understand there was an independent team appointed a few days after our daughter disappeared,' Margot Balkwill said.

'And who was it who reported their findings to you?' Cassian Pewe asked.

'Well,' she said, 'it was Roy.'

Pewe opened his arms. 'There, you see, is the problem. Normally when a wife goes missing, her husband is instantly the prime suspect, until cleared. From what I have read and heard, it doesn't seem to me that your son-in-law was ever formally regarded as a suspect.'

'Are you saying that you regard him as a suspect now?' Derek asked.

He picked up his teacup and again Pewe noticed the tremor. He wondered whether the man was nervous or it was the onset of Parkinson's.

'I wouldn't go so far as to say that, at this stage.' Pewe smiled smugly. 'But I'm certainly going to take radical steps to eliminate him from suspicion – which is something that has clearly not yet been done.'

Margot Balkwill was nodding. 'That would be good.'

Her husband nodded, also.

'Can I ask you both a very personal question? Has either of you ever, for a moment, suspected that Roy might be hiding something from you?'

There was a long silence. Margot furrowed her eyebrows, pursed her lips, then clenched and opened her hands several times. They were coarse hands, Pewe noticed, a gardener's hands. Her husband sat still, his shoulders hunched, as if being slowly crushed by a huge, unseen weight.

'I think you should understand,' Margot Balkwill said, 'that we don't have any animosity towards Roy.' She spoke like a schoolmistress delivering a report to a parent.

'None,' Derek said emphatically.

'But,' she said, 'a little bit of you can't help wondering . . . Human nature. How well do any of us really know anyone. Isn't that right, Officer?'

'Oh, absolutely,' Pewe agreed silkily.

In the silence that followed Margot Balkwill picked up her spoon and stirred her tea. Pewe noticed that although she didn't take sugar, this was the third time now she had stirred it. 'Was there ever anything you noticed in the way Roy treated your daughter?' he asked. 'Anything that bothered you? I mean, would you say they had a happy marriage?'

'Well, I don't think it's easy for anyone being married to a police officer. Particularly an ambitious one like Roy.' She looked at her husband, who shrugged assent. 'She had to put up with being on her own a lot. And being disappointed at the last minute when he got called out.'

'Did she have her own career?'

'She worked for an accountant in Brighton for a few years. But they were trying for a child and nothing was happening. The doctor told her she should do something less stressful. So she left, got a part-time job as a receptionist at a medical centre. She was between jobs when she . . .' Her voice tailed off.

'Disappeared?' Pewe prompted.

She nodded, tears welling in her eyes.

'It's been hard on us,' Derek said. 'Particularly hard on Margot. She and Sandy were very close.'

'Of course.' Pewe pulled out his notebook and made some jottings. 'How long were they trying for a child?'

'Several years,' Margot replied, her voice choked.

'I understand that's hard on a marriage,' Pewe said.

'Everything's hard in a marriage,' Derek said.

There was a long silence.

Margot sipped her tea, then asked, 'Are you implying there is more behind this than we've been told?'

'No, I wouldn't want to speculate at this stage. I simply have to say that the methodology underpinning the investigation of your daughter's disappearance is, in my view as an officer of some nineteen years' experience in the top police force in the UK, wanting. That's all.'

'We don't suspect Roy,' Margot Balkwill said. 'Just so you don't jump to the wrong conclusions.'

'I'm sure you don't. Perhaps I should make one thing clear from the outset. My investigation is not a witch hunt. It is merely about closure. Enabling you and your husband to move on.'

'That will depend, won't it, on whether our daughter is alive or dead?'

'Absolutely,' Cassian Pewe said. He drank some more of his tea, then cleaned his teeth with his tongue. He pulled his card from his pocket and laid it on the table. 'If there is anything, at any time, you think of that might be helpful for me to know, call me.'

'Thank you,' Margot Balkwill said. 'You are a good man. I can feel it.'

Pewe smiled.

51

OCTOBER 2007

Abby blinked, waking up from a confusing dream to a strange whirring sound. Her stomach was hurting. Her face felt numb. She was freezing cold. Shivering. Staring at cream wall tiles. For a moment she thought she was in a plane, or was it a cabin on a ship?

Then the steady, slow realization that something was very wrong. She couldn't move. She smelled plastic, grout, tile cement, disinfectant.

Now it was coming back. And with an explosion of swirling darkness inside her, she remembered.

Fear shimmied through her. She tried to raise her right arm to touch her face. And that was when she realized she couldn't move.

Or open her mouth.

Her head was pulled back so much her neck was hurting and something hard was sticking into her back. It was the cistern, she realized. She was seated on the lavatory. It was hard to see anything except straight ahead and she had to strain her eyes to look down. When she did, she became aware she was naked, bound with grey gaffer tape around her midriff, her breasts, her wrists and ankles, her mouth and, she assumed, because that was what it felt like, her forehead.

She was in the guest shower room of her flat. Staring at

the walk-in shower cabinet, with a packet of expensive soap, never unwrapped, in the dish, a sink and a few towel rails, and the beautifully tiled walls, in cream with Romanesque tiles and a dado rail. There was a door to her right, through to the tiny utility room, in which were crammed a washing machine and tumble dryer, and at the back of which was a fire escape door out on to the stairwell. The main door out on to the hallway, to her left, was ajar.

She began to shake, then nearly vomited with fear. She didn't know for how long she had been imprisoned in here, in this small, windowless room. She tried to shift her position, but the bindings were too secure.

Had he gone? Taken everything and just left her here like this?

Her stomach was hurting. The tape had been put on so tightly, she was losing feeling in some parts, and had pins and needles in her right hand. The hard seat was digging into her bum and thighs.

She was trying to remember what was behind the toilet, so that she could work out what the tape was fixed to behind her. But she couldn't picture it.

The light was on, which kept the extractor fan running, she realized, making that steady, gloomy whirr.

Her fear turned to despair. He had gone. After all that she'd been through, and now this. How had she let this happen? How had she been so stupid? How? How? How?

Her despair turned to anger.

Then back to fear again as she saw a shadow moving.

52

11 SEPTEMBER 2001

Seated on the edge of the L-shaped sofa in the living room, Lorraine unscrewed the cap of a miniature vodka bottle and tipped the contents over the ice cubes and lime slice in her glass. Her sister had come round earlier with an entire plastic bag full of miniatures. Mo seemed to have a never-ending supply and Lorraine assumed she snaffled them from the bar of whatever flight she was on.

It was 9 o'clock. Almost dark outside. The news was still on. Lorraine had been watching it, through her tears, all day. The repeat images of the horror, repeat statements of the politicians. Now there was a group of people in a studio in Pakistan: a doctor, an IT consultant, a lawyer, a vociferous woman television documentary maker, a company director. Lorraine could not believe her ears. They were saying what had happened today in America was a good thing.

She leaned forward and crushed out her cigarette into an ashtray that was overflowing with butts. Mo was in the kitchen making a salad and heating up some pasta. Lorraine looked at these people, listening to them, bewildered. They were intelligent people. One of them was laughing. There was joy on his face.

'It's about time the United States of America realized they need to stop beating up on the rest of the world. We don't want their values. Today they've learned that lesson. Today it was their turn to have a bloody nose!'

The woman documentary maker nodded and expanded his argument forcefully.

Lorraine looked at the phone handset beside her. Ronnie had not called. Thousands of people were dead. These people were happy? People jumping out of skyscrapers. A *bloody nose*?

She picked up the phone handset, pressed it to her sodden cheeks. *Call, Ronnie darling, call. Please call. Please call.*

Mo had always been protective towards Lorraine. Although only three years older, she treated her as if there was a whole generation between them.

They were actually very different people. Not just their hair colouring – Mo's was almost jet black – and appearance, but their attitude to life and their luck. Mo had a shapely, rounded, naturally voluptuous figure. She was gentle. Life fell into her lap. Lorraine suffered five years of humiliating, cripplingly expensive – and ultimately unsuccessful – in vitro fertilization treatment. Mo could get pregnant by just thinking about her husband's dick.

Mo'd had three children, one after the other, who were all growing up into nice people. She was happy with her quiet, unassuming draughtsman husband and her small, pleasant home. Sometimes Lorraine wished she could be like her. Content. Instead of the yearnings – cravings – she had for a better lifestyle.

'Lori!' Mo shouted excitedly from the kitchen.

She came running into the room and, for a moment, Lorraine's hopes soared. Had she glimpsed Ronnie on the news?

But Mo's face was a mask of shock as she appeared. 'Quick! Someone's stealing your car!'

Lorraine leaped off the sofa, jammed her feet into her loafers, ran to the front door and pulled it open. There was a low-loader truck with amber flashing lights on the roof, parked just past her short driveway. Two men, rough-looking types, were winching her convertible BMW up metal ramps on to the truck.

'Hey!' she shouted, running down towards them, livid. 'What the hell do you think you're doing?'

They carried on winching up the car, which moved steadily forward, jerking along the ramp. As Lorraine approached, the taller one stuffed a grimy hand into his front pocket and pulled out a sheaf of papers. 'Are you Mrs Wilson?'

Uneasy, suddenly, her confidence eroding, she replied, 'Yes?'

'Your husband is Mr Ronald Wilson?'

'Yes, he is.' Her defiance was returning.

He showed her the documents. Then, his tone softening, almost apologetic, he said, 'Inter-Alliance Autofinance. I'm afraid we are repossessing this vehicle.'

'What do you mean?'

'No payments have been made for six months. Mr Wilson's in breach of the terms.'

'There must be a mistake.'

'I'm afraid not. Your husband's ignored three warning letters that have been sent to him. Under the terms of the hire purchase, the company is legally entitled to repossess this vehicle.'

Lorraine burst into tears as the rear wheels of the blue BMW went over the top of the ramp and on to the flatbed. 'Please – you've seen the news today. My husband is there.

He's in – in New York. I'm trying to get hold of him. I'm sure we can sort this out.'

'He'll have to speak to the company tomorrow, madam.' There was some sympathy in the man's voice, but he was firm.

'Look – I – please leave the car here tonight.'

'I'll give you a number you can call tomorrow,' he said.

'But – but – I won't have a car. How am I supposed to manage? I – I've got things in the car. CDs. Parking vouchers. My sunglasses.'

He gestured. 'Go ahead. You can take those.'

'Thanks,' she said. 'Thanks a million.'

53

OCTOBER 2007

Shaking in terror, Abby watched the creeping shadow, heard the squeak of a trainer on the shiny hall floorboards, followed by the rustle of paper.

Then Ricky appeared.

He stood in the doorway and leaned casually against the jamb, his leather motorcycling jacket unzipped, a grimy white T-shirt beneath. He had several days' growth of stubble and his hair was greasy, and looked as if it had been flattened down on his head by the helmet. He seemed different from the last time she had seen him. He no longer had the air of a relaxed surfer dude, but one of a haunted man. He had aged in just a couple of months. He had lost weight and his face was haggard, with black rims and heavy bags beneath his eyes. He smelled rank.

Christ, how had she ever fancied him?

He was smiling, as if reading her mind.

But it wasn't a smile she knew. Not a *Ricky* smile. It was more like a mask he had pulled on. She caught a glimpse of his watch. It was 10.50. Had she been unconscious for nearly four hours?

Then she saw the Jiffy bag. He held it up, nodded and turned it upside down, allowing the contents, Friday's *Times* and *Guardian* newspapers, to fall out and on to the floor.

'It's good to see you again, Abby,' he said. His voice wasn't smiling.

She tried to speak, to ask him to untie her, but all she could do was make a muffled sound from her throat.

'Glad you feel the same! I'm just a bit confused about why you want to courier someone old newspapers in a Jiffy bag.' He looked at the address. *Laura Jackson. 6 Stable Cottages, Rodmell.* 'Old friend of yours? But why would you want to send her old newspapers? Doesn't make a huge amount of sense to me. Unless of course I'm missing something. Am I missing something? Perhaps they can't get newspapers delivered in Rodmell?'

She stared at him.

He tore the bag in half. Fluff poured out. Then, being careful to take only small strips at a time, he ripped the rest of the bag apart. When he had finished, he shook his head and let the last piece fall to the floor. 'I've read both the newspapers. No clues there either. But hey, none of that really matters now, does it?'

He locked on to her eyes, staring her out, still smiling. Enjoying himself.

Abby was thinking fast. She knew what he wanted. She also knew that, to get it, he was going to have to let her speak. She racked her petrified mind, thinking desperately. But she wasn't getting any traction.

He disappeared for a few moments, returning with her large blue suitcase, and laid it down on the floor, in full view of the door. Then he knelt and unzipped it and raised the lid.

'Nice packing,' he said, staring at the contents. 'Very neat and tidy.' His voice turned bitter. 'But I suppose you've had plenty of practice at packing and running in your life.'

Again his grey eyes locked on to hers. And she saw something in them that she had never seen before. Something new. There was darkness in them. A real darkness. As if his soul was dead.

He began to unpack, one item at a time. First he took a warm knitted jumper that was folded on top of her wash and make-up bags. He unfolded it unhurriedly, checking it carefully, turning it inside out, then, when he was satisfied, he threw it over his shoulder.

She wanted to pee badly. But she was determined not to humiliate herself in front of him. Nor to give him the satisfaction of seeing her fear. Instead she held on and watched him.

He was taking his time, being incredibly, agonizingly slow. Almost as if he sensed that need she had.

She could see from his watch it was almost twenty minutes by the time he had finished unpacking, discarding the last item, her travel hair dryer, which he sent skidding down the corridor, banging against the skirting board.

All the time she kept trying to move. Nothing gave. Nothing. Her wrists and her ankles were hurting like hell. Her bum was numb, and she was having to clench her knees together to fight the need to pee.

Without a word, he pushed the suitcase aside and walked away down the corridor. She had a raging thirst, but that was the least of her problems. She had to get free. But how?

She peed. At least she was still able to do that, he hadn't taped that up as well. Then she felt better. Exhausted, her head was throbbing, but now she could think a little more clearly.

If she could get him to take the tape off she could at least talk to him, try to reason with him.

Maybe even cut a deal.

Ricky was a businessman.

But that would depend. How hard he looked.

He was coming back now. Holding a tumbler of whisky on the rocks in his hand and smoking a cigarette. The sweet, rich smell tantalized her. She would have given almost anything for just one drag. And a drink. Of anything.

He rattled the ice cubes, then his nostrils twitched. He stepped forward and reached past her. She heard a clank, then the lavatory flushed and she felt spots of cold water splashing her backside.

'Dirty cow,' he said. 'You ought to flush the toilet when you use it. You like to flush other people down the toilet.' He flicked ash on to the floor. 'Got yourself a nice pad here. Doesn't look much from the street.' He paused and reflected. 'But on the other hand, I don't suppose my van looks much from up here.'

The word hit her like a punch. *Van.* That old white van? The one that had not moved? Had she been so stupid that she'd not thought about that possibility?

She tried pleading with her eyes. But all he did was look back mockingly, drink more whisky, smoke the cigarette down to the butt and trample it on the floor.

'Right, Abby, you and I are going to have a little chat. Very simple. I ask you questions, you move your eyes right for *yes*, left for *no*. Any part of that you don't understand?'

She tried to shake her head, but couldn't. She could move it only a fraction to the right and left.

'No, Abby, you didn't hear me right. I said move your *eyes*, not your *head*. Like to show me you've got that?'

After some moments' hesitation, she moved her eyes to the right.

'Good girl!' he said, as if he was praising a puppy. '*Very* good girl!'

He put his glass down, pulled out another cigarette and gripped it between his lips. Then he picked his glass up, shaking the ice cubes. 'Nice whisky,' he said. 'Single malt. Expensive. But I don't suppose money is much of a problem for you, right?'

He knelt, so he was at eye level, and inched forward, until he was eyeballing her from just a few inches away. 'Eh? Money? Not a problem for you?'

She stared rigidly ahead, shivering from the cold.

Then he took a drag of his cigarette and blew the smoke straight in her face. The smoke stung her eyes. 'Money?' he said again. 'Not a problem for you, right?'

Then he stood up. 'The thing is, Abby, not many people know you are here. Not many people at all. Which means no one's going to miss you. No one's going to come looking for you.' He drank some whisky. 'Nice shower,' he said. 'No expense spared. I expect you'd like to enjoy it. Well, I'm a fair man.'

He rattled the ice cubes hard, staring at the glass, and for a moment Abby thought he was actually going to cut her a deal.

'Here's my offer to you. Either I hurt you until you give it all back to me. Or you just give it back to me.' He smiled again. 'Strikes me as a no-brainer.'

He took a slow, relaxed drag on his cigarette, as if enjoying her eyes watching him, enjoying the knowledge that she was probably desperate for one. He tilted his head and allowed the blue smoke to curl out of his mouth and drift upwards.

'Tell you what,' he said. 'I'll let you sleep on it.'

Then he shut the door.

54

OCTOBER 2007

Roy Grace sat at the work station in Major Incident Room One, nursing the mother, father, brother, sister, uncle, grandson, first cousin and second cousin-once-removed of all hangovers. His mouth was like the bottom of a parrot's cage and it felt as if a chainsaw was blunting its teeth on a steel spike inside his head.

His one consolation was that Glenn Branson, seated diagonally opposite him, looked like he was suffering too. What the hell had come over them last night?

They'd gone to the Black Lion for a quick drink, because Glenn wanted to talk to him about his marriage. They had staggered out some time around midnight, having drunk – how many whiskies, beers, bottles of Rioja? Grace did not even want to think about it. He vaguely remembered a taxi ride home, and that Glenn was still with him because his wife had told him she didn't want him coming home in the state he was.

Then they had drunk more whisky and Glenn had started riffling through his CDs, criticizing his music, as he always did.

Glenn had still been there this morning, in the spare room, moaning about his blinding headache and telling Grace he was seriously thinking of ending it all.

'The time is 8.30, Tuesday 23 October,' Grace read from his briefing notes.

His policy book, and his notes, typed out half an hour earlier by his MSA, sat in front of him, along with a mug of coffee. He was maxed out on paracetamols, which weren't working, and he was chewing mint gum to mask his breath, which he was sure must reek of alcohol. He had left his car at the pub last night and decided a walk there to get it, later this morning, would do him some good.

He was starting to get seriously worried about his lack of self-control over drinking. It didn't help that Cleo drank like a fish – he wondered if it was to help her cope with the horrors of her work. Sandy liked an occasional glass of wine or two at weekends, or a beer on a hot evening, but that was all. Cleo, on the other hand, drank wine every night and seldom just one glass, except when she was on call. They would often go through a bottle of wine, on top of a whisky or two – and sometimes make good progress on a second bottle, as well.

At his recent medical, the doctor had asked him how many units of alcohol he drank a week. Lying, Grace had said seventeen, under the impression that around twenty was a safe number for a male. The doctor had frowned, advising him to cut down to under fifteen. Later, after a quick check on a calculator programme he had found on the internet, Grace discovered his average weekly intake was around forty-two units. Thanks to last night, this week's would probably be double that. He vowed silently never to touch alcohol again.

Bella Moy, opposite him, was already stuffing her face with Maltesers at this early hour. Although she never normally offered them around, she pushed the box towards Grace.

'I think you need a sugar hit, Roy!' she said.

'Does it show?'

'Good party?'

Grace shot a glance at Glenn. 'I wish.'

He removed his chewing gum, ate a Malteser, followed, moreishly, by another three. They didn't make him feel any worse. Then he swigged some coffee and popped the gum back in his mouth.

'Coca-Cola,' Bella said. 'Full strength – not the Diet one. That's good for a hangover. And a fried breakfast.'

'There's the voice of experience,' Norman Potting interrupted.

'Actually I don't do hangovers,' she said dismissively to him.

'Our virtuous virgin,' Potting grumbled.

'That's enough, Norman,' Grace said, smiling at Bella before she rose any further to the bait.

He then returned to the task in hand, reading out the information Norman Potting had produced at the previous evening's briefing meeting, that Joanna Wilson's husband, Ronnie, had died in the World Trade Center on 11 September 2001. When he had finished, he turned to Potting. 'Good work, Norman.'

The DS gave a noncommittal grunt, but looked pleased with himself.

'What information do we have on Joanna Wilson? Any family that we can talk to?' Grace asked.

'I'm working on it,' Potting said. 'Her parents are dead, I've managed to establish that. No siblings. I'm trying to find out if she had any other relatives.'

Shooting a glance at Lizzie Mantle, his deputy SIO, Grace said, 'OK, in the absence of immediate family we need to focus our enquiries on the Wilsons' acquaintances and friends. Norman and Glenn can concentrate on that. Bella, I want you to contact the FBI through the American Embassy in London, see if you can find any record of Joanna Wilson entering the USA during the 1990s. If she was intending to work there, she would have required a visa. Ask the FBI to check all records and computer databases to see if they can find any record of her living there during that period.'

'Do we have a point person at the embassy?' she asked.

'Yes. I know Brad Garrett in the Legal Attaché's Office. He'll give you any help you need. If you have a problem, I also have two friends in the District Attorney's Office in New York. Actually, the smart thing might be to go straight to them. It'll cut out some red tape. When we need the formal evidence, we will of course go through all the right channels.' Then he thought for a moment. 'Leave Brad to me. I'll give him a ring and run things past him.'

Then he turned to DC Nicholl. 'Nick, I want you to do a nationwide search on Ronnie Wilson. See if there's anything on him cross-border.'

The young DC nodded. He looked as exhausted and pale-faced as usual. No doubt he had spent another sleepless night experiencing the joys of fatherhood, Grace thought.

He turned back to Lizzie Mantle. 'Anything you would like to add?'

'I'm thinking about this Ronnie Wilson character,' she said. 'On the balance of probability, he's got to be our number-one suspect at this point.'

Grace popped the gum from his mouth and dropped it in a bin close to his feet. 'I agree,' he said. 'But we need to know more about him and his wife, understand their life together. See if we can find a motive. Did he have a lover? Did she? See what we can eliminate.'

'Once you eliminate the impossible, whatever remains, no matter how improbable, must be the truth,' Norman Potting cut in.

There was a brief moment of silence. Potting looked as pleased as hell with himself.

Then Bella Moy looked at him and said acidly, '*Sherlock Holmes*. Very good, Norman. You and he are about the same generation.'

Grace shot her a warning glance, but she shrugged and ate another Malteser. He turned to Emma-Jane Boutwood. 'E-J, I also want you to take charge of drawing the family tree on the Wilsons.'

'Actually, I have something to report,' Norman Potting said. 'I did my homework last night on the PNC. Ronnie Wilson had form.'

'Previous?' Grace said.

'Yes. He was a frequent flyer with Sussex Police. First time on the radar was 1987. He worked for a dodgy second-hand car dealership that was clocking cars, bunging written-off ones back together.'

'What happened?' Grace asked.

'Twelve months, pope on a rope. Then he popped up again.'

Bella Moy interrupted him. 'Excuse me – did you say *pope on a rope*?'

'Yes, gorgeous.' Potting mimed being hung from a rope around his neck. 'Suspended sentence.'

'Any chance you could speak in a language we all understand?' she retorted.

Potting blinked. 'I thought we did all understand cockney rhyming slang. That's what villains speak.'

'In movies from the 1950s,' she said. '*Your* generation of villains.'

'Bella,' Grace cautioned gently.

She shrugged and said nothing.

Norman Potting continued. 'In 1991, Terry Biglow went down for four years. Knocker boy, ripping off old ladies.' He paused and looked at Bella. '*Knocker* boy. All right with that? I'm not talking about boobies.'

'I know what *knocker boys* are,' she said.

'Good,' he continued. 'Ronnie Wilson worked for him. Got charged as his accomplice, but a smart brief got him off on a technicality. I spoke to Dave Gaylor, who was the case officer.'

'Worked with Terry Biglow?' Grace said.

Everyone in the room knew the name Biglow. They were one of the city's long-established crime families. Several generations into everything from drug dealing, stolen antiques and call girls to witness intimidation, they were just plain trouble in all its forms.

Grace looked at DI Mantle. 'Seems you could be right, Lizzie. There's enough there at least to announce we have a suspect.'

Alison Vosper would like that, he thought. She always liked that phrase, *We have a suspect.* It made her in turn look good to her boss, the Chief Constable. And if her boss was happy, then she was happy.

And if she was happy, she tended to stay out of his face.

55

11 SEPTEMBER 2001

Refreshed after a shower, which had washed the grey dust out of his hair and helped him to partly sober up, Ronnie lounged on the pink candlewick bedspread with the two cigarette burn holes. His thirty-dollar-a-night room did not run to a headboard, so he lay back against the bare wall, studying the news on the fuzzy screen of the clapped-out television and smoking a cigarette.

He watched the two planes repeatedly crash into the Twin Towers. The burning Pentagon. The solemn face of Mayor Giuliani praising the NYPD and the fire officers. The solemn face of President Bush declaring his War on Terrorism. The solemn faces of all the grey ghosts.

The dim, low-wattage bulbs added to the gloominess of this room. He had drawn the drab curtains over his view across the alleyway to the wall of the next-door house. At this moment the whole world beyond his little room seemed solemn and gloomy.

However, despite the raging headache from all the vodka he had drunk, he did not feel gloomy. Shocked at all that he had seen today, at all that had happened to his plans, yes. But here in this room he felt safe. Cocooned in his thoughts. The realization that the opportunity of a lifetime had presented itself to him.

He realized, also, that he had left more stuff behind in

his room at the W. His plane tickets, as well as his passport, and some of his underwear. But instead of being concerned, he was rather pleased.

He looked down at his mobile phone, checking for the thousandth time that it was switched off. Getting paranoid that it might, somehow, of its own volition, have switched itself back on. That suddenly Lorraine's voice would be on the other end, screaming with joy or, more likely, cursing him for not having called her.

He saw something scurrying across the carpet. It was a dark brown roach, about half an inch long. He knew that cockroaches were among the few creatures that could survive a nuclear war. They had reached perfection through evolution. Survival of the fittest.

Yep, well, he was pretty fit too. And now that his plan was taking shape, he knew exactly what his first step was going to be.

He walked over to the waste bin and removed the plastic bag that lined it. Then he took the red folder from his briefcase and dropped it in, figuring he was unlikely to be mugged for the contents of a plastic bag. He was well aware of the risk he had run towing his briefcase and suitcase all this way. He stopped and listened. The item of news he was most interested in was now coming up on the television. The repeated information that all non-military flights in and out of America were grounded. Indefinitely.

Perfect.

He pulled on his jacket and left the room.

It was 6.45. Dusk was beginning to fall, but it was still broad daylight as he walked along, swinging the carrier bag at his side, retracing his steps to the busy main street with the L-Train overpass.

He still hadn't eaten anything since breakfast, but he wasn't hungry. He had a job to do first.

To his relief, Mail Box City was still open. He crossed the street and went in. To his right was the floor-to-ceiling wall of metal safe-deposit boxes. At the far end, the same long-haired man he had seen earlier was busy on one of several internet terminals. Two empty phone booths were beyond him. To Ronnie's left, three people were queuing at the counter. The first, a man in a white hard hat and dungarees, held out a strange-looking passbook and was receiving a wad of banknotes. Behind him stood a grim-faced old woman in a denim skirt, and behind her was a strung-out girl with long orange hair who kept looking around with blank, glazed eyes, rotating her hands every few moments.

Ronnie joined the queue behind her. Five minutes later the grizzled man behind the counter handed him a key as thin as a razor blade, and a slip of paper, in exchange for fifty dollars. 'Thirty-one,' he said in guttural English, and jerked a finger. 'One week. You come back, otherwise open box. Take. Understand?'

Ronnie nodded and looked at the slip of paper. The date and time, down to the minute, were printed on it. Along with the expiry date.

'No drugs.'

'Understood.'

The man gave him a long, sad stare, his demeanour softening suddenly. 'You OK?'

'Yep, I'm OK.'

The man nodded. 'Crazy. Crazy today. Why they do this to us? It's crazy, yes?'

'Crazy.'

Ronnie turned away, found his deposit box and unlocked it. It was deeper than he had imagined. He slid his package in, then glanced around to make sure no one was observing him, closed the door and locked it. He had a sudden thought and went back to the counter. Having paid for thirty minutes' internet connection time, he sat down at a terminal and logged on to Hotmail.

Five minutes later he was all set up. He had a new name, a new email address. This was the start of his new life.

And now, he realized, he was ravenous. He left the store and went in search of a burger and fries. And a gherkin. For some reason, he suddenly could have killed for a gherkin. And fried onions. Ketchup. The works. And a Coke.

Champagne would come later.

56

OCTOBER 2007

'Come in,' Alison Vosper said, in response to the knock on her door.

Cassian Pewe had selected his clothes carefully for this meeting. His sharpest blue suit, his best white shirt, his favourite tie, pale blue and white geometrics. And he had sprayed on so much Calvin Klein Eternity cologne he smelled like he had been marinated in the stuff.

You could always tell when you really connected with someone, and Pewe knew that he had with this particular lady Assistant Chief Constable from the very first time they met. It was at a Metropolitan Police conference on counter-terrorism and the Islamic threat in Britain's cities back in January. He had sensed more than a frisson of sexuality between them. He was quite sure that the reason she had so enthusiastically and proactively encouraged his move to the Sussex CID – and championed his promotion to Detective Superintendent – was because she had extracurricular activities in mind.

Quite understandably, of course. He knew just how attractive to women he was. And throughout his career to date he had always focused on the women in power in the police force. Not all were malleable; in fact some were as steely as their male counterparts, if not more so. But a fair percentage were normal women, intelligent and strong, but with emotional vulnerabilities. You just had to press the right buttons.

Which made the coldness of the ACC's reaction as he entered her office all the more surprising.

'Take a seat,' she said, without looking up from the array of morning papers fanned out on her desk like a poker hand. 'Or perhaps I should say, "Take a *pew.*"'

'Oh, that's very witty,' Pewe cooed.

But no smile cracked her icy expression. Seated behind her huge rosewood desk, she continued reading an article in the *Guardian*, holding him at bay with her elegantly manicured hand.

He eased himself down into the black leather armchair. Although it was four months since the taxi he had been travelling in had been T-boned by a stolen van, fracturing his left leg in four places, it was still painful to stand for prolonged periods of time. But he kept that to himself, not wanting to risk his future career chances by being marked as a semi-invalid.

Alison Vosper continued reading. Pewe looked at the framed photographs of her husband, a burly, shaven-headed police officer several years older than her, and her two children, boys in school uniform wearing rather goofy spectacles.

Several framed certificates bearing her name hung on the walls, along with a couple of old Brighton prints, one of the racecourse, the other of the long-gone chain pier.

Her phone rang. She leaned forward and stared at the display, then hoisted it from its cradle, barked, 'I'm in a meeting, call you back,' replaced it and continued reading. 'So, how are you getting on?' she asked suddenly, still reading.

'So far, great.'

She glanced up and he tried to hold and maintain eye contact, but, almost immediately, she looked down at something else on another part of her desk. She reached over, picked up and then shuffled through some sheets of typewritten papers, a report of some kind, as if she was trying to find something. 'I understand you've been allocated cold cases?'

'Yes.'

She was dressed in a short, tight-fitting black jacket over a white, Mandarin-collared blouse, which was closed at the neck by an opal in a silver clasp. Her breasts, which he had fantasized about, were almost flattened. Then she looked at him and smiled. A long, almost come-on smile.

Instantly he melted. Then lost eye contact again as she looked down and began shuffling through the papers once more.

There was something intensely fragrant about her, he thought. She wasn't beautiful, but he was powerfully attracted. Her skin was silky white and even the small wart just above the neckline of her blouse, her one tiny blemish, intrigued him. She was wearing a citrus fragrance that was setting off fireworks deep in his belly. She looked pure, and strong, and exuded authority. He wanted to go around the far side of that desk, rip her clothes off and roll around with her on the carpeted floor.

He was getting an erection at the thought.

And she was still looking down at her desk, shuffling through the damn papers!

'It's good to see you again,' he said gently, as a prompt.

He left an expectant gap. Was she feeling the same way about him and just being coy? Maybe she was going to suggest a place where the two of them could meet later for a drink. Somewhere cosy.

He could invite her over to his pad at the Marina. With its view of the yachts, it was pretty cool.

Now she was reading the *Guardian* again.

'Are you looking for something?' he asked. 'Is there some mention of Sussex Police?'

'No,' she said dismissively. 'Just trying to catch up on the day's news.' Then, without looking up, she said, 'I presume you're starting an audit of how many cold cases are outstanding?'

'Well,' he said, 'well, yes, absolutely.'

'Murders, suspicious deaths? Long-term missing persons? Other undetected serious crimes?'

'All of those.'

She moved on to the *Telegraph* and scanned the front page.

He stared at her uncertainly. There was an invisible barrier between them and he felt completely thrown. 'Look, I – I was wondering if I could speak to you off the record.'

'Go ahead.' She turned several pages in rapid succession as he spoke.

'Well, I know I'm meant to report to Roy Grace, but I have concerns about him.'

Now he had her full attention. 'Go on.'

'You know about his missing wife, of course,' he said.

'The entire force has lived with it for the past nine years,' she replied.

'Well, I went to interview her parents last night. They are deeply concerned. They don't feel that anyone in Sussex Police has carried out an impartial investigation.'

'Can you elaborate?'

'Yes. Well, here's the thing. In all that time, the only officer in Sussex Police who has taken responsibility for reviewing the investigation into her disappearance is Roy himself. To me, that doesn't sit right. I mean, that wouldn't have happened in the Met.'

'So what are you saying?'

'Well,' Pewe continued unctuously, 'her parents are deeply uncomfortable about this. Reading between the lines, I think they suspect Roy is hiding something.'

She looked at him for some moments. 'And what do you think?'

'I'd like your permission for me to prioritize this. Dig further. Use my discretion to take whatever investigatory steps I consider necessary.'

'Granted,' she said. Then she looked back down at her papers and dismissed him with a single wave of her hand. The one with the diamond solitaire and wedding band.

When he stood up, his hard-on had gone but he felt a whole new kind of excitement.

57

OCTOBER 2007

The light and the extractor fan had been on for what seemed like hours and hours. In the tiny, windowless room, Abby had lost all track of time. She didn't know if it was still the middle of the night or morning. Her mouth and throat were parched, she was ravenously hungry and almost every part of her body was numb or hurting from the bindings.

She was shivering with cold in the constant icy draught. She desperately needed to blow her nose, which was blocked and getting increasingly hard to breathe through. No air at all came in through her mouth and, breathing faster and faster, she was sensing another panic attack coming on.

She tried to calm herself down, to slow her breathing. She was beginning to feel she wasn't totally inside her body, that she was dead and floating above it. As if the naked person bound with tape was someone else, not her any more.

She was dead.

Her heart was pounding. Hammering. She tried to say something to herself and heard the muffled humming sound inside her mouth. *I am still alive. I can feel my heart.*

Inside her skull, she could feel a band tightening around her brain. She felt clammy and unable to focus her eyes clearly. Then she began shaking uncontrollably. A cold sweat of fear erupted on her skin as the thought hit her like a sledgehammer.

What if he has gone and left me here?

To die . . .

When she had first met Ricky she thought that, like Dave, his violence was just big talk, swagger, keeping up with their gangster friends. Then one night when she was with him, he'd caught a spider in the bathtub and burned each of its legs off with a cigarette lighter, then left it, alive in a glass jar, to die of thirst or hunger.

The realization that he was quite capable of doing the same to her made her struggle against the bonds with a sudden, new urgency. Her panic was deepening.

Concentrate.

Focus.

Remember it is just a panic attack. You are not dying. You are not out of your body. Say the words.

She breathed in, out, in, out. *Hi,* she thought the words. *I am Abby Dawson. I am fine. This is just a wonky chemical reaction. I'm fine, I am in my body, I am not dead, this will pass.*

She tried to focus on each of the bindings in turn, starting with the one around her forehead. Her neck was increasingly painful from her head being pulled back so far. But try as hard as she could, she could not move it an inch in any direction.

Next she tried her hands, which were taped to her thighs. Her fingers were splayed out and taped too, making it impossible to get a purchase on anything. She tried to move her legs, but they were taped together so hard they felt like they were in a cast. Nothing gave. There was no slack anywhere.

Where had he learned about bindings? Or had he just winged it as he went along? Smiling as he worked?

Oh yes, smiling for sure.

And she could hardly blame him.

She was wishing desperately, suddenly, that she had never agreed to this. She wasn't strong enough, she realized. Nor smart enough. How the hell had she ever thought she could succeed? How could she have been so stupid?

A clank interrupted her thoughts, then the squeak of a rubber shoe and a shadow fell across the door. Ricky was looking down at her, holding a large, plastic ASDA carrier bag in one hand and a tall, white mug of coffee in the other. She could smell the aroma. God, that was so good.

'Hope you had a good night's rest, Abby. I want you fresh for today. Did you?'

She made a lowing moan.

'Yes, sorry about the tape. But the walls in this place aren't that thick. I can't take any risks, I'm sure you understand. So – maybe the bed was a little hard? Still, very good for your posture, that position. Straight back. Did anybody ever tell you about the importance of good posture?'

She said nothing.

'No, well, I don't suppose the word *straight* features much in your vocabulary.' He put the carrier bag down on the floor. It made a heavy clank, followed by the rattle of metal objects inside.

'I've brought along a few things. I've never actually done torture before. Seen it in films, of course. Read about it.'

Her throat tightened.

'I just want you to understand, Abby, that I don't have to hurt you. All you have to do is tell me where it is. You know, what you took from me. Like, my entire stash.'

She was silent. Trembling.

He picked up the bag and shook it, with a loud, metallic rattle. 'Got all kinds of stuff in here, but most of it's pretty primitive. Got a power drill that could go right through your kneecaps. I've got a packet of needles and a small hammer. Could whack those up inside your fingernails. Got some pliers for your teeth. Or we could be a bit more cultural.'

He put his hand in his pocket and pulled out a black iPod. Then he held it up close to her eyes. 'Music,' he said. 'Have a listen.'

He inserted the ear-pieces, checked the display and pressed the start symbol. Then he turned up the volume.

Abby heard a song she recognized but could not immediately name.

'"Fool for Love",' Ricky helped her. 'Could be me, really, couldn't it?'

She looked at him, almost incoherent with terror, not sure what reaction he was expecting. And trying not to let him see how scared she was.

'I like this record,' he said. 'Do you? Remember, eyes right for *yes*, left for *no*.'

She moved her eyes right.

'Good, now we're cooking with gas! So, is it here, or somewhere else? How about I make the question simple. Is it here, in this flat?'

She moved her eyes left.

'OK. Somewhere else. Is it in Brighton?'

She moved her eyes right.

'In a safe-deposit box?'

Again she moved her eyes right.

He dug his left hand into the pocket of his jeans and pulled out a small, thin key. 'Is it this key?'

Her eyes told him it was.

He smiled. 'Good. Now all we need to establish is the bank and the address. Is it NatWest?'

Eyes left.

'Lloyds TSB?'

Eyes left.

'HSBC?'

Her eyes moved left. And she nixed Barclays too.

'OK, I think I get it,' he said, and moved away from the doorway. A short while later he returned holding a copy of the *Yellow Pages*, open at the listings page for security companies. His finger ran down, stopping and getting a negative from Abby at each name. Then it came to Southern Deposit Security.

Her eyes moved right.

He studied the name and address, as if memorizing it, then closed the directory.

'OK, good. All we need now is to establish a few more details. Would the account be in the name of Abby Dawson?'

Eyes left.

'Katherine Jennings?'

Her eyes went right.

He smiled, looking much happier now.

Then she stared at him, trying to signal. But he wasn't interested.

'Hasta la vista, baby!' he said cheerily. 'That's from one of my favourite movies. Remember?' He peered at her intently.

She moved her eyes right. She remembered. She knew this film, this line. It was Arnie Schwarzenegger in *The Terminator*. She knew what it meant.

See you later!

58

OCTOBER 2007

After the briefing meeting, Roy Grace retreated to the quiet sanctuary of his office and spent a few moments looking out of the window, across the main road at the ASDA car park, and the ugly slab building of the supermarket itself cutting off what would have been a fine view across the city of Brighton and Hove he loved so much. At least he could actually see some sky, and for the first time in several days patches of it were blue, with rays of sun breaking through the cloud.

Nursing the hot mug of coffee that Eleanor had just brought him, he glanced down at the plastic trays containing his prized collections – three dozen vintage cigarette lighters that he hadn't yet put up on display and a fine selection of international police caps.

Lying beside his stuffed brown trout, which he used to teach young detectives a lesson, in an analogy between fishing and patience, was a new addition, a birthday present from Cleo. It was a stuffed carp, in a display case, at the base of which was engraved the legend – a terrible pun – *Carpe diem.*

His briefcase sat open on the table, together with his mobile, his dictating machine and a bunch of transcripts relating to the court hearings he was helping to prepare, one of which he had to go through this morning, because the CPS lawyer was on his back for it.

What's more, thanks to his promotion, he now had new stacks of files, growing by the minute, that Eleanor was bringing in and placing on every available flat surface. They contained case summaries of all the major crimes that Sussex CID were currently investigating, which he now had to review.

He made a list of everything he needed to follow up on *Operation Dingo*, then he went through the transcript, which took him an hour. When he had finished, he pulled out his notebook and, starting at the back, read his most recent jotting. His handwriting was bad, so he took a moment to decipher it and remember.

> Katherine Jennings, Flat 82, Arundel Mansions,
> 29 Lower Arundel Terrace.

He stared at it blankly, for some moments. Waiting for his brain's synapses to kick in and provide him with some recollection of why he had written that down. Then he remembered Kevin Spinella cornering him after the press briefing yesterday. Telling him something about her being freed from a trapped lift and that she had seemed frightened about something.

Most people trapped in a lift would have been frightened. Mildly claustrophobic and with a fear of heights, he probably would have been too. Scared witless. Still, you never knew. He decided to do the dutiful thing and report it to East Brighton District. He dialled the internal number of the most efficient officer he knew there, Inspector Stephen Curry, gave him the woman's name and address, and explained the provenance.

'Don't make it a priority, Steve. But maybe have one

of your beat officers swing by some time, make sure all is OK.'

'Absolutely,' said Stephen Curry, who was sounding rushed. 'Leave it with me.'

'With the greatest pleasure,' Grace said.

Having hung up, he looked down at the workload on his desk and decided he would stroll down later this morning, towards lunchtime, to collect his car. Take in a bit of fresh air. Enjoy a rare bit of sunshine and try to clear his head. Then make his way downtown to see if he couldn't find one or two of Ronnie Wilson's old acquaintances. He had a good idea where to start looking.

59

12 SEPTEMBER 2001

Ronnie spent a restless night lying between unwashed nylon sheets, trying to cope with a foam pillow that felt as if it was filled with rocks and a mattress whose springs bored into him like corkscrews. He had a choice between keeping the window shut and enduring the air-conditioning unit that made a noise like two skeletons fighting in a metal shed, or opening it and being kept awake by the non-stop wailing of distant sirens and the chop of helicopters.

At a few minutes to 6 he lay wide awake, scratching one of several tiny red bites on his leg. He soon discovered more that were itching like fury on his chest and stomach.

He fumbled on the bedside table for the remote and switched the television on. The urgency of the outside world suddenly filled his room. Images of New York were on the screen. There were distraught-looking people, women and men, holding up hand-made boards, placards, signs, some with photographs, some with just names, in red or black or blue writing, all asking, HAVE YOU SEEN?

A newscaster appeared, giving an estimate of the numbers dead. Emergency phone numbers to call ran along the bottom, as well as more breaking news.

All kinds of bad stuff.

Bad stuff was churning around inside his head too, together with everything else that had been in the mix all night long. Thoughts, ideas, lists. Lorraine. Donald Hatcook. Flames. Screams. Falling bodies.

His plan.

Was Donald OK? If he had survived, was there any guarantee he would agree to back his biodiesel venture? Ronnie had always been a gambling man and he didn't reckon the odds on that were as good as the odds on his new plan working. So far as he was now concerned, alive or dead, Donald Hatcook was history.

Lorraine would be hurting. But in time she would understand that there was *no gain without pain.*

One day the silly cow would understand – one day soon, when he showered her in fifty-quid notes, bought her everything she ever wanted and more!

They would be rich!

Just had to suffer some pain now.

And be very, very careful.

He looked at his watch to double-check: 6.02. It took a few moments for his tired, jet-lagged brain to work out whether the UK was ahead in time or behind. Ahead, he finally decided. So it would be just after 11 in the morning in Brighton. He tried to think what Lorraine would be doing. She'd have phoned his mobile, phoned the hotel, phoned Donald Hatcook's office. She might be round at her sister's house, or, more likely, her sister would be round at theirs.

A police officer was speaking now, straight at the television. He was saying volunteers were needed to come and help out on the *pile.* They needed people down in the disaster area to help with the digging, to hand out water. He looked exhausted, as if he had been up all night. He looked like a man stretched to breaking point from tiredness and emotion and just sheer workload.

Volunteers. Ronnie thought about that for some moments. *Volunteers.*

He climbed out of bed and stood in the puny shower, feeling strangely liberated, but nervous. There were a thousand and one ways he could screw this up. But also there were ways he could be smart. Really smart. *Volunteers.* Yes, that had something! That had currency!

Drying himself, he focused on the news, watching a New York channel, wanting to see what was predicted for the city today. The other shoe that was going to drop that people were talking about? Meaning more attacks. Or was business going to get back to normal today? At least in some parts of Manhattan?

He needed to know, because he had transactions to make. His new life was going to require funding. You had to speculate to accumulate. Stuff he needed was going to be expensive and, wherever he got it, he would have to pay in cash.

The item he wanted was coming up on the news now. The parts of New York that would be closed off and the parts that were open. What was running on the transit system. It seemed there was a lot, that most of it was operating. The anchor woman was saying, solemnly, that yesterday the world had changed.

She was right, he thought, but for many today it would be business as usual. Ronnie was relieved about that. After his binge in the bar yesterday, his evening meal and his advance on the room, his resources were down to about three hundred and two dollars.

The reality of that was hammering home. Three hundred and two dollars to last him until he could make a transaction. He could pawn his laptop, but that was too risky. He knew, to his own cost, when the computer at the car dealership had been seized a few years back, that it was almost impossible to wipe a computer memory clean. His laptop would always be traceable back to him.

They were talking about volunteers wanted for the *pile* on the screen again now. *Volunteers,* he thought. The idea was taking root, exciting him.

Now, thanks to the morning news, he had another piece of his plan in place.

60

OCTOBER 2007

Sussex House had originally been acquired as the headquarters for Sussex CID. But recently, despite the fact that the building was bursting at the seams, a uniformed district, East Brighton, had been squeezed into the premises as well. The Neighbourhood Specialist Team officers, involved in community-orientated problem-solving, occupied a tight space behind double doors leading directly off the reception area.

One downside of this location for Inspector Stephen Curry was that every morning he needed to be in two places at once. He had to be here for his daily briefing with the duty Neighbourhood Policing Team inspector, which ended just after 9 o'clock, and then he had a mad dash through the Brighton rush hour to be at Brighton Police Station in John Street for the daily 9.30 review meeting chaired by the Superintendent Crime and Operations for Brighton and Hove Division.

A strong-framed man of thirty-nine with hard-set good looks and a youthful air of enthusiasm about him, Curry was in even more of a rush than usual today, looking anxiously at his watch. It was 10.45. He had just returned to his office at Sussex House from John Street, to deal with a couple of urgent matters, and was about to fly back out of the door when Roy Grace phoned him.

He carefully wrote down the name *Katherine Jennings* and the address in his notebook, then told Grace he would get someone from his Neighbourhood Specialist Team to stop by the place.

As the matter didn't sound urgent, he decided it could wait till later. Then he jumped up, grabbed his cap off the door, and hurried out.

61

12 SEPTEMBER 2001

Lorraine was sitting once again at the kitchen table in her white towelling dressing gown, a cigarette in her mouth and a cup of tea in front of her. Her head was pounding and she was bleary-eyed, not fully with it, from an almost sleepless night. Her heart felt like a lead weight in her chest and she had a sick feeling in the pit of her stomach.

She tapped the cigarette on the ashtray, sending a quarter-inch of ash tumbling in to join the four fresh butts already there this morning. The *Daily Mirror* lay beside her and the news was on television, but for the first time since yesterday afternoon, her mind was on something else.

In front of her lay the post that had arrived that morning, as well as yesterday's and Monday's. Plus more opened post she had found in Ronnie's bureau in the small spare room upstairs he used as his office.

The letter she was looking at now was from a debt-collection agency called EndCol Financial Recovery. It was acknowledging an agreement Ronnie appeared to have entered into to pay off the hire-purchase payments on the large-screen television in the living room. The next one was from another debt-collection agency. It informed Ronnie that the phone line to the house was going to be disconnected if the outstanding balance of over six hundred pounds was not paid within seven days.

Then there was the letter from Her Majesty's Revenue & Customs, demanding that nearly eleven and a half thousand pounds be paid within three weeks or a distraint order would be made.

Lorraine shook her head in disbelief. Half the letters were demands for payment on overdue bills. And one, from his bank manager, told him that his request for a further loan had been rejected.

The worst letter of all was from the building society. She had found it in his bureau and it informed Ronnie that they were foreclosing on the mortgage and commencing court proceedings to repossess the house.

Lorraine crushed out the cigarette, buried her face in her hands and sobbed. All the time thinking, *Why didn't you tell me this, Ronnie darling? Why didn't you tell me the mess you – we – are in? I could have helped, gone out and got a job. I might not have earned much, but it would have helped. It would have been better than nothing.*

She shook another cigarette out and stared numbly at the screen. At the people in New York walking around with their placards, their photographs of lost loved ones. That's what she needed to do, she knew. She had to get over there and find him. Maybe he'd been injured and was lying in a hospital somewhere . . .

He was alive, she felt it in her bones. He was a survivor. All these debts, he would deal with them. If Ronnie had been here last night, he'd never have let them take the car. He'd have cut a deal, or found some cash, or torn the fuckers' throats out.

For the millionth time, she dialled his number. And it went straight to his voicemail. Not his voice, just an impersonal one telling her sorry, the person she had called was not available and inviting her to leave a message.

She hung up, sipped her tea, then lit the cigarette and coughed. A deep, hacking cough which made her eyes water. They were now showing the smouldering rubble, the skeletal walls, the whole apocalyptic scene of what had been, until yesterday morning, the World Trade Center. She tried to work out from the images now on the screen – first a tight shot of a fireman in the foreground wearing a face mask, stumbling across a hillock of shifting, smoking masonry, then a much wider shot showing a slab maybe a hundred feet high and a flattened cop car – where the South Tower had been. What was left of it. When had Ronnie got out of it and how?

Her front doorbell rang. She froze. Then there was a sharp rap.

Shit. Shit. Shit.

She slunk upstairs and into the front bedroom, the one that Ronnie used, and peered down. There was a blue van outside in the street, blocking her drive, and two burly men were standing outside her front door. One had a shaven head and was wearing a parka and jeans; the other, with close-cropped hair and a large gold earring, was holding a document.

She lay still, almost holding her breath. There were more raps on the door. The bell rang again, twice. Then, finally, she heard the van drive off.

62

OCTOBER 2007

Tosser!

Cassian Pewe had been in Sussex House for a couple of days, but it had taken about three minutes for Tony Case, the Senior Support Officer, to sum him up.

Case, a former police officer himself, ran the administration for this building and the three other buildings that housed between them all the Major Incident Suites in Sussex – at Littlehampton, Horsham and Eastbourne. Among his duties were performing risk assessments for raids, budgeting forensic requirements and new equipment, and general compliance, as well as ensuring that the people who worked here had everything they needed.

Such as picture hooks.

'Look,' Pewe said, as if he were addressing a flunky, 'I want that picture hook moved three inches to the right and six inches higher. OK? And I want this one moved exactly eight inches higher. Understand? You don't seem to be writing any of this down.'

'Perhaps you'd like me to get you a supply of hooks, a hammer and a ruler, then you could put them up yourself?' Case suggested. It was what every other officer did, including the Chief Superintendent.

Pewe, who had removed his suit jacket and hung it over his chair, was wearing red braces over his white shirt.

He strutted around the room now, twanging them. 'I don't do DIY,' he said. 'And I don't have time. You must have someone here to do stuff like this.'

'Yes,' Tony Case said. 'Me.'

Pewe was looking out of the window at the grim custody block. The rain was stopping. 'Not much of a view,' he moaned.

'Detective Superintendent Grace was quite happy with it.'

Pewe went a strange colour, as if he had swallowed something to which he was allergic. 'This was *his* office?'

'Yes.'

'It's really a lousy view.'

'Perhaps if you call ACC Vosper, she'll have the custody block demolished for you.'

'That's not funny,' Pewe said.

'Funny?' Tony Case said. 'I'm not being funny. I'm at work. We don't do humour here. Just serious police work. I'll go and get you a hammer – if no one's nicked it.'

'And what about my assistants? I've requested two DCs. Where will they be seated?'

'No one told me anything about two assistants.'

'I need some space for them. They will have to sit somewhere fairly near me.'

'I could get you a smaller desk,' Tony Case said. 'And put them both in here.' He left the room.

Pewe couldn't work out whether the man was being facetious or was for real, but his thoughts were interrupted by the phone ringing. He answered it with an important-sounding, 'Detective Superintendent Pewe.'

It was a controller. 'Sir, I have an officer at Interpol on the line. On behalf of the Victoria Police in Australia.

He asked specifically for someone working on cold-case inquiries.'

'OK, put him through.' He sat down, taking his time about it, and put his feet up on his desk, in a space between bundles of documents. Then he brought the receiver to his ear. 'Detective Superintendent Cassian Pewe,' he said.

'Ah, good morning, ah, Cashon, this is Detective Sergeant James Franks from the Interpol bureau in London.'

Franks had a clipped public school accent. Pewe didn't like the way desk-jockey Interpol members tended to think they were superior and ride roughshod over other police officers.

'Let me have your number and I'll call you back,' Pewe said.

'That's OK, you don't need to do that.'

'Security. It's our policy here in Sussex,' Pewe said importantly, getting pleasure out of exercising his little bit of power.

Franks repaid the compliment by making him listen to an endless loop of 'Nessun dorma' for a good four minutes before he finally came back on the line. He would have been even happier had he known it was a song that Pewe, a classical music and opera purist, particularly hated.

'OK, Cashon, our bureau's been contacted by police outside Melbourne in Australia. I understand they have the body of an unidentified pregnant woman recovered from the boot of car – been in a river for some two and a half years. They've obtained DNA samples from her and the foetus, but they have not been able to get any match off their Australian databases. But here's the thing . . .'

Franks paused and Pewe heard a slurp, as if he was swigging some coffee, before he resumed.

'The woman has silicone breast implants. I understand these are all printed with the manufacturer's batch number and each of them has a serial number that's kept in the hospital register under the recipient's name. This particular batch of implants was supplied to a hospital called the Nuffield in Woodingdean, in the city of Brighton and Hove, back in 1997.'

Pewe took his feet off the table and looked around hopelessly for a notebook, before using the back of an envelope to scribble down a few details. He then asked Franks to fax through the information on the implants and the DNA analysis of both the mother and the foetus, promising that he would start making enquiries right away. He then pointed out rather crisply that his name was *Cassian,* not *Cashon,* and hung up.

He really did need a junior officer to assist him. He had far more important things to deal with than a floater in an Australian river. One of them *much* more important.

63

OCTOBER 2007

Abby was laughing. Her father was laughing too.

'You stupid girl, you did that deliberately, didn't you?'

'No I didn't, Daddy!'

Both of them stood back, staring at the partially tiled bathroom wall. White tiles with a navy-blue dado rail and a scattering of navy tiles as relief, one of which she had just put on backwards, so that the coarse grey underside was now visible, looking like a square of cement.

'You're meant to be helping me, young lady, not hindering me!' her dad admonished.

She burst into loud giggles. 'I didn't do it deliberately, Daddy, honestly.'

For an answer, he patted her squarely on the forehead with his trowel, depositing a small lump of grout.

'Hey!' she cried. 'I'm not a bathroom wall, so you can't tile me.'

'Oh yes, I can.'

Her father's face darkened and the smile faded. Suddenly it wasn't him any more. It was Ricky.

He was holding a power drill in his hand. Smiling, he squeezed the trigger. The drill whined.

'Right knee or left knee first, Abby?'

She began shaking, her body still held rigid by her bonds, her insides twisting, shrinking back, screaming silently.

She could see the spinning drill bit. Corkscrewing towards her knee. Inches from it. She was screaming. Her cheeks popping. Nothing coming out. Just an endless, trapped moan.

Trapped in her throat and in her mouth.

He lunged forward with the drill.

And as she screamed again, the light changed suddenly. She smelled the sharp, dry smell of fresh grout, saw cream wall tiles. Hyperventilating. There was no Ricky. She could see the carrier bag lying where he had left it, untouched, just beyond the doorway. She felt slippery with perspiration. Heard the steady whirr of the extractor fan, felt the cold draught from it. The insides of her mouth were feeling stuck together. She was so parched, so terribly parched. Just one drop. One small glass of water. Please.

She stared at the tiles again.

God, the irony of being imprisoned in here. Facing these tiles. So near. So damned near! Her mind was all over the place. Somehow she had to get to Ricky. Had to get him to remove the tape from her face. And if he was rational, when he returned, that's exactly what he would have to do.

But he wasn't rational.

And thinking about that now chilled every cell in her body.

64

12 SEPTEMBER 2001

Wide awake and feeling mentally alert, despite his tired eyes, Ronnie stepped out of the front door of the rooming house shortly after 7.30. Immediately, he noticed the smell. There was a hazy, metallic blue sky and there should have been a dewy freshness in the morning air. But instead a pungent, sour reek filled his nostrils.

At first he thought it must be coming from the garbage cans, but as he walked down the steps and along the street it stayed with him. A suggestion of something that was damp and smouldering, something chemical, sour and cloying. His eyes hurt too, as if there were tiny pellets of sandpaper in the haze.

On the main drag, there was a strange atmosphere. It was Wednesday morning, midweek, yet there were hardly any cars about. People were walking slowly, with drawn, haggard expressions, as if they too had not slept well. The whole city seemed to be in a state of deepening shock. The numbing events of yesterday had now had time to work through everyone's psyche and were bringing a new, dark reality this morning.

He found a diner, displaying, among all its Russian signs in the window, the English words stencilled in red letters on illuminated plastic, ALL DAY BREAKFAST. Inside, he could see a handful of people, including two cops, were eating in silence, watching the news on the television high on one wall.

He sat in a booth towards the rear. A subdued waitress poured him coffee and a glass of iced water, while he looked blankly at the Russian menu, before realizing there was an English version on the reverse. He ordered fresh orange juice and a pancake stack with bacon, then watched the television while he waited for his food to arrive. It was hard to believe that it was only twenty-four hours since his breakfast yesterday. It felt like twenty-four years.

After leaving the diner, he walked the short distance down the street to Mail Box City. The same young man was seated at one of the internet terminals, pecking at the keys, and a thin, dark-haired young woman in her early twenties, who seemed on the verge of crying, was staring at a website on another. A nervous-looking bald man in dungarees, who had the shakes, was removing items from a holdall and inserting them into a deposit box, looking furtively over his shoulder every few moments. Ronnie wondered what he had in that bag, but knew better than to stare.

He was now part of the world of transient people, the dispossessed, the poor and the fugitives. Their lives centred around places like Mail Box City, where they could store or hide their meagre stashes and collect their post. People didn't come here to make friends, but to remain anonymous. Which was exactly what he needed.

He looked at his watch. It was 8.30. A half-hour or so before the people he wanted to speak to would be at their offices – assuming they were in today. He paid for an hour of internet time and sat down at a terminal.

*

At 9.30 Ronnie entered one of the hooded phone booths against the end wall, put a quarter in the slot and dialled the first of the numbers on the list he had just made from his internet search. As he waited, he stared at the perforations in the sound-deadening lining of the booth. It reminded him of a prison phone.

The voice at the other end startled him out of his reverie: 'Abe Miller Associates, Abe Miller speaking.'

The man was not discourteous, but Ronnie didn't feel any depth to his interest or any hunger for a deal. It was as if, he thought, Abe Miller figured that the world might very well end one day soon, so what did making a buck mean any more? In fact, what was the point of anything? That was how Abe Miller sounded to him.

'An Edward, one pound, unmounted, mint,' Ronnie said, after introducing himself. 'Perfect gum, no hinge.'

'OK, what are you looking for?'

'I have four of them. I'd take four thousand each.'

'Whee, that's a little steep.'

'Not for their condition. Catalogue's over double that.'

'Thing is, I don't know how all this that's going on right now will play out on the market. Stocks are on the floor – know what I'm saying.'

'Yeah, well, these are better than stocks. Less volatile.'

'I'm not sure about buying anything right now. Guess I'd prefer to wait a few days, see how the wind blows. If they're in as good condition as you say they are, right now I could maybe go to two. No more than that. Two.'

'Two thousand bucks each?'

'Couldn't manage any more, not now. If you want to wait a week and see, maybe I can improve a little. Maybe not.'

Ronnie understood the man's reticence. He knew he

had probably picked the worst morning since the day after the Wall Street Crash of 1929 to try to do business anywhere in the world, and worst of all in New York, but he didn't have any choice. He did not have the luxury of time. It seemed to him that this was the story of his life. *Buy at the top of the market, sell at the bottom.* Why was the world always fucking dumping on him?

'I'll get back to you,' Ronnie said.

'Sure, no worries. What did you say your name was?'

Ronnie's brain raced, momentarily forgetting the name he'd used for his hotmail account. 'Nelson,' he said.

The man perked up a little. 'You any relation to Mike Nelson? From Birmingham? You're English, right?'

'Mike Nelson?' Ronnie cursed silently. Not good to have another person in this game with a similar name. People would remember – and at this moment what he needed was for people to forget him. 'No,' he said. 'No relation.'

He thanked Abe Miller and hung up. Then, thinking about the name, he decided maybe it was OK to keep it. If there was another trader with a similar name, people might think he was related and treat him more respectfully from the start. This was a business that relied heavily on reputation.

He tried six more dealers. None of them were inclined to better his first offer, and two of them said they weren't going to buy anything at the moment, which panicked him. He wondered whether the market might go even flatter, and if it would be wise to take the offer he'd had from Abe Miller while it was still on the table. *If*, twenty-five minutes on in this uncertain new world, it *was* still on the table.

Eight thousand dollars. They were worth twenty, at least. He had a few others with him, including two Plate 11 and unmounted mint Penny Blacks, with gum on the back.

In a normal market he'd be looking for twenty-five thousand dollars a plate, but God knows what they were worth now. No point even trying to sell them. They were all he now had in the world. They were going to have to tide him over for a long time.

Possibly a very long time.

65

OCTOBER 2007

When Roy Grace had started his career he worked as a beat copper in central Brighton, then for a brief time in the CID with the drugs surveillance unit. He knew most of the faces and names of the street dealers, and some of the major users, and had busted most of them at one time or another.

It was normally only the smaller people who got caught – the *low-hanging fruit.* Frequently the police ignored them, watching them instead, even making friends with some of them in the hope that they would lead to the bigger fish, the middlemen, the suppliers and, very occasionally, a major consignment. But every time the police achieved a result and took out a handful of players, there were always new ones waiting in the wings.

At this moment, though, as he parked his Alfa Romeo in the Church Street NCP and switched off the engine, killing the Marla Glen song that was playing, the Brighton drugs underworld might suit his immediate purposes well.

Wearing a light mackintosh over his suit, he walked down through the lunchtime crowds starting to emerge from their offices, past cafés and sandwich bars and the Corn Exchange, and made a left turn into Marlborough Place, where he stopped, pretending to make a phone call. The area immediately to the north of here, and across the

London Road to the east, had long been the downtown domain of the street dealers.

It took him less than five minutes to spot two shabbily dressed men in a hurry, walking faster than everyone else, easy targets. He set off after them, but kept a good distance back. One was tall and thin, with rounded shoulders, and was wearing a windcheater over grey trousers and trainers. The shorter, stockier man, who was wearing a tracksuit top over shell-suit bottoms and black shoes, walked in a strange strutting motion, arms out wide, and was shooting a worried glance over his shoulder every few moments, as if to check he wasn't being followed.

The taller one carried a plastic bag, almost certainly with a can of lager inside it. Street drinking was illegal in the city, so most street people kept an open can in a plastic bag. They were walking really fast, either in a hurry to get money, in which case they were about to commit an offence – maybe a bag snatch, or some shop-lifting – or on their way to meet a dealer and buy their day's supply, Grace supposed. Or they could be dealers going to meet a customer.

Two single-decker red and yellow buses thundered past, followed by a Streamline taxi and then a line of private cars. Somewhere a siren wailed and both men's heads twitched. The stocky one only ever seemed to look over his right shoulder, so Grace kept to the left, close to the shop fronts, shielding himself behind people as much as he could.

The two men turned left into Trafalgar Street and now Grace was starting to feel even more certain about his hunch. Sure enough, in a couple of hundred yards they turned left and entered their destination.

Pelham Square was a small, elegant square of Regency

terraced houses, with a railed park in the centre. The benches near the Trafalgar Street entrance had always been a popular lunch spot for local office workers on fine days. Now, with the workplace smoking ban, they seemed even more popular. Few of the people eating their sandwiches or having a lunchtime cigarette took any notice of – or indeed even noticed – the ragbag assortment of people clustered around another bench at the far end of the park.

Grace leaned against a lamppost and observed them for some moments. Niall Foster was one of three people sitting on the bench, drinking beer like all the others from a concealed can in his carrier bag. A man in his early forties with a sullen, mean face beneath a strange haircut that looked like a monk's tonsure gone wrong, he was wearing a singlet, despite the chill breeze, over blue dungarees and workman's boots.

Grace knew him well enough. He was a burglar and a small-time drugs dealer. He'd be the one serving up now, for sure, to the sad group of people around him. Next to him on the bench was a grimy, strung-out-looking woman with matted brown hair. Beside her sat an equally grubby man in his thirties, who kept putting his head between his knees.

The two men he had been following walked up to Foster. It was a textbook *migration*. Foster would have told each of the users to meet him here, in this park, at this exact time. If he then became nervous that he was being watched, he would abort, leave the park, select a new location and phone each of his customers to come there instead. Sometimes there could be several such migrations before dealers felt comfortable. And often they would have a young assistant to do the serving up for them. But Foster was cheap, he probably didn't want to pay anyone. And besides, he knew the system. He was fully aware that he was small fry and would simply swallow the packets of whatever drug he was dealing, if challenged, and retrieve them from the lavatory later.

Niall Foster looked over in his direction and as Grace moved up the pavement, not wanting to be spotted, he found himself almost colliding head on with the man he had come to find.

It had been a few years, but even so Grace was shocked by how much the old villain had aged. Terry Biglow was a scion of one of Brighton's bottom-feeder crime families. The Biglows' history reached back to the razor gangs, who fought turf wars over protection rackets in the 1940s and 1950s, and there were plenty of people in Brighton and Hove who would once have been scared by the mere mention of the name. But now most of the older members of the family were dead, while the younger ones were either serving long prison sentences or were fugitives in Spain. The remnants still in the city, like Terry, were busted flushes.

Terry Biglow had started life as a knocker boy, then he had become a fence and sometime drugs dealer. He used to cut a mean, dapper figure, with a slick haircut brushed up in a quiff and cheap, sharp shoes. He must be in his mid to late sixties now, Grace thought, but he could have passed for a decade more.

The old rogue's hair was still tidily coiffed, but it looked greasy and threadbare, and had turned a listless grey. His rodent-like face was sallow and thin to the point of being emaciated, while his sharp little teeth were the colour of rust. He wore a shabby grey suit with the trousers fastened by a cheap belt far too high up his chest. He seemed to have shrunk several inches too and he smelled musty. The only signs of the original Terry Biglow were the big gold watch and a massive emerald ring.

'Mr Grace, Detective Sergeant Grace, nice to see yer! What a surprise!'

Actually not that much of a surprise, Roy Grace nearly said. But he was pleased at the ease with which it all seemed to be dropping into his lap on this visit downtown.

'It's Detective *Superintendent* now,' he corrected.

'Yeah, course it is! I was forgetting.' Biglow's voice was small and reedy. 'Promoted. I heard you was, yeah. You deserve it, Mr Grace. Sorry, sir, Detective – Detective Superintendent. I'm clean now. I found God in prison.'

'He was doing time too, was he?' Grace retorted.

'Don't do none of that stuff no more, sir,' Biglow said, deadly serious, completely missing – or ignoring – Grace's joke.

'So it's just coincidence you're standing outside the park while Niall Foster serves up inside, is it, Terry?'

'Total coincidence,' Biglow said, his eyes shiftier than ever. 'Yeah, coincidence, sir. Me and my friend – we're just on our way to lunch, just passing.'

Biglow turned to his companion, who was as shabbily dressed. Grace knew the man: Jimmy Bardolph, who used to be a henchman for the Biglows. But not any more, he imagined. The man stank of alcohol, his face was covered in scabs and his hair was awry. He didn't look as if he'd had a bath since his afterbirth had been washed off.

'This is my friend, Detective Superintendent Grace, Jimmy. He's a good man, always fair to me. He's a cop you can trust is Mr Grace.'

The man extended a veined, filthy hand from the overlong sleeve of his raincoat. 'Nice to meet yer, Officer. Perhaps you could help me?'

Ignoring it, Grace turned back to Biglow. 'I need to have a chat with you about an old friend of yours – Ronnie Wilson.'

'Ronnie!' Biglow exclaimed.

Out of the corner of his eye, Grace could see that Foster had very definitely clocked him now and was hot-footing it across the park. The dealer sidled out of the entrance, shot Grace a wary glance and set off down the street, half walking, half running, lifting his mobile phone to his ear as he went.

'Ronnie!' Biglow repeated. He gave Grace a wistful smile and shook his head. 'Dear old Ronnie. He's dead, you know that, don't you? God rest his soul.'

The fresh air was not doing it for Grace's headache, so he decided to follow Bella's earlier recommendation about hot, greasy food. 'Have you had lunch?' he asked.

'Nah, we was just on our way to dinner now.' Terry Biglow smiled suddenly, as if pleased with the alibi that had just presented itself. 'Yeah, you see, that's why Jimmy and I – why we is here. Just walking down to the café, it being a nice morning and that.'

'Good. Well, in that case, lead the way. I'm buying.'

He followed them down the street, Jimmy moving in jerky little steps, like a clockwork toy that needed rewinding, and into a workmen's café.

66

OCTOBER 2007

Abby heard the slam of a door. The front door. For an instant her hopes rose. Could it by some miracle be the caretaker?

Then she heard the squeak of the shoes. Saw his shadow first.

Ricky came into the bathroom like a thunderbolt and she felt the crack of his hand on her face. She flinched inside her bindings.

'You fucking little bitch!'

He slapped her again, even harder. She hardly recognized him. He was in disguise, wearing a blue baseball cap pulled low over his face, and dark glasses, and had a heavy beard and moustache. He stepped out of the room and she watched, through smarting eyes, as he picked up the bag in the hallway and emptied its contents on the floor.

A power drill fell out. A large pair of pincers. A hammer. A bag of hypodermic syringes. A razor-bladed block cutter.

'Which one would you like me to start with, bitch?'

A moan of terror yammered in her throat. She felt her insides loosening. She tried to signal with her eyes. To plead with him.

He put his face right in front of hers. 'Did you hear me?'

She tried to remember which way he had told her to move her eyes to signal *no*. Left. She moved them left.

He knelt and picked up the block cutter, bringing the blade tight up to her right eyeball. Then he turned it and pressed it flat, covering her eye. She could felt the cold steel against her brow. She began hyperventilating in terror.

'Shall I cut one of your eyes out? Take it with me? Would that work? It will be even darker then.'

She signalled *no* desperately. *No, no, no.*

'I could try, couldn't I? I could take it with me and see what happens.'

No, no, no.

'Very clever. Biometrics. *Iris recognition.* You think that's very smart, don't you? Lock it all away in a safe-deposit box that requires iris recognition to access. Well, how about I just cut your fucking eye out and take that with me, see if it recognizes it? If not, I'll come back for the other one.'

Again she signalled frantically. *No, no, no.*

'Of course, if that doesn't work we're both fucked, because you'll be blind and I'll be no better off. And you know that, don't you?'

Suddenly he removed the blade. Then, in one sudden movement, he ripped the tape away from her mouth.

She cried out in agony. It felt as if he had torn off half the skin on her face. She gulped air down her parched throat. Her face was on fire.

'Talk to me, bitch.'

Her voice came out as a croak. 'Please can I have some water? Please, Ricky.'

'Oh, that's wonderful!' he said. 'That's rich! You steal everything I have, make me chase you halfway around the world, and what's the first thing you have to say to me?'

He mimicked her voice. '"Oh, please, Ricky, can I have a glass of water?"' He shook his head. 'What would you like? Sparkling or plain? Tap or bottled? How about the toilet water you keep pissing in? Would that be OK? Would you like some ice and lemon in it?'

'Anything,' she croaked.

'I'll get you some in a minute,' he said. 'What you should have done is fill in the room service breakfast menu and hung it on the door last night. Then you'd have had everything you wanted this morning. But I guess you were a bit tied up, ripping your old love Ricky off.' He grinned. '*Tied up.* That's quite funny, isn't it?'

She said nothing, trying hard to think clearly, to make sure she said the right thing when she spoke and didn't antagonize him further. It was good, she thought, that he was letting her speak finally. She knew how desperately he wanted back what she had taken.

And he wasn't a fool.

He needed her. In his mind that was the only way he was going to get it. Whether he liked it or not, he was going to have to cut a deal with her.

Then he held up his mobile phone to her ear and pressed a button. A recording began to play. It lasted just a few seconds, but they were enough.

It was herself and her mother speaking. A phone conversation they had had on Sunday, she remembered clearly. She could hear her own voice talking.

'Listen, Mum, it won't be long now. I've been in touch with Cuckmere House. They've got a beautiful room with a view of the river coming free in a few weeks' time and I've reserved it. I've looked it up on the internet and it really does look lovely. And of course I'll come over and check it out and help you move in.'

Then Abby heard her mother replying. Mary Dawson, her brain sharp despite her crippling illness, retorted, 'And where are you going to get the money from, Abs? I've heard these places cost a fortune. Two hundred quid a day, some of them. More even.'

'Don't worry about the money, Mum, I'm taking care of it. I—'

The recording stopped abruptly.

'That's what I like about you, Abby,' Ricky said, pressing his glaring face up close to her own. 'You're all heart.'

67

OCTOBER 2007

The interior of the café was a fug of frying grease. Taking his seat opposite the two men, Grace reckoned that just breathing in here could raise anyone's cholesterol up to heart-attack levels. But he went ahead and ordered egg, bacon, sausage and chips, fried bread and a Coke, glad that neither Glenn Branson nor Cleo was around to chide him about his diet.

Terry Biglow ordered egg and chips, while his vacant friend, Jimmy, just ordered a cup of tea and kept giving Grace imploring looks, as if the Detective Superintendent was the only man on the planet who could save him from something that he didn't seem very clear about. Himself, most likely, Roy thought, watching him slip a half-bottle of Bells from his coat pocket and take a long swig, and clocking the prison tattoos on his knuckles. One dot for each year inside. He counted seven.

'I'm on the straight and narrow now, Mr Grace,' Terry Biglow suddenly said.

He had dots on his knuckles too, and the tail of a serpent on the back of his hand, its body disappearing up his sleeve.

'So you told me. Good.'

'Me brother's very ill. Pancreas cancer. Do you remember me uncle, Eddie, Mr Grace? Sorry, *Inspector* Grace?'

Grace did indeed, more clearly than he cared to. He had never forgotten taking a statement from one of Eddie Biglow's victims. His face had been ripped open in jagged lines by broken glass, down both sides from the hairline to the chin, because he had complained when Biglow barged in front of him at the bar of a pub.

'Yes,' he said. 'I remember him.'

'Actually,' Biglow went on, 'I've got a bit of cancer myself.'

'I'm sorry to hear that,' Grace said.

'Me tummy, you know?'

'Bad?' Grace asked.

Biglow shrugged, as if it was only minor. But there was fear in his eyes.

Jimmy nodded sagely and took another swig. 'I dunno who'll look after me when he's gone,' he whined to Grace. 'I need protecting.'

Grace gave him a cursory shrug with his eyebrows, then took his Coke from the waitress and immediately drank some. 'You and Ronnie Wilson were mates, weren't you, Terry?'

'Yeah, we was once, yeah.'

'Before you went to jail?'

'Yeah, before then. I took the rap for him, you know.' He stirred sugar into his tea wistfully. 'I did an' all.'

'You knew his wife?'

'Both his wives.'

'*Both?*' Grace said, surprised.

'Yeah. Joanna and then Lorraine.'

'When did he remarry?'

He scratched the back of his head. 'Cor, that was a few years after Joanna left him. She was a looker, Joanna was, a stonker! But I didn't like her much. Gold-digger, she was.

Latched on to Ronnie cos he was flash – but she didn't realize he didn't have much money.' He tapped the side of his nose. 'Not a good businessman, Ronnie. Always talked big, always had big schemes. But he didn't have – what's it called – the *nose*, the Midas touch. So when Joanna sussed that out, she legged it.'

'To where?'

'Los Angeles. Her mum died and she inherited a bit from the house. Ronnie woke up one morning and she was gone. Just left a note. Gone to try to make it in the movies as an actress.'

Their food arrived. Terry smothered his chips in vinegar, then shook out half the contents of the salt cellar on to them. Grace poured some brown sauce on to his plate, then picked up the tomato-shaped ketchup container. 'Who did she keep in touch with after she went to LA?'

Biglow shrugged and speared a chip with his fork. 'No one, I don't think. Wasn't no one down here liked her. None of us. My old lady couldn't stick her. And she didn't have no interest in making friends with us.'

'Was she from down here?'

'Nah, London. I think he met her at a lap-dancing place in London.'

Another chip met the same fate.

'What about his second wife?'

'Lorraine. She was all right. She was a good looker too. Took him a while to marry her – had to wait two years, I think, to get a divorce through from Joanna, cos of her desertion.'

Very difficult to get someone who is rotting in a storm drain to sign divorce papers, Grace thought.

'Where can I find Lorraine?'

Biglow gave him a strange look.

'I do need looking after, Mr Grace,' whined Jimmy again.

Biglow turned to his friend and pointed at his own face. 'See the lips moving? Means I'm still talking, so give it a rest, all right.' He turned to Grace. 'Lorraine. Yeah, well, if you want to find her you'll have to get yerself a boat and a deep-sea diving suit. She topped herself. Went overboard the Newhaven–Dieppe ferry one night.'

Grace suddenly lost all interest in his food. 'Tell me more.'

'She was depressed, in a terrible state after Ronnie died. He left her in a right old mess, financially like. The mortgage company took the house and the finance people took just about everything else, except for a few stamps.'

'Stamps?'

'Yeah, they was Ronnie's thing. Traded them all the time. Told me once he preferred them to cash, more portable.'

Grace thought for a moment. 'I thought I'd read that 9/11 victims' families got quite big compensation payments. Didn't she?'

'She never said nothing about that. She sort of became a recluse, you know, just kept her distance. Like retreated into a shell. When they took everything, she moved into a little rented flat down Montpelier Road.'

'When did she die?'

He thought for a moment. 'Yeah. It was November – 9/11 happened in 2001, so this would have been November 2002. Christmas was coming up. Know what I mean? Difficult time, Christmas, for some people. Jumped overboard from the ferry.'

'Was the body found?'

'I dunno.'

Grace made some notes, while Biglow ate. He picked at his own meal, his concentration now elsewhere. *One wife sets off to America and ends up in a storm drain in Brighton. The second jumps off a cross-Channel ferry.* A lot of questions were now filling his head. 'Did they have children?'

'Last time I saw Ronnie he said they was trying. But they was having fertility problems.'

Grace thought some more. 'Other than you, who were Ronnie Wilson's closest friends?'

'We wasn't that close. We was friends, but not close. There was old Donald Hatcook – Ronnie was with him, apparently, in his office on 9/11. Up in one of them towers of the World Trade Center. Donald made it big, poor bastard.' He thought for a moment. 'And Chad Skeggs. But he emigrated, didn't he, went to Australia.'

'Chad Skeggs?'

'Yeah.'

Grace remembered the name; the man had been in trouble years back, but he couldn't recall why.

'See, they've all gone. It would have been the Klingers here, I s'pose. Yeah, Steve and Sue Klinger, know them? Live in Tongdean.'

Grace nodded. The Klingers had an ostentatious house in Tongdean Avenue. Stephen had been, as the euphemism goes, a *person of interest to the police* for as long as Grace had been in the force. It was a widely held view that Klinger, who had started life as a car dealer, had not made his money legitimately and that his nightclubs, bars, coffee houses, student rental properties and moneylending businesses were all money-laundering fronts for his real business: drugs. But so far, at least, if he was a drugs overlord, he ran a tight ship and had ensured nothing could ever be traced back to him.

'Ronnie and he started out working together,' Biglow continued. 'Then they got into trouble over a bunch of clocked cars. I don't remember what happened exactly. The business disappeared overnight – the garage burned down with all the records. Sort of convenient. There weren't no charges never brought.'

Grace added Steve and Sue Klinger's names to the list of people to be interviewed by his team. Then he cut off a corner of fried bread and dunked it in an egg.

'Terry,' he said, 'what was your take on Ronnie?'

'How d'yer mean, Mr Grace?'

'What kind of a bloke was he?'

'Fucking psycho,' Jimmy chipped in suddenly.

'Shut it!' Biglow turned on him. 'Ronnie wasn't no psycho. But he had a temper, I'll grant you that.'

'He was a fucking psycho,' Jimmy insisted.

Biglow smiled at Grace. 'He was a little sick in the head at times, you know, sort of his own worst enemy. He was angry at the world cos he wasn't succeeding, not like some of his friends – know what I mean?'

Like you? Grace wondered privately. 'I think so.'

'Know what my dad said about him once?'

Grace, chewing on a piece of fatty sausage, shook his head.

'He said he was the kind of bloke who could follow you in through a turnstile and come out in front of you without having paid!' Biglow chuckled. 'Yeah, that was our Ronnie all right. God bless his soul!'

68

12 SEPTEMBER 2001

Ronnie was feeling a whole lot better now that he had money in his pocket again. In the left-hand pocket of his suit jacket, to be precise. *Holding folding,* he liked to call it. And he kept his left hand in there, holding the folded wad of crisp new one-hundred-dollar bills tightly, never once letting go, all the way back in the L-Train from midtown Manhattan to Brighton Beach station, where he got off.

Still without removing his hand, he walked the short distance back to Mail Box City and stashed five thousand and six hundred of those dollars safely away in his deposit box. Then he walked back along the street until he found a clothing store, where he bought a couple of white T-shirts, a change of socks and underpants, a pair of jeans and a lightweight bomber jacket. A short distance further along he went into a souvenir store and bought himself a black baseball cap emblazoned with the words BRIGHTON BEACH. Then he popped into a sports outfitters and bought a cheap pair of trainers.

He stopped at a stall to pick up a hot corned beef sandwich with a gherkin the size of a small melon and a Coke for his lunch, then returned to his rooming house. He punched on the television and changed into his new kit, putting all his old clothes into one of the plastic bags his new gear had come in.

He ate his sandwich watching television. There wasn't much that he hadn't seen on the news already, just recaps, images of George Bush declaring his War on Terrorism, and comments from other world leaders. Then images of joyous people in Pakistan, jumping up and down in the street, laughing, proudly displaying crude, anti-American banners.

Ronnie was actually feeling rather pleased with himself. His tiredness had gone and he was on a high. He had done something brave: he had ridden into the war zone and back out again. He was on a roll!

He finished his meal, then scooped up the bag containing his old clothes and headed out of the door. A short distance down the street, he crammed the bag into a stinking garbage can that was already nearly full to the brim with rotting foodstuff. Then, with a spring in his step, he made for the Moscow bar.

It was just as empty as yesterday, but he was pleased to see that his new best friend, Boris, was sitting on what looked like the same bar stool he had sat at yesterday, cigarette in hand, mobile phone pressed to his ear and a half-full bottle of vodka in front of him. All that was different was his T-shirt, which today was pink and carried the legend, in gold lettering, *Genesis World Tour.*

The same shrimp of a barman was there, wiping glasses with a dishcloth. He acknowledged Ronnie with a nod of recognition.

'You back,' he said in his broken English. 'Thought you maybe gone to help.' He pointed at the television screen. 'They needing volunteers,' he said. 'They needing people help dig bodies out. I thought maybe you gone to do that.'

'Maybe,' Ronnie said. 'Maybe I will do that.'

He hauled himself on to the bar stool next to his friend and waited for him to finish his call, which sounded like some kind of business deal, then slapped him on the back. 'Hey, Boris, how you doing?'

Ronnie received a resounding thump in return, which felt like it had dislodged several of his fillings.

'My friend! How you doing? You found the place last night? It was OK?'

'It was fine.' Ronnie leaned down and scratched a particularly itchy bite on his ankle. 'Terrific. Thank you.'

'Good. For my friend from Canada, nothing is too much trouble.'

Without any prompt, the barman produced a shot glass and Boris immediately filled it to the brim.

Holding it daintily between his finger and thumb, Ronnie raised it to the level of his lips. '*Carpe diem!*' he said.

The vodka went down well. It had a lemon flavour, which he found instantly addictive. The second one went down even better.

The Russian waved an admonishing hand in front of Ronnie's face, then he raised his glass, staring Ronnie in the eye, the rubble in his mouth formed into a smile. 'Remember yesterday, what I tell you, my friend?'

'What was that?'

'When you toast in Russia, you drink entire glass. All way down. Like this!' Boris drained the glass.

*

Two hours later, after exchanging more and more outrageous stories about their backgrounds, Ronnie was reeling, barely able to remain on the bar stool. Boris seemed to have fingers in a range of dubious activities, which included importing fake designer-brand perfumes and colognes, fixing green cards for Russian immigrants, and acting as some kind of middleman for Russian hookers who wanted to work in America. Not a pimp, he assured Ronnie. No, no, absolutely, one hundred per cent not a pimp.

Then suddenly he put an arm around Ronnie and said, 'I know, my friend, you are in trouble. I help you! There is nothing I can't help you with!'

Ronnie saw to his horror that Boris was refilling the glasses yet again. The television screen was going in and out of focus. Could he trust this guy? He was going to have to trust someone and, at least to his addled brain at this moment, Boris did not seem like a bloke to make moral judgements.

'Actually,' he said, 'I need another favour.'

The Russian didn't take his eyes from the television screen, where Mayor Giuliani was talking.

'For my Canadian friend, any favour. What I can do?'

Ronnie removed his baseball cap and leaned closer, lowering his voice to a whisper.

'Do you know anyone who could create a new passport – and a visa?'

The Russian gave him a stern look. 'What you think this place is? An embassy? This just a bar, man. OK?'

Ronnie was shaken by the man's vehemence, but then the Russian gave him a broad grin.

'Passport and visa. Of course. Don't you worry. Whatever you want, I fix for you. You want passport, visa, no problem. I got a friend can fix this. He can fix you anything. So long you got money?'

'How much money?'

'Depends how difficult the visa. I give you his name. Me, I don't want nothing, OK?'

'You're very kind.'

The Russian then raised his glass. '*Carpe diem!*'

'*Carpe diem!*' Ronnie replied.

The rest of the afternoon became a complete blur.

69

OCTOBER 2007

Abby peered numbly through the windscreen of the grey rental Ford Focus. She hadn't thought it possible for the nightmare to worsen, but now it had.

There was a broad stretch of clear blue sky over them as they headed up the A27 Brighton bypass, with Patcham to their right and rolling open downland countryside to their left. Freedom, she thought, still a prisoner, although her bonds had been removed and she was now in jeans, a pullover and fleece jacket and trainers. The grass looked lush and green from all the recent heavy rain, and if it hadn't been for the whirr of the car's heater fan blowing in welcome warm air, it could have been summer outside with that sky. But inside her heart, it was darkest winter.

To have got that recording, she realized, he must have bugged her mother's phone.

Seated beside her, Ricky drove in angry silence, careful to keep within the speed limit, not taking any risks of getting stopped. It was an anger that had been simmering for two long months. The slip road was coming up ahead. He moved the indicator stalk. He'd already been here once this morning, he knew the way. She listened to the steady tick-tick-tick and watched the light winking on the dash.

Now she'd drunk some water and eaten a hunk of bread and a banana she was feeling more human and could think more clearly, despite being sick with fear for her mother – and for herself. How had Ricky found her mother? Presumably the same way he had found her, whatever that was. She was racking her brains, trying to think if she had left some clue back in Melbourne. How the hell could he have got her address? Not that difficult, she supposed. He knew her last name and she had probably mentioned at some point that her widowed mother now lived in Eastbourne. How many Dawsons were there in the Eastbourne phone directory? Probably not that many. Certainly not to a determined man.

He wasn't answering any questions.

Her mother was a defenceless woman. Almost crippled by multiple sclerosis, she was still just about mobile, but not for much longer. And although she was fiercely independent, she had no physical strength. An infant could have overpowered her, which made her extremely vulnerable to any intruder, yet she flatly refused to wear a panic button. Abby knew that a neighbour looked in on her occasionally and she had a friend she went to bingo with on Saturday evenings. Other than that, she was alone.

Now Ricky had her address and, knowing what a sadist he was, that frightened her more than anything. She had the feeling he wouldn't be content with just getting everything back; he would want to hurt her and her mother too. He would know, from the conversations they'd had in Australia when she had opened up to him, trying to gain his confidence, the love she felt for her mother, and her guilt at abandoning her, moving to the other side of the world, just when she needed Abby the most. He would *enjoy* hurting her mother to get at her.

They were now approaching a small roundabout. He took the second right turn off it and started going down a hill. To their right was a view for several miles across fields and housing estates. To their left was the Hollingbury industrial estate, a sprawling cluster of superstores, 1950s factories and warehouses converted into offices, and modern industrial units. One of the buildings, partially obscured from their view by an ASDA supermarket, was the headquarters of Sussex CID, but Abby did not know that. Even if she had, she could not take the risk of going in there. Regardless of what Ricky had done to get his money, she was a thief. She had stolen a great deal from him, and just because the person you stole from was a criminal, that did not exonerate your behaviour.

Besides, if they blew the whistle on each other, they would lose everything. They were in a kind of Mexican standoff at the moment. But equally she knew that if she did give him back what he wanted, there was no good reason for him to keep her alive. And plenty not to.

She saw a massive edifice carrying the sign, BRITISH BOOKSHOPS, then the *Argus* building, a Matalan sign, then they passed a Renault dealership. Almost missing the turn, Ricky cursed, braked sharply and swung the wheel, making the tyres squeal. He drove too quickly down a sharp incline, then had to bring the car to an abrupt halt inches from a truck-sized Volvo, with a tiny woman behind the wheel, which had pulled straight out of the car park in front of a row of stores.

'Stupid fucking cow,' he mouthed at her, and the woman responded by tapping the side of her head. For a moment Abby thought – hoped – that he was going to get out of the car and start a barney.

Instead the Volvo roared off and they drove on down the incline, past the car park and the rear of a warehouse. Then they went through a gateway with massive steel doors and large CCTV warning signs on either pillar, into a yard where there were several armoured cash-transporter vans and trucks parked. Each was in a distinctive livery of black paint with gold lettering showing a shield interwoven with a chain and the name SOUTHERN DEPOSIT SECURITY.

Then they headed towards a single-storey, modern building with tiny slit-like windows that gave it the air of a fortress. Which is what it was.

Ricky parked in a bay marked VISITORS and switched off the engine. Then he turned to Abby.

'Try anything clever and your mother's dead. You understand that?'

She choked out a terrified, 'Yes.'

And all the time she was thinking. Trying to plan in her mind how she was going to play this. Trying to visualize the next few minutes. Doing her best to think it through, to remind herself of her strengths.

So long as she had what he wanted, he was going to have to negotiate. It didn't matter how much he blustered, that was the truth of the matter. That had kept her alive and intact until now, no question about it. With luck, it was what would keep her mother alive. She hoped.

She did have a plan, but she hadn't thought it through, and it all started coming unstitched inside her head as she climbed out of the car. She suddenly became a jelly, a bag of quivering nerves, and had to grip the roof of the car for a moment, almost certain she was going to throw up.

After a couple of minutes, when she felt a bit better, Ricky took her arm and they walked to the entrance, like any couple coming to make a deposit, or a withdrawal, or just to check out the family silver. But as she shot him a sideways stony glance, she felt revulsion, wondering how she had ever stooped to do all she had done with him.

She pressed the entryphone buzzer beneath the imperious gaze of two CCTV cameras and gave her name. Moments later the door clicked open and they passed through two sets of security doors into an austere foyer that gave the impression it had been hewn from granite.

Two burly, unsmiling uniformed security guards stood just inside the door, and two more manned the counter behind a glass shield. She walked up to one of them and spoke through the perforations, wondering, suddenly, whether to try to signal distress to him, then thinking better of it.

'Katherine Jennings,' she said in a shaky voice. 'I want to access my safe-deposit box.'

He pushed a register under the bottom of the shield. 'Please fill this in. Are both of you going in?'

'Yes.'

'I'll need both of you to fill it in, please.'

Abby filled in her name, the date and the time, then handed the register to Ricky, who did the same. When he had finished, he pushed it back under the shield and the guard typed into a terminal. Some moments later, he pushed printed name tags, encased in plastic and with lapel clips, across the counter.

'You know what to do?' he asked Abby.

She nodded and walked to the security door to the right of the counter. Then she put her right eye up close to the biometric retinal scanner and pressed the green button.

After some moments the lock clicked. She pushed the heavy door open, held it for Ricky and they both went through. There was a cement staircase in front of them. She went down, hearing Rick's steps close behind her. At the bottom there was a massive steel door with a second biometric scanner. She placed her right eye up close and again pressed the green button. There was a sharp click and she pushed this door open.

They entered a long, narrow, icily cold vault. It was a good hundred feet long and twenty feet wide, lined floor-to-ceiling on both sides and at the far end with steel safe-deposit boxes, each bearing a number.

The ones on the right were six inches deep, the ones on the left were two feet deep and the ones at the far end were six feet high. She wondered again, as she had the last time she came here, just what exactly might be in those, and indeed what treasures, legally obtained or otherwise, might be behind any of these locked doors.

Holding the key, Ricky greedily scanned the numbers on the boxes. 'Four-two-six?' he said.

She pointed, down towards the far end, on the left, and watched as he almost ran the last few yards.

Then he slipped the thin, flat key into the vertical slot and gave it a tentative twist. He could feel the cam of the well-oiled lock revolving smoothly. He turned the key through one complete revolution, listening for each of the pins moving in turn. He liked locks, always had, and understood how most of them worked. He gave the key a pull, but the door did not move. It had a more complex mechanism inside than he'd imagined, he realized, turning the key another complete revolution and sensing more pins moving. He pulled again.

Now the heavy metal door swung open and he peered inside. To his utter astonishment, it was empty.

He spun around, swearing loudly at Abby. And found himself swearing at an empty room.

70

OCTOBER 2007

Abby sprinted. She had run most mornings in Melbourne and, despite having done little exercise in the past couple of months, she was still in reasonable shape.

She ran flat out without looking back, across the tarmac parking area of Southern Deposit Security, past the vans and trucks, out through the gates and up the hill. Then, just before she turned right through the shrubbery lining the car park by the row of stores, she shot a glance over her shoulder.

Ricky had not appeared yet.

She trampled through the bushes, only to narrowly avoid being struck by a people carrier driven by a harassed-looking woman as she dashed across the lanes of the car park towards the front entrance of an MFI store. She stopped when she reached it and looked back.

Still no sign of him.

She entered the building, briefly aware of the distinct, rich smell of new furniture, and raced through it, dodging around customers as she passed showroom displays of office furniture, living-room furniture, bedroom furniture. She found herself, almost at the rear of the store, in the bathroom section. There were showers all around her. A classy looking walk-in one to her right.

She looked back down the aisle. No Ricky.

Her heart was crashing around as if it had broken loose inside her chest. She was still holding the plastic Southern Deposit Security identity tag in her hand. Ricky had not allowed her to take her handbag with her from the flat, but she had managed to conceal her mobile phone, by stuffing it down her front, with some cash and her credit card, as well as a key to her mother's flat. She'd switched the phone off just in case, by a billion to one chance, it rang. Now she retrieved it and switched it back on. As soon as it powered up, she rang her mother's number.

No answer. She had begged her mother for months to get voicemail, but she still had not done anything about it. After numerous rings, the tone turned to a flat whine. She tried again.

There was a slatted wooden bench in one of the walk-in showers, flipped up against the wall. She went into it, pulled the bench down and sat holding the phone to her ear, listening to the unanswered ringing. Thinking. Thinking.

She was in total panic.

All her stalling tactics were now exhausted. She had not thought this through. She wasn't capable of thinking anything through at the moment. All she could do was run on autopilot, dealing with one minute at a time.

Ricky had threatened to harm her mother. A sick, elderly lady. Her bargaining power was that she still had in her possession the riches Ricky desperately wanted. She needed to keep reminding herself that she held all the nuts.

Ricky could bluster all he wanted.

I hold everything he wants.

Except . . .

She sank her face into her hands. She wasn't dealing with someone normal. Ricky was more like a machine.

The voice almost made her jump out of her skin.

'Are you OK? Can I help you, madam?'

A young assistant in a suit and tie, with a lapel badge giving his name as Jason, was standing at the entrance to the shower. She looked up at him.

'I – I . . .'

He had a kind face and suddenly she felt close to tears. Thinking rapidly, a half-formed plan vaguely taking shape, sounding as weak as she could, she said, 'I don't feel very well. Is it possible someone could call me a taxi?'

'Yeah, of course.' He looked at her in concern. 'Would you rather an ambulance?'

She shook her head. 'No, a taxi, thanks. I'll be fine when I get home. I just need to lie down.'

'We have a staff rest area,' he said in a sympathetic voice. 'Would you like to go there and wait?'

'Yes, thank you. Thank you very much.'

Glancing around warily for any sight of Ricky, she followed him through a side door and into a tiny canteen, where there was a row of chairs against the wall with a low table in front of them, some tea- and coffee-making equipment, a small fridge and a biscuit tin.

'Would you like anything?' he asked. 'Some water?'

'Water,' she said, nodding her head.

'I'll phone a taxi, then I'll get you some water.'

'Do you have a side entrance it could come to? I – I'm not sure I could make it all the way back through the store.'

He pointed at a door she hadn't noticed, which had an illuminated FIRE EXIT sign above it.

'Staff entrance,' he said. 'I'll tell it to come there.'

'You're very kind.'

*

Ten minutes later, Jason came to tell her the taxi was outside. She drained the last of her water, then, acting the part of the sick lady, walked slowly out through the door and climbed into the rear of a turquoise and white Streamline taxi, thanking the young assistant again for his kindness.

The driver, an elderly man with a shock of white hair, closed the door for her.

She gave him the address of her mother's flat in Eastbourne before sinking down low in her seat, so she could just see out but hopefully not be seen, and pulling her jacket up over her head.

'Like me to put the heating up higher?' the driver asked.

'I'm fine, thanks,' she replied.

She looked hard for Ricky or the rental Ford as they drove out through the car park. No sign of him. Then, at the top of the incline, as they reached the junction with the main road, she saw the car. The driver's door was open and Ricky was standing beside it looking around. His face, beneath his baseball cap, was a mask of fury.

She shrank down, below the level of the window, and covered her head completely with her jacket. Then she waited until she felt the taxi pulling away, making a right turn up the hill, before sitting far enough up to be able to see out of the rear window. Ricky was looking away from her, scanning the car park.

'Please go as quickly as you can,' she said. 'I'll give you a good tip.'

'I'll do my best,' the driver said.

She heard classical music playing on the radio. Something she recognized: Verdi's 'Chorus of the Hebrew Slaves'. Ironically, this was one of her mother's favourite pieces. A curious coincidence. Or was it a sign?

She believed in omens, always had. She had never bought into her parents' religious convictions, but she had always been superstitious. How strange it was that this was playing, right at this moment.

'Nice music,' she said.

'I can turn it down.'

'No, please, turn it up.'

The driver obliged.

She dialled her mother's number again. As it started ringing, she heard the insistent beep of an incoming call. Which could only be one of two people. The wording *Private number* appeared.

She hesitated. Tried to think clearly. Could it be her mother? Unlikely, but . . .

But . . .

She continued hesitating. Then she accepted the call.

'OK, bitch, very funny! Where are you?'

She hung up. Shaking. The sick feeling back in the pit of her stomach.

The phone rang again. Same *Private number*. She killed it.

And again.

Then she realized she could play this a lot more cleverly and waited for it to ring again.

But it remained silent.

71

13 SEPTEMBER 2001

Nothing in his life prepared Ronnie for the devastation that lay ahead of him as he made his way from the subway station towards the vicinity of the World Trade Center. He'd thought he had some idea of what it might be like from all he had seen on Tuesday with his own eyes, and on television subsequently, but experiencing it now was shaking him to the core.

It was just past noon. His hangover from his drinking binge with Boris yesterday wasn't helping and the smell of the dusty air was making him very queasy. It was the same rank stench that he'd woken up to in Brooklyn these past two days, but far stronger here. A slow line of emergency and military vehicles moved down the street. A siren wailed in the distance and there was a constant cacophony of roaring and clattering from helicopters hovering what seemed like just feet above the tops of the skyscrapers on either side of him.

At least the time he had invested in his new best friend had not been in vain. Indeed, he was beginning to look upon him as his local Mr Fixit. The forger Boris had recommended lived just a ten-minute walk from his new lodgings. Ronnie had been expecting to enter dingy, back-street premises and find a wizened old man with an eye-piece and inky fingers. Instead, in a smart, bland office in a modernized walk-up, he had met a good-looking, expensively suited and very pleasant Russian man of no more than thirty, who could have passed for a banker or a lawyer.

For five thousand dollars, fifty per cent in advance, which Ronnie had handed over, he was going to provide Ronnie with the passport and the visa he wanted. Which left Ronnie with about three thousand dollars net. Enough to tide him over for a while, if he was careful. Hopefully the stamp market might recover soon, although the world stock markets were still in freefall today, according to the morning news.

But all this was small beer compared to the riches that awaited him if his plan succeeded.

A short distance ahead there was a barrier across the road, with the bar raised for the convoy of vehicles to pass through. Two young soldiers manned it, facing his way. They wore dusty combat fatigues and GI helmets, and were holding machine guns in an aggressive stance, as if they were intending to find something to shoot at soon in the new War on Terrorism.

A crowd of what looked like tourists, among them a group of young Japanese teenagers, stood staring, taking photographs of just about everything – the dust-coated store fronts, the sheets of paper and flakes of ash that lay ankle deep in places on the street. There seemed to be even more grey dust than on Tuesday, but the ghosts were less grey. They looked more like people today. People in shock.

A woman in her late thirties with matted brown hair, wearing a smock and flip-flops, with tears streaming down her cheeks, was weaving in and out of the crowd, holding up a photograph of a tall, good-looking man in a shirt and tie, saying nothing, just looking at each person in turn, silently imploring one of them to give a sudden nod of recognition. *Yeah, I remember that guy, I saw him, he was fine, he was heading . . .*

Just before he reached the soldiers, he saw on his left a hoarding with dozens of photographs taped to it. Most were close-ups of faces, a few of them mounted on Stars and Stripes backgrounds. They had clear cellophane wrapped round to rainproof them and all bore a name and handwritten messages, the most common of which was: HAVE YOU SEEN THIS PERSON?

'I'm sorry, sir, you can't go past here.' The voice was polite but firm.

'I've come down to work on the pile,' Ronnie said, putting on a phoney American accent. 'I heard they're needing volunteers.' He looked at the soldiers quizzically, glancing warily at their guns. Then, in a choked voice, he said, 'I got family – in the South Tower on Tuesday.'

'You and most of New York, buddy,' said the older of the soldiers. He gave Ronnie a smile, a kind of helpless, we're-all-in-this-shit-together smile.

A backhoe excavator, followed by a bulldozer, rumbled through the barrier.

The other soldier pointed a finger down the street. 'Make a left, first left, you'll see a bunch of tents. They'll kit you out, tell you what to do. Be lucky.'

'Yeah,' Ronnie said. 'You too.'

He ducked under the barrier and, after only a few more strides, the whole vista of the devastated area started opening up before him. It reminded him of pictures he had once seen of Hiroshima after the atomic bomb.

He turned left, unsure of his bearings, and followed the street for a short distance. Then, ahead of him, the Hudson suddenly appeared, and right by the river he saw a whole makeshift encampment of stalls and tents at the edge of a massive area of rubble.

He walked past an upturned sports utility vehicle. A shredded fireman's jacket lay on the ground near it, yellow bands on the grey, dusty, empty uniform. One sleeve had been ripped off and lay some distance from it. A fireman in a dusty blue T-shirt, sitting on a small mound of rubble, was holding his head in one hand, a water bottle in the other, looking as if he couldn't take much more.

In a momentary respite from the helicopters, Ronnie heard new sounds: the roar of lifting gear, the whine of angle cutters, drills, bulldozers, and the intermittent warble, wails and shrieks of mobile phones. He saw an ant-line of people, many in uniforms and hard hats, entering the cluster of tents. Others were queuing at stalls made from trestle tables. There were new smells here too, of spit-roasted chicken and burgers.

In a daze, he suddenly found himself in line, passing a stall where someone handed him a bottle of water. At the next stall he received a face mask. Then he went into a tent, where a smiling, long-haired guy who looked like a superannuated hippie, handed him a blue hard hat, a torch and a spare supply of batteries.

Cramming his baseball cap into his pocket, Ronnie put on his face mask and then the hard hat. He passed another stall, where he declined an offer of socks, underwear and work boots, and continued out of the rear entrance. Then he followed the ant-line past the blackened shell of a building. An NYPD cop in a hard hat and a filthy blue stab vest trundled past on a green tractor, towing what looked like plastic body bags.

Beyond a blackened leafy tree, Ronnie saw a bird flying above a skeleton in the sky. One massive wall of a structure rose at a precarious angle, like the Leaning Tower of Pisa, all the glass gone from the windows, which were still otherwise intact, and the forty or fifty floors of offices that should have been beside it gone, collapsed.

He was stumbling over the roofs of smashed police cars and then across the underbelly of a half-buried fire truck. Every now and then from somewhere under the rubble there was the sound of a mobile phone ringing. Small teams of people were digging frantically and shouting. Dog handlers were dotted around, with German Shepherds, Labradors, Rottweilers and other breeds he didn't recognize straining on their leashes, sniffing.

He continued forward, passing a swivel chair covered in dust, with an equally dusty woman's jacket slung over the back. There was a telephone handset on a cord entwined around it, dangling from the seat.

He saw something glinting. Looking closer, he realized it was a wedding band. Near it he saw a smashed wrist watch. Chains of people were pulling out pieces of rubble, passing them back. He stepped aside, watching, taking it all in, trying to understand the pattern of what was going on. Eventually he realized there was no real pattern. There were just people in uniforms around the edges, holding huge black garbage sacks that people were bringing things they found to.

In front of him he saw what at first he thought was a broken waxwork. Then he realized, to his revulsion, that it was a severed human hand. He felt his breakfast rising up his throat. He turned away and swigged some of his water, feeling the dry dust dissolving in his mouth.

He noticed a sign painted in red on a brown hoarding at the edge of the devastation. It read GOD BLESS FDNY & NYPD.

Again there were all kinds of drained-looking people stumbling around the perimeter of the site, holding up photographs. Men, women, children, some of them small kids, mingling with all the different uniformed rescue services in helmets, masks, respirators.

He walked past a burnt cross, having to concentrate to keep his balance on the shifting mass beneath him. He saw a crane bent like a dead T. Rex. Two men in green surgical scrubs. He passed an NYPD officer in a blue helmet with a miner's lamp, and what looked like mountaineering gear slung from his belt, cutting into the rubble with a motorized angle grinder.

A Stars and Stripes flag leaned out of the rubble at a drunken angle, as if someone had just conquered this place.

It was total and utter chaos. And seemingly uncoordinated.

It was perfect, Ronnie thought.

He glanced over his shoulder. The long ant-line stretched, never-ending, behind him. He stepped aside, letting it continue past him, and moved further away. Then, surreptitiously, and with some small regret, he dropped his mobile phone on to the rubble and trod it in. He stamped on it and took a few steps forward. Next, he pulled his wallet out of his jacket and checked through it, removing the dollar bills and jamming them in the rear pocket of his jeans.

He left his five credit cards, his RAC membership card, his Brighton and Hove Motor Club membership card and, after some moments of thought, his driving licence as well.

Unsure whether he could smoke here or not, he discreetly put a cigarette in his mouth, pulled out his lighter and cupped his hands over the flame. But instead of lighting his cigarette, he began singeing the edges of his wallet. Then he dropped that into the rubble also and stamped it in, hard.

Then he lit his cigarette and smoked it gratefully. When he had finished, he ducked down and retrieved his wallet. Then he retraced his steps and picked up his mobile phone. He carried them across to one of the makeshift repositories for recovered items.

'I found these,' he said.

'Just drop them in the bag. All gonna be gone through,' an NYPD woman officer told him.

'They might help identify someone,' he said, just to be certain they took notice.

'That's what we're here for,' she assured him. 'We gotta lotta people missing from Tuesday. Lotta people.'

Ronnie nodded. 'Yep.' Then, to further double-check, he pointed at the bag. 'Someone's logging everything?'

'You bet. All gonna be logged, honey. Every damned item. Every shoe, every belt buckle. Anything you can find out there, you just hand it in.'

'All of us got family in there – somewhere,' the officer continued, waving her hand expansively at the devastation in front of them. 'Every damn person in this city got a loved one in there.'

Ronnie nodded and moved away. It had been much easier than he had thought.

72

OCTOBER 2007

'Here,' Abby said. 'Just past the lamppost on the left.' She glanced again over her shoulder out of the rear window. No sign of Ricky's car or him. But it was possible he could have come a quicker route, she thought. 'Could you drive past, turn left and go around the block, please.'

The taxi driver obliged. It was a quiet, residential area, close to Eastbourne College. Abby scanned the streets and parked cars carefully. To her relief, she could see no sign of Ricky's rental car or him.

The driver brought her back into the wide street of semi-detached red-brick houses, at the end of which, totally out of character with the area, was the 1960s low-rise block of flats where her mother lived. It had been built cheaply at the time and four decades of battering from the salty Channel winds had turned it into an eyesore.

The driver double-parked alongside an old Volvo estate. The meter was reading thirty-four pounds. She handed the driver two twenty-pound notes.

'I need your help,' she said. 'I'm giving you this now just so you know I'm not doing a runner on you. Don't give me any change, I want you to keep the meter running.'

He nodded, giving her a worried look. She shot another glance over her shoulder, but still she wasn't sure.

'I'm going inside the building. If I don't come back out

in five minutes, OK, exactly *five minutes,* I want you to dial 999 and get the police here. Tell them I'm being attacked in there.'

'Want me to come in with you?'

'No, I'm OK, thanks.'

'You got boyfriend troubles? Husband?'

'Yes.' She opened the door and climbed out, looking back down the street. 'I'm going to give you my mobile number. If you see a grey Ford Focus – a four-door, clean-looking, with a bloke in it wearing a baseball cap, call me as quickly as you can.'

It took him several agonizing moments to find his pen, then, with the slowest handwriting she had ever seen, he began jotting down the numbers.

Once he'd finished, she hurried to the entrance door of the building, unlocked it and went into the dingy communal hallway. It felt strange being back here again – nothing seemed to have changed. The linoleum on the floor, which looked as if it had been there since the building was put up, was immaculately clean, as ever, and the same metal pigeonholes were there for mail, with what could even have been the same pizza, Chinese, Thai and Indian takeaway advertising leaflets poking out of several of them. There was a strong reek of polish and of boiled vegetables.

She looked at her mother's mail box, to see if it had been emptied, and to her dismay saw several envelopes wedged into it, as if there was no further room inside. One of them, almost hanging out, was a Television Licence Renewal reminder.

The post was one of the highlights of her mother's day. She was a competition fanatic, subscribing to a number of magazines that included them, and she had always been good at them. Several of Abby's childhood treats and even holidays had been from competitions her mother had won and half the things her mother now owned were prizes.

So why had she not yet collected her post?

With her heart in her mouth, Abby hurried along the hallway to the door of her mother's flat at the rear of the building. She could hear the sound of a television on in another flat somewhere above her. She knocked on the door, then opened it with her key without waiting for a reply.

'Hi, Mum!'

She heard the sound of voices. A weather report.

She raised her voice. 'Mum!'

God, it felt strange. Over two years since she had been here. She was well aware of the shock her mother was going to get, but she couldn't worry about that now.

'Abby?' Her mother's voice sounded utterly astonished.

She hurried in, through the tiny hallway and into the sitting room, barely noticing the smell of damp and body odour. Her mother was on the couch, thin as a rake, her hair lank and greyer than she remembered, wearing a floral dressing gown and pompom slippers. She had a rose-patterned tray, which Abby remembered from her childhood, balanced on her knees. An open tin of rice pudding sat on it.

Torn-out newspaper and magazine competitions were spread all over the carpeted floor, and the lunchtime weather forecast was on the Sony wide-screen television, which Abby recalled her winning, perched clumsily on a metal drinks trolley, which was another prize.

The tray crashed to the floor. Her mother looked as if she had seen a ghost.

Abby ran across the room and threw her arms around her mother.

'I love you, Mum,' she said. 'I love you so much.'

Mary Dawson had always been a small woman, but now she seemed even smaller than Abby remembered, as if she had shrunk during these past two years. Though she still had a pretty face, with beautiful pale blue eyes, she was much more wrinkled than last time Abby had seen her. She hugged her tightly, tears streaming down her face, wetting her mother's hair that smelled unwashed, but smelled of her mother.

After her father had died, horribly but mercifully quickly from prostate cancer ten years ago, Abby had hoped for a while that her mother might find someone else. But when the disease was diagnosed, that hope went.

'What's going on, Abby?' her mother quizzed, then added, with a sudden twinkle, 'Are we going to be on *This Is Your Life*? Is that why you're here?'

Abby laughed. Then, clutching her mum tightly, realized it had been a long, long time since she had last laughed. 'I don't think it's on any more.'

'No prizes on that show, Abby dear.'

Abby laughed again. 'I've missed you, Mum!'

'I miss you too, my darling, all the time. Why didn't you tell me you were coming back from Australia? When did you get home? If I'd known you were coming I'd have tidied myself up!'

Suddenly remembering the time, Abby glanced at her watch. Three minutes had elapsed. She jumped up. 'I'll be back in a sec!'

She hurried outside, looking warily each way up and down the street, then went over to the taxi and opened the front passenger door. 'I'll be a few more minutes, but the same applies. Call me if you see him.'

'If he turns up, miss, I'll beat the crap out of him!'

'Just call me!'

She returned to her mother.

'Mum, I can't explain it all now. I want to call a locksmith and get a new lock put on your door, and a safety chain and a spyhole. I want to try to get it done today.'

'What's going on, Abby? What is it?'

Abby went over to the phone and picked up the cradle, turning it upside down. She didn't know what a bug looked like, but she could see nothing underneath it. Then she looked at the handset and couldn't see anything wrong with that either. But what did she know?

'Do you have any other phones?' she asked.

'You're in trouble, aren't you? What is it? I'm your mum, tell me!'

Abby knelt down and picked up the tray, then went to the kitchen to find a cloth to clear up the spilt rice pudding.

'I'm going to buy you a new phone, a mobile. Please don't use this one any more.'

As she started wiping the mess off the carpet, she realized it was the old carpet from the sitting room at their home in Hollingbury. It was a deep red colour, with a wide border of entwined roses in green, ochre and brown, and was frayed to the point of baldness in some patches. But it was comforting to see it, taking her back to her childhood.

'What is it, Abby?'

'Everything's OK.'

Her mother shook her head. 'I may be a sick woman, but I'm not stupid. You're frightened. If you can't tell your old mum, who can you tell?'

'Please just do what I say. Have you got a *Yellow Pages*?'

'In the middle drawer of the bottom half,' her mother said, pointing at a walnut tallboy.

'I'll explain everything later, but I don't have time now. OK?' She went over and found the directory. It was a few years out of date, but that probably didn't matter, she decided, flipping it open and leafing through until she found the *Locksmith* section.

She made the call, then told her mother someone would be here later this afternoon from Eastbourne Lockworks.

'Are you in trouble, Abby?'

She shook her head, not wanting to alarm her mother too much. 'I think someone is stalking me – someone who wanted me to go out with him, and he's trying to get to me through you, that's all.'

Her mother gave her a long look, as if showing she didn't fully believe the story. 'Still with that fellow Dave?'

Abby replaced the cloth in the kitchen sink, then came back and kissed her mother. 'Yes.'

'He didn't sound a good 'un to me.'

'He's been kind to me.'

'Your father – he was a good man. He wasn't ambitious, but he was a good person. He was a wise man.'

'I know he was.'

'Remember what he used to say? He used to laugh at me doing the competitions and tell me that life wasn't about getting what you wanted. It was about wanting what you have.' She looked at her daughter. 'Do you want what you have?'

Abby blushed. Then she kissed her mother again on both cheeks. 'I'm close. I'll be back with a new phone within the hour. Are you expecting anyone today?'

Her mother thought for a moment. 'No.'

'The friend of yours, the neighbour upstairs who pops by sometimes?'

'Doris?'

'Do you think she could come and sit with you until I get back?'

'I may be sick, but I'm not a total invalid,' her mother said.

'It's in case *he* comes.'

Again her mother gave her a long look. 'Don't you think you should tell me the full story?'

'Later, I promise. What flat is she in?'

'Number 4, on the first floor.'

Abby hurried out and ran up the stairs. Emerging on the first-floor hallway, she found the flat and rang the bell.

Moments later she heard the clumsy rattle of a safety chain and wished that her mother had one of those right now. Then the door was opened a few inches by a statuesque white-haired woman, with distinguished features that were partly obscured by a pair of dark glasses the size and shape of a snorkelling mask. She was dressed in an elegant knitted two-piece.

'Hello,' she said in a very posh accent.

'I'm Abby Dawson – Mary's daughter.'

'Mary's daughter! She talks so much about you. I thought you were still in Australia.' She opened the door wider and peered closer, putting her face almost inches from Abby's. 'Excuse me,' she said. 'I have macular degeneration – I can only see well out of one corner of my eye.'

'I'm sorry,' Abby said. 'You poor thing.' Abby felt she should be more sympathetic but she was anxious to press on. 'Look, I wonder if you could do me a favour. I have to dash out for an hour and – it's a long story – but there's an old boyfriend who's making my life hell, and I'm worried he might turn up and abuse Mum. Is there any chance you could sit with her until I get back?'

'Of course. Would you prefer she came up here?'

'Well, yes, but she's expecting the locksmith.'

'OK, don't worry. I'll be right down in a couple of minutes. I'll fetch my stick.' Then, her voice darkening with good-humoured menace, she added, 'If this fellow turns up he'll be sorry!'

Abby hurried back downstairs and into her mother's flat. She explained what was happening, then said, 'Don't answer the door to anyone until I get back.'

She then hurried out into the street and climbed into the back of the taxi.

'I need to find a mobile phone shop,' she told the driver. Then she checked her pocket. She had another hundred and fifty pounds in cash. It should be enough.

*

Parked carefully out of sight behind a camper van to the right, on the cross-street, Ricky waited for them to drive off, then started his engine and followed, staying a long way back, curious to know where Abby was heading.

At the same time, keeping a steadying hand on the GSM 3060 Intercept he had placed on the passenger seat beside him, he replayed her call to Eastbourne Lockworks and memorized the number. He was glad he had the Intercept with him, he hadn't wanted to risk leaving such a valuable piece of kit in the van.

He called the locksmith and politely cancelled the appointment, explaining that the lady, his mother, had forgotten she had a hospital appointment this afternoon. He would call back later and arrange a new time for tomorrow.

Then he rang Abby's mother, introduced himself as the manager of Eastbourne Lockworks and apologized profusely for the delay. His staff were attending an emergency. Someone would be there as soon as possible, but it might not be until early evening, at the earliest. Otherwise it would be first thing tomorrow morning. He hoped that would be all right. She told him that would be fine.

The taxi driver drove cretinously slowly, which made following at a safe distance easy, the vehicle's bright turquoise and white livery and the sign on its roof making it easy for Ricky to spot. After ten minutes it started driving even more slowly down a busy shopping street, the brake lights coming on several times before it finally pulled over outside a phone shop. Ricky swerved sharply into a parking bay and watched Abby run into the shop.

Then he switched off his engine, pulled a Mars bar out of his pocket, ravenously hungry suddenly, and settled down to wait.

73

OCTOBER 2007

Something was nagging Inspector Stephen Curry when he returned to his office from the Neighbourhood Policing meeting, which had gone on much longer than expected.

It had turned into a sandwich lunch meeting as well, covering a broad range of issues, from two illegal traveller encampments that were causing problems at Hollingbury and Woodingdean, to the creation of an intelligence report on the city's latest teenage gangs and a plague of happy-slapping incidents associated with them. These violent incidents were becoming an increasingly large problem, with youths filming the attacks and then posting them as trophies on social networking sites such as Bebo and MySpace. Some of the worst attacks had taken place in schools, been picked up on by the *Argus* and had a real impact on children and worried parents.

It was coming up to 2.30 p.m. and he had a ton of stuff to get through today. He had to leave earlier than usual – it was his wedding anniversary and he had promised Tracy faithfully – absolutely one hundred per cent faithfully – that he would not be late home.

He sat at his desk and ran his eyes down the log on the screen of all incidents in his area during the past few hours, but there was nothing he needed to get involved with right now. All emergency calls had been responded to without delays and there were no significant critical incidents which would sap resources. It was just the usual assortment of minor crimes.

Then, remembering Roy Grace's call earlier, he opened his notebook and read the name *Katherine Jennings* and the address he had written down. He had just seen one of the early-turn Neighbourhood Policy Team sergeants, John Morley, come in, so he picked up the phone and asked him to have someone from the Neighbourhood Team go and see the woman.

Morley crooked the phone into his shoulder and picked up a pen, his left hand marking his place in a crime file he was reviewing relating to a handover prisoner arrested by the night shift. Then he flipped over a small scrap of paper on his desk, on which he'd written a vehicle registration number earlier, and jotted the name and address down.

The sergeant was young and bright, with his buzz cut and stab vest making him look harder than he actually was. But, like all of his colleagues, he was stressed from being overworked, because they were short of staff.

'Could be any number of reasons why she was agitated by that jerk Spinella. He agitates me.'

'Tell me about it!' Curry concurred.

A couple of minutes later, Morley was about to transfer the details to his notebook when his phone rang again. It was an operator in the Southern Resourcing Centre, asking the sergeant to take command of a grade-one emergency. An eight-year-old mis-per. Vanished from her school this afternoon and not with her family.

Within moments the shit hit the fan. Morley radioed first his duty inspector, then barked instructions on his radio phone to his team of officers and PCSOs who were out and about in the city. While doing this, he ran to the back of the cluttered room, which contained half a dozen communal metal desks, boxes of supplies, and a row of pegs and hooks for jackets, hats and helmets, and grabbed his cap.

Then, taking a couple of constables who had arrived early for the afternoon shift, he headed for the door at a semi-run, still talking into his phone.

As the three of them passed his desk, the draught of air lifted the scrap of paper with Katherine Jennings's name and address up, off the flat surface, and it fluttered to the floor.

Ten minutes later an MSA entered the room and put several copies of the latest directive on diversity training within the police force down on Sergeant Morley's desk for him to distribute. As she was about the leave, she noticed the scrap of paper lying on the floor. She stooped down, picked it up and dropped it, dutifully, in the waste-paper basket.

74

OCTOBER 2007

The fresh air and the greasy fry-up had done the trick for his hangover, Roy Grace decided, feeling almost human again now as he walked back up Church Street and entered the NCP multistorey car park.

He stuck his ticket in the machine, wincing as he always did each time he parked here at the extortionate amount that appeared on the display, then climbed the steps up towards his level, thinking about Terry Biglow.

Maybe he was going soft, because he actually found himself feeling a little sorry for the man – although not for his vile companion. Biglow had once had a bit of style and he was one of the last of a generation of old-school villains who respected the police, if nothing else.

The poor bastard didn't look as if he was long for this world. What did a man like him think as he approached the end of his life? Did he care that he had totally squandered it, contributing nothing to the world? That he had played a part in ruining countless other lives, ending up with nothing, absolutely nothing? Not even his health . . .

Grace unlocked his car, then sat inside and ran through his notes from the encounter. Partway through, he phoned Glenn Branson and gave him the news that Ronnie had had a second wife, called Lorraine. Then he told him to take Bella Moy and interview the people Terry Biglow said had been Ronnie Wilson's best friends, the Klingers. Stephen Klinger currently ran a large antiques emporium in Brighton and should be easy enough to find.

As he hung up, his phone rang. It was Cleo.

'How's your hangover, Detective Superintendent Grace?' she asked.

It was strange, he thought. Sandy had always called him just *Grace* and now occasionally Cleo did it too. At the same time, he found it endearing.

'Hangover? How do you know about that?'

'Because you rang me from the pub about 11.30 last night, slurring undying love for me.'

'I did?'

'Uh oh, memory loss. Must have been a seriously bad session.'

'It was. Five hours of Glenn Branson's marital woes. Enough to drive any man to drink.'

'Starting to sound to me like his marriage is terminal.'

'Yep, heading that way.'

'I – ah – need a favour,' she said, her tone changing, suddenly all sweetness and light.

'What kind of a favour?'

'An hour of your time, between 5 and 6.'

'What do you want me to do?'

'Well, I've just had to go and bring in a particularly unpleasant suicide – a fellow who put a twelve-bore in his mouth in his garden shed – and the Coroner's not happy with the circumstances. She wants a Home Office pathologist – so our good friend Theobald is coming to do the PM this afternoon. Which means I can't take Humphrey to dog training.'

'Dog training?'

'Yes, so I thought it might be a good opportunity for you and Humphrey to bond.'

'Cleo, I'm right in the middle of a really—'

Cutting him short, she said, 'Your murder investigation – she's been dead for ten years. One hour isn't going to make a huge difference. Just one hour, that's all I'm asking for. It's the first day of a new course and I'd really like Humphrey to be there from the start. And because I know you're going to do it, because you're such a lovely man, I'm offering you a very sweet reward!'

'Reward?'

'OK. Dog training's from 5 o'clock to 6 . . . Here's the deal. You take Humphrey and in exchange I'll cook you Thai-style stir-fried tiger prawns and scallops.'

Instantly she had him hooked. Cleo's prawn and scallop stir-fry was one of the best dishes in her amazing repertoire. It was almost to die for.

Before he had time to comment, she added, 'I've also got a rather special bottle of Cloudy Bay Sauvignon Blanc I've popped in the fridge for you as a treat.' She paused and then, in a deeply seductive voice, said, 'And . . .'

'*And?*'

There was a long silence. Just the hiss of static from the phone.

'What's the *and*?' he asked.

Even more seductively, she said, 'That's for your imagination.'

'Did you have anything particular in mind?'

'Yes, lots . . . We have the whole of last night to catch up on as well as tonight. Think you can rise to the occasion, with your hangover and all?'

'I think I could.'

'Good. So, you give Humphrey a treat and I'll give you one in exchange. Deal?'

'Shall I bring some biscuits?'

'For Humphrey?'

'No, for you.'

'Sod you, Grace.'

He grinned.

'Oh, and one other thing – don't get tooooo aroused. Humphrey likes chewing on hard things.'

75

OCTOBER 2007

He could have done with another Mars bar – he was starving – but Ricky didn't want to risk leaving the car to buy one, in case he missed her. Christ, it was over half an hour since she had gone into the mobile phone shop – what was the bitch doing in there? No doubt dithering about which colour to buy.

The cab would be costing a bloody fortune! And whose money would she be using to pay for it?

His, of course.

Was she doing it deliberately to make him angry, knowing that he would be watching somewhere?

She would pay for this. Every which way. And then some.

She would scream apologies to him. Over and over and over. Before he was finished with her.

A shadow fell across his nearside window. Then he saw a traffic warden's face peering in. He put down the window.

'I'm picking up my mother,' Ricky said. 'She's disabled – won't be a few minutes.'

The warden, a lanky youth with a sullen face and his cap at a jaunty angle, was not impressed. 'You've been here half an hour.'

'She's driving me nuts,' Ricky said. 'She's suffering dementia – first stages.' He tapped his watch. 'Got to get her to the hospital. Just give me a couple more minutes.'

'Five minutes,' the warden said, and swaggered off. He then stopped by the car in front and began tapping out a ticket on his machine.

Ricky watched his altercation moments later with the returning owner, an irate-looking woman, and continued to watch his slow progress into the distance. He realized, with a shock, that another twenty minutes had passed.

Jesus, how long do you need to buy a fucking phone?

Another five minutes went by. Followed by another. Suddenly the taxi drove off and was swallowed by the traffic.

Ricky did a double-take. Had he missed her? Had the warden moved the taxi on?

He started the car and followed. Several vehicles in front, the taxi headed down to the sea, then turned right. Keeping his distance, staying several vehicles back, he followed the imbecilic, moronic, geriatric, dithering fool of a driver at a pace where he was likely to be overtaken by a tortoise. They went along the seafront, then up the winding hill into wide, open national park and farmland, and along towards the cliff-top beauty and favoured suicide spot of Beachy Head.

A double-decker bus was on his tail, pushing for him to speed up. 'Come on, fuckwit!' he shouted through the windscreen at the cab. 'Put your fucking foot down!'

Still at the same speed, he passed the Beachy Head pub, following the winding road towards Birling Gap, then up through East Dean village. The agony continued through more open countryside, winding past the Seven Sisters and into Seaford. Then on, past the Newhaven ferry port, and up the hill into Peacehaven. A long-haired young man and a girl stood on a street corner in the distance waving and, to Ricky's astonishment, the FOR HIRE light suddenly came on and the taxi pulled over.

He pulled over too and a line of traffic that had built up behind him shot past.

He watched the couple get into the back.

The taxi had been empty.

He'd been following an empty taxi.

Shit, shit, shit.

Oh, you little bitch, now you've really fucking done it.

76

OCTOBER 2007

A scarlet-haired bimbo dressed in skimpy purple, with legs up to her neck and massive boobs spilling out of her bra, winked at Roy Grace.

He took hold of the card and, as the angle changed, the other eye winked at him. He grinned and opened it. A cheesy voice, which was a bad imitation of some female vocalist he could not immediately place, began singing 'Happy Birthday'.

'This is wonderful!' he said. 'Who did you say it was for?'

With her tall, leggy good looks, DC Esther Mitchell was, no contest, currently the best-looking detective in the whole of Sussex House. She was also one of the cheeriest.

'It's for DI Willis,' she said breezily. 'His fortieth.'

Grace grinned. Baz Willis, an overweight slug who should never, in anyone's opinion, have been promoted to the rank of Detective Inspector, was a renowned groper. The card was therefore eminently fitting. He found a space between the dozen or so other signatures, scrawled his name on it and handed it back to her.

'He's having a party. Open bar at the Black Lion tonight.'

Grace grimaced. The Black Lion in Patcham, Sussex House's local, was one of his least favourite pubs and the thought of two consecutive nights there was more than his constitution could handle – besides he had a far, far better offer.

'Thanks, I'll swing by if I can,' he said.

'Someone's organizing a minibus – if you want to book on that—'

'No, thanks,' he said, and shot a glance at his watch. He needed to leave in five minutes, to get sodding little Humphrey to his dog-training class. Then he gave her a smile. She had a nice energy about her and had managed to make herself popular – and not just for her looks – in the short while she had been here.

'Oh, and Detective Superintendent Pewe asked me to check with you about travel arrangements for Australia.'

'What?'

'Sorry – I've been seconded to work with him, along with DC Robinson, on his cold-case files.'

'Did you say *Australia*?'

'Yes, he wanted me to ask you which airlines Sussex Police has business-class deals with.'

'Business-class deals?' he said. 'Where does he think he is? A law firm?'

She grinned, looking embarrassed. 'I – er – I assumed you knew about this.'

'I'm just dashing out,' Grace said. 'I'll stop by his office.'

'I'll tell him.'

'Thanks, Esther.'

She gave him a look as she left his office. It was an *I-don't-like-him-either* acknowledgement.

*

Five minutes later, Grace entered his old office with its crappy view of the custody block. Cassian Pewe was sitting there, in his shirtsleeves, making what was clearly a personal call. Grace didn't give a toss about his privacy. He pulled one of the four chairs away from the tiny, round conference table and plonked it directly in front of Pewe's desk, then sat down.

'I'll call you back, my angel,' Pewe said, looking warily at Grace's glowering face. He hung up and beamed. 'Roy! Good to see you!'

Grace cut to the chase. 'What's this about Australia?'

'Ah, I was just going to come and tell you. There's something I'm looking into today for the Victoria police in Melbourne – well, the Melbourne area – that I've just learned has a connection to your *Operation Dingo*. Bit of a coincidence, the name, *Dingo* – that's an Australian wild dog, isn't it?'

'What connection? And what are you doing getting a DC running round asking about travel policy? That's what MSAs are for.'

'I think someone's going to have to go to Australia, Roy – thought I might do it myself—'

'I don't know what happens in the Met, but just so you know for future reference, Cassian, in Sussex we spend our money on policing, not turning police officers into fat cats on ratepayers' money. We fly economy, OK?'

'Of course, Roy,' Pewe said, giving him an oily smile. 'It's just a long journey if someone's got to do a day's work at the end of it.'

'Yep, well, that's tough. We're not operating a holiday company here.'

And the only way you're going to Australia, Detective Superintendent Pewe, if I have anything to do with it, is by digging your way there with a spade! Grace thought. 'Do you want to tell me what the connection with my case is?'

Pewe said, 'I've got information about Lorraine Wilson, Ronnie Wilson's second wife, that I think you will find interesting. It has a bearing on Ronnie Wilson. Could lead you to him.'

'Yes, well, you're clearly not up to speed on Ronnie Wilson. He died in the World Trade Center on 9/11.'

'Actually,' Cassian Pewe said, 'I have evidence that might suggest otherwise.'

77

OCTOBER 2007

Ricky followed the taxi along the main drag of Peacehaven. He was tempted to grab the driver by the throat next time he stopped and grill him about Abby.

But what would the man know? The smart little bitch had probably given him a big tip to sit there and sod off after an hour, that's all he would know, and the last thing Ricky needed right now was every cop in Brighton looking out for his face, to bring him in on an assault charge. He had something much more important to think about at this moment. Several things, in fact.

The first was that Abby knew he had recorded her phone conversation with her mother. But she would not have known how he did it. Probably she would suspect he had somehow bugged her mother's phone.

Now the penny dropped!

That was why she had gone to a phone shop, to get her mother a new phone!

He had been realizing for some time now just how dangerously thorough Abby was. What about her own phone? He dialled the number.

After two rings it was answered. A tentative young male voice.

'Yeah?'

'Who the fuck's that?' Ricky demanded.

The connection was terminated. He dialled again. The connection was terminated again the moment it began to ring. As he suspected, the bitch had ditched her phone. Which meant she now had a new one.

You are really trying my patience.

And where are you?

A speed camera flashed at him, but he didn't give a toss. Where had she gone in that hour? What had she used the time for?

A few miles on, the taxi turned off, but he barely noticed. He was driving along Marine Parade now, passing the elegant Regency façades of Sussex Square. In a minute he would be approaching Abby's street. He pulled over to the side, stopped the car and killed the engine, needing to think this through carefully.

Where had she hidden the stash? She didn't need much space. Just enough room to conceal an A4 envelope. The package she'd tried to send via the courier was a decoy. Why? To get him to follow the courier? So she could retrieve it and disappear? He'd made a big error, he realized, sending her that text. His intention had been to flush her out, but he had not reckoned on her being so devious.

But the fact she had tried to send the decoy package told him something, when he added that together with the empty deposit box. Had she been hoping that he would follow the decoy, leaving her free to run with the package and put it in the safe-deposit box at Southern Deposit Security? Why else would it be empty? The only possible reason, surely, was that she hadn't been able to get the package to the place yet. Or that she had recently withdrawn it.

Unless she had another deposit box somewhere else, it was most likely still somewhere in her flat.

He'd spent the night going through her belongings, including all her clothes that he had removed. He'd also taken her passport, which would at least stop the bitch from getting out of the country in a hurry.

Surely if there was another deposit box somewhere he'd have found the key or a receipt? He'd searched every damn inch of the flat, moved all the furniture, levered up every loose floorboard. He'd even taken the backs off the televisions, ripped open the soft furnishings, unscrewed the ventilation grilles, dismantled the light fittings. From his days of dealing in drugs, he knew just how thoroughly police would take a place apart, and all the kinds of hiding places a smart dealer would use.

Another possible option was that she had left it with a friend. But the name on the package she'd given to the courier was a dummy, he'd checked that one out. He suspected she had been avoiding contacting anyone here. If she hadn't even told her mother she was back, he doubted she would want word to get out among her friends.

No, he was becoming increasingly convinced that she still had it all in the flat.

Despite all her clever ploys, as Ricky well knew, everyone has an Achilles heel. Any chain is only as strong as its weakest link. An army can only march as fast as its slowest soldier.

Abby's mother was both her weak link and her slowest soldier.

Now he knew exactly what he had to do.

*

The Renault van outside Abby's flat, which had not been driven in a while, was reluctant to start. Then, just as the battery started fading and he was beginning to think this was not going to work, it fired and spluttered into oily, smoky life.

He drove it out of the parking space and replaced it with the rental Ford. Now, when Abby came back here, she would spot the car and think he was in there. He smiled. For the immediate future she would not be entering the flat. There was no residents' parking sticker on the rental car, so it would probably be given a ticket at some point, and maybe get clamped, but what the hell did that matter?

He removed the GSM 3060 Intercept from the Ford and put it in the van. Then he drove off back towards Eastbourne, stopping only to pick up a takeaway burger and a Coke. He felt happier now. Confident that he was close to having the situation back under control.

78

OCTOBER 2007

At 6.30 p.m. the fourth briefing meeting of *Operation Dingo* commenced. But as Roy Grace began reading his summary to his assembled team, he hesitated, noticing that Glenn Branson was staring at him a bit strangely and twitching his nostrils, as if he was trying to send him a signal.

'Is there a problem?' Grace asked him.

Then he noticed several of the others gathered around the work station seemed to be looking at him strangely too.

'You smell a bit fruity, boss,' Glenn said. 'If you don't mind me being personal. Not your usual brand of cologne, if you get my drift. Have you stood or sat in something?'

Grace realized to his horror what the DS was driving at. 'Oh, right, I apologize. I – just got back from a dog-training class. The little bugger threw up all over me in the car. I thought I'd managed to wash it off.'

Bella Moy delved into her handbag and handed Grace a perfume spray. 'This'll drown it,' she said.

Grace hesitantly sprayed his trousers, shirt and jacket.

'Now you smell like a bordello,' Norman Potting commented.

'Well, thank you very much,' Bella said, glaring at him indignantly.

'Not that I would know, of course,' Potting mumbled,

in a feeble attempt at retrieving the situation. Then he added, 'I read recently that Koreans eat dogs.'

'That's quite enough, Norman,' Roy Grace said sternly, returning to his typed agenda. 'OK, Bella, first can you report on your findings so far about Joanna Wilson ever going to America? My guy hasn't come up with anything.'

'I contacted the officer in the New York District Attorney's Office you suggested, Roy. He sent me an email an hour ago, saying that prior to 9/11 all immigration was handled by the Immigration and Naturalization Agency. It's different since. They're merged with US Customs and are now called Immigration Customs Enforcement. He says that unless she had gone in on a visa for an extended stay, there would be no records. He's checked back through those for the 1990s and she doesn't show up as having gone in on a visa, but he says there's no way of finding out whether she ever went there or not.'

'OK, thanks. E-J, how are you progressing with the family tree? Did you track down any of Joanna Wilson's relatives?'

'Well, she doesn't seem to have had many. I've found a gay stepbrother – who's a piece of work. He goes under the name of Mitzi Dufors, is nudging sixty, wears studded leather hot-pants and is covered in piercings. He does some kind of a drag act in a Brighton gay club. Didn't have many flattering words to say about his late stepsister.'

'You can't trust middle-aged men in leather hot-pants,' Norman Potting interjected.

'Norman!' Grace said, firing a warning shot across his bows.

'You're not exactly a fashion guru yourself, Norman,' Bella retorted.

'OK, both of you, enough!' Grace said.

Potting shrugged like a petulant child.

'Anything else from her stepbrother?'

'He said Joanna inherited a small house in Brentwood from her mother, about a year before she went to America. He reckoned she took the sale proceeds to fund her acting career there.'

'We should try to find how much money was involved and what happened to it. Good work, E-J.'

Grace made some notes, then moved on to Branson. 'Glenn, did you and Bella get hold of the Klingers?'

Branson grinned. 'I think we got Stephen Klinger at a good time, after lunch – pissed as a fart and well chatty. Told us that no one liked Joanna Wilson much – she sounds like she was a real slapper. She gave Ronnie a right old song and dance, and no one cared too much when she ditched him – or so it seemed – and went off to the States. He confirmed that Ronnie had married again, after dutifully waiting out the legal period for desertion, to Lorraine. When Ronnie died she was inconsolable. What made it worse for her, if that's possible, is that he left her up shit creek financially.'

Grace made a note.

'Her car got repossessed, then her house. Sounds like Wilson was a man of straw. Had nothing, no assets at all. His widow ended up getting evicted from her posh house in Hove and moved into a rented flat. Just over a year later, in November 2002, she left a suicide note and jumped off the Newhaven–Dieppe ferry.' He paused. 'We went and saw Mrs Klinger as well, but she more or less confirmed what her husband told us.'

'Any of her relatives able to verify her state of mind?' Grace asked.

'Yeah, she's got a sister who works as a hostess for

British Airways. I just talked to her. She was at work and couldn't really speak. I've got an appointment to see her tomorrow. But she also pretty well confirmed what Klinger said. Oh, yeah, and she said she took Lorraine to New York as soon as flights were running again. They spent a week traipsing around the city with a big photograph of Ronnie. Them and a million others.'

'So she's convinced Ronnie died in 9/11.'

'No question,' Glenn said. 'He was at a meeting in the South Tower with a guy called Donald Hatcook. Everyone on the floor Donald Hatcook was on perished – almost certainly instantly.' Then he looked at his notes. 'You asked me about this geezer Chad Skeggs?'

'Yes, what did you find out?'

'He's wanted for questioning by Brighton CID regarding an allegation of indecent assault on a young woman back in 1990. The girl's story is that they left the club and went back together, and then she was badly beaten up by him. It could be linked to an S&M scenario. Possible that she initially went along with it and then he wouldn't stop. It was a very nasty assault, together with an allegation of rape. But it was decided at the time that it wasn't in the public interest to go to Australia and bring him back. I don't think we'll be seeing him in England again, not unless he's very stupid.'

Grace turned to DC Nicholl. 'Nick, what do you have to report?'

'Well,' he said, 'it's actually quite interesting. After I did a nationwide search on Wilson, which didn't come up with anything we didn't already know, I decided that a businessman like him, with his smart house in Hove 4, was likely to have some life insurance. I did some digging and discovered Ronnie Wilson had a life insurance policy of just over one and a half million quid with the Norwich Union, taken out in 1999.'

'Presumably his widow didn't know this?' Grace said.

'I think she did,' Nick Nicholl said. 'They paid out to her in full in March 2002.'

'When she was in a rented flat, in distress?' Grace asked.

'There's more,' the DC said. 'In July 2002, ten months after her husband died, Lorraine Wilson received a payment of two and a half million dollars from the 9/11 compensation fund.'

'Three months before she jumped off the ferry,' Lizzie Mantle said.

'*Allegedly* jumped off the Newhaven–Dieppe ferry,' Nick Nicholl said. 'She is still officially recorded as a Sussex Police missing person. I've checked the file and the investigators at that time were not entirely convinced that she had killed herself. But the trail went cold.' Then he added, 'The insurance investigator assigned to the claim on Ronnie Wilson's policy wasn't happy either. But there was a lot of political pressure to pay out quickly to the survivors of 9/11 victims.'

'Two million five hundred thousand dollars – with the exchange rate back in those days, that would have been worth close to one and three-quarter million quid,' Norman Potting said.

'So she died in abject poverty, with over three million in the bank?' Bella said.

'That amount of moolah would buy you a lot of Maltesers,' Norman Potting said to her.

'Except the money wasn't in the bank,' Nick Nicholl said. He held up two folders. 'Managed to get these a bit quicker than we should have done, thanks to Steve.'

He waved a hand in acknowledgement to thirty-year-old DC Mackie, seated further down the table, dressed in jeans and an open-neck white shirt.

Mackie spoke with quiet authority and had a tidy, efficient air about him, which Grace liked. 'My brother works for HSBC. He fast-tracked my request.'

Nick Nicholl then removed a sheaf of documents from one folder. 'These are all the joint-account statements of Ronnie and Lorraine Wilson going back to 2000. They show an ever-increasing overdraft, with just occasional small amounts coming in.' He put them back in the folder and raised the second one. 'This is much more interesting. It's a bank account opened in Lorraine Wilson's sole name in December 2001.'

'For the life insurance money, presumably?' Lizzie Mantle said.

Nick Nicholl nodded and Grace was impressed. Normally the young man lacked self-confidence, but at this moment he seemed really together.

'Yes, that was deposited in March 2002.'

'I don't understand how it was paid out that fast,' Lizzie Mantle queried. 'I thought if there was no body found, there was a seven-year-wait before a missing person could be declared dead.' As she spoke she deliberately avoided Roy Grace's eyes, knowing what a sensitive issue this was for him personally.

'There was an international agreement, thanks to an initiative from Mayor Giuliani,' Steve Mackie said, 'to waive this period for the families of 9/11 victims and fast-track payments.'

Nick Nicholl laid out several of the bank statements in front of him, like a dealer in a card game. 'But this is where it gets interesting. The entire amount of that payment of one and a half million pounds was withdrawn in different-sized chunks, in cash, over the next three months.'

'What did she do with it?' Grace queried.

Nick Nicholl raised his hands. 'Her sister was totally and utterly gobsmacked when I told her. Just didn't believe it. She said that Lorraine was relying on handouts from her and from friends.'

'And what about the 9/11 compensation payout?' Grace asked.

'That went into her account in July 2002.' Nicholl held up the relevant statement. 'Then the same thing happened. The money was withdrawn in different chunks, in cash, between then and a few weeks before she left the suicide note.'

The whole team was frowning. Glenn Branson tapped his teeth with a ballpoint pen. Lizzie Mantle, busy for a moment jotting down a note, looked up.

'And we have no idea what this money was being used for?' she asked. 'Did she tell anyone at the bank what the cash was for? Presumably some questions would have been asked with that amount going to her in cash.'

'The bank has a policy to check whether clients are under any kind of duress when withdrawing large sums in cash,' DC Mackie said. 'When she was asked about it, she said the bank had not supported her when her husband had died and she was damned if she was leaving the money with them.'

'Sounds a feisty lady,' Lizzie Mantle said.

'Do we have a bit of a pattern forming here?' Norman Potting asked. 'Wilson's first wife inherits, tells her friends she is off to America, and ends up in a storm drain. Then his second wife inherits and ends up in the Channel.'

Nodding at him, Grace decided it was time to add his

latest information, courtesy of Cassian Pewe. 'This may shed some light on things,' he said. 'Last month police in Geelong, near Melbourne, Australia, found the body of a woman in the boot of a car in a river,' he said. 'Forensic reports estimate she has been dead for a maximum of two years. The woman had breast implants, which were traced to a batch delivered to the Nuffield Hospital here in Woodingdean in June 1997. The recipient of the ones matching the serial number was Lorraine Wilson.'

He paused to let this sink in.

'So – she like swam from the English Channel to Australia and then up a river?' Glenn Branson said. 'With three million quid in folding in her bathing costume.'

'And that's not all,' Roy Grace went on. 'She was four months pregnant. The Australian police were not able to find any DNA match on their records for the mother, or a familial match for the father, and wondered if there might be anything on the National UK DNA Database. We're waiting to hear now. Hopefully we'll know tomorrow if there is any match on either.'

'Seems like we have a problem, Houston,' Norman Potting said.

'Or perhaps a lead,' Grace corrected him. 'The post-mortem in Melbourne indicated the probable cause of death was strangulation,' he continued. 'They arrived at this conclusion because Lorraine Wilson's hyoid bone – the U-shaped bone at the base of the neck – was broken.'

'Which was the same probable cause of death for Joanna Wilson,' said Nick Nicholl.

'Well remembered,' Grace said. 'You're on peak form today, Nick. I'm glad your sleepless nights haven't dulled your wits!'

Nicholl blushed, looking pleased with himself.

'Ronnie Wilson's not done badly for a dead man,' Norman Potting said. 'Managing to strangle his wife.'

'We don't have enough evidence to make that assumption, Norman,' Grace said, although privately he was wondering. He glanced at his agenda. 'OK, so this is what's going to happen. If she spent over three million quid in cash, in the space of a few months, someone will know about it. Glenn and Bella, I want you to prioritize that. Start with the Klingers again. Find out everything you can about the circles the Wilsons moved in. What did they spend money on? Did they gamble? Did they buy a place abroad? Or a boat? Three and a quarter million quid is a lot of money – and its value was even more five years ago.'

Branson and Bella nodded.

'Steve, can you use your banking fast-track to find out what happened to Joanna Wilson's inheritance? I appreciate we're talking ten years back and there may not be any records. Just do all you can.'

Grace paused to check his notes, then went on. 'I'm flying to New York tomorrow to see what I can find. I'm intending to fly back overnight, Thursday night, and be here for Friday morning. I want you, Norman and Nick, to go to Australia.'

Potting looked pleased as punch at the news, but Nicholl seemed worried.

'Reservations have been made for you on a flight out tomorrow evening. You'll lose a day and get there for early Friday morning, Melbourne time. You could have a full day's investigation and, with the time difference, be able to report back to us by our morning briefing here on Friday. You look like you're fretting about something, Nick. Can you not tear yourself away from your paternal duties?'

The DC nodded.

'You OK about going?'

He nodded again, more vigorously this time.

'Either of you been there before?'

'No, but I've got a cousin in Perth,' Nick Nicholl said.

'That's almost as far from Melbourne as Brighton is,' Bella said.

'So I wouldn't have time to go and see him?'

'You're not going on a vacation. You're going to get a job done,' Grace chided.

Nick Nicholl nodded.

'Following a dead woman's footsteps,' Norman Potting said.

And, Grace had a hunch, maybe following a dead man's too.

79

OCTOBER 2007

Roy Grace went straight from the briefing meeting to his office and phoned Cleo, telling her he would be later than planned as he needed to finish off here, then go home and pack a bag.

He had been to New York on several previous occasions. A couple of them were with Sandy – once for Christmas shopping and once for their fifth wedding anniversary – but the rest of the times were for work, and he always enjoyed visiting the city. He was particularly looking forward to seeing his two police friends there, Dennis Baker and Pat Lynch.

He'd met them seven years ago when, as a Detective Inspector, he'd gone to New York on a murder inquiry. That had been the year before 9/11. Dennis and Pat were then officers in the NYPD, working in Brooklyn, and had been among the first police officers on the scene at 9/11. He doubted there were two men better qualified in the whole of New York City to help him find the truth about whether or not Ronnie Wilson had perished on that dreadful day.

Cleo was fine, all sweetness and light, *just get here when you can*. And, she assured him, she had a very, very, very sexy treat awaiting him. Knowing from past experience just how good her sexy treats were, he decided it would be well worth the dry-cleaning bill from little Humphrey's dog training and projectile-vomiting session.

He turned his attention first to his emails. He replied to a couple of urgent ones and decided to leave the rest for his plane journey in the morning.

Then, just as he was making a start on his paperwork, there was a rap on the door and, without waiting for an answer, Cassian Pewe came in with a pained expression on his face. He stood in front of Grace's desk, suit jacket slung over his shoulder, top button of his shirt open, expensive-looking tie at half mast.

'Roy, excuse me, sorry to bounce in on you, but I'm rather hurt.'

Grace raised a finger, finished reading through a memo, then looked up at him. 'Hurt? I'm sorry. Why?'

'I just heard you are sending DS Potting and DC Nicholl to Melbourne tomorrow. Is that right?'

'Yes, absolutely right.'

Pewe tapped his own chest. 'What about me? I started this. Surely I should be one of those going?'

'I'm sorry – what do you mean, you *started* it? I thought all you did was take a call from Interpol?'

'Roy,' he said, in an imploring tone that suggested Grace was his very, very best friend ever, 'it was my initiative that got everything moving so fast.'

Grace nodded, irritated by the man's attitude and the interruption. 'Yes, and I appreciate that. But you have to understand we operate on teamwork here in Sussex, Cassian. You're in charge of cold cases – I'm running a live inquiry. The information you've given me may be very helpful and your swift action has been noted.'

Now fuck off and let me get on with my work, he wanted to say, but didn't.

'I appreciate that. I just think that I should be one of the team going to Australia.'

'You are better off being deployed here,' Grace said. 'That's my call.'

Pewe glared at him and, in a fit of sudden pique, snapped back, 'I think you might regret that, Roy.'

Then he stormed out of Grace's office.

80

OCTOBER 2007

Tuesday evening, 8 o'clock. Ricky sat in his van in darkness, back at the same cross-street vantage point opposite Abby's mother's flat where he had waited earlier. From here he could see both the front entrance and the street she would have to use if she tried sneaking out of the rear fire-escape door.

The chill was really seeping into his bones. He just wanted to get everything back, get Abby out of his face and get the fuck out of this godforsaken damp, freezing country and into some sunshine.

He'd hardly seen a soul in the past three hours. He seemed to remember Eastbourne had a reputation as a retirement town where the average age was either dead or nearly dead. Tonight it felt as if everyone was dead. Street-lighting fell on empty pavements. *Fucking waste,* he thought. *Someone should talk to this place about its carbon footprint.*

Abby was inside, in the warm with her mother. He had a feeling she would be staying there tonight, but he did not dare leave his post and go to find a pub and have a drink or three until he was sure.

About two hours ago he'd picked up the signal from her new mobile phone when she'd made a call to her mother's new phone to test its ring tone and volume, and to give it her number. Now, thanks to that call, he had both of their numbers logged.

When they were testing the phones he heard the television in the background. It sounded like some soap opera, with a man and a woman bickering in a car. So the bitch and her mother were settled in for a cosy evening in front of the telly, in a warm flat, charging two new mobile phones that had been bought with his money.

The Intercept beeped busily. Abby was phoning rest homes, looking for somewhere that would take her mother in immediately for four weeks, until a room in the place she had chosen came available.

She was interrogating them about nursing care, doctors, mealtimes, ingredients of the food, exercise, about whether there was a pool, a sauna, whether they were near a main road or somewhere quiet, gardens with wheelchair access, were there private bathrooms? Her list went on and on. Thorough. As he had learned to his bitter cost. She was a thorough bitch.

And whose money would be paying for it?

He listened to Abby making appointments to go and see three places in the morning. He presumed she would leave her mother behind. That she had not forgotten the locksmith was coming.

By the time he had finished with her, it wouldn't be a rest home she was needing. It would be a chapel of rest.

81

OCTOBER 2007

At 8.20 the next morning, Inspector Stephen Curry, accompanied by Sergeant Ian Brown, entered the small conference room in the custody block behind Sussex House. He was clutching today's morning briefing notes, which comprised a comprehensive review of all priority crimes that had occurred in the district over the last twenty-four hours.

They were joined by Sergeant Morley and the second early-shift sergeant, a short, stocky officer with a fierce crew cut and even fiercer enthusiasm for her work called Mary Gregson.

They immediately got down to the job in hand. Curry started to go through all the critical serials. There had been an ugly racist incident, with a young Muslim student badly beaten up outside a late-night takeaway in Park Road, Coldean, on his way back to the university; a traffic fatality involving a motorcyclist and a pedestrian on Lewes Road; a violent mugging on the Broadway in Whitehawk; and a young man beaten up in Preston Park in a homophobic incident.

He went through all of them with a toothcomb, working out areas of threat, making sure, in his terminology, that he didn't *drop a bollock* which could be kicked into touch by the Superintendent at the 9.30 review.

Then they moved on to the current district mis-pers

and agreed lines of enquiry. Mary brought up the details of a bail returning to be charged later that day, and reminded Curry that he had an 11 a.m. with a Crown Prosecution Service solicitor, about a suspect they had arrested after a spate of handbag thefts the previous set of shifts.

Then the Inspector suddenly remembered something else. 'John – I spoke to you yesterday about visiting a lady down in Kemp Town. I didn't see that on the list – what was her name? – Katherine Jennings. Any follow-up?'

Morley suddenly blushed. 'Oh, God, sorry, boss. I haven't done anything about it. That Gemma Buxton incident came in and – I'm sorry – I gave that priority over everything. I'll put it on the serial and get someone down there this morning.'

'Good man,' Curry said, then looked at his watch again. Shit. Nearly 9.05. He jumped up. 'See you later.'

'Have a nice time with the headmaster,' Mary said with a cheeky grin.

'Yeah, you might be teacher's pet today!' Morley said.

'With someone whose memory's as crap as yours on the team?' he retorted. 'I don't think so.'

82

OCTOBER 2007

Ricky slept fitfully, dozing off after the several pints of beer he had treated himself to in a busy seafront pub and waking with a start every time he saw headlights or heard a vehicle, or footsteps, or a door close. He sat in the passenger seat just so he didn't look like a drunk driver, should an inquisitive policeman come by, only leaving the van a couple of times to urinate in an alley.

He drove off again in the darkness, at 6 a.m., in search of a workmen's café, where he had some breakfast, and was back at his observation post again within the hour.

How the hell had he got himself into this situation? he asked himself repeatedly. How had he let himself be duped by this bitch? Oh, she'd played it so cutely, coming on to him, playing the horny little slut to perfection. Letting him do everything he wanted with her and pretending to enjoy it. Maybe she was really enjoying it. But all the time she was pumping him so subtly for information. Women were smart. They knew how to manipulate men.

He'd made the damned mistake of telling her, because he wanted to show off. He thought it would impress her.

Instead, one night when he was coked out of his tree and rat-arsed drunk, she cleaned him out and ran. He needed it back desperately. His finances were shot to hell, he was up to his ears in debt and the business was not working out. This was his one chance. It had fallen into his lap, then she had snatched it and run.

There was one thing in his favour, though: the world in which she was running was smaller than she thought. Anyone she went to, with what she had, would ask questions. A lot of questions. He suspected she had already begun to find that out, which was why she was still around, and now her problems had been further complicated by his arrival in Brighton.

*

At 9.30 a local Eastbourne taxi pulled up outside the front door of the block of flats. The driver got out and rang the bell. A couple of minutes later, Abby appeared. On her own.

Good.

Perfect.

She was going to the first of the three appointments at rest homes she had made for this morning. Leaving Mummy alone, under strict instructions no doubt not to answer the door to anyone but the locksmith.

He watched Abby climb in and the taxi drive off. He didn't move. He knew how unpredictable women could be and that she might easily be back in five minutes for something she had forgotten. He had plenty of time. She'd be gone an hour and a half, minimum, and more likely three or more. He just had to be patient for a little while longer to ensure the coast was clear.

Then he would not need very long at all.

83

OCTOBER 2007

Glenn Branson pressed the bell and stood back a couple of feet, so that the security camera could get a good look at him. The wrought-iron gates jerked a few times, then began silently to swing open. The DS climbed back into the pool car and drove through two impressive brick pillars on to the circular in-and-out drive, the tyres crunching on the gravel. He pulled up behind a silver Mercedes sports and a silver S-class saloon, parked side by side.

'It's all right, this place, don't you think?' he said. 'Matching *his* and *hers* Mercs and all.'

Bella Moy nodded, some of the colour just starting to return to her face. Glenn's driving totally terrified her. She liked Glenn and didn't want to offend him, but if she could have taken a bus back to the office, or walked there barefoot on burning coals, she would have done.

The palatial house was partly faux-Georgian, and partly faux-Greek temple, with a columned portico running along the entire width of the front. Ari would die for this place, Glenn thought. Funny, when they'd first got married she hadn't seemed interested in money at all. That had all changed around the time Sammy, who was now eight, started going to school. No doubt talking with the other mums, seeing some of their fancy cars, going to some of their flash houses.

But houses like this fascinated him too. It seemed to Glenn that houses gave off auras. There were plenty of others in this area, and elsewhere in the city, that were every bit as large and swanky, but they gave the impression of being lived in by ordinary, decent citizens. Just occasionally you saw a place like this one now, which seemed somehow *too* flash, and sent out signals, wittingly or unwittingly, that it had not been acquired by honest money.

'Would you like to live here, Bella?' he asked.

'I could get used to it.' She smiled, then looked a tad wistful.

He shot her a sideways glance. She was a nice-looking woman, with a cheery face beneath a tangle of brown hair and no ring on her wedding finger. She always dressed in slightly dowdy clothes, as if not interested in making the best of herself, and he longed to give her a makeover. Today she was wearing a white blouse under a plain navy V-neck sweater, black woollen trousers, solid black shoes and a short green duffel coat.

She never talked about her private life and he often wondered what she went home to. A guy, a woman, a group of flatmates? One of his colleagues had once said that Bella looked after her elderly mum, but Bella never mentioned this.

'I can't remember where it is you live,' he said as they climbed out of the car. A gust of wind lifted the tails of his camel coat.

'Hangleton,' she said.

'Right.'

That sort of fitted. Hangleton was a pleasant, quiet residential sprawl on the west of the city, bisected by a motorway and a golf course. Lots of small houses and bungalows and neatly tended gardens. It was exactly the kind of quiet, safe area a woman might live in with her elderly mother. He suddenly had an image in his mind of a sad-looking Bella at home, caring for a sick, frail lady, munching away on her Maltesers as a substitute for any other kind of a life. Like a forlorn, caged pet.

He rang the bell and they were ushered in by a Filipino maid, who led them through into a high-ceilinged orangery, with a view down across terraced lawns containing an infinity swimming pool and a tennis court.

They were ushered into armchairs arranged around a marble coffee table and offered drinks. Then Stephen and Sue Klinger came in.

Stephen was a tall, lean, rather cold-looking man in his late forties, with greying wavy hair brushed harshly back, and his cheeks were a patchwork of purple drinker's veins. He was wearing a pinstriped suit and expensive-looking loafers, and glanced at his watch the moment after he shook Branson's hand.

'I'm afraid I have to be away in ten minutes,' he said, his voice hard and bland, very different from the Stephen Klinger they had interviewed yesterday in his office after what had clearly been a very heavy lunch.

'No problem, sir, we just have a few more quick questions for you and some for Mrs Klinger. We appreciate your taking the time to see us again.'

He gave Sue Klinger an appreciative second glance and she smirked slyly, as if noticing. She was a serious looker, he thought. Early forties, in great shape, dressed in a brown brushed-cotton designer tracksuit and trainers that looked like they were fresh out of their box.

And she had real *come-to-bed* eyes. Which he caught

twice in fast succession and then did his best to ignore, opening his notebook, deciding to focus on Stephen Klinger's eyes, which might be easier to read.

The maid came in with coffee and water.

'Can I just recap, sir? How long had you and Ronnie Wilson been friends?' Branson asked.

Klinger's eyes moved to his left, a fraction. 'We go – went – back to our late teens,' he said. 'Twenty-seven – no – thirty years. Roughly.'

As a double check, Glenn said, 'And you told us yesterday that his relationship with his first wife, Joanna, had been difficult, but it was better with Lorraine?'

Again the eyes moved to the left a fraction before he spoke.

This was a neurolinguistic experiment Glenn had learned about from Roy Grace, and he sometimes found it of great assistance in assessing whether someone was telling the truth in an interview. Human brains were divided into left and right hemispheres. One was for long-term memory storage, while in the other the creative processes took place. When asked a question, people's eyes almost invariably moved to the hemisphere they were using. In some people the memory storage was in the right hemisphere and in some the left; the creative hemisphere would be the opposite one.

So now he knew that when Stephen Klinger's eyes moved to the left in response to a question they were moving to his memory side, which meant he was likely to be telling the truth. So if his eyes moved right, then that meant he was likely to be lying. It wasn't a failsafe technique but it could be a good indicator.

Leaning forward, as the maid put down his cup and saucer, and a china jug of milk, Branson said, 'In your opinion, sir, do you think Ronnie Wilson would have been capable of murdering either of his wives?'

The look of shock on Klinger's face was genuine. As was the double-take on his wife's. His eyes stayed dead centre as he replied. 'Not Ronnie, no. He had a temper on him, but . . .' He shrugged, shaking his head.

'He had a kind heart,' Sue added. 'He liked to look after his friends. I don't think – no, definitely, I don't think so.'

'We have some information we'd like to share with you, in confidence at this stage, although we will be making a statement to the press in the next few days.'

Branson glanced at Bella, as if offering her the opportunity to speak, but she signalled back she was happy for him to continue.

He poured some milk into his coffee, then said, 'It doesn't seem that Joanna Wilson ever made it to America. Her body was found in a storm drain in the centre of Brighton on Friday. She'd been there for a long time and she appears to have been strangled.'

Now both of them looked genuinely shocked.

'Shit!' Sue said.

'Is that the one that was in the *Argus* on Monday?' Stephen wondered.

Bella nodded at him.

'Are you saying that – that – Ronnie had something to do with it?' he asked.

'If I may continue for a moment, sir,' Branson pressed, 'we learned yesterday that Lorraine Wilson's body has also been found.'

Sue Klinger blanched. 'In the Channel?'

'No, in a river outside Melbourne, in Australia.'

Both Klingers sat looking at him in stunned silence. Somewhere in the house a phone started ringing. No one made any move to answer it. Glenn drank some of his coffee.

'*Melbourne?*' Sue Klinger said eventually. '*Australia?*'

'How on earth did she get there from the English Channel?' Stephen asked, looking totally astonished.

The ringing stopped. 'The post-mortem has shown that she has only been dead for two years, sir – so it doesn't look as if she did commit suicide by jumping into the Channel back in 2002.'

'So she did it by jumping into a river in Australia instead?' Stephen said.

'I don't think so,' Glenn replied. 'Her neck was broken and she was in the boot of a car.' He held back the rest of the information he had.

Both the Klingers sat very still, absorbing the impact of what they had just heard. Finally Stephen broke the silence. 'By whom? Why? Are you saying the same person killed Joanna and Lorraine?'

'We can't tell at this stage. But there are some similarities in the way they both appear to have been killed.'

'Who – who would have killed Joanna – and then Lorraine?' Sue asked. She began twisting a gold bracelet on her wrist round and round nervously.

'Were either of you aware that Joanna Wilson inherited a house from her mother, which she sold shortly before her death?' Glenn asked. 'It netted an amount of approximately one hundred and seventy-five thousand pounds. We are now trying to track down what happened to that money.'

'Probably went to pay off Ronnie's debts the moment it came into her account,' Stephen said. 'I liked the old bugger but he wasn't too clever with money, if you know what I mean. Always wheeling and dealing, but never getting it quite right. He wanted to be a much bigger player than he had the ability for.'

'That's a bit harsh, Steve,' Sue commented, turning to face her husband. 'Ronnie had good ideas.' She looked at the two detectives and tapped her head. 'He had an inventive mind. He once invented a gizmo for extracting air from wine bottles that had been opened. He was in the process of patenting it when that – what's it called? – Vacu Vin came out and cleaned up in the market.'

'Yeah, but the Vacu Vin was plastic,' Stephen said. 'Ronnie made his out of brass, the stupid sod. Anybody could have told him that metals react with wine.'

'You said yourself at the time you thought it was smart, didn't you?'

'Yeah, but I wouldn't invest in any business Ronnie was running. Done it twice before and both went down the toilet.' He shrugged. 'You need more than a good idea to make a business work.' He glanced at his watch and looked a little agitated.

'Mr and Mrs Klinger,' Bella said, 'did you have any idea that Lorraine had come into a substantial amount of money in the months before she – *seemingly* – ended her life?'

Sue shook her head vigorously. 'No way. I'd have been the first to know. Ronnie left her in a terrible mess, poor thing. She had to go back to work at Gatwick. She couldn't get any credit because of all the judgements against Ronnie. She couldn't even scrape enough cash together to buy a car. I even lent her a few hundred quid to tide her over at one point.'

'Well, this may come as a surprise to you both,' Glenn

said, 'but Ronnie Wilson had a life insurance policy with the Norwich Union which paid out just over one and a half million pounds to Lorraine Wilson in March 2002.'

Their shock was palpable. Then he added to it.

'Further, in July 2002, Mrs Wilson received a payment of nearly two and a half million dollars from the 9/11 compensation fund. About one and three-quarter million pounds at the exchange rate at that time.'

There was a long silence.

'I don't believe it. I just don't believe—' Sue shook her head. 'I know at the time she disappeared the police officers we spoke to didn't seem entirely convinced that she had committed suicide by jumping off the boat. They didn't say why. Perhaps they knew something then that we didn't. But Stephen and I, and all her friends, were convinced she was dead, and none of us has heard a single word from her since.'

'If what you are saying is true, that's—' Stephen Klinger broke off in mid-sentence.

'She withdrew all of it, in cash, in different amounts, between the time she received the money and her disappearance in November 2002,' Bella said.

'Cash?' Stephen Klinger echoed.

'Would either of you have any idea if the Wilsons – or more likely Ronnie – were being blackmailed by anyone?' Glenn asked.

'Lorraine and I were very close,' Sue said. 'I think she'd have told me – you know – confided in me.'

The way she confided in you about the three and a quarter million quid! Glenn thought.

Stephen Klinger suddenly stabbed a finger in the air. 'There's one thing – could be that Ronnie had taught her this. He liked to trade stamps.'

'Stamps?' Glenn said. 'Like postage stamps, you mean?'

He nodded. 'Big-ticket ones. He always traded them for cash. Reckoned it was harder for the Revenue to keep tabs on him.'

'Three million plus pounds would be an awful lot of stamps,' Bella said.

Stephen shook his head. 'Not necessarily. I remember Ronnie opening his wallet one night in a pub and showing me this one stamp, all in tissue paper, just *one* stamp he'd paid *fifty grand* for. Reckoned he had a buyer who would pay sixty for it. But knowing his luck, he probably ended up getting forty.'

'Would you have any idea where Mr Wilson did his stamp trading?'

'There's a few local dealers he told me he used, for smaller stuff. I know he dealt with a place called Hawkes down Queen's Road sometimes. And with one or two places in London, and in New York, as well. Oh yeah, and he used to talk about some big player who deals from home – can't remember his name – he's just around the corner in Dyke Road. Someone at Hawkes would be able to tell you.'

Glenn noted the name down.

'He did say that at the top end of the market it's a very small world. If any dealer made a large sale, everyone in the business would know about it. So if she spent that kind of money on stamps, someone's going to remember.'

'And presumably,' Bella said, 'someone would also remember if she sold them.'

84

OCTOBER 2007

It was Duncan Troutt's first day on patrol as a fully fledged police officer. He felt rather proud, rather self-conscious and, in truth, a little nervous of screwing up.

At five feet nine inches tall and just under ten stone, he cut a slight figure, but he knew how to look after himself. A long-time fan of martial arts, he had attained a whole raft of certificates in kickboxing, taekwondo and kung fu.

His girlfriend, Sonia, had given him a framed poster which read:

YEA, THOUGH I WALK ALONE THROUGH THE SHADOW OF
THE VALLEY OF DEATH, I FEAR NO EVIL, FOR I AM
THE MEANEST SON OF A BITCH IN THE VALLEY.

Right now, at 10 a.m., the Meanest Son of a Bitch in the Valley was at the junction of Marine Parade and Arundel Road, at the eastern extremity of Brighton and Hove. Not exactly a valley. Not even a small dip, really. The streets were calm at the moment. In another hour or so the drug addicts would be starting to surface. One statistic that the local tourist board did not like to advertise was that the city had the second largest number of injecting drug users – and drug deaths – per capita in the UK. Troutt had been warned that a disproportionately large share of them appeared to live on his beat.

His radio crackled and he heard his call sign. He answered it with excitement and heard the voice of Sergeant Morley.

'All OK, Duncan?'

'Yes, Sarge. So far, Sarge.'

The area of Troutt's beat extended from the Kemp Town seafront back to the Whitehawk estate, which housed, historically, some of the city's roughest and most violent families – as well as many decent folk. And recent community policing initiatives were resulting in big and positive changes. The warren of terraced streets in between contained the transients' world of rooming houses and cheap hotels, a prosperous urban residential community, including one of the largest gay communities in the UK, and dozens of restaurants, pubs and smaller independent shops. It was also home to several schools as well as the city's hospital.

'Need you to check out a person of concern. A woman reportedly in an anxious state.' He then outlined the circumstances.

Troutt pulled out his brand-new notebook and wrote down the name, *Katherine Jennings*, and her address.

'This has come from the Inspector, and I think it's come down from someone high up in the brass, if you know what I mean.'

'Absolutely, Sarge. I'm very close – will attend now.'

With a new urgency to his stride, he strutted along blustery Marine Parade and turned left away from the seafront.

The address was a mansion block of flats, eight storeys,

and there was a builder's lorry, as well as a van from a lift company, double-parked in the street. He passed a grey Ford Focus that had a parking ticket taped to its windscreen, crossed over and walked up to the front entrance, stepping aside to let two men carry in a large sheet of plasterboard. Then he looked at the doorbell panel. There was no name against number 82. The PC pressed it. There was no answer.

At the bottom of the panel was a bell for the caretaker, but as the front door was wedged open he decided to go in. There was an OUT OF ORDER sign taped across the front of the lift, so he took the stairs, treading carefully up the trail of dust sheets, slightly irritated that the shoes he had carefully polished last night were getting caked in dust. He heard hammering and banging and the sound of drilling directly above him, and on the fifth floor he had to negotiate an obstacle course of building materials.

He walked on up and reached the eighth floor. The door to Katherine Jennings's flat was directly in front of him. The sight of three separate locks on it, along with the spyhole, aroused his curiosity. Two was not unusual, as he knew from his experience of visiting homes that had suffered repeated break-ins in the Brighton crime hotspots. But three was excessive. He peered more closely at them, noting that they all looked substantial.

You are worried about something, lady, he thought to himself, as he rang the bell.

There was no answer. He tried a couple more times, waiting patiently, then decided to go and have a chat with the caretaker.

As he reached the small downstairs lobby, two men came in. One was in his thirties, with a pleasant demeanour, wearing a boiler suit with *Stanwell Maintenance* embossed on the breast pocket, and a tool-belt. The other was a bolshy-looking man in his sixties, in dungarees over a grimy sweatshirt. He was holding an old-fashioned mobile phone and had a blackened fingernail.

The workman gave Troutt a bemused smile. 'Gosh, you came quickly!'

The older man held up his phone. 'I only phone you, what, less than one minute!' His guttural accent made it sound like a complaint.

'Phoned me?'

'About the lift!'

'I'm sorry,' Troutt said. 'You are?'

'The caretaker.'

'I'm afraid I'm actually here on other business,' Troutt said. 'But I'm more than happy to try to help if you'd like to tell me the problem.'

'It's very simple,' the younger man said. 'The lift mechanism's been tampered with. Vandalized. Sabotaged. And the alarm and the phone in the lift – the wire's been cut.'

Now he had Troutt's full attention. The PC pulled his notebook out.

'Can you give me some details?'

'I can bloody show you. How technical-minded are you?'

Troutt shrugged. 'You can try me.'

'I need to take you to the motor room to show you. There are syringes on the floor. More importantly someone has tampered with the brake mechanism while the lift was in operation.'

'All right. First, I need to talk to this gentleman for a moment.'

The workman nodded. 'I'm just going to move my van. Bloody wardens round here are like the Gestapo.'

As he walked off, Troutt addressed the caretaker. 'You have a resident in flat 82 – Katherine Jennings?'

'She new. Been there only a few weeks. Short let.'

'Can you tell me anything about her?'

'I not speak much to her, except Sunday, after she was stuck in the lift. She got plenty money, I can tell you the rent she pay.'

'Who do you think vandalized the lift? Local yobs? Or something to do with her?'

The caretaker shrugged. 'I think maybe he no wants to admit there's a mechanical problem. Maybe he protect himself or his company?'

Troutt nodded, not rising to this. He would form his own judgement after visiting the motor room with the engineer.

'So you don't know what she does for a living?'

The caretaker shook his head.

'Is she married? Any kids?'

'She on her own.'

'Do you have any idea about her movements?'

'I'm at the other end of the block, I don't see the tenants in this wing unless they have a problem. She in trouble with the police?'

'No, nothing like that.' He gave the man a reassuring smile. 'I should introduce myself – PC Troutt. I'm one of your new neighbourhood officers.' He fished out a card.

The caretaker took it and looked at it dubiously, as if it was from a double-glazing salesman. 'I hope you come down here on Friday and Saturday nights, late. Last Friday night we have little bastards set light to a dustbin,' he grumbled.

'Yes, well, that's exactly the sort of thing this new initiative is all about,' the young PC said earnestly.

'I believe when I see it.'

85

OCTOBER 2007

'Yo, old-timer, taken off yet?'

Grace, standing in his socks at Gatwick Airport's South Terminal, watched his shoes appear on the conveyor belt on the far side of the scanner. Holding his mobile phone to his ear he replied, 'Only my sodding shoes, so far. It pisses me off, this,' he went on. 'Have to remove more and more bloody clothes every time you fly. Just because some loony tried to set light to his laces about five years ago! And I've had to check my overnight bag in, because it's too big for the new regulations, which means I'm going to have to wait for it at the other end. Bloody waste of time!'

'So, you had a bad night, did you?'

Grace grinned at the memory of a very sweet night with Cleo. 'Actually, no. It was a lot better than the night before. I didn't get shit-faced with some miserable git pouring out his woes to me.'

Ignoring the barb, the DS retorted, 'And the dog didn't throw up on you again?'

Grace, who was wearing a suit because he wanted to look businesslike when he arrived in New York, struggled to lace up his right shoe while keeping the phone wedged to his ear. He gave up trying to do it standing up and sat down. 'No, it just did a dump on the floor instead.'

'You all right, man? Your voice sounds muffled.'

'I'm fine, I'm trying to put my fucking shoes back on. Are you phoning about anything important or is this just a social chat?'

'What do you know about stamps?' Branson asked.

'First or second class?'

'Very funny.'

'I can tell you a bit about British Colonials,' Grace said. 'My dad collected them – first-day covers. Used to get them for me when I was a boy. They're worthless. My mum asked me to take his whole collection to a dealer after he died – they wouldn't give me two beans for them. If you're thinking of a hobby, you could try collecting butterflies – or what about trainspotting?'

'Yeah, yeah! Finished?'

Grace grunted.

'Listen, me and Bella have just been with the Klingers, right? That cash, all those transactions Lorraine Wilson made – that three million plus quid, yeah? I think she may have been buying stamps.'

'You do?'

Grace suddenly stopped tying his shoe and concentrated. He was thinking back to the conversation he'd had with Terry Biglow on Tuesday.

She was . . . in a terrible state after Ronnie died . . . the mortgage company took the house . . . the finance people took just about everything else, except for a few stamps.

'Yeah. Stephen Klinger said to me that it was a small world, the high-end stamp trade. Like, everyone knew everyone.'

'Did he give you a list of local dealers?'

'Some names, yeah.'

'Listen, Glenn. When you get any tight-knit group, they tend to close ranks, as much to protect themselves as anyone they're giving information about. So go in and break their balls, understand?'

'Uh huh.'

'Tell them this is a murder inquiry, so if they withhold any information they could end up being charged as accessories after the fact. Ram that down their throats.'

'Yes, boss man. Have a nice flight. Give my love to the Big Apple. Enjoy.'

'I'll send you a postcard.'

'Don't forget to put a stamp on it.'

86

OCTOBER 2007

Bella radioed one of the researchers in the *Operation Dingo* incident room and asked her to compile a complete list of all stamp dealers in the Brighton and Hove area. Then, with Glenn driving again, they headed for Queen's Road and the dealer Stephen Klinger had mentioned.

Just down from the station, Hawkes looked like one of those places that have been there for ever. It had the kind of window display that never changed but was just added to from time to time. It was full of boxed coin sets, medals, first-day covers in plastic envelopes and old postcards.

They hurried inside, out of the hardening drizzle, and saw two women in their thirties who could be sisters, both fair-haired and good-looking, not the image Branson had in his mind of a stamp dealer at all. He'd imagined stamps to be a rather nerdy male domain.

The women were deep in conversation and didn't acknowledge the detectives, as if used to time-wasting browsers. Glenn and Bella glanced around, politely waiting for them to finish. The shop was even more cluttered inside, with much of the floor space taken up with trestle tables on which were cardboard boxes filled with vintage saucy postcards and bygone Brighton scenes.

The women stopped talking suddenly and turned to look at them. Branson pulled out his warrant card.

'I'm Detective Sergeant Branson of Sussex CID and this is my colleague, Detective Sergeant Moy. We'd like to have a word with the proprietor. Would that be one of you?'

'Yes,' said the older-looking one, pleasantly, but slightly reserved. 'I'm Jacqueline Hawkes. What is this about?'

'Do the names Ronnie and Lorraine Wilson mean anything to you?'

She looked surprised and shot a glance at the other woman. 'Ronnie Wilson? Mum used to deal with him some years back. I remember him well. He was often in and out, haggling. He's dead, isn't he? He died in 9/11, I seem to remember.'

'Yes,' Bella said, not wanting to give anything away.

'Was he a big trader? At a high level?' Branson asked. 'You know, very rare stamps?'

She shook her head. 'Not here. We don't deal much at the top end – we don't have that kind of stock. We're just high street retail, really.'

'What kind of values do you go up to?'

'Small stuff, mostly. Stamps with a value of a few hundred pounds are about the highest we get involved with. Unless someone comes in with an obvious bargain, then we might go up a bit.'

'Did Lorraine Wilson ever come in here?' he said.

Jacqueline thought for a moment, then nodded. 'Yes, she did – I can't remember when exactly. Not that long after he died, I think it must have been. She had some stamps of her husband's she wanted to sell. We bought them – not a huge amount – a few hundred pounds' worth, from memory.'

'Did she ever talk to you about dealing in a much larger amount? Spending serious money?'

'What kind of *serious* money?'

'Hundreds of thousands.'

She shook her head. 'Never.'

'If someone came to see you wanting to buy, say, several hundred thousand pounds' worth of stamps, what would you do?'

'I'd direct them to an auction house in London or to a specialist dealer, and hope he'd be decent enough to give me a bit of comission!'

'Who would you send them to in this area?'

She shrugged. 'There's really only one person in Brighton who deals at the level you're talking about. That's Hugo Hegarty. He's getting on a bit, but I know he's still trading.'

'Do you have an address for him?'

'Yes. I'll get it for you.'

*

Dyke Road, which turned seamlessly into Dyke Road Avenue, ran like a spine from close to the centre of the city right up to the edge of the Downs, and formed part of the border between Brighton and Hove. Apart from a couple of sections where it was lined with shops, offices and restaurants, for much of its length it was residential, with detached houses that got progressively swankier away from the city centre.

To Bella's relief the traffic was heavy, forcing Glenn to drive at a sedate crawl. Calling out the numbers, she said, 'Coming up on the left.'

There was an in-and-out driveway, which seemed an almost mandatory status symbol for this neighbourhood. But, unlike at the Klingers' house, there were no electric gates, just wooden ones that did not look as if they had been closed in years. The drive was completely cluttered with cars, so Branson parked outside, putting two wheels on the pavement, aware that he was obstructing a cycle lane, but not able to do much about it.

They walked in, edging past an elderly BMW convertible, an even older Saab, a grimy, grey Aston Martin DB7 and two Volkswagen Golfs. He wondered if Hegarty traded in cars as well as stamps.

They ducked into the shelter of a porch and rang the bell. When the imposing oak door was opened, Glenn Branson did an immediate double-take. The man who answered was a dead ringer for one of his favourite film actors of all time, Richard Harris. He was so startled that for a moment he was lost for words as he fumbled for his warrant card.

The man had one of those craggy faces Glenn found hard to put an age to. He could have been anywhere between mid-sixties and late seventies. His hair, closer to white than grey, was long and rather unkempt, and he was dressed in a cricket sweater over a sports shirt and tracksuit bottoms.

'Detective Sergeant Branson and Detective Sergeant Moy from Sussex CID,' Glenn said. 'We'd like to have a word with Mr Hegarty. Is that you?'

'Depends which Mr Hegarty you're after,' he said with an evasive smile. 'One of my sons or me?'

'Mr *Hugo* Hegarty,' Bella said.

'That's me.' He looked at his watch. 'I've got to leave in twenty minutes to play tennis.'

'We only need a few minutes, sir,' she said. 'We want to talk to you about someone we believe you had dealings with some years ago – Ronnie Wilson.'

Hugo Hegarty's eyes narrowed and he looked very concerned suddenly. 'Ronnie. Good God! You know he's dead?' He hesitated before stepping back and saying, in slightly more affable tones, 'Do you want to come in? It's a foul day.'

They entered a long, oak-panelled hall hung with fine oil paintings, then followed Hegarty through into a similarly panelled study with a studded crimson leather sofa and a matching recliner armchair. There was a view out through the leaded-light windows on to a swimming pool, a large lawn bordered by autumnal-looking shrubs and bare flowerbeds, and the roof of a neighbour's house beyond the closeboard fence. Directly above them was the whine-thump whine-thump of a vacuum cleaner.

It was an orderly room. There were shelves laden with what looked like golfing trophies and a mass of photographs on the desk. One was of a handsome, silver-haired woman, presumably Hegarty's wife, and others showed shots of two teenage boys, two teenage girls and a baby. Next to the blotter on the desk was an enormous magnifying glass.

Hegarty pointed them to the sofa, then perched on the edge of the armchair. 'Poor old Ronnie. Terrible business, all that. Just his luck to be there on that one day.' He gave a nervous laugh. 'So, how can I help you?'

Branson noticed a row of thick, heavy-looking, Stanley Gibbons stamp catalogues and a row of another dozen or so other catalogues lining the bookshelves. 'It's concerning an inquiry we're carrying out which has some links to Mr Wilson,' he replied. 'You trade in valuable stamps, we've been told. Is that correct, sir?'

Hegarty nodded, then scrunched up his face in a slightly dismissive way. 'Maybe not so much now. The market's very difficult. I do more with property and stocks and shares than with stamps these days. But I still dabble a bit. I like to keep my finger on the pulse.'

He had a twinkle in his eye, which Branson liked. Richard Harris had had that same twinkle – it was part of the great actor's magic. 'Would you say you did a substantial amount of business with Mr Wilson?'

Hegarty shrugged. 'A fair bit, on and off over the years. Ronnie wasn't the easiest person to deal with.'

'In what way?'

'Well, you know, to put it crudely, the provenance of some of his stuff was iffy. I've always been careful to protect my reputation, if you get my drift.'

Branson made a note. 'Do you mean you felt some of his dealings were dishonest?'

'Some of what he had I wouldn't buy at any price. I used to wonder sometimes where he got the stamps he brought to me and whether he'd actually paid what he claimed he had for them.' He shrugged. 'But he had a fair grasp of the business, and I sold him some good things too. He always paid cash on the nail. But . . .' His voice trailed away and he shook his head. 'To be honest, I have to say he wasn't my favourite customer. I try to look after people I do business with. You can trade with someone a thousand times, I always say, but you can only screw them once.'

Glenn smiled, but said nothing more.

Bella tried to move things on. 'Mr Hegarty, did Mrs Wilson – Mrs Lorraine Wilson – contact you at all after his death?'

Hegarty hesitated for a second, his eyes shooting warily at each of them in turn, as if the stakes had suddenly been raised. 'Yes, she did,' he answered decisively.

'Can you tell us why she contacted you?'

'Well, I suppose it doesn't matter now – she's also been dead a long while. But I was sworn to secrecy by her, you see.'

Remembering Grace's instructions, Branson put things as tactfully to the man as he could. 'We are dealing with a murder inquiry, Mr Hegarty. We require all the information you can give us.'

Hegarty looked shocked. 'Murder? I had no idea. Oh dear. Gosh. Who – who is the victim?'

'I'm afraid I cannot disclose that at the moment.'

'No, right, of course,' Hegarty said. He had blanched visibly. 'Well, let me get this straight in my head.' He thought for a moment. 'The thing was, she came to see me – I suppose it was about February or March in 2002 that would be – or perhaps April – I can check that for you from my records. She said that her husband had left massive debts when he died and every penny they had had been taken and their house had been repossessed. It sounded a bit brutal, to be frank, to hound a widow like that.'

He looked at them as if for support, but got no reaction.

He went on, 'She told me she'd just discovered she was due some money from a life insurance policy and was scared about his creditors getting hold of that too. Apparently she was a joint signatory on a number of personal guarantees. So she wanted to convert it into stamps, which she thought – quite rightly – would be easier to hide. Something I think she had learned from her husband.'

'How much money was it?' Bella asked.

'Well, the first lot was one and a half million, give or take a few bob. And then she came into the same amount or even a bit more again months later, from the 9/11 compensation fund, she told me.'

Branson was pleased that the amounts Hegarty stated tallied with their earlier information. It suggested he was telling the truth.

'And she asked you to convert it all into stamps?' he asked.

'It sounds easier than it was,' he said. 'That kind of spending draws attention, you see. So I fronted the purchases for her. I spread the money around the stamp world, saying I was buying for an anonymous collector. That's not unusual. In recent years the Chinese have gone bananas for quality stamps – the only bad thing is that some dealers are flogging them rubbish.' He raised a cautionary finger. 'Even some of the most respected dealers.'

'Can you provide us with a list of all the stamps you sold to Mrs Wilson?' Bella asked.

'Yes, but you'll have to give me a little time. I could make a start after my game – could let you have it by around teatime this afternoon. Would that be OK?'

'Perfect,' Branson said.

'And what would be extremely useful,' Bella added, 'is if you could let us have a list of all the people she could have gone to who would have had the money to buy them later on, when she needed the cash.'

'I can give you the dealers,' he said. 'And a few individual collectors like myself. Not so many of us as there were. I'm afraid quite a few of my old friends in this game are now dead.'

'Do you know any dealers or collectors in Australia?' she asked.

'Australia?' He frowned. 'Australia? Now, wait a minute. Of course, there was someone Ronnie knew from Brighton who emigrated out there, some years back, in the mid-1990s. His name was Skeggs. Chad Skeggs. He's always dealt in big numbers. He operates a mail order business from Melbourne. Sends me a catalogue every now and then.'

'Do you ever buy from him?' Glenn asked.

Hegarty shook his head. 'No, he's dodgy. Tucked me up once. I bought some pre-1913 Australian stamps from him, I seem to recall. But they weren't in anything like the condition he'd told me over the phone. When I complained, he told me to sue him.' Hegarty raised despairing hands in the air. 'The amount wasn't worth it and he knew that. A couple of grand – it would have cost me more than that in legal fees. I'm amazed the blighter's still in business.'

'Anyone else in Australia you can think of?' Bella asked.

'Tell you what I'll do, I'll give you a full list this afternoon. Want to pop back around, say, 4?'

'Fine, thank you, sir,' Branson said.

As they all stood up, Hegarty leaned forward conspiratorially, as if for their ears only. 'I don't suppose you can help me,' he said. 'I got flashed by one of your cameras – along Old Shoreham Road – a couple of days ago. You couldn't have a word in someone's ear for me, could you?'

Branson looked at him, astonished. 'I'm afraid not, sir.'

'Ah, well, not to worry. Just thought I'd ask.'

He gave them a rueful smile.

87

OCTOBER 2007

Abby sat in the back of the taxi, re-reading a new text that had just come in. It lifted her spirits and made her smile.

> *Remember . . . Work like you don't need the money. Love like you've never been hurt. Dance like nobody is watching.*

The driver lifted her spirits too. He used to be a boxer, he said, never made the big time but did a bit of training now, encouraging kids into the sport. He had a flattened boxer's face, she thought, as if at some point in his life he'd hit a concrete wall, face-first, at about a hundred miles an hour. He told her during the journey back from the third rest home she had visited that morning that he too had an elderly mother with health problems, but couldn't afford the charges of these homes.

Abby couldn't think of a quotation to text back, so instead she just said:

> *Soon! I can't wait. I miss u soooo much. Xxxxxx*

It was shortly after 1 o'clock as they pulled up outside her mother's apartment block. Abby looked around, checking for any sign of Ricky, but the coast looked clear. She asked the driver to wait and keep the meter running. The first two places she'd seen this morning were horrible, but the third was fine and, most importantly, it seemed secure. Best of all, it had a vacancy. Abby decided she was going to take her mum there right now.

All she needed to do was throw a few things in a bag. She knew how slow her mum was, but she would do it all for her and hustle her out. Her mum might not like it, but she would have to lump it for a few weeks. At least she would be safe there. Abby could not go on relying indefinitely on the services of her mum's new minder, the redoubtable Doris – whose last name she didn't even know.

With her mother secure, she could put into action the plan she'd been figuring out during the past few hours. The first part of which was to get as far away from here as possible. The second was to find someone she could take into her confidence. But she would need to trust them totally.

How many strangers could she trust to hold everything she had in the world and not run off with it like she had?

This cab driver seemed a good type. She had a feeling she could trust him if she needed to. But would he be able to keep Ricky at bay on his own, or would he need a couple of others with him? Which meant she would be putting her trust in one person she had known for thirty minutes and others she had never met. That was too big a gamble after all she had gone through to get this far.

At this moment, though, she didn't have a huge number of other options. The rent on the flat was paid in advance for three months, with two still to run, and that had taken the biggest bite out of her cash reserves. And the one-month payment in advance for her mother's room at the Bexhill Lawns Rest House this morning hadn't helped. She had enough credit left on her card to see her through a couple of months, if she holed up in a cheap hotel somewhere. After that she would need to get at her resources. And to do that she had to evade Ricky.

She thanked God for the sheer luck she hadn't yet transferred them to her newly acquired safe-deposit box.

She should have realized, from all she knew about Ricky, that he was a wizard with electronics. He'd boasted to her one night that he had front desk staff at half the top hotels in Melbourne and Sydney working for him, passing him the returned plastic room keys of guests who had checked out. Those keys contained their credit card details and their home addresses. He had a willing buyer for the information, he'd told her, and the scam, or rather, *data service,* as he liked to call it, netted him far more than his legitimate business.

She let herself in the front entrance and walked along the corridor to her mother's flat. She had rung her mother twice to check she was OK. The first time had been at about 10.30, when her mother told her the locksmith had rung to say he would be there by 11. And the second time was an hour ago, when she said the man was there.

Abby was dismayed to discover that her key still unlocked the door. More worryingly, she saw no sign of any workman having been there at all. She called out anxiously, then hurried across the hallway and into the sitting room.

To her astonishment, the carpet had been removed. The red carpet she remembered from her childhood, that she had cleaned the spilt rice pudding off yesterday, was gone. All that remained were some patches of worn-out underlay on top of bare, rough boards.

For a moment her whole world skewed as she tried to make a connection between having new door locks and the need to take up a carpet. Something felt totally wrong.

'Mum! Mum!!!!' she called out, in case her mother was in the kitchen, or the loo, or the bedroom.

Where was Doris? Hadn't she promised to stay in her mother's flat with her?

She ran, in growing panic, into each room in turn. Then she rushed out of the flat, tore up the staircase two steps at a time and rang the bell of Doris's flat. Then she knocked on the door with her fist as well.

After what felt like an eternity, she heard the familiar rattle of the safety chain and, as before, the door opened a few inches. Doris, in her massive dark glasses, peered out warily, then gave her a welcoming smile and opened the door wider.

'Hello, my dear!'

Abby was instantly relieved by the cheeriness of the greeting and for an instant felt sure that Doris was going to say her mother was up here in her flat.

'Oh, hi, I just wondered if you knew what was going on downstairs.'

'With the locksmith?'

So he had arrived. 'Yes.'

'Well, he's getting on with the work, dear. He seems a very charming young man. Is anything wrong?'

'You checked his ID, like I told you?'

'Yes, dear, he had a card from the company. I had my magnifying lens with me to make sure I could read it. Lockworks, wasn't it?'

At that moment, Abby's phone started ringing. She looked down at the display and saw it was her mother's new number. She looked back at Doris.

'It's OK, thanks.'

Doris raised a finger. 'There's something burning on the stove, dear. Pop back up if you need me.'

Abby took the call as Doris closed the door.

It was her mother's voice. But it was all trembling and wrong, and breathless, as if she was reading from a script.

'Abby,' she said. 'Ricky wants to speak to you. I'm going to put him on. Please do exactly what he tells you.'

Then the line went dead.

Abby frantically redialled. It went straight to voicemail. Then almost instantly she had another incoming call. The display read: *Private number calling.*

It was Ricky.

88

OCTOBER 2007

'Where's my mother?' Abby yelled into the phone before Ricky had a chance to speak. 'Where is she, you bastard? WHERE IS SHE?'

A door behind her opened and an elderly man peered out, then closed it again loudly.

Distraught now, in retrospect, that she had been so stupid as to leave her mother with this old woman, Abby hurried to the relative privacy of the stairwell.

'I want to speak to her now. Where is she?'

'Your mother is fine, Abby,' he said. 'She's as snug as a bug in a rug – in case you were wondering where it had gone.'

With the phone clamped to her ears, she tripped back downstairs and into her mother's flat, closing the door behind her. She walked through into the sitting room, staring at the bare boards showing through the underlay again. Tears were streaming down her face. She was shaking, starting to feel disassociated, the first signs of a panic attack coming on.

'I'm calling the police, Ricky,' she said. 'I don't care about anything else any more. OK? I'm going to call the police right now.'

'I don't think so, Abby,' he said calmly. 'I think you are too smart to do that. What are you going to say to them?

I stole everything this man had and now he's caught up with me and he's taken my mother as hostage. You have to be able to account for things, Abby. In the western world today, with all the money-laundering regulations, you have to be able to account for substantial possessions and amounts of money. How are you going to account for what you've got, on the earnings of a Melbourne bar waitress?'

She screamed back down the phone, 'I don't care any more, Ricky. OK?'

There was a brief silence. Then he said, 'Oh, I think you do. You didn't do what you did to me on a sudden impulse. You planned this long and hard, you and Dave, didn't you? Any position he didn't tell you to shag me in, or was it just me who got fucked?'

'This has nothing to do with my mother. Bring her back. Bring her here and we'll talk.'

'No, you bring me everything you've taken and then we'll talk.'

The panic attack was worsening. She was taking deep gulps of air. Her head was burning. She felt as if she was half floating out of her body, that her body was going to die on her. She tripped sideways, hit the end of the sofa, clung desperately to one of the arms, then swung herself down on to it and sat there giddily.

'I'm hanging up now,' she gasped, 'and I'm calling the police.'

But even as she said the words she could feel that some of the conviction had gone from her voice, and that he could feel it too.

'Yeah, and then what?'

'I don't care. I don't bloody care!' Like a child having a tantrum, she repeated several times, louder each time, 'I don't bloody care!'

'You should. Because they're going to find a chronically ill woman who has committed suicide, and her daughter a thief, with a cock-and-bull story about the man she stole from, and the man who put her up for it isn't exactly in a position to enter any witness box to back her up. So think your way out of that one, smart bitch. I'm going to leave you to calm down now and I'm going to brew your mum a nice cup of tea, and then I'll call you back.'

'No – wait—' she shouted.

But he had hung up.

Then, suddenly, she remembered the taxi waiting outside, with the meter running.

89

OCTOBER 2007

Roy Grace sent Cleo a brief text telling her he had arrived as he stood waiting for the baggage carousel to start up. By his calculation, it would be 6.15 p.m. in the UK. Fifteen minutes before the start of the evening briefing meeting on *Operation Dingo.*

He called DI Lizzie Mantle to get an update, but both her direct landline and mobile numbers went to voicemail. Next he tried Glenn Branson, who answered on the second ring.

'Got your shoes back on?'

'Yeah, I phoned to tell you that. Thought you might be pleased.'

'So where are you? You've arrived, right? JFK Airport?'

'Newark. Just waiting for my bag.'

'All right for some, swanning off to New York, leaving us all here at the coal face.'

'I would have sent you to Australia, but I didn't think in your current situation that would have been too clever.'

'At this moment, the further away I am from Ari, the happier she is. Anyhow, more on that when you get back.'

Spare me, Grace thought. And whilst he would do anything to help this man he loved so much, he was always nervous about giving him – or indeed anyone else – advice on matters that could affect their lives. What the hell did he know? And what kind of an example had his own marriage been? But he said none of this now.

'So, tell me, what updates?' he said.

'Well, we've actually been hard at work while you've been lounging back, swigging champagne and watching movies for the past seven hours.'

'I've been in cattle class, fighting off cramp, listeria and deep-vein thrombosis. And my headset didn't work. Other than that, you're pretty close.'

'It's tough at the top, Roy. Isn't that what they say?'

'Yeah, yeah. This is costing a fortune. Cut the chat!'

Branson reported on their visits to the stamp dealer Hawkes and Hugo Hegarty.

Grace listened intently. 'So it really is stamps! She converted the whole lot into stamps!'

'That's right. Portability. All the money-laundering regulations. They have sniffer dogs at airports that are trained to smell cash. And three and a quarter million in cash takes up a lot of space. But that value in stamps would take up just a couple of A4 envelopes.'

'Do we have any idea what she did with them?'

'No. Not so far. Anyhow, then we went to see Lorraine Wilson's sister.'

'What did she have to say?'

'Quite a lot, actually.'

There was a beep and the carousel started moving. Grace was jostled by two hugely fat men, then an old woman backed a luggage cart into his legs. He stepped back and away from the crowd swarming around the conveyor, to a place where he had some space but could still see the bags. He knew from a stint at Gatwick Airport some years ago that theft of luggage from conveyor belts was common.

'There's a lot of noise your end,' Branson said.

'I can hear you OK. Tell me?'

'First thing is, the sister went to New York with Lorraine Wilson a week after 9/11 – just as soon as they could get a flight. They went to the hotel Ronnie was staying at, the W.'

'The W?' Grace queried. 'The W what?'

'That's its name.'

'Just W?'

'Old-timer, you spend your life under a stone or what? You need to employ me as your full-time style guru. The W is a chain. They're, like, considered über-cool hotels.'

'Yeah, well, my salary doesn't run to über-cool hotels.'

'I can't believe you haven't heard of them.'

'Well, there you go, yet another of life's many unsolved mysteries. Anything you want to tell me about it, other than that I haven't heard of it?'

'Yeah, quite a bit. So, some of his belongings were still in the room, and the management weren't too happy, because the credit card he'd given had maxed out on them.'

'They didn't make any allowance for the fact that he was dead?'

'I presume they didn't know at that point. He'd booked in for just two nights and left an opened credit card slip with them. Anyhow, the thing is that his passport and airline ticket back to the UK were still in the safe.'

To his relief, Grace suddenly saw his bag appear. 'Hang on a tick.' He hurried forward to grab it, then said, 'OK, go on.'

'So then they went to Pier 92, where the NYPD had set up a kind of bereavement centre. People were bringing stuff like hairbrushes, so they could get the DNA of probable victims to help identify the bodies, or the body parts. They were also displaying personal items that had been recovered. Lorraine went there with her sister, but the police hadn't recovered anything belonging to her husband that could identify him, at that stage.'

Grace lugged his bag away from the crowd to a quieter spot, then had to wait for a tannoy announcement to end before he could ask, 'What about the money Lorraine received?'

'I'll come to that – and I gotta dash in a minute to the briefing.'

'Tell DI Mantle to call me afterwards.'

'I will. But you've got to hear something first. We have a big development! So, anyhow, Lorraine blags fifteen hundred dollars from the officer at Pier 92. They were doling the dough out to anyone who'd lost someone and was suffering financial hardship.'

'Fair enough at that time. She'd been left up shit creek financially, right?'

'Yes. Then a couple of weeks after they get back to the UK, her sister said Lorraine got a phone call – a fire-damaged wallet containing Ronnie Wilson's driving licence and a mobile phone identified as belonging to him were handed in by rescue workers digging in the rubble at Ground Zero. Photographs of them and the contents of the wallet were sent over to her so she could formally identify them.'

'Which she was able to do?'

'Yep. Now, the cash she got – the big payments of the life insurance, then the compensation – here's the thing. Her sister was astonished when we told her. Like more than astonished, like blown-fucking-away astonished.'

'Acting?'

'Not in my view, nor Bella's. She swung between astonishment and anger. I mean, she blew her rag at one point, saying she'd cleaned out her own savings to help Lorraine – and that was long after, according to the bank records, Lorraine had had the first lump of moolah in.'

'So no honour among sisters then?'

'Seems like it was one-way between these two. But I've got the best to come for you. You're going to love this.'

There was another tannoy announcement. Grace yelled for Branson to wait until it had stopped.

'The lab's come back this afternoon with a familial DNA match on the foetus Lorraine Wilson was carrying. I think we've got the father!'

'Who?' Grace asked excitedly.

'Well, if we are right, it is none other than Ronnie Wilson.'

Grace was silent for a moment, adrenaline surging. Thrilled that his hunch seemed to have been right. 'How good a match?'

'Well, this particular *familial* match means we have half of the father's DNA. There could be other matches. But considering who the mother is, I'd say the chances of it being anyone else are too remote to be worth considering.'

'Where did Ronnie's DNA come from?'

'From a hairbrush his widow took the NYPD when she went to New York. That profile was passed back to the British police, as routine, and entered on the National Database.'

'Which means,' Grace said, 'that either our friend Mr Wilson had left behind some frozen sperm which his wife, who wasn't quite so dead as she appeared, had implanted. Or . . .'

'Me, I favour the *or* option,' Branson said.

'Certainly looks favourite from where I'm standing,' Grace replied.

'And you're standing a lot closer than me, old-timer. With your shoes on or off.'

90

OCTOBER 2007

Abby heard a phone ringing somewhere, close and insistent. Then she realized, with a start, that it was her own. She sat up, confused, trying to work out where she was. The phone continued to ring.

There was chill air on her face, but she was perspiring heavily. She was in darkness, just shadows all around her in a ghostly orange haze. A spring creaked beneath her as she moved. She was sitting on a sofa in her mother's flat, she realized. Christ, how long had she been asleep?

She looked around, fearful that Ricky had come back and was in here. She could see the glow of the phone's display and reached for it. The coils of fear rising in her stomach worsened when she saw the words: *Private number*. The time on the display read 18.30.

She brought the phone to her ear. 'Yes?'

'Had a good think about it, have you?' Ricky said.

Panic raced through her brain. Where the hell was he? She had to get away from here quickly. She was a sitting duck in this place. Did he know where she was at this moment? Was he outside somewhere?

She waited a moment before replying, trying to collect her thoughts. She decided to keep the lights off, not wanting to show him she was here, in case he was out in the street watching. There was enough glow penetrating the net curtains, from the street light outside the window, to see all she needed in here at the moment.

'How is my mother?' she demanded, and heard the tremble in her voice.

'She's fine.'

'She's got no resistance. If you let her get cold, she could get pneumonia—'

Interrupting, Ricky replied, 'Like I told you, she's snug as a bug in a rug.'

Abby did not like the way he said those words. 'I want to speak to her.'

'Of course you do. And I want what you've stolen from me. So it's very simple. You bring it back, or you tell me where it is, and your mum can go home with you.'

'How do I know I can trust you?'

'That's rich, coming from you!' he sneered. 'I don't think you know the meaning of that word.'

'Look, what happened happened,' she said. 'I'll give you back what I've got left.'

The pitch of his voice changed to alarm. 'What do you mean *what you've got left*? I want it all. Everything. That's the deal.'

'You can't have it. I can only give you what I've got.'

'That's why it wasn't in the safe-deposit box, right? You spent it?'

'Not all of it,' she gambled.

'You callous bitch. You'd let me kill your mother, wouldn't you? You'd let me kill her rather than give it back to me! That's how much money means to you.'

'Yes,' she said. 'You're quite right, Ricky. I would.'

Then she hung up on him.

91

OCTOBER 2007

Abby ran across the dark room, stumbling over a leather pouffe, and groped her way into the bathroom. She found the sink and threw up into it, her stomach jangling, her nerves shot to pieces.

She rinsed the vomit away, washed her mouth and switched on the light, breathing deeply. *Please don't let me have another panic attack.* She stood clutching the sides of the sink, her eyes watering, terrified that Ricky was going to smash his way in here at any moment.

She had to get away from here, and she had to remember why she was doing this. *Quality of life for her mother.* That's what it was all about. Without the money, her mother's last years were going to be unimaginably grim. She had to keep hold of that.

And to think about what lay beyond for her: Dave waiting for the text to say they were good to go.

She was just one transaction away from giving her mother a future worth living. One plane ride away from the life she had always promised herself.

Ricky was nasty. A sadist. A bully. But a killer? She didn't think so.

She knew she had to stand up to him, show strength back. That was the only language a bully understood. And he wasn't a stupid man. He wanted everything back.

There was no value to him in harming an elderly, sick lady.

Please God.

Abby went back to the sitting room waiting for him to ring. Ready to kill the call when he did. Then, heart in her mouth, terrified she was making a big mistake, she crept out of the apartment into the even darker corridor and up the fire exit stairs to the first floor.

*

A few minutes later, from the phone in Doris's flat, she was dialling a different number. The call was answered by a well-spoken male voice.

'Is it possible to speak to Hugo Hegarty?' she asked.

'Indeed, you are speaking to him.'

'I apologize for calling you in the evening, Mr Hegarty,' Abby said. 'I have a collection of stamps that I want to sell.'

'Yes?' He drew the word out so it sounded deeply pensive. 'What can you tell me about them?'

She itemized each stamp, describing it in detail. She was so familiar with them, they had become as clear as a photograph in her memory. He interrupted her a couple of times, asking for specific information.

When she had finished, Hugo Hegarty fell strangely silent.

92

OCTOBER 2007

Sitting in his van at the remote campsite he had found on the internet, Ricky was deep in thought. The rain drumming down on the roof was good cover. No one was going to go traipsing around in the darkness in a muddy field, poking their nose into things that didn't concern them.

This place was perfect. Just a few miles along the Downs from Eastbourne, on the outskirts of a picture postcard village called Alfriston. A campsite in a large, wooded field half a mile up a deserted farm track, behind a rain-lashed tennis club.

This wasn't the time of the year or the weather for tennis or camping, which meant no prying eyes. The owner didn't look the prying type either. He'd driven up with two small boys who were squabbling in the car, taken his payment of fifteen pounds for three nights in advance and shown Ricky where the toilets and shower were. He'd given him a mobile phone number and said he might be back some time tomorrow in case anyone else showed up.

There was only one other vehicle on the site, a large camper van with Dutch plates, and Ricky was parked well away from it.

He had food, water, milk – stuff he'd picked up from a petrol station shop – enough to keep them going for a while. He popped the lid of a can of lager and downed half the contents in one long draught, wanting some alcohol to calm his nerves. Then he lit a cigarette and took three long puffs in quick succession. He wound down the window a fraction and tried to flick the ash out, but the wind blew it straight back in on his face. He closed the window and, as he did so, his nose twitched. Some unpleasant smell had come in from outside.

He took another drag on the cigarette and another swig of the lager. He was deeply disturbed by the call with Abby just now. By the way she had hung up on him. By the way he kept misreading the bitch.

He was scared that she meant what she had said. The words were replaying over and over in his head.

I'll give you back what I've got left.

How much had she spent? Blown? She must be bluffing. It was impossible that she had got through more than a few thousand during the time she had been on the run. She was bluffing.

He would have to raise the stakes. Call her bluff. She might think she was tough, but he had his doubts.

He finished the cigarette and tossed the butt outside. Then, as he closed the window, his nostrils twitched again. The smell was getting stronger, more insistent. It was coming from inside the van, very definitely. The distinct sour reek of urine.

Oh, for fuck's sake, no!

The old woman had wet herself.

He snapped on the interior light, scrambled out of his seat and into the rear of the van. The woman looked ridiculous, her head poking out of the top of the rolled-up carpet like some ugly, hatching chrysalis.

He pulled the gaffer tape away from her mouth as gently as possible, not wanting to hurt her more than was necessary; she was already in a high state of distress and he was scared that she might die on him.

'Have you wet yourself?'

Two small, frightened eyes peered at him. 'I'm ill,' she said, in a weak voice. 'I'm incontinent. I'm sorry.'

Sudden panic gripped him. 'Does that mean you're going to do the other thing too?'

She hesitated, then nodded apologetically.

'Oh, that's great,' he said. 'That's just great.'

93

OCTOBER 2007

As Glenn Branson was walking back to his desk after the 6.30 p.m. briefing on *Operation Dingo*, his mobile phone rang. The caller ID showed an unfamiliar Brighton number.

'DS Branson,' he answered. Then immediately recognized the rather smart voice at the other end.

'Oh, Detective Sergeant, apologies for calling you a bit late.'

'No problem at all, Mr Hegarty. What can I do for you?' Glenn continued walking.

'Is this a good moment?'

'Absolutely fine.'

'Well, the damnedest thing just happened,' Hugo Hegarty said. 'You remember when you and your very charming colleague came back this afternoon, I gave you a list? A list and description of all the stamps I purchased for Lorraine Wilson back in 2002?'

'Yes.'

'Well – look – this could just be one of those strange coincidences, but I've been in this game for too long and I really don't think it is.'

Glenn reached the doorway of Major Incident Room One, and stepped inside. 'Uh huh.'

'I've just had a phone call from a woman – sounded like a young woman, and rather nervous. She asked me if

I would be able to sell a collection of high-value stamps that she has. I asked her to give me the details and what she described is exactly – and I mean *exactly* – what I purchased for Lorraine Wilson. Less just a few, which may have been sold off along the way.'

Still holding the phone to his ear, Branson went over to his work station and sat down, absorbing the significance of this. 'Are you really sure it's not just coincidence, sir?' he asked.

'Well, they are mostly rare plates of mint stamps, desirable for all collections, plus some individual stamps. I doubt I would be able to remember from five years ago whether the postage marks on these are the same. But to give you a bit of a steer, there are two Plate 77 Penny Reds – I believe the last sale price fetched one hundred and sixty thousand pounds. There were several Plate 10 and Plate 11 Penny Blacks – they're worth between twelve and thirteen thousand pounds each – very easily tradable. Then quite a substantial quantity of Tuppenny Blues, plus a whole raft of other rarer stamps. It might be coincidence if she had just one or two of these, but the same items, the same quantities?'

'It does sound a little strange, sir, yes.'

'To be honest,' Hegarty said, 'if I hadn't gone through the files today to compile the list for you, I doubt I would have remembered it was such an exact match.'

'Sounds like that might have been a stroke of good fortune. I appreciate your telling us. Did you ask her where she obtained them?'

Hegarty dropped his voice, as if nervous of being overheard. 'She said she'd inherited them from an aunt in Australia and that someone she'd met at a party in Melbourne told her I was one of the dealers she should talk to.'

'You, rather than anyone in Australia, sir?'

'She said she was told that she would get a better price in the UK or in the States. As she was moving back here to look after her elderly mother, she thought she would try me first. She's coming over tomorrow morning at 10 o'clock to show me them. I thought I would ask her a few discreet questions then.'

Branson looked at his notes. 'Do you have an interest in buying them?'

He could almost feel the twinkle in Hegarty's eyes as the man replied.

'Well, she said she was in a hurry to sell – and that's usually the best time to buy. Not many dealers would have the kind of ready cash needed to buy this lot in one go – it would be more usual to break it up into auction lots. But I'd want to ensure they were all certificated. I'd hate to part with all that money and get a knock on my front door from you boys a few hours later. That's why I rang you.'

Of course. This isn't about Hugo Hegarty being a dutiful citizen. It's about him protecting his own backside, Glenn Branson thought. Still, such was human nature, so he could hardly blame the man.

'Roughly what value would you put on these, sir?'

'As a buyer or a seller?' Now he was sounding even more wily.

'As both.'

'Well, total catalogue value at today's prices, we're looking around four – four and a half million. So, as a seller, that's what I would be aiming to achieve.'

'Pounds?'

'Oh yes, pounds.'

Branson was astonished. The original three and a quarter million pounds Lorraine Wilson had come into had gone up by around thirty per cent – and that was after a substantial number of them, probably, had been sold off.

'And as a buyer, sir?'

Suddenly Hegarty sounded reticent. 'The price I'd be willing to pay would depend on their provenance. I'd need more information.'

Branson's brain was whirring. 'She's coming to you at 10 tomorrow morning? That's definite?'

'Yes.'

'What's her name?'

'Katherine Jennings.'

'Did she give you an address or phone number?'

'No, she didn't.'

The DS wrote the name down, thanked him and hung up. Then he pulled his keyboard closer, tapped the keys to call up the serials log and entered the name *Katherine Jennings*.

Within a few seconds a match came up.

94

OCTOBER 2007

Roy Grace sat in the back of the unmarked grey Ford Crown Victoria. As they headed into the Lincoln Tunnel he wondered whether, if you were a seasoned enough traveller, you could identify any city in the world just from the sound of the traffic.

In London the constant petrol roar and diesel rattle of engines and the whine-swoosh of the new generation of Volvo buses dominated. New York was completely different, mostly the steady tramp-tramp-tramp of tyres on the ribbed or cracked and lumpy road surfaces, and the honking of horns.

A massive truck behind them was honking now.

Detective Investigator Dennis Baker, who was driving, raised a hand up to the interior mirror and flipped him the bird. 'Go fuck yourself, asshole!'

Grace grinned. Dennis hadn't changed.

'I mean, for Chrissake, asshole, what you want me to do? Drive over the top of the dickhead in front or what? Jesus!'

Long used to his work buddy's driving, Detective Investigator Pat Lynch, seated alongside him in the front passenger seat, turned without comment to face Roy. 'It's good to see you again, man. Long time. Wayyyyy too long!'

Roy felt that too. He'd liked these guys from the moment they first met. Back in November 2000 he had been sent to New York to question a gay American banker whose partner had been found strangled in a flat in Kemp Town. The banker was never charged, but died from a drugs overdose a couple of years later. Roy had worked with Dennis and Pat for some while on that case and they'd stayed in touch.

Pat wore jeans and a denim jacket over a beige shirt, with a white T-shirt beneath that. With his pockmarked face and lanky, boyish haircut, he had the rugged looks of a movie tough guy, but he had a surprisingly gentle and caring nature. He had started life as a stevedore in the docks and his tall, powerful physique had stood him in good stead for that work.

Dennis wore a heavy black anorak, embossed with the legend *Cold Case Homicide Squad* and the NYPD shield, over a blue shirt, and also had on jeans. Shorter than Pat, wirier and sharp-eyed, he was heavily into martial arts. Years ago he had achieved 7th dan in Ruy Te and Isshinryu styles of Okinawan karate, and was something of a legend in the NYPD for his street-fighting skills.

Both men had been at the Brooklyn Police Station on Williamsburg East at 8.46 on the morning of 9/11, when the first plane had struck. Being literally one mile away, across the Brooklyn Bridge, they headed over there immediately, with their chief, and arrived just as the second plane struck, crashing into the South Tower. They had spent the following weeks as part of the team sifting through the rubble at Ground Zero, in what they had described as the 'Belly of the Beast'. Dennis had then transferred to the crime scene tent and Pat to the bereavement centre on Pier 92.

In the ensuing years both men, previously extremely fit, had developed asthma, as well as trauma-related mental health problems, and had transferred from the rough and tumble world of the NYPD to the calmer waters of the Special Investigations Unit at the District Attorney's Office.

Pat brought Grace up to speed on their current work, which was mostly transporting and interrogating mobsters. They now knew the US underworld as well as anybody. Pat talked about how the Mafia no longer had the *juice* it used to have. Villains flipped easier today than they used to. Who wouldn't try to cut a deal, Pat said, when looking at the wrong end of a twenty-year to life sentence?

Hopefully they'd find in the next twenty-four hours someone who'd known Ronnie Wilson, someone who had helped him. If anyone could help him to look for someone who, Grace was becoming increasingly certain, had deliberately disappeared during 9/11 and its aftermath, it was these two.

'You're looking younger than ever,' Pat said, suddenly changing the subject. 'You must be in love.'

'That wife of yours, she still never turned up, right?' Dennis asked.

'No,' was his short answer. He'd rather not talk about Sandy.

'He's just envious,' Pat said. 'Cost him a fortune to get rid of his!'

Grace laughed and at that moment his phone beeped with an incoming text. He looked down.

> *Glad u there safe. Miss u. Humphrey misses u too.*
> *No one 2 throw up on. XXX*

He grinned, instantly feeling a pang of longing for Cleo. Then he remembered something. 'If we've got five minutes, could we go into one of those big Toys "R" Us places? I'll get my god-daughter's Christmas present. She's into something called Bratz.'

'Biggest one's in Times Square, we can swing by there now, then go on to W, where we thought we'd start,' Pat said.

'Thanks.' Grace stared out of the window. They were going up an incline, past precarious-looking scaffolding. Steam rose from a subway vent.

It was a crisp autumnal afternoon, with a clear blue sky. Some people were wearing coats or heavy jackets, and as they got further into the centre of Manhattan everyone looked as if they were in a hurry. Half the men scurrying past were dressed in suits with tieless shirts and wore worried frowns. Most of them had a mobile clamped to one ear and carried in their other hand a Starbucks coffee with a brown collar around it, as if that was a mandatory totem.

'So, Pat and I, we worked out a pretty good programme for you,' Dennis said.

'Yeah,' Pat confirmed. 'Although we're now working for the DA we're happy to run you around as a favour for a friend and a fellow cop.'

'I really appreciate it. I spoke to my FBI guy in London,' Grace replied. 'He knows I'm here and what I'm doing. If my hunches work out, we may well have to come back formally to the NYPD.'

Dennis hit the horn at a black Explorer in front of them that had put its flashers on and half pulled over, looking for something. 'Fuck you! Come on, asshole!'

'We've booked you into the Marriott Financial Center – that's right down by Ground Zero, in Battery Park City. Figure that'll be a good base, as we can get to most places you might want to check out easily enough from there.'

'Give you some atmosphere too,' Dennis said. 'It was badly damaged. All brand new now. You'll be able to see the work going on at Ground Zero.'

'You know they're still finding body parts,' Pat said. 'Six years on, right? Found some last month on the roof of the Deutsche Bank Building. People don't realize. They got no fuckin' idea the force of what happened when those planes hit.'

'Right opposite the Medical Examiner's Office they got a tented-off area with eight refrigerated trucks inside,' Dennis said. 'They've been there for – what – six years now. Twenty thousand unidentified body parts in there. Can you believe that? Twenty thousand?' He shook his head.

'My cousin died,' Pat went on. 'You knew that, right? He worked for Cantor Fitzgerald.' He held up his wrist to reveal a silver bracelet. 'See that, it has his initials. *TJH.* We all got one, wear it in his memory.'

'Everyone in New York lost someone that day,' Dennis said, swerving to avoid a jay-walking woman. 'Shit, lady, you want to know what the fender of a Crown Victoria feels like? I can tell you, it don't feel too good.'

'Anyhow,' Pat said, 'we've been doing as much as we could before you got here. We checked out the hotel where your Ronnie Wilson stayed. Same manager's still there, so that's good. We've fixed for you to meet him. He's happy to talk to you, but there's no change from what we already know. Some of Wilson's stuff was still in his room – his passport, tickets, a few underclothes. That's all now in one of the 9/11 victim storage depots.'

Grace's phone rang suddenly. Excusing himself, he answered it. 'Roy Grace?'

'Yo, old-timer, where are you now? Having an ice cream on top of the Empire State Building?'

'Very droll. I'm actually in a traffic jam.'

'OK, well, I have another development for you. We're working our butts off here while you're having fun. Does the name Katherine Jennings ring a bell?'

Grace thought for a moment, feeling a little weary, his brain less sharp than usual after the flight. Then he remembered. It was the name of the woman in Kemp Town that the *Argus* reporter, Kevin Spinella, had given him. The name he had passed on to Steve Curry.

'What about her?'

'She's trying to sell a collection of stamps worth around four million pounds. The dealer she's gone to is Hugo Hegarty and he recognizes them. He hasn't seen them yet, only spoken to her over the phone, but he's convinced, all bar a few that are missing, that these are the stamps he purchased for Lorraine Wilson back in 2002.'

'Did he ask the woman where she got them from?'

Branson repeated what Hegarty had told him, then added, 'There's a serial on Katherine Jennings.'

'Mine,' Grace said. He fell silent for some moments, thinking back to his conversation on Monday with Spinella. The reporter had said Katherine Jennings seemed agitated. Would having four million pounds' worth of stamps in your possession make you agitated? Grace reckoned he'd be feeling pretty relaxed, having that kind of loot, so long as it was in a safe place.

So what was she agitated about? Something definitely smelled wrong.

'I think we should put surveillance on her, Glenn. And we have the advantage of knowing where she lives.'

'She may have done a runner from there,' Branson

replied. 'But she's made an appointment to go to Hegarty's house tomorrow morning. And she's bringing him the stamps.'

'Perfect,' Grace said. 'Get on to Lizzie. Tell her we've had this conversation and I'm suggesting trying to get a surveillance team to pick her up at Hegarty's house.' He looked at this watch. 'There's plenty of time to get that in place.'

Glenn Branson looked at his watch too. It wasn't going to be a simple matter of a two-minute call to Lizzie Mantle. He was going to have to write out a report detailing the reasons for requesting a surveillance unit and its potential value to *Operation Dingo*. And he was going to have to prepare the briefing. He wasn't going to make it home for hours yet. It would mean another bollocking from Ari.

Nothing new there.

When Roy Grace ended the call, he leaned forward. 'Guys,' he said, 'do you have someone who can put together a list of stamp dealers here?'

'Starting a new hobby, are you?' quipped Dennis.

'Just stamping out crime,' Grace retorted.

'Shit, man!' Pat said, turning to face him. 'Your jokes don't get any better, do they?'

Grace smiled sardonically. 'Sad, isn't it?'

95

OCTOBER 2007

The air stewardess was going through the safety demonstration. Norman Potting leaned over to Nick Nicholl, seated next to him near the rear of the 747, and said, 'It's all a load of rubbish, this safety stuff.'

The young Detective Constable, who was terrified of flying but hadn't wanted to admit that to his boss, was hanging on to every word that was coming out through the speakers. Turning his face away to avoid the full blast of Potting's bad breath, he peered upwards, working out exactly where his oxygen mask would be dropping from.

'The brace position – you know what they don't tell you?' Potting went on, undeterred by Nicholl's lack of reaction.

Nicholl shook his head, now watching and memorizing the correct way to tie the tapes on the life jacket.

'It might save you in some situations, I grant you. But the thing they don't tell you,' Potting said, 'is the brace position helps preserve your jawbone intact. Makes identifying all the victims from their dental records much easier.'

'Thanks a lot,' Nicholl muttered, observing the stewardess now pointing out where he would find his whistle.

'As for the life jacket, that's a laugh, that is,' Potting carried on. 'Do you know how many passenger airliners in the entire history of aviation have ever successfully made an emergency landing on water?'

Nick Nicholl was thinking about his wife, Jen, and his small son, Ben. He might never see either of them again.

'How many?' he gulped.

Potting touched the tip of his own thumb with his index finger, forming a circle. 'Zero. Zilch. Nada. Not one.'

There's always a first time, Nicholl thought, clinging tightly to the thought; clinging to it as if it were a liferaft.

Potting starting reading a men's magazine he had bought in the airport. Nicholl studied the laminated safety card, checking the position of the nearest exits, glad to see that they were only two rows behind him. He was glad too that he was near the rear of the plane; he remembered a newspaper account of an air disaster in which the tail section broke off and all the passengers inside it survived.

'Phoaaaawwww!' Potting said.

Nicholl looked down. His colleague had the magazine open at a nude centre-spread. A blonde with pneumatic breasts was lying spread-eagled on a four-poster bed, her wrists and ankles secured by lengths of black velvet to the posts. Her pubic hair was a tidily shaved Brazilian and the pink lips of her vulva were prominently exposed, as if they were the buds of a flower placed between her legs.

A stewardess walked past, checking passengers had their seat belts on. She stopped to peer down at Nicholl and Norman Potting, then moved smartly on.

Nick felt his face burning with embarrassment. 'Norman,' he whispered, 'I think you should put that away.'

'Hope we find a few like her in Melbourne!' Potting said. 'We could have a bit of sport, you and me. I fancy that Bondi Beach.'

'Bondi Beach is in Sydney, not Melbourne. And I think you embarrassed the stewardess with that.'

Unabashed, Potting traced his fingers over her curves. 'She's a bit of all right, she is!'

The stewardess was coming back. She gave both of them a cursory, rather frosty glance and hurried past.

'I thought you were a happily married man, Norman,' Nicholl said.

'The day I stop looking, lad,' he said, 'that's the day I want someone to take me out into a field and shoot me.' He grinned and, to Nicholl's relief, he turned the page. But the DC's relief was only fleeting.

The next page was much worse.

96

OCTOBER 2007

Abby was on the train heading to Brighton, a lump deep in her throat. Her stomach was knotted. She was trembling, trying to stop herself crying, struggling to hold it all together.

Where was her mother? Where had the bastard taken her?

Her watch said 8.30. Almost two hours since she'd put the phone down on Ricky. She dialled her mother's number yet again. Once more it went to voicemail.

She wasn't sure exactly what medication her mother was on – there were antidepressants, plus pills for muscle spasm, constipation, anti-reflux – but she doubted very much that Ricky would care about that. Without them, her mother's condition would deteriorate rapidly, and she would start to have mood swings, from euphoria one second to a deeply distressed state the next.

Abby cursed her stupidity for leaving her mother so exposed. She should have just bloody well taken her.

Call me, Ricky. Please call me.

She was bitterly regretting hanging up on him, realizing she hadn't thought it through properly. Ricky knew she would be the first to panic, not him. But he would have to call her, he would have to make contact. A frail, sick old lady was not the prize he wanted.

She took a taxi from the station and got out at a convenience store close to her flat, where she bought a small torch. Keeping to the shadows, she turned into her street and saw, under the glare of a street light, Ricky's rental Ford Focus. It was clamped. Large police stickers were fixed to the windscreen and driver's-side window, warning that the owner should not attempt to move it.

She walked warily to the car. Glancing around to make sure she wasn't being watched, she removed the parking ticket from beneath the windscreen wiper and, using her torch, read the time it had been issued: 10.03 a.m. So the car had been here all day. Which meant he hadn't used it to transport her mother. Of course not – he had the van.

But presumably he was intending to return. Maybe he was already there. Somehow she doubted that. She was sure he had a place in the city, if only a lock-up.

The windows of her flat were all dark. She crossed the street to the entrance and pressed the bell of Hassan, hoping he was home. She was in luck. There was a crackle followed by his voice.

'Hi, it's Katherine Jennings from Flat 82. Sorry to bother you, but I've forgotten my front door key. Could you let me in?'

'No problem!'

Moments later there was a sharp buzz and she pushed the door open. As she entered, she saw a stack of junk mail crammed in her letter box. Better not to touch it, she decided, not wanting to leave any indications that she had been here.

The lift had a large OUT OF ORDER sign taped across the doors. She began climbing the dimly lit stairs, stopping on each floor to listen for any movement, wishing she had her Mace spray with her. On the third floor she started to smell freshly sawn wood, from the builders in the flat above. She climbed one more floor, then her nerve began failing her, so she was tempted for a moment to knock on Hassan's door and ask him to come up with her.

Finally, she reached the top. She stopped to listen for any noise. There were two other flats on this floor, but she had never met anyone coming or going in the brief time she had been here. She could hear nothing. Total silence. She went over to the fire reel that was fixed to the wall and began to unwind the hose. After five loops, she saw the set of spare keys lying where she had hidden them. She rewound the hose, pushed open the fire door and went through onto her landing.

Then stood still, feeling very scared now. What if he was in there?

Of course he wasn't. He was with her mother in whatever lair he had imprisoned her. All the same, she slipped in each key as silently as possible, turning the locks and opening the door quietly, not wanting to announce her presence.

Shadows jumped at her as she stepped inside. She left the door ajar behind her and the lights off. Then she slammed the front door hard, to flush him out if he was in here and had maybe fallen asleep, and immediately opened it again. She slammed it and opened it a second time. Total silence.

She shone the torch beam along the corridor. The plastic bag of tools Ricky had brought to threaten her with – probably nicked from the builders downstairs – was still lying on the floor outside the guest shower room.

Keeping all the lights off just in case he was outside somewhere, watching, she went through the whole flat, room by room. She came across her Mace on the coffee table in the sitting room and jammed it in her pocket. Then she hurried back to the front door and put the safety chain across.

Thirsty and hungry, she gulped down a Coke and a peach yoghurt from the fridge, then went through into the guest shower room, closed the door and switched on the light. There was no exterior window in this room, so it was safe.

Stepping past the lavatory and the huge glass shower wall, she opened the door to the tiny utility room, crammed with the washing machine and tumble dryer. Up on the shelf to the left were her own tools. She pulled down a hammer and chisel and carried them back into the shower room.

Then she took one brief, proud last look at her fine handiwork, placed the blade of the chisel against the grout between two tiles halfway up the wall and hit it hard. Then again.

Within a few minutes she had removed enough of the tiles and could reach into the false wall behind them. She felt deep relief as her fingers touched the waterproof protective bubble wrap, which she had carefully wound around the A4 Jiffy bag before putting it here the day she had moved in.

The landlord wouldn't be too impressed with the damage to the bathroom wall. If she'd had the time, thanks to the skills she had learned from her father, she could have fixed it so perfectly he would never have seen the joins. But at this moment a few damaged tiles was the least of her problems.

She changed her underwear, packed her suitcase for

the second time this week with everything she thought she might need, then logged on to the internet and looked up cheap hotels in Brighton and Hove.

When she had made her choice, she phoned for another taxi.

97

OCTOBER 2007

The old woman was turning out to be more of a problem than Ricky had imagined. He stood in the tiny kitchenette area of the wooden building that served as the tennis club pavilion, toilet and shower facility for the campsite.

She'd been in the bloody toilet for over fifteen minutes now.

He stepped out of the door, into the pouring rain, beginning to think that killing her might be the best option, and peered across the field, anxiously, at the Dutch camper van. The lights were on behind drawn curtains. He just hoped to hell they didn't decide to come and use these facilities while she was in here. Although he was confident she was scared enough of his threats not to say anything to anyone, or do anything stupid.

Another five minutes passed. He glanced at his watch again. It was 9.30. Three hours since Abby had hung up on him. Three hours in which she would have been thinking about what had happened. Coming to her senses?

Now would be a good moment, he decided.

He flipped open the lid of his phone and texted Abby the photograph he had taken a little earlier, of her mother's head poking out of the top of the carpet roll.

He sent the words with it:

Snug as a bug in rug.

98

OCTOBER 2007

Roy sat with Pat and Dennis at a wooden table in the restaurant area of the huge, open-plan Chelsea Brewing Company, which was owned by Pat's cousin. To his right was a long wooden bar, and behind him were rows of gleaming copper vats as tall as houses, and miles of stainless-steel and aluminium piping and tubing. With its acres of wooden flooring and immaculate cleanliness, it had the feel more of a museum than a busy working enterprise.

Visiting had become a ritual, a compulsory watering-hole stop during every trip Roy made to New York. Pat was clearly proud of his cousin's success and enjoyed giving an Englishman a run for his money with American-brewed beer.

There were six different varieties in sampler glasses in front of each of the three police officers. The glasses were positioned on a round blue spot on the specially designed table mat that gave the names of the beers. Pat's cousin, also called Patrick, a stocky, bespectacled and intense man in his forties, was talking Roy through the different brewing processes for each one.

Roy was only half listening. He was tired; it was late according to UK time now. Today had yielded nothing – just one blank after another. Apart from the successful purchase of a precocious-looking Bratz for his god-daughter. In his view the doll looked like a Barbie that was working in the sex trade. But, as he reflected, what did he know about the tastes of nine-year-olds?

The hotel manager of the W had little to add to what Grace already knew other than, for what it was worth, Ronnie had watched a pay-per-view porn movie at 11 o'clock that last night.

And no one at any of the seven stamp dealers they had visited this afternoon had recognized either Wilson's name or his photograph.

As Pat's cousin intoned on about the science behind the beer Roy liked best, Checker Cab Blond Ale, he stared out of the window into the night. He could see the rigging of yachts in the marina and further, beyond the darkness of the Hudson, the lights of New Jersey. It was so vast, this city. So many people coming and going. Live here, like any big city, and you'd see thousands of faces every day. How likely was it that he could find anyone who would remember one face from six years back?

But he had to try. Knocking on doors. The good old-fashioned-policing way. The chances of Ronnie being here were slim. More likely he was in Australia – certainly the latest evidence pointed that way. He tried to do a quick calculation of the time zones in his head, while Patrick moved on to explaining how the subtle caramel flavours of Sunset Red Ale were achieved.

It was 7 o'clock in the evening. Melbourne was ten hours ahead of the UK, so how many did that make it ahead of New York, which was five hours ahead – no – behind the UK? Christ, the calculation was doing his head in.

And all the time he kept nodding politely at Patrick.

It was fifteen hours ahead, he worked out. Mid-morning. Hopefully, ahead of Norman and Nick's visit, the Melbourne police would make a start on checking whether Ronnie Wilson had entered Australia at any point since September 2001.

There was something else, he suddenly remembered, surreptitiously pulling out his notebook and flicking back a couple of pages to the notes he had taken at his meeting with Terry Biglow, the list of Ronnie Wilson's acquaintances and friends. *Chad Skeggs,* he had written down. *Emigrated to Oz.* As a result of what Branson had told him, and the likelihood that Ronnie Wilson was in Australia, he was going to make finding Chad Skeggs a priority for Potting and Nicholl.

Patrick finally finished and went off to get Roy his own personal jug of Checker Cab. The three detectives each raised a glass.

'Thanks for your time, guys, I appreciate it,' Grace said. 'And I'm buying.'

'You're in my cousin's place,' Pat said. 'You don't pay a dime.'

'When you're with us in New York, you're our guest,' Dennis said. 'But shit, buddy, when we come to England you'd better take out a second mortgage!'

They laughed.

Then Pat looked sad suddenly. 'You know, did I ever tell you that thing about 9/11, about the *feelgood* dogs?'

Grace shook his head.

'They had people bring dogs along – to the pile, you know, the Belly of the Beast. They were just for the workers there to stroke.'

Dennis nodded, concurring. 'That's what they called 'em – *feelgood* dogs.'

'Kind of like therapy,' Pat said. 'We were all finding such horrible things. They figured, we stroke the dogs, it's a good feeling, contact with something living, something happy.'

'You know, I think it worked,' Dennis said. 'That whole thing, 9/11, you know, it brought a lot of good out in people in this city.'

'And it brought the scumbags out too,' Pat reminded him. 'At Pier 92 we were giving cash handouts between fifteen hundred and two and a half thousand bucks, depending on their needs, to help people in immediate hardship.' He shrugged. 'Didn't take the scumbags long to hear about this. We had several came and scammed us, telling us they had lost family, when they hadn't.'

'But we got them,' Dennis said with grim satisfaction. 'We got 'em after. Took a while, but we got every damned one of them.'

'But there was good that came out of it,' Pat said. 'It brought some heart and soul back to this city. I think people are a little kinder here now.'

'And some people are a lot richer,' Dennis said.

Pat nodded. 'That's for sure.'

Dennis chuckled suddenly. 'Rachel, my wife, she's got an uncle over in the Garment District. He has an embroidery business, makes stuff for the souvenir shops. I stopped by to see him a couple of weeks after 9/11. He's this little Jewish guy, right, Hymie. He's eighty-two years old, still works a fourteen-hour day. The nicest guy you'd ever want to meet. His family escaped the Holocaust, came out here. There isn't anybody he wouldn't help. Anyhow, I walk in there and I never saw the place so busy. Workers everywhere. T-shirts, sweatshirts, baseball caps, all piled up, people stitching, ironing, machining, bagging.'

He sipped some beer and shook his head.

'My uncle had had to take on extra staff. Couldn't cope with all the orders. It was all Twin Towers commemorative stuff he was making. I asked him how it was going. He sat there in the middle of all this chaos and he looked at me with this little smile on his face and he said business was good, it had never been better.' Dennis nodded, then gave a wry shrug, 'You know what? There's always a buck in tragedy.'

99

2 NOVEMBER 2001

Lorraine lay in bed, wide awake. The sleeping pills the doctor had prescribed for her were about as effective as a double espresso.

The television was on in the room, the shitty little portable that had been in the guest bedroom, the only one that hadn't been repossessed by the bailiffs, as there wasn't any money owing on it. There was an old film playing. She hadn't caught the title, but she kept the set on all the time, as if the screen was wallpaper. She liked the light from it, the noises, the company.

Steve McQueen and Faye Dunaway were playing chess in a swish pad with moody lighting. There was a seriously erotic, charged atmosphere between them, with all kinds of nuances.

She and Ronnie used to play games together. She recalled those early years, when they had been crazy about each other and did wild things sometimes. They played strip chess, and Ronnie always wiped her out, leaving her naked and himself fully clothed. And strip Scrabble.

Never again. She sniffed.

She found it hard to focus on anything clearly. Hard to get her head around anything. She just kept thinking about Ronnie. Missing him. Dreaming of him on the rare occasions she slept long enough to dream. And in the dreams he was alive, smiling, telling her she was a silly cow for thinking he was dead.

She was still shaking from the contents of the FedEx envelope that had arrived at the end of September, containing photographs of Ronnie's wallet and his mobile phone. It was the picture of the singed wallet that was the worst. Had he been burned to death?

A massive wave of grief flooded through her suddenly. She started crying. Clinging to the pillow, she sobbed her heart out. 'Ronnie,' she murmured. 'Ronnie, my darling Ronnie. I loved you so much. So much.'

After some minutes she calmed down and lay back, watching the movie flickering on the screen. And then, to her complete and utter terror, she suddenly saw her bedroom door opening. A figure was coming in. A tall, black shadow. A man, his face almost in total darkness inside a cagoule hood. He was striding towards her.

She scrambled back in the bed in terror, reaching out to her bedside table for something to use as a weapon. Her glass of water went crashing to the floor. She tried to scream, but only the faintest sound blurted out before a hand clamped over her mouth.

And she heard Ronnie's voice. Sharp and hushed.

'It's me!' he said. 'It's me! Lorraine, babe, it's me. I'm OK!'

He took his hand away and tossed back the cagoule hood.

She snapped on the bedside light. Stared at him in utter disbelief. Stared at a ghost who had grown a beard and shaved his head. A ghost who smelled of Ronnie's skin, of Ronnie's hair, of Ronnie's cologne. Who was cupping her face with hands that felt like Ronnie's hands.

She stared at him with complete and utter bewilderment, joy steadily catching fire inside her. 'Ronnie? It's you, isn't it?'

'Course it's me!'

She stared back. Open-mouthed. Stared. And stared. Then she shook her head, silent for some moments.

'They all said – they said you were dead.'

'That's good,' he said. 'I am.'

He kissed her. His breath smelled of cigarettes, alcohol and something slightly garlicky. At this moment it was the most beautiful smell in all the world.

'They sent me pictures of your wallet and your phone.'

His eyes lit up like a child. 'Fuck! Brilliant! They found them! That is so fucking great!'

His reaction confused her. Was he joking? Everything at this moment was confusing her. She touched his face, tears starting to roll down her cheeks.

'I can't believe it,' she said, caressing his cheeks, touching his nose, his ears, stroking his forehead. 'It's you. It's really you.'

'Yes, you daft cow!'

'How – how did you – how did you survive?'

'Because I thought about you and I wasn't ready to leave you.'

'Why – why didn't you call? Were you hurt?'

'It's a long story.'

She pulled him towards her and kissed him. Kissed him as if she was discovering his mouth for the first time, exploring every part of it. Then she pulled back her face for a moment, grinning almost breathlessly.

'It really is you!'

His hands had found their way inside her nightdress

and were exploring her breasts. When she'd first had her boob job, they had driven him wild for a time, then he seemed to lose interest in them, the way he had lost interest in just about everything. But tonight this apparition, this Ronnie in her bedroom, was a totally different man. The old Ronnie she remembered from happier times. Ronnie who had died and come back?

He was undressing. Unlacing his trainers. Dropping his trousers. He had a massive erection. He pulled off his cagoule, his black polo-neck sweater, peeled off his socks. Now he pulled back the bedclothes and roughly pushed her nightdress up over her thighs.

Then he knelt over her and began to make her wet with his fingers, finding her sweet spot the way he used to, so brilliantly, finding it, working it, moistening his finger from his lips and from herself, setting the fire raging in her now. He leaned forward, untying the front of her nightdress, freeing her breasts, then kissing each of them for a long time, in turn, still working on her with his fingers.

Then his cock, bigger, harder than it had felt in years, hard as a stone, was pushing deep up inside her.

She screamed out in joy. 'RONNIE!'

Instantly he pressed a finger to her lips. 'Ssshhh!' he said. 'I'm not here. I'm just a ghost.'

She wrapped her arms around his head, pulled his face as close to hers as she could, feeling the bristles of his beard on her skin and loving it, and pushed against him, pushed and pushed and pushed, feeling him further, deeper, then deeper still inside her.

'Ronnie!' she panted into his ear, breathing faster and faster, climaxing now, and feeling him exploding inside her.

They both lay very still, gulping down air. The film was

still playing on the television. The fan heater was steadily blowing out air, with an intermittent rattle.

'I never realized ghosts got horny,' she whispered. 'Can I summon you up every night?'

'We need to talk,' he said.

100

OCTOBER 2007

PC Duncan Troutt felt a little less self-conscious this morning, his second day as a fully fledged police officer. And he was rather hoping for more action than yesterday, when he had spent most of his time giving directions to foreign students and introducing himself to some of the businesses on his beat, in particular to the manager of an Indian takeaway who had been beaten up recently, in an attack that had been filmed on a mobile phone camera and ended up on YouTube.

Turning into Lower Arundel Terrace shortly after 9 o'clock, he decided he would pay Katherine Jennings another visit in the hope of catching her in. He'd read on the log before setting out this morning that a fellow officer on the evening shift had tried her twice, at 7 p.m. and again at 10 p.m., with no luck. A call to Directory Enquiries had not yielded any phone number for someone of that name at that address, listed or unlisted.

As he walked down the pavement, observing each of the houses in turn and checking each of the parked cars for signs of break-ins or vandalism, two seagulls screeched above him. He glanced up at them and then stared for a moment at the dark, threatening sky. The streets were still glossy from last night's rain and it looked as if it might start again at any moment.

Shortly before reaching the front entrance of number 29

he noticed, on the opposite side of the road, a grey Ford Focus that had been clamped. The car rang a bell from yesterday. He recalled seeing it there with a ticket on the windscreen. He crossed over, lifted the ticket from under the wiper blade, shook raindrops off its wet cellophane wrapper and read the date and time on it. It had been issued at 10.03 a.m. yesterday. Which meant it had been here for over twenty-four hours.

There could be all kind of innocent explanations. Someone who hadn't realized these streets required residents' parking permits was the most likely. It could possibly be an abandoned stolen car. The biggest significance to him was its location, close to the flat of the woman he had been asked to check up on, who had seemingly disappeared, if only temporarily.

He radioed in for a PNC check on the car, then crossed back over and rang Katherine Jennings's doorbell. As before, there was no answer.

Then, deciding he would try again later, he continued on with his patrol, down to Marine Parade, where he turned left. After a few minutes, his radio crackled into life. The Ford Focus was registered to Avis, the car rental company. He thanked the operator and considered this new information carefully. People who rented cars often flouted traffic regulations. Maybe whoever had rented this one couldn't be bothered with the hassle of getting it unclamped. Or hadn't had the time.

But there still just *might* be a link to Katherine Jennings, however small the odds. As the first spots of rain fell, he radioed his immediate superior, Sergeant Ian Brown from the East Brighton District crime desk, and reported his concerns about the vehicle, asking if someone could contact Avis and find who the renter was.

'It's probably nothing, sir,' he added, concerned not to make a fool of himself.

'You're quite right to check like this,' the Sergeant reassured him. 'A lot of good police work comes from the smallest details. No one's going to chew you out for being over-observant. Miss something that matters and that's a whole different story!'

Troutt thanked him and continued on his way. Thirty minutes later the Sergeant radioed him back. 'The car's been rented by an Australian called Chad Skeggs. Lives in Melbourne, Australian licence.'

Troutt ducked into a porch to shelter his notebook from the rain and dutifully wrote the name down on his pad, spelling it back for him.

'Does the name mean anything to you?' the Sergeant asked him.'

'No, sir.'

'Me neither.'

All the same, Sergeant Brown decided to log it on the serial. Just in case.

101

OCTOBER 2007

Abby sat in silence in the back of the taxi in the pouring rain, staring at the display of her mobile phone.

The bubble-wrapped envelope was sandwiched between her pullover and the T-shirt beneath. She had a belt tucked tightly around her midriff to prevent the package from falling out – and from being visible to anyone. And she felt the reassuring bulge of the Mace in the front pocket of her jeans.

The driver turned right off Hove seafront by the statue of Queen Victoria and headed up the Drive, a wide street lined on both sides with expensive apartment blocks. But she saw nothing outside the windows of the vehicle. In fact, she saw barely anything at all. There was only one image in front of her raw eyes; one image burning in her mind.

The photograph on her mobile of her mother's head sticking out of the top of the rolled-up carpet. And the words beneath:

Snug as a bug in a rug.

Her emotions were in meltdown. She see-sawed from blind fury at Ricky to the most terrible fear for her mother's life.

And the guilt that she had caused this.

She was so tired, she was finding it hard to think straight. She had been wide awake throughout the night. Wired. Listening to the endless traffic on the seafront, a pebble's throw from her hotel window. Sirens. Trucks. Buses. A car alarm that kept going off. The early-morning cries of the gulls. She'd ticked off each long hour. Each half-hour. Each quarter-hour.

Waiting for Ricky to call.

Or at least to send a text saying something else. But there had been nothing. She knew him. Knew this kind of psychological game was his style. He enjoyed waiting games. She remembered the second time she had gone to his apartment. Their second *secret* date, or so he thought, and she had been stupid – or naïve – enough to let him try bondage on her. The bastard had tied her up naked, in a cold room, brought her to just short of a climax with a vibrator, then slapped her and left her in the room for six hours, gagged. Then he'd returned and raped her.

Afterwards he told her it was what she had wanted.

And she had totally failed on that occasion to get what *she* – or more accurately *Dave* – had wanted. It had taken a lot longer.

Her concern at this moment was that she did not know his limits – she suspected that he had none. She believed that Ricky was quite capable of killing her mother to get everything back. And that he could kill her too.

And probably enjoy it.

She was trying to imagine the distress her mother was in at this moment, when she realized, with a start, they had arrived at Hegarty's imposing house.

She paid the driver, peered carefully out of the rear window and then the front. She saw a British Telecom truck a short distance away, which looked as if it was doing some kind of a repair, and a small blue car parked partially on the kerb a short distance further on. But no sign of Ricky's Ford Focus or him.

She double-checked the number of the house, wishing she had remembered to pack her small umbrella. Then, head bowed against the rain, she hurried through the open gates, past a cluster of cars and into the dark porch. She stood there a moment, extricating the package from her midriff and tidying her clothes, then rang the bell.

A couple of minutes later she was seated on a large crimson leather sofa in Hegarty's study. The dealer, dressed in a baggy checked shirt, elephant cords and leather slippers, sat at his desk, scrutinizing each stamp with an enormous, tortoiseshell-rimmed magnifying glass.

It always excited her to see the stamps, because there was such a mystique about them. They were so tiny, so old, so delicate, and yet so valuable. Most of them were black or blue or a rusty red colour, bearing the head of Queen Victoria. But there were other colours and other sovereigns' heads.

Hegarty's wife, a handsome, smartly dressed woman in her sixties, with elegantly coiffed hair, brought Abby a cup of tea and a plate of digestive biscuits, then went out again.

There was something about the man's demeanour that was making her feel uncomfortable. Dave had told her to bring them here, that Hugo Hegarty was the dealer who would give her the best price and ask the fewest questions, so she had to trust that was the case. But she had a bad feeling about him that she couldn't quite put her finger on.

She needed to sell them urgently. The sooner she banked the money, the better her bargaining position with Ricky would be. All the time she had them, he had something on her. If he wanted to cut up really rough, he could go to the police. Then they would all be losers, but she believed he was spiteful enough to do that rather than be shafted.

Without the stamps, though, he would have nothing to substantiate his story. And meanwhile she would have the money safely tucked away, hidden by a firewall of nominee trustees in a bank in Panama, a tax haven that did not cooperate with authorities in other countries.

In any case, possession was nine-tenths of the law.

It had been a mistake to wait. She should have sold them as soon as she arrived in England, or in New York. But Dave had wanted to wait until they were sure Ricky had no idea where she was. Now that strategy had backfired badly.

Suddenly Hegarty's phone rang. 'Hello?' he answered. Then his voice suddenly sounded stiff and a little awkward. He shot a glance at Abby, then said, 'Just hold on a sec, would you? I'm going to take this in another room.'

*

Glenn Branson was sitting at his desk, phone to his ear, waiting for Hugo Hegarty to come back on the line.

'Sorry about that, Sergeant,' Hegarty said after what felt like a couple of minutes. 'The young lady was in my office. I presume this is about her?'

'It could be, yes. I just happened to be checking this morning's serials – the log of everything that's reported – and I've come across something that might be significant. Of course it might be nothing at all. You gave us a name yesterday, sir – a Mr Chad Skeggs.'

Wondering what was coming next, Hegarty responded with a hesitant, 'Yes.'

'Well, we've just had a report that a vehicle rented by

someone of this name, an Australian from Melbourne, has been seen opposite the flat where Katherine Jennings lives.'

'Oh, really? How very interesting. How very interesting indeed!'

'Do you think there's a possible connection, sir?'

'I would certainly say so, Sergeant, in the way that you might connect a rotting fish with a bad smell.'

102

3 NOVEMBER 2001

Some time during the early hours of the morning, as Lorraine lay awake, listening to Ronnie snoring, her joy and relief that he was alive started turning to anger.

Later, when he was awake, insisting on keeping the curtains drawn in the bedroom and the blinds down in the kitchen, she rounded on him at the breakfast table. Why had he put her through all this suffering? Surely he could have made one quick phone call, explaining everything, and then she wouldn't have been to hell and back for almost two months.

Then she began crying.

'I couldn't take the risk,' he said, cradling her face in his arms. 'You've got to understand that, babe. Just one call from New York showing up on your bill could have created questions. Insurance investigators are all ex-cops – they're no fools. And I had to know you were acting the grieving widow.'

'Yeah, I sodding acted that all right,' she said, dabbing her eyes. Then she took out a cigarette. 'I should get a bloody Oscar.'

'You're going to deserve one by the time we're through.'

She gripped his strong, hairy wrist, pulled it tightly against her face. 'I feel so safe with you, Ronnie. Please don't go. You could hide here.'

'Yeah, sure.'

'You *could*!'

He shook his head.

'Can't we do anything so we don't lose this place? Tell me again, what money's going to come in?' She lit the cigarette and inhaled deeply.

'I've got a life insurance policy, with Norwich Union, for one and a half million pounds. You'll find the policy in a deposit box at the bank. The key's in my bureau. Sounds like there's going to be special dispensation for 9/11 victims. The insurance companies are going to pay out on the policies, even where bodies haven't been found, instead of the statutory seven-year wait.'

'One and a half million! I could take the policy to the bank manager. He'd let me stay on!'

'You can try, but I know what that bastard'll say. He'll tell you there's no certainty they'll pay out, or when, and that insurance companies always wriggle.'

'So this one might wriggle?'

'Nah, it'll be OK, I reckon. Too emotive, this situation. But they'll give you a good grilling, for sure. So make sure you stick to your story. Appear helpful, but say the minimum you have to. Then there's going to be the 9/11 compensation fund. I'm told we could be looking at two and a half million dollars.'

'*Two and a half million?*'

He nodded excitedly.

She stared at him, doing a quick calculation in her head. 'That would be about one and three-quarter million pounds? So we're talking about three and a quarter million quid, give or take?'

'Give or take, yeah. And tax-free. For one year of pain.'

She sat still for some moments. When she finally spoke there was a tinge of awe in her voice. 'You're unbelievable.'

'I'm a survivor.'

'That's why I love you. Why I've always believed in you. I have, you know, haven't I?'

He kissed her. 'You have.'

'We're rich!'

'Nearly. We will be. Softly, softly catchee monkey . . .'

'You look strange with a beard.'

'Yeah?'

'Sort of younger.'

'And less dead than old Ronnie?'

She grinned. 'You were a lot less dead last night.'

'I waited a long time for that.'

'And now you're talking about waiting a year? Maybe longer?'

'The compensation fund will pay out fast to hardship cases. You're a hardship case.'

'They'll prioritize Americans before foreigners.'

He shook his head. 'Not what I've heard.'

'Three and a quarter million quid!' she said again dreamily and rolled the ash off her cigarette into the saucer.

'That'll buy you a lot of new frocks.'

'We'd need to invest it.'

'I've got plans. The first thing we have to do is get it out of the country – and you.'

He jumped up, went into the hall and returned with a small knapsack. From it he removed a brown envelope, which he put on the table and pushed towards her.

'I'm not Ronnie Wilson any more. You're going to have to get used to that. I'm now David Nelson. And in a year's time you won't be Lorraine Wilson any more.'

Inside the envelope were two passports. One was Australian. The photograph was a barely recognizable one of herself. Her hair had been changed to dark brown, cut short, and she'd been given a pair of glasses. The name inside said *Margaret Nelson.*

'There's a visa stamp in there for permanent residence in Australia. Valid for five years.'

'*Margaret?*' she said. 'Why Margaret?'

'Or Maggie!'

She shook her head. 'I have to be *Margaret – Maggie*?'

'Yes.'

'For how long?'

'For ever.'

'Great,' she said. 'I don't even get a choice in my own name?'

'You didn't when you was born, you stupid cow!'

She said the name aloud, dubiously, '*Margaret Nelson.*'

'Nelson's a good name, classy!'

She shook a second passport out of the bag. 'What's this?'

'It's for when you leave England.'

Inside was a photograph of her again, but in this one she had grey hair and looked twenty years older. The name said *Anita Marsh.*

She looked at him in bewilderment.

'I worked it out. The best way to disappear. People remember good-looking women, blokes in particular. They don't remember little old ladies, they're almost invisible. When the time comes you're going to buy two tickets in advance on the Newhaven–Dieppe ferry for a night-time crossing. One ticket in your name, one in Anita Marsh's name. And you're going to book a cabin in Anita Marsh's name. OK?'

'Want me to write this down?'

'No. You're going to have to memorize it. I'll be contacting you. I'll go through it all plenty of times more with you before then. What you're going to do is leave a suicide note – you're going to write that you can't bear life without me, you're miserable being back at work at Gatwick, life sucks – and the doctor'll be able to back it up that you were on antidepressants, all that stuff.'

'Yeah, well, he won't be lying about that.'

'So you get on the ferry as Lorraine Wilson, looking as beautiful as you can, and make sure plenty of people see you. You dump your bag, with a change of clothes, in the cabin booked in Anita Marsh's name. Then you go to the bar and you start giving the impression that you are sad, and drinking heavily, and not in any mood to talk to anyone. The crossing's four and a quarter hours, so you have plenty of time. When you are out in mid-Channel, leave the bar and tell the barman that you are going out on the deck. Instead, you go down to the cabin and transform yourself into Anita Marsh, with a wig and old-lady clothes. Then you take your clothes, your passport and your mobile phone and you drop them over the side.'

Lorraine stared at him in utter astonishment.

'In Dieppe you take a train to Paris. There you rip up your Anita Marsh passport and buy a plane ticket to Melbourne as Margaret Nelson. I'll be waiting for you at the other end.'

'You've thought of bloody everything, haven't you?'

He could not immediately tell whether she was pleased or angry.

'Yeah, well, I haven't exactly had much else to do.'

'Promise me one thing – all this money – you're not planning to sink it into a scheme, are you?'

'No way. I've learned my lesson, babe. I been giving it

a lot of thought. The problem is, once you get into debt, you're on a spiral. Now we're free, we can start again. Start in Australia and then maybe go off somewhere else, live life in the sun. Sounds good to me! We can eventually put the money in the bank, live off the interest.'

She looked at Ronnie dubiously.

He pointed at the envelope. 'There's something else in there for you.'

She pulled out a slim cellophane bag. Inside was an assortment of loose stamps.

'To help tide you over,' he said. 'Expenses. And give yourself a couple of treats to cheer yourself up. There's a 1911 Somerset House One Pound – that's worth about fifteen hundred quid. There's an 1881 One Penny that you should get about five hundred quid for. There's about five grand's value in total. Take them to this guy I know – he'll give you the best price. And when the big money comes through, he's the guy you get to convert it into stamps. He's straight. We'll get the best value from him.'

'And he knows nothing?'

'God, no.' He tore off a blank strip from the back of *Hello!* magazine on the kitchen table and wrote down the name *Hugo Hegarty*, with the man's phone number and address on it. 'He should be sorry when you tell him about me. I was a good customer.'

'We've had a few letters of sympathy and cards over the past weeks.'

'I'd like to see those, read what everyone says about me.'

'Nice things.' She gave a sad laugh. 'Sue was saying I needed to start thinking about a funeral. Wouldn't have needed a very big coffin, would we? For a wallet and a mobile phone.'

They both giggled. Then she dabbed away more tears that had started rolling down her face.

'At least we can laugh about it,' she said. 'That's good, isn't it?'

He walked around the table to her and hugged her hard. 'Yep. That's good.'

'Why Australia?'

'It's far enough away. We can be anonymous there. Also, I've got an old mate who went out there years ago. I can trust him – he'll convert the stamps back into cash, no questions asked.'

'Who's that?'

'Chad Skeggs.'

She looked at him with a startled expression, as if she had just been shot. '*Ricky* Skeggs?'

'Yeah. You went out with him before me, didn't you? He used to have all his birds call him *Ricky*. Like it was a special privilege. *Chad* in business, *Chad* to his mates, but *Ricky* to his birds. He was always very particular about things.'

'It's the same name,' she said. 'They're both versions of Richard.'

'Yeah, whatever.'

'No, it's not actually *whatever*, Ronnie. And I didn't *go out* with him. I went on just one date. He tried to rape me, remember? I told you all about it.'

'Yeah – rape used to be his idea of foreplay.'

'I'm serious. Surely I told you the story. Back in the early 1990s, he had a Porsche. Took me out one night—'

'I remember that Porsche. A 911 Targa. Black. I worked for Brighton Connoisseur Cars – we rebuilt it after it had been written off – wrapped around a tree. We spliced the rear end together with the front end of another one. Flogged it to him cheap. It was a fucking death trap!'

'You sold that to your friend?'

'He knew it was dodgy and not to drive it too fast. He just used it for posing – and pulling dolly birds like you.'

'Yes, well, after a few drinks at the bar I thought he was taking me to eat something. Instead he drove me up on the Downs, told me he allowed the girls he screwed to call him Ricky, then he unzipped himself and told me to suck him off. I couldn't believe it.'

'Crude bastard.'

'Then when I told him to take me home, he tried to drag me out of the car, said I was an ungrateful bitch and he was going to show me what a proper shag was. I scratched the side of his face, then I hit the horn and suddenly there were headlights coming towards us. He panicked and drove me home.'

'And?'

'He didn't say a word. I got out of the car and that was it. I used to see him around town from time to time, always with a different woman. Then someone told me he'd gone to Australia. Not far enough in my view.'

Ronnie sat in awkward silence. Lorraine crushed out her cigarette, which was burnt down to the filter, and lit another one. Finally Ronnie spoke. 'He's all right, Chad is. He was probably just pissed that night. Got a big ego, always had. You'll find he's mellowed now, with age.'

Lorraine was silent for a long while.

'It'll be all right, babe,' Ronnie said. 'It'll work out. How many people get a chance of a totally new start in life?'

'Some start,' she said bitterly. 'Where the person we are going to be totally dependent on once tried to rape me.'

'You have a better plan?' Ronnie snapped suddenly. 'You have a better plan, tell me?'

Lorraine looked at him. He seemed different from before he'd gone to New York. And not just physically. It wasn't just the beard and the shaven head, something else seemed to have changed. He seemed more assertive, harder.

Or maybe, because of the long absence, she was seeing him as he actually was for the first time.

No, she told him reluctantly, she didn't have a better plan.

103

OCTOBER 2007

Abby, waiting on the leather sofa in Hugo Hegarty's study, blew on her tea and sipped it. Then she took a biscuit. She hadn't eaten any breakfast and felt in need of a sugar hit. Hegarty seemed to have been gone a long time before he finally returned.

'Sorry about that,' he said politely, and sat back down behind his desk. Then he looked at the stamps again for some moments. 'These are all excellent quality,' he said. 'Mint condition. This is a very substantial collection.'

Abby smiled. 'Thank you.'

'And you're looking to sell it all?'

'Yes.'

'What price do you have in mind?'

'The catalogue value is just over four million pounds,' she replied.

'Yes, that would be about right. But I'm afraid no one's going to pay you catalogue prices. Anyone who buys these will want a margin. And the better the provenance, the lower the margin, of course.'

'Are you willing to buy them?' she asked. 'At a discounted price?'

'Can you explain to me in more detail how they came to be in your hands? You said, last night, you were clearing out your aunt's house?'

'Yes.'

'In Sydney, Australia?'

She nodded.

'What was your aunt's name?'

'Anne Jennings.'

'And do you have anything that can show me the chain of title?'

'What do you need?'

'A copy of her will. Perhaps you could get her lawyer to fax it to me? I don't know what time of day it is there now.' He glanced at his watch. 'Middle of the night, I think. He could do that tomorrow.'

'And how much would you pay me for the collection?'

'With kosher chain of title? I'd be prepared to pay around two and a half. Million.'

'And without? Cash on the nail, now?'

He shook his head with a wry smile. 'Not the way I operate, I'm afraid.'

'I was told you were the man I should come and see.'

'No, not me, not any more. Look, young lady, I'll give you some advice. Break this collection down. This is too big. People are going to ask you questions. Break it right down. There are a few dealers here in the UK. Take one plate to one of them, another plate to another one. Maybe go to a few dealers abroad. Haggle with them. You don't have to take their prices if you don't like them. Sell them quietly, over a couple of years, and that way you won't pop up on any radar.'

He gathered the stamps up carefully, almost reverentially, and slipped them all back in their protective sheets.

Gutted, Abby said weakly, 'Can you recommend any dealers here in the UK to me?'

'Yes, well, let me think.' He reeled off several names as

he began putting the stamps back into the Jiffy bag. Abby wrote them down. Then he added, as if it was an afterthought, 'Of course, there is someone else who springs to mind.'

'Who?'

'I hear Chad Skeggs is in town,' he said, giving her a hard stare.

And she couldn't help it. Her face turned the colour of a beetroot. Then she asked if he would call her a taxi.

*

Hugo Hegarty saw Abby to the front door. There was a frosty silence between them and she could not think of anything to say that would break it, other than a lame, 'It's not what you think.'

'That's the problem with Chad Skeggs,' he retorted. 'It never is.'

When she had left, he went straight back to his study and phoned Detective Sergeant Branson again. He didn't have a lot more to add to his previous conversation, other than to give him the name of the young woman's aunt, Anne Jennings.

Anything he could do, anything at all, to get one back on Chad Skeggs would not, in his view, be enough.

104

OCTOBER 2007

Abby opened the rear door of the taxi, deeply distressed by the encounter with Hugo Hegarty, and shot a bleak glance through the pouring rain up and down Dyke Road Avenue.

The British Telecom van was still there and the small, dark blue car was still parked further along. She climbed in the back of the taxi and pulled the door shut.

'The Grand Hotel?' the woman driver checked.

Abby nodded. It was the wrong address, which she had given deliberately when she phoned from Hegarty's office, not wanting him to know where she was staying. She would bail out somewhere before there.

She sat back, thinking. No word from Ricky. Dave was wrong. It was going to be a lot harder to sell the stamps than he had told her. And it was going to take much longer.

Her phone started ringing. The caller display showed it was her mother. She felt sick with fear as she answered, clamping the phone tightly to her ear, aware that the driver would be listening.

'Mum!' she said.

Her mother sounded disoriented and deeply distressed. Her breathing coming in short bursts. 'Please, Abby, please, I've got to get my medication, I'm getting—' She stopped and drew her breath in sharply, then let out a gasp. 'The spasms. I've – please – you shouldn't have taken them. It's wrong—' She let out another gasp.

Then the call terminated.

Abby redialled frantically, but it just went straight to voicemail, as before.

Shaking, she stared at her phone's display, expecting it to come back to life at any moment with a call from Ricky. But it remained silent.

She closed her eyes. How much could her mother take? How much more could she put her through?

Bastard. You bastard, bastard, bastard, bastard, bastard.

Ricky was smart. Too bloody smart. He was winning. He knew she wouldn't be able to sell the stamps easily and that therefore she almost certainly still had them all. Her plan to palm him off with a small cash payment, telling him that she'd transferred the bulk to Dave, was now out of the window.

She didn't know what to do any more.

She looked at the phone again, willing it to ring.

Actually there was one thing she could do, and she had to do it as fast as possible. She had to stop her mother's suffering, even if that meant making a deal with Ricky. Which was going to mean giving him what he wanted. Or at least pretty much everything.

Then she had a thought. Leaning forward to speak to the driver, she said, 'Do you know any local stamp dealers?'

The name on the driver's ID card read 'Sally Bidwell'.

'There's one in Queen's Road, just down from the station, called Hawkes. I think there's one out in Shoreham. And I'm sure there's one in the Lanes, down Prince Albert Street,' Sally Bidwell said.

'Take me to Queen's Road,' Abby said. 'That's nearest.'

'A collector, are you?'

'I just dabble,' Abby said, reaching inside her coat and unbuckling her belt.

'More of a boy's hobby, I always thought.'

'Yes,' Abby said politely.

She retrieved the Jiffy bag, held it down, below the line of sight of the interior mirror, and shuffled through the contents, looking for some of the lower-value items. She pulled out a block of four stamps with Maltese crosses on them that were worth about a thousand pounds. Also, there were some blocks of stamps featuring Sydney Harbour Bridge that were worth about four hundred pounds a sheet. She kept these out, then replaced the rest in the Jiffy bag and belted it back securely under her pullover.

A few minutes later the taxi pulled up outside Hawkes. Abby paid and climbed out, keeping the stamps safely dry, in their cellophane, inside her coat. A bus rumbled by, then she fleetingly noticed a small blue car passing her, with two men in the front, a Peugeot or a Renault, she thought. The passenger was talking on his mobile phone. The car looked very similar to the one that had been parked near Hegarty's house. Or was she being paranoid?

There were no customers in the shop. A woman with long fair hair was seated at a table, reading a copy of the local newspaper. Abby rather liked the slightly ramshackle feel of the place. It didn't seem precious, didn't feel the kind of place where you were likely to get asked all sorts of difficult questions about provenance and chain of title.

'I have some stamps I'm interested in selling,' she said.

'Do you have them with you?'

Abby handed them to her. The woman put the paper aside and took a cursory look at the stamps.

'Nice,' she said, in a friendly tone. 'Haven't seen any of these Sydney Harbour ones in a while. Let me just go and check on a few things. OK if I take them with me into the back?'

'Fine.'

The woman carried them through an open door and sat at a desk, over which was a large magnifying plate. Abby watched her put the stamps on the desk and then start to examine each of them carefully.

She glanced at the front page of the *Argus*. The headline read:

SECOND MURDERED WOMAN LINKED TO 9/11 VICTIM

Then she saw the photographs beneath. And froze.

The smallest showed a beautiful but hard-looking blonde in her late twenties, gazing seductively into the camera lens as if she wanted to have sex with whoever was behind it. The caption at the bottom read *Joanna Wilson.* The largest photograph showed another woman, in her late thirties. She had wavy blonde hair and was attractive, with a pleasant, open smile, although there was something slightly bling-looking about her, as if she had money but not much style. The name beneath the photograph was *Lorraine Wilson.*

But it was the photograph of the man in the centre that Abby was staring at. Totally fixated. She looked at his face, then his name, *Ronald Wilson*, then his face. Then his name again.

She read the first paragraph of the story:

> The body of a 42-year-old woman, found in the boot of a car in a river outside Geelong, near Melbourne, Australia, five weeks ago, has been identified as that of Lorraine Wilson, widow of Brighton businessman Ronald Wilson, one of the 67 British citizens known to have perished in the World Trade Center on 9/11.

She skimmed through it again. It felt as if someone had suddenly dimmed the lights inside her. Then she read on:

> The skeletal remains of Joanna Wilson, 29, were discovered in a storm drain by workmen digging the foundations for the New England Quarter development, in central Brighton, last Friday. She had been Wilson's first wife, DI Elizabeth Mantle, of Sussex CID, the Senior Investigating Officer, confirmed to the *Argus* this morning.
>
> Sussex Police are mystified by forensic evidence indicating that Lorraine Wilson's body had been in the Barwon river for approximately two years. As reported by this newspaper at the time, it was believed that Mrs Wilson had committed suicide in November 2002, when she disappeared from the Newhaven–Dieppe ferry during a night crossing, although the Coroner returned an open verdict.
>
> DI Mantle said that investigations into her 'suicide' were being reopened immediately.

Abby looked at each of the photographs again in turn. But it was the man in the centre her eyes went back to. Suddenly the floor she was standing on seemed to slope away from her. She took a couple of steps to the left, to avoid falling over, and gripped the edge of a table. The walls seemed to be moving, swirling past her.

A disembodied voice asked, 'Are you all right? Hello?'

She saw the woman, the fair-haired stamp dealer, standing in a doorway. She saw her go past her eyes as if she was the attendant on a fairground carousel. She came round again.

'Would you like to sit down?' the voice said.

The carousel was slowing now. Abby was shivering and sweating at the same time.

'I'm OK,' she gasped, looking at the paper again.

'Interesting story,' the woman said, nodding at the paper, then looking at her again, concerned. 'He was in the stamp trade. I knew him.'

'Ah.'

Abby stared at the photo again. She barely heard the woman's words as she offered her two thousand, three hundred and fifty pounds for the stamps. She took the money, in cash, in fifty-pound notes, and crammed them into her pockets.

105

OCTOBER 2007

Abby walked out into the street in a daze. Her phone started ringing, but it was several moments before she even noticed.

'Yes, hello?' Abby blurted.

It was Ricky. She could barely hear him as traffic roared past. 'Wait,' she said, hurrying down the street through the rain until she saw a covered doorway. Ducking into it, she said, 'I'm sorry, what did you say?'

'I'm worried about your mum.'

It took her a moment to be able to reply. To swallow the sob back down her gullet. To slow her breathing down.

'Please,' she gasped. 'Tell me where she is, Ricky, or bring her back to me.'

'She needs her medication, Abby.'

'I'll get it. Just tell me where to bring it.'

'It's not that simple.'

A bus stopped in a line of traffic right in front of her. Its engine made it too noisy to speak or hear. She stepped out into the rain again, hurried back up the street and ducked into another shop entrance. She didn't like the way he said *not that simple*.

She had a sudden, terrible panic that her mother was dead. Had the spasm killed her, since they had spoken just a short while ago?

She began crying, she couldn't help it. The shock of what she had read and now this. She was so far out of her depth.

'Is she all right? Please just tell me if she's all right.'

'No, she's not all right.'

'But she's alive.'

'For the moment.'

Then he ended the call.

'No!' she cried out. 'No! Please!'

She stood leaning against the front door of the shop, not caring whether anyone inside was looking at her or not, rain and tears stinging her eyes, almost blinding her. But not so much that she didn't see a small brown car drive slowly past.

There were two men inside, the one in the passenger seat on his phone. Both men had short hair: one was totally shaven, the other had a crew cut. Military types. Or *police* types.

They looked at her the same way as the two men she had seen drive past in the blue car, before she had gone into Hawkes. Her time on the run had sharpened her awareness of everything around her. Something just felt wrong about these two cars.

Each with the passenger on his phone.

Each looking in her direction as they drove past.

Had Hugo Hegarty phoned the police? Was she under surveillance?

Both cars were in heavy traffic southbound. Were there any others? Northbound? On foot?

She stared wildly in every direction, then sprinted north, ducking left down an alley and easing past a row of stinking dustbins. Across the next street she saw an alley running up between two houses. She shot a glance over her shoulder but could see no one following, so dashed into that narrow space. The rain was easing a little. Her brain was racing. She knew this area like the back of her hand, because for a time, in her previous incarnation, she had lived in a flat near the Seven Dials.

She ran fast, checking every few steps that the package was still firmly at her midriff and that the money was safely wedged in her pockets, then checking over her shoulder. She sped up a tree-lined street of terraced houses, with few people out and about in this horrible weather to notice her. The exercise and the pattering of rain on her face helped to clear her head a little.

Helped her to think.

Abby headed uphill, towards the Dials, then turned right, along another residential street, and emerged above the station. Standing back, out of sight from the road, she watched several cars and commercial vehicles go past, then dashed across Buckingham Road and into another street directly above the station. She ran down that, and again, being careful to wait, crossed another main road, New England Street, and ran on uphill again, through a maze of terraced residential streets and forests of estate agents' boards.

She got a stitch and stopped for some moments, then carried on at walking pace, gulping down air, perspiring heavily. The rain had stopped almost completely now and there was a strong breeze, which felt good and cooling on her face.

She was thinking clearly now, more clearly than for some hours, as if the shock of what she had seen in the *Argus* had rebooted her clogged hard drive. Striding purposefully, she kept to the back streets, checking behind her constantly for any sign of a blue or a brown car, or any other car with two people in, but she saw nothing that bothered her.

Had Ricky seen the *Argus*? Would the story be in other papers also? He would see it, for sure. Wherever he was, he would have papers, radio, television.

She went into a newsagent's and flicked quickly through some of the national dailies. None of them was carrying the story yet. She bought a copy of the *Argus*, and stood outside the shop, staring for a long time at the face of the man on the front page. Her emotions were in complete turmoil.

Then, still rooted to her spot in the street, she re-read the entire story. It filled in the gaps in Dave's past. The silences, the evasive answers, the rapid changing of the subject every time she brought it up. And the remarks Ricky made, testing her on how much she knew about Dave.

How much did Ricky know about him?

She walked along a few paces, then sat down on a damp doorstep, head in her hands. She felt more scared than she had ever been in her life. Scared not just for her mother, but for the whole future.

Life's a game, Dave liked to tell her. Liked to remind her. *A game.* This had all started as a game.

Some game.

Life's not about victims, Abby. It's about winners and losers.

Tears were misting her eyes again. Her mother's pitiful voice was ringing in her ears, in her heart. She dialled her mother's number, then Ricky's, to no avail.

Ring back. Please ring back. I'll make a deal.

After some minutes she stood up and walked down a hill, then along a street with the railway track of the London–Brighton line visible through railings beyond. She continued down stone steps, along a short tunnel and up to the ticket office of Preston Park Station.

It was a small commuter station, busy in the rush hour, deserted at most other times of the day. If the police were following her, if they had seen her downtown, near Brighton Station, that was where they might watch out for her. They were less likely to be here, she decided.

Life's a game.

She studied the timetable, working out a route that would get her to Eastbourne, avoiding Brighton Station, and then to Gatwick Airport, which was now part of the new plan crystallizing in her head.

Her phone suddenly beeped. She pulled it out, hoping desperately it was a message from Ricky, but it wasn't. It said:

Silence is golden? X

She suddenly realized she hadn't responded to his last text. She thought for some moments, then replied:

Problemo. x

A few minutes later, as she was stepping on to the train, her phone beeped again, with a reply.

Love, like a river, will cut a new path whenever it meets an obstacle.

She settled in her seat, too shaken up to think of a quote back. Instead she replied with a single x.

Then she stared bleakly out of the window at the chalk escarpment rising on either side of her as the train pulled out of the station. She was engulfed in icy, dark fear.

106

OCTOBER 2007

The interior of the Marriott Financial Center hotel had a cool, slightly Zen aura, Roy Grace thought, as he left the checkout desk and carried his bag across the foyer. And it all felt very fresh. Table lamps that looked like inverted opaque Martini glasses. Slim white vases on black tables, from which sprouted tall stems so elegant, so perfect, they seemed to have been designed rather than to have grown.

He found it hard to believe that this place, right on the edge of Ground Zero, had been badly damaged in 9/11. It felt important, solid, indestructible, as if it had always been here and always would be.

He walked past a cluster of businessmen in dark suits and ties, talking earnestly. Pat Lynch was waiting for him, standing on a red rug in the middle of the cream marble floor. He was dressed casually, in a sleeveless green flak jacket, over a black T-shirt, blue jeans and stout black shoes. Roy could see the bulge where his gun was.

Pat raised his hands. 'All done and dusted? Dennis is parked up outside. We're all set.'

Grace followed him into the revolving door. The world changed abruptly as he stepped out the other side into the damp, October morning. Traffic several lines deep trundled past. A cement mixer chuntered in front of him. A doorman, his elegance marred by a plastic shower cap over his peaked uniform cap, held open the door of a yellow cab for three Japanese businessmen.

As they walked a short distance along the pavement to the Crown Victoria, Pat pointed up at a wide expanse of sky. It was bounded by a thin scattering of skyscrapers on one side and the much denser mass of downtown New York on the other. Steam or smoke poured from a low-rise green building that was shaped like a vent. Almost directly in front of them was what looked like a makeshift bridge across the street.

'See that space, buddy?' Pat said, pointing at the sky.

Grace nodded.

'That's where our towers were.' He shot a glance at his watch. 'Half an hour earlier than this, on the morning of 9/11, you'd have been looking at the World Trade Center. You wouldn't have sky, you'd have seen those beautiful buildings.'

Then he walked Roy past the car to a street corner and pointed to the blackened hulk of a high-rise to his right, from which hung massive strips of some dark material covering the outside like giant black vertical Venetian blinds.

'I told you about the Deutsche Bank Building, right, where they recently found more body parts? That's it. We just lost two firemen there, back in the summer – back in August. And you know the thing about those two men? They were both at Ground Zero on 9/11. They went into the World Trade Center. They survived that. Then they died here six years later.'

'Very sad,' Roy said. 'And ironic.'

'Yeah, ironic. Makes you wonder sometimes if this whole place is jinxed – you know, cursed.'

They climbed into the Crown Victoria. A brown UPS

truck was trying to reverse into a tight space in front of them. Dennis, behind the wheel, raised a cheery hand to Roy.

'Hey! How's it goin'?' Then he looked back at the UPS truck, which had just mounted the kerb for the second time, perilously close to a letter box, and was now inching forward again. 'Hey, come on, lady, it's a van you're driving, not a fucking elephant!'

It began reversing again. Even closer to the letter box.

'Shit, lady!' Dennis said. 'Mind that post box! Damage that and it's a federal fucking offence!'

'So, more stamp dealers?' Pat said, trying to focus on the task ahead.

'I have another six on my list.'

'You know, if we don't get lucky today, we can broaden the search for you,' Pat said. 'Dennis and I, we can take care of it.'

'I appreciate that.'

'It's no big deal.'

Dennis drove them past Ground Zero. Grace stared at the steel fences, the concrete barriers, the mobile storage and office units, the cranes rising like giraffe necks, the banks of floodlights on tall poles. The area was vast. Almost beyond-comprehension vast. He kept thinking of the two men's description of it as the Belly of the Beast. But it was a strangely quiet beast now. There wasn't the usual din that came from most construction sites. Despite all the work that was going on, it felt almost reverentially quiet.

'You know, I've been thinking about this woman in Australia, right? In the river,' Pat said, turning again to look at Roy.

'You have a theory?'

'Sure. She was hot, OK, so she dove into this river,

didn't realize there was a car under the surface, with its trunk popped open. She dove straight into the trunk and snapped her neck. The impact caused the car to rise and fall a little. The water pressure and the current swung the lid shut. Boom!'

'It's a no-brainer!' Dennis grinned.

'Yeah, that's what it is,' Pat said. 'A no-brainer.'

'You want us to solve your problem cases for you, just send us the files,' Dennis said.

Grace tried to ignore their banter and to concentrate on thinking through the latest information he had received from Glenn Branson. They had spoken a few minutes before he left the hotel. Glenn told him that Hawkes had paid two thousand, three hundred and fifty pounds to Katherine Jennings for a few stamps, after Hegarty had refused to play ball. Then, after she left the dealer, the surveillance team had lost her.

Had she rumbled the surveillance unit? Grace wondered. Unlikely, as they were pretty good. Although it was always possible. Then another thought crossed his mind. Chad Skeggs's rental car parked outside her flat. She had not been back to her flat while the car was there. Was it Chad Skeggs she was running from?

The stamp dealer had told Glenn that Katherine Jennings seemed scared and very nervous. Tomorrow morning, when it was daytime again in Melbourne, they would find out whether anyone called Anne Jennings had died recently there and, if she had, whether she had been wealthy enough to have owned three million plus pounds' worth of stamps and forgotten about them.

It was starting to seem as if Kevin Spinella's instinct about this woman had been right.

Suddenly, Dennis braked hard. Roy peered out of the

window, wondering where they were. An Oriental-looking man walked by dressed in white chef's overalls, with a baseball cap perched the wrong way round on his head. It was a narrow street with brownstones on both sides and a row of garishly coloured awnings over shop fronts. Just beyond them was another awning, this one in elegant black with white lettering. It read: ABBE MILLER ASSOCIATES. STAMPS AND COINS.

Dennis stopped the car in front of a no-parking sign right outside, and shoved a large cardboard sign, bearing the crudely stencilled word POLICE, under the windscreen. Then the three of them went into the premises.

The interior felt plush, reminding Grace of an old-fashioned gentlemen's club. It was panelled in dark, glossy wood, there were two black leather armchairs and thick carpet, and a strong smell of furniture polish. Only the glass-fronted cabinets, containing a small selection of very old-looking stamps, and the glass-topped counter, containing a row of coins on purple velvet, indicated it was a business.

As the front door closed behind them, a tall, hugely overweight man of about fifty, with a big welcoming smile on his face, materialized through a concealed door in the panelling. Dressed in keeping with the premises, he was parcelled in a well-cut, chalk-striped three-piece suit and sported a striped college tie. His head was almost completely bald, except for a narrow fringe like a pelmet halfway up his forehead that looked faintly comical, and it was impossible to tell where his triple chin ended and his neck began.

'Good morning, gentlemen,' he said affably, in a higher-pitched voice than Grace had expected. 'I'm Abe Miller. How can I help you today?'

Dennis and Pat showed their shields and introduced Roy Grace. Abe Miller remained completely affable, showing no disappointment that they were not customers.

Grace, thinking the man looked too big and too clumsy to handle items as delicate as rare stamps and coins, showed him the three different photographs of Ronnie Wilson that he had brought. To his excitement he saw a glimmer of recognition in Abe Miller's face. The dealer took a second look at them, and a third.

'He was believed to be in New York around the time of 9/11,' Grace prompted.

'I've seen him.' He nodded thoughtfully. 'Let me think.' Then he raised a finger in the air. 'You know, I'm pretty sure I remember this guy. Know why?' He looked at each of the three policemen.

Grace shook his head. 'No.'

'Because I think he was the first person to walk in here after 9/11.'

'His name is Ronald Wilson,' Grace said. 'Ronald or *Ronnie*.'

'Name doesn't ring a bell. But let me check something in back. Just give me two minutes.'

He disappeared through the hidden door and returned a minute later holding an old-fashioned index card, with notes on it written in ink.

'Right here,' he said. He put the card down and read from it, for a moment. 'Wednesday 12 September 2001.' Then he looked up at the three of them again. 'I bought four stamps from him.' He continued reading. 'Each of them an Edward, one pound, unmounted, mint. Perfect gum, no hinge.' Then he grinned mischievously. 'Paid him two thousand bucks each. I got a bargain!' He looked at his card again. 'Sold 'em on just a few weeks later. Made a good profit. Thing was, he shouldn't have sold them, not that day. Hell, we all thought maybe the world was going to end.'

Then Abe Miller looked at the card again and frowned. 'You said *Ronald Wilson*?'

'Yes, Grace replied.

'Nope, no, sir. That was not his name. Not the name he gave me. I wrote down here *David Nelson*. Yep, that was his name. *Mr David Nelson*.'

'Did he give you an address or a phone number?' Grace asked.

'No, sir, he did not.'

*

As soon as they were back out on the street, Grace called Glenn Branson. He told him to get Norman Potting and Nick Nicholl to make it their first priority to find out whether there were immigration records going back to 2001, and if so, whether any *David Nelsons* show up on them.

He felt good about the meeting he had just had. But the one shadow, as Glenn picked up on, and which he had already thought about, was whether Ronnie Wilson was still using that name if and when he went to Australia. Maybe by then he had become yet another person.

But an hour later, as they were about to enter the slate-blue and grey Medical Examiner's Office, Glenn Branson phoned, sounding excited. 'We have a development!'

'Tell me?'

'I said earlier that we'd lost Katherine Jennings, right? That she gave the surveillance team the slip. Well, get this. She walked into John Street Police Station an hour ago.'

The words were like an electric shock. 'What? Why?'

'She says her mother's been kidnapped. A sick little old lady. A guy's threatening to kill her.'

'Have you spoken to her?'

'A CID officer spoke to her down there – and discovered the man she is accusing of the kidnap is none other than Chad Skeggs.'

'Shit!'

'I thought you'd like it.'

'So what's happening now?'

'I've sent Bella, along with a Family Liaison Officer, Linda Buckley, to bring her up here. I'm going to see her with Bella when she gets here.'

'Call me as soon as you've spoken to her.'

'What time are you flying back?'

'Leaving at 6 o'clock – that's 11 o'clock tonight your time.'

Branson's voice changed suddenly. 'Old-timer, I might need to crash at your place tonight. Ari's doing her tank. I didn't get home until midnight last night.'

'Tell her you're a police officer, not a fucking baby-sitter!'

'You tell her. Want me to call her, put her on the line?'

'The key's in the usual place,' Grace said hastily.

107

OCTOBER 2007

Abby's phone remained silent. It seemed that her lifeline to the world had flat-lined. It was almost three hours since she had heard from Ricky.

She stared bleakly out of the window of the empty railway carriage, clutching the plastic bag into which she had scooped all the medicines she could find in her mother's bathroom and bedroom. She told Doris that she was putting her mother in a rest home because she was worried about her ability to look after herself, and that she would phone her with her mother's new address and phone number. Doris said she was sad to lose her neighbour, but that her mum was lucky to have such a lovely, caring daughter to look after her.

Some irony, Abby thought.

More and more of the sky was turning blue. Large clouds scudded across it as if they were on some urgent mission. It was becoming a fine, blustery autumn afternoon. The kind of weather in which she loved walking along the seafront, particularly the under-cliff walk at Black Rock, past the Marina and towards Rottingdean.

Her mother used to enjoy that walk too. Sometimes, they would do it as a family on a Sunday afternoon, her mother, her father and herself. She loved it when the tide was in, waves exploding on the groynes and sometimes smashing up against the sea wall itself, hurling spray over them.

And there was a time, somewhere back there in the mists of her childhood, that she remembered she had felt content. Was that before she had started going with her father to the big houses he did work in? Before she saw there were people who were different, who had lives that were different?

Was it then? Her personal tipping point?

In the distance to her left she could see the soft hills of the Downs as the train headed back towards Brighton. To where so many memories of her life lay. Where her friends still lived. Friends who didn't know she was here. Whom she would have loved to see. More than ever she craved the company of her friends now. To pour her heart out to someone not involved in all this. Someone who could think clearly and tell her whether she was mad or not. But it was too late for that, she feared.

Friends were the one part of life that was not a game. But sometimes it was necessary to discard them, however hard that was.

Her eyes started watering. She had a sick feeling in the pit of her stomach. She'd eaten nothing all day except for the one digestive biscuit at Hugo Hegarty's house, and she'd drunk a Coke on Gatwick Station platform a short while ago. She was too knotted up for anything more.

Please phone.

They were passing through Hassocks. A short while later they entered Clayton Tunnel. She listened to the roar of the train exploding off the walls. Saw her own pale, scared reflection staring back in the window.

When they emerged back into light – the sloping greenery of Mill Hill to her right, the London Road to her left – she saw to her dismay that she had a missed call.

Shit.

No number.

Then it rang again. It was Ricky.

'I'm getting increasingly worried about your mother, Abby. I'm not sure she's going to survive much longer.'

'Please let me speak to her, Ricky!'

There was a brief silence. Then he said, 'I don't think she's up to speaking.'

A new, darker slick of fear spread through her. 'Where are you?' she said. 'I'll come to you. I'll meet you anywhere, I'll give you everything you want.'

'Yes, Abby, I know you will. We're going to meet tomorrow.'

'Tomorrow?' she screamed at him. 'No fucking way! We're going to do it now, please. I have to get her to hospital.'

'We'll do it when it suits *me.* You've inconvenienced me quite enough. Now you can have a taste of what it feels like.'

'This isn't inconvenience, Ricky. Please, for God's sake. This is a sick old lady. She hasn't done anything wrong. She hasn't harmed you. Take it out on me, not her.'

The train was slowing down, approaching Preston Park, where she wanted to get off.

'Unfortunately, Abby, it's her that I have, not you.'

'I'll swap places.'

'Very funny.'

'Please, Ricky, let's just meet.'

'We will meet, tomorrow.'

'No! Now! Please, today. Mum might not survive until tomorrow.' She was getting hysterical.

'That would be too bad, wouldn't it? For her to have died knowing her daughter is a thief.'

'God almighty, you are a callous bastard.'

Ignoring the remark, Ricky said, 'You're going to need a car. I've posted the key of the Ford I rented to your flat. It will be there in the morning.'

'It's been clamped,' she said.

'Then you'll just have to rent something yourself.'

'Where are we going to meet?'

'I'll phone you in the morning. Go hire a car tonight. And have the stamps with you, won't you?'

'Please can we meet now, this afternoon?'

He ended the call. The train jolted to a halt.

Abby climbed out of her seat and made her way unsteadily along to the exit, holding tightly on to her handbag and the plastic bag with one hand and the handrail with the other as she climbed down on to the platform. It was 4.15.

Got to hold it together, she thought. *Got to. Somehow. Somehow.*

Oh, Jesus, how?

She thought she was going to throw up as she left the station and walked over to the taxi rank. To her dismay, there were no cabs waiting. She looked at her watch, anxiously, then called the number of one of the local companies. Then she called another number, one she had called earlier. The same male voice answered. 'South-East Philatelic.'

It was the one stamp dealer in the city whose name Hugo Hegarty had omitted to give her.

'It's Sarah Smith,' she said. 'I'm on my way over, just waiting for a taxi. What time do you close?'

'Not till 5.30,' the man said.

An anxious fifteen minutes later the taxi appeared.

108

OCTOBER 2007

The Witness Interview Suite at Sussex House comprised two rooms. One was the size of the sitting room of a very small house. The other, which could just fit two people side by side, was used solely for observation.

The larger room, in which Glenn Branson sat with Bella Moy and a very distressed-looking 'Katherine Jennings', contained three bucket-shaped armchairs, upholstered in red, and a bland coffee table. Branson and Abby each had a mug of coffee in front of them and Bella was sipping a glass of water.

Unlike most of the gloomy interview rooms down at the well-worn Brighton Central Police Station in John Street, this one felt bright and actually had a view.

'Are you happy for this to be recorded?' Branson asked, nodding up at the two wall-mounted cameras pointing down at them. 'It's standard procedure.' What he did not add was that sometimes a copy of the tape would be given to a psychologist for profiling. You could learn a lot from just the body language of some witnesses.

'Fine,' she said, her voice barely a whisper.

He studied her carefully for some moments. Despite her face being drained and all scrunched up in misery, she was an extremely good-looking young woman. Late twenties, he guessed. Black hair that was cut a little severely and almost certainly dyed, because her eyebrows were much lighter. Her face was classically beautiful, with high cheekbones, a large forehead and an exquisite nose, small, finely chiselled and very slightly turned up. It was the kind of nose that less fortunate women paid thousands of pounds to plastic surgeons to try to achieve. He knew that because Ari had shown him an article on nose jobs once, and he had looked for signs of surgery on women's noses ever since.

But the young woman's most striking feature was her eyes. They were emerald green, mesmerizing, feline eyes. Even with her wretched expression, they still sparkled.

And she knew how to dress. In designer jeans, ankle-length boots – admittedly scuffed and dusty – a belted, black, knitted polo neck beneath a long, expensive-looking fleece-lined jacket, she was pure class. A few inches taller and she could have stepped off a catwalk.

Branson was about to start the interview when the young woman raised a hand. 'It's actually not my real name that I gave you. I think I ought to clarify. It's Abby Dawson.'

'Why were you using a different name?' Bella asked gently.

'Look, my mother's dying. She's in terrible danger. Could we just – just—' She put her hands over her face. 'I mean, do we need to go through all this? Can't we just – just do that later?'

'I'm afraid we do need to get all the facts, Abby,' Bella said. 'Why the name?'

'Because . . .' She shrugged. 'I came here, back to England, to try to escape from my boyfriend. I thought it would make it harder for him to find me with a different name.' She shrugged again and gave a sad smile. 'I was wrong.'

'OK, *Abby*,' Glenn said, 'would you like to tell us exactly what has happened? Everything we need to know about yourself, your mother and the man you say has kidnapped her.'

Abby pulled a tissue out of her brown suede handbag and dabbed her eyes. Glenn wondered what was in the plastic groceries bag that lay on the floor beside it.

'I was left a collection of stamps. I didn't know anything about them – but by coincidence I was going out with – dating – this guy Ricky Skeggs in Melbourne, who was in the rare stamp and coin business in quite a big way.'

'Is he connected to *Chad* Skeggs?' Branson asked.

'It's the same person.'

'*Chad* and *Ricky* are both derivatives of *Richard*,' Bella said to Glenn.

'I didn't know that.'

'I asked Ricky to take a look at them and tell me if they were worth anything,' Abby continued. 'He took them away, then gave them back to me a couple of days later. He said there were a few individual stamps that were worth something, but most of them were replicas of rare stamps, collectable, but not valuable. He said he could probably get a couple of thousand Australian dollars for the lot.'

'OK,' Glenn said. Her eyes made him uneasy, they were all over the place. He felt he was getting a rehearsed performance, not something from the heart. 'Did you believe him?'

'I didn't have any reason not to,' Abby replied. 'Except I've never been a very trusting person.' She shrugged again. 'It's not in my nature. So I'd made photocopies of all the stamps before I gave them to him. When I checked with the ones he gave me back, they all looked the same, but there were subtle differences. I confronted him and he told me I was being delusional.'

'That was smart that you made the copies,' Bella commented.

Abby looked at her watch anxiously, then sipped some coffee. 'Anyhow, I was glancing through one of the specialist magazines in Ricky's flat a day or so later, and read an article about a rare stamp auction in London. It was about a Plate 77 Penny Red that went for a record price of one hundred and sixty thousand pounds. And I recognized it as looking similar to the plate of Penny Reds I had. I checked the newspaper photo against my own stamps and to my relief I could see they were very similar but not absolutely identical, so it wasn't mine he had sold. But I then panicked that Ricky was going to try to sell them.'

'Why did you think that?' Bella probed.

'There was something about the way he acted over the stamps that made me very uncomfortable. I just *knew* he was lying to me.' She shrugged. 'Anyhow, a couple of days later he was blasted out of his skull on cocaine – he snorted it all the time – and then early in the morning he crashed out into a deep sleep. I went on to his computer – he'd left it logged on – and I found several emails to dealers around the world, offering stamps that were clearly mine for sale. He was very clever. He'd broken them down into individual stamps and plates so they couldn't be identified as one collection.'

'Did you confront him?' Glenn asked.

She shook her head. 'No, he'd boasted to me the first time we met how easy stamps were to conceal, that they were a great way of laundering money and transporting it around the world. That even if you got stopped, most customs officers wouldn't have a clue there was any value to them. He said the best place to hide stamps was inside a book – a hardback novel, anything like that, which would protect them. So I just searched his bookshelves. And I found them.'

Bella smiled.

Branson watched Abby's face, her eyes, absorbing it, but not comfortable. This wasn't the whole story. There was something she was omitting, but he had no idea what. Clearly, she was smart.

'What happened then?' he asked.

'I did a runner. I took the stamps, crept home, packed a bag and flew to Sydney on the first flight I could get in the morning. I was scared because I thought he would come after me – he's extremely sadistic. I made my way to England via Los Angeles and then New York.'

'Why didn't you go to the police in Melbourne and report what he had done?' Glenn asked.

'Because he scared me,' she said. 'And he's very clever. He's very good at lying. I was worried he would spin the police a story and get them back. Or that he would come after me and hurt me. He'd already hurt me once.'

Glenn and Bella shot each other a knowing glance, remembering Chad Skeggs's history with the police in Brighton.

'And I needed the value from them badly,' Abby said. 'My mother is extremely sick – she's got multiple sclerosis. I need the money to pay for her to be in a home.'

Glenn picked up on the way she said that last sentence. Nothing he could put his finger on, but she said it in a strange way, as if that would be justification for any action. And it just struck him as strange that she said the word *need.* If someone took something that belonged to you, it wasn't a question of whether you *needed* it. You had a *right* to it.

'Are you saying it will cost millions to keep your mother in a rest home?' Bella said.

'She's only sixty-eight, although she looks a lot older,' Abby replied. 'It could be for twenty years, maybe more. I don't know what it will cost.' She sipped some coffee. 'Why does that have any relevance? I mean – if we don't do something quickly, she won't survive. She won't.' She buried her face in her hands again and sobbed.

The two detectives shot each other a glance. Then Glenn Branson asked, 'Did you ever meet someone called David Nelson?'

'David Nelson?' She frowned, dabbing her eyes, then shook her head. 'The name rings a bell, I think.' She hesitated, then went on, 'David Nelson? I think Ricky may have mentioned the name.'

Branson nodded. She was lying.

'And the stamps – are they here in England now?' he asked.

'Yes.'

'Where?'

'Safe, under lock and key.'

He nodded again. Now she was telling the truth.

109

OCTOBER 2007

All Nick Nicholl wanted at this moment was a good night's sleep. His problem was that it was 8.30 in the morning and he was in the back of a blue unmarked Holden police car, in brilliant sunshine, heading away from the airport complex towards downtown Melbourne. They were on a wide, multi-lane highway which, to his eyes, could as easily have been in the USA as in Australia, except that the driver, Detective Sergeant Troy Burg, was sitting on the right.

Some of the road signs looked similar to those in the UK, but some were a different colour, blue and orange a lot of them, he noticed, and the speed limits were in kilometres. He stared at a slim black box on top of the dash, at a touch-screen computer mounted on the front binnacle and at the big shiny buttons all around it. It was like an adult version of a child's computer. Although Ben wasn't old enough yet, Nick was already looking at educational toys for him.

He was missing him. Missing Jen. The prospect of spending the weekend in Australia without them, with just bloody Norman Potting for company, filled him with dread.

The avuncular Detective Senior Sergeant George Fletcher, in the front passenger seat, seemed well briefed and got straight down to business after a few pleasantries. His taciturn colleague, a decade younger, drove in silence.

Both the Australian detectives wore freshly pressed white shirts, patterned blue ties and dark suit trousers.

Potting, dressed in what looked like a demob suit, had briefly lit up his pipe the moment they stepped out of the airport terminal and he now emitted a rank odour of unaired fabric, tobacco and stale alcohol fumes into the car. But he seemed remarkably breezy after the lengthy journey, and the young Detective Constable, also in a suit and tie, envied the older man's constitution for that.

'OK,' Fletcher said, 'we haven't had a lot of time to prepare but we've made a start on all the lines of enquiry. First thing we can report on is the trawl of immigration records for people with the name David Nelson who have entered Australia since 11 September 2001. We have one that is particularly interesting in terms of your time profile. On 6 November 2001, a David Nelson arrived in Sydney on a flight from Cape Town, South Africa. His date of birth puts him at the right age.'

'Did he give an address?' Norman Potting asked.

'He came in on an Australian passport with a five-year residence visa, so we didn't require that information. We're now checking our Law Enforcement Assistance Programme. That will tell us if he has a driving licence and any vehicles registered in his name. It will also tell us any known alias he may have used and his last known address.'

'He could be anywhere, couldn't he?'

'Yes, Norman,' Nick Nicholl reminded him, 'but we know that he had one old friend, Chad Skeggs, in Melbourne, so there's a good chance he came here – and might still be here. If you are going to do a disappearing act and fetch up in a new country, you need someone you can depend on, someone you can take into your confidence.'

Potting considered this. 'It's a valid point,' he conceded

a tad grudgingly, as if he didn't want to be outsmarted in front of these seasoned detectives by his junior.

Troy Burg said. 'And we're checking the Revenue to see which David Nelsons have a TFN.'

'TFN?' Potting queried.

'Tax File Number. You'd need that for employment.'

'Legitimate employment, you mean?'

Burg gave a wry smile.

'We have something else that could be a connection,' George Fletcher said. 'Mrs Lorraine Wilson committed suicide on the night of Tuesday 19 November 2002, correct?'

'Allegedly,' Potting said.

Four days later, on 23 November, a Mrs Margaret Nelson arrived in Sydney. Could be nothing,' he said. 'But the age on her passport is about right.'

'It's not that common a name,' Nicholl said.

'It's not,' Detective Senior Sergeant Fletcher said. 'It's not rare, but it's not common, I'd say.'

'I think we should run through the agenda we put together, see if it works for you guys,' Troy Burg said.

'So long as it includes beer and tottie, it works for me,' Potting said, and chuckled. '*Tinnies,* isn't that what you call 'em?'

'You mean girls or beer?' Fletcher grinned at him, eyes twinkling good-humouredly.

In the distance, Nick Nicholl could see a cluster of jagged high-rise buildings.

'You guys are in for a treat tomorrow. George's going to cook for you. He's a genius. He should have been a chef, not a cop,' Burg said, becoming animated for the first time.

'I can't boil an egg,' Potting said. 'Never could.'

'I think you'll want the best part of a week here to get through everything,' George Fletcher said.

Nick Nicholl groaned inwardly at the thought.

'We've been given a list of what you need to see,' Fletcher said. 'You just tell us if you want to skip some of it. We're going to take you out to the Barwon river, where Mrs Wilson's body was found. Then you might want to see the car – we have that in the pound.'

'What are the ownership records on the vehicle she was found in?' Nick Nicholl asked.

'The car had false number plates and its serial numbers had been filed off. I don't think we're going to get much from it.' Moving on, he said, 'I imagine you will want to see Mrs Wilson's remains so we've set up a meeting with the pathologist.'

'Sounds good,' Potting said. 'But I want to start with Chad Skeggs.'

'We're going there now,' Burg said.

'You guys like red wine?' George Fletcher said. 'Australian Shiraz? It's Friday, so Troy and I thought we'd take you to a place for lunch that we like.'

At this moment, Nick Nicholl felt desperately in need of black coffee, not any kind of alcohol.

'You bet,' Potting said.

'George knows his way around Australian Shiraz,' Troy Burg said.

'Are we going to see you over the weekend too, Troy?' Potting asked.

'Sunday,' George said. 'Troy's busy tomorrow.'

'I'll take you guys to the river on Sunday,' Troy said. 'Show you where the car was found.'

'We couldn't do that tomorrow?' Nicholl asked, anxious not to waste any precious time.

'He's busy most Saturdays,' George Fletcher said. 'Tell them what you do on Saturdays, Troy?'

After some moments, reddening a little, the Australian Detective Sergeant said, 'I play the banjo at weddings.'

'You're joking?' Norman Potting said.

'He's in big demand,' George Fletcher said.

'It's how I switch off.'

'What do you play?' Norman Potting asked. '"Duelling Banjos"? Ever see that film *Deliverance*?'

'Uh huh, I saw that.'

'When those hillbillies tie the guy to the tree and butt-fuck him? With the banjo music playing?'

Burg nodded.

'That's what they should have at weddings, not the "Wedding March",' Potting said. 'When a man gets married that's what happens to the poor sod. His wife ties him to a tree and butt-fucks him.'

George Fletcher laughed genially.

'Know the similarity between a hurricane and a woman?' Potting asked, on a roll now.

Fletcher shook his head.

'I think I heard this,' Burg murmured.

'When they come, they're wet and wild. When they go, they take your house and car.'

Nick Nicholl stared out of the window miserably. He'd already heard the joke on the plane. Twice. He saw a row of low-rise apartment blocks ahead. They were driving down a street of single-storey shops. A white tram crossed in front of them. A short while later they crossed the Yarra river and passed a geometric building in a wide plaza that looked like it was an arts centre. Now they were entering a busy downtown area.

Troy Burg made a left turn into a narrow, shaded street and parked outside a shop advertising itself as a bottle store. As Nick Nicholl climbed out of the car he saw the shop had a bay-windowed, Regency front that looked as if it had been modelled on one of the antiques shops in Brighton's Lanes. The window was filled with displays of rare stamps and coins. In gold Olde Worlde lettering above he read: CHAD SKEGGS, INTERNATIONAL COIN AND STAMP DEALERS AND AUCTIONEERS.

They went inside and a bell pinged. Behind the glass-topped display counter, showing more stamps and coins, stood a skinny, tanned youth in his early twenties with spiky, bleached blond hair and a large gold earring. He was dressed in a T-shirt with a surf board emblazoned on it and faded jeans, and he greeted them as if they were long-lost friends.

George Fletcher showed him his ID. 'Is Mr Skeggs in?'

'No, mate, he's away on business.'

Norman Potting showed him a photograph of Ronnie Wilson and watched the man's eyes. He had never got the hang of Roy Grace's technique for sussing a liar, but he reckoned he was pretty good at telling, anyway.

'Have you ever seen this man?' he asked.

'No, mate.' Then the Australian touched his nose, a dead giveaway.

'Take another look.' Potting showed him two more photographs.

He looked even more awkward. 'No.' He touched his nose again.

'I think you have,' Potting said insistently.

Cutting in, George Fletcher said to the assistant, 'What's your name?'

'Skelter,' he replied. 'Barry Skelter.' He made it sound like a question.

'OK, Barry,' George Fletcher said. He pointed to Potting and Nicholl. 'These gentlemen are detectives from England, helping Victoria Police on a murder inquiry. Do you understand that?'

'Murder inquiry? Right, OK.'

'Withholding information in a murder inquiry is an offence, Barry. If you want the technical legal term, it is *perverting the course of justice.* In a murder inquiry that carries a likely minimum sentence of five years' imprisonment. But if the judge wasn't happy, you could be looking at ten to fourteen years. I just want to make sure you are quite clear about that. Are you clear about that?'

Skelter suddenly changed colour. 'Can I see those photographs again?' he asked.

Potting showed them to him again.

'Actually, you know, I can't swear, but there is a resemblance to one of Mr Skeggs's customers, now I come to think about it.'

'Would the name *David Nelson* help you think about it a bit more clearly?' Potting asked.

'David Nelson? Oh yeah. David Nelson! Of course. I mean, he's changed a bit since these were taken. You see, that's why I kind of didn't recognize him immediately. You get my drift?'

'We're drifting with you all the way,' Potting said. 'Now let's just drift along to your customer address book, shall we?'

*

Outside afterwards, Norman Potting turned to George Fletcher. 'That was brilliant, George,' he said. 'Ten to fourteen years. Is that right?'

'Shit,' he said, 'I don't know. I made it up. But it worked, right?'

For the first time since he had set foot in Australia, Nick Nicholl smiled.

110

OCTOBER 2007

The landscape changed rapidly. Ahead of them, Nicholl saw the glimmering water of the ocean. The wide street they were driving down had a resort feel to it, with bleached, low-rise buildings on either side. It reminded him of some of the streets on the Costa del Sol in Spain, which was pretty much the limit of his previous travel horizons.

'Port Melbourne,' George Fletcher said. 'This is where the Yarra river comes out into Hobson's Bay. Expensive property round here. Young, wealthy community. Bankers, lawyers, media types, those kinds of people. They buy nice flats overlooking the bay before they get married, then graduate to something a little bigger further out.'

'Like you,' Troy ribbed his colleague.

'Like me. Except I could never afford to be here first.'

They parked outside yet another bottle store, then walked up to the smart entrance of a small apartment block and George rang the bell for the caretaker.

The door clicked open and they went into a long, smartly carpeted corridor that was freezing cold from the air-conditioning. After a few moments, a man in his mid-thirties with a shaven head, wearing a purple T-shirt, baggy shorts and Crocs, strutted up to them. 'How can I help you?'

George again showed the man his ID. 'We'd like to have a word with one of your residents, Mr Nelson, in Flat 59.'

'Flat 59?' he said cheerily. 'You beat me to it.' He raised a clutch of keys in his hand. 'I was about to go up there myself. Had a few complaints from the neighbours about a smell. At least, they think it may be coming from there. I haven't seen Mr Nelson in a while and he hasn't picked up his post in several days.'

Potting frowned. Reports of smells from neighbours were rarely good news.

They entered the lift and travelled up to the fifth floor, then went out into the corridor, which smelled strongly of new carpet and nothing else. But as they walked along it, towards the flat at the far end, their nostrils started picking up something very different.

It was a smell with which Norman Potting had long if uncomfortably been acquainted. Nick Nicholl less so. The heavy, cloying stench of decaying flesh and internal organs.

The caretaker gave the four detectives a *hope-for-the-best* raise of his eyebrows, then opened the front door. The stench became instantly stronger. Nick Nicholl, covering his nose with his handkerchief, brought up the rear.

It was stiflingly hot inside, the air-conditioning evidently not on. Nicholl stared around apprehensively. It was a nice pad in anybody's terms. White rugs on polished boards and smart modern furniture. Unframed erotic canvases lined the walls, some showing women's loins, others abstract.

The smell of rotting flesh hung heavily in the corridor, getting denser with every step the five men took forward. Nick, increasingly uncomfortable about what they were going to find, followed his colleagues into an empty master bedroom. The huge bed was unmade. An empty tumbler lay on the table, along with a digital clock radio that appeared to be off.

They walked through into what looked like a den converted from a spare room. A hard-drive back-up sat on a desk, along with a keyboard and a mouse, but no computer. Several cigarette butts lay in an ashtray and had evidently been there a while. The window looked across to the grey wall of the building opposite. There was a pile of bills on the side of the desk.

George Fletcher lifted one of them. It had large red printing on it.

'Electricity,' he said. 'Final reminder. Several weeks ago. That's why it's so hot. They've probably cut him off.'

'I've had the landlords on my back about Mr Nelson,' the caretaker prompted. 'He's behind with the rent.'

'Badly?' Burg asked him.

'Several months.'

Nick Nicholl was looking around for family photographs, but could not see any. He stared at a stack of bookshelves, noticing that alongside the volumes of stamp catalogues there were several collections of love poems and a dictionary of quotations.

They entered a large, open-plan living and dining room, with a view across a wide balcony with a barbecue and loungers on it, and a neighbour's rooftop tennis court, to the harbour. Nick could just make out the hazy silhouette of industrial buildings on the far shore.

He followed the three detectives through into a smart but narrow kitchen, and by then he was having to pinch his nose against the worsening smell. He heard the buzz of flies. A mug of tea or coffee sat on the draining board with mould on top of it and there was rotten fruit, covered in grey and green mould, in a wire basket. A wide, dark stain lay on the floor at the base of the swanky silver fridge-freezer unit.

George Fletcher pulled open the bottom door of the refrigerator and suddenly the smell got even worse. Staring at the green, decaying cuts of meat that lined the freezer shelves, he said, 'Lunch is off, guys.'

'I think someone must have told Mr Nelson we were coming,' Troy Burg said.

Fletcher closed the door. 'He's gone all right.'

'Done a runner, you think?' Norman Potting said.

'I don't think he's planning to come back any time soon, if that's what you mean,' the Detective Senior Sergeant replied.

111

OCTOBER 2007

The plane landed at Gatwick at 5.45, twenty-five minutes early, thanks to a tail wind, as the captain proudly reported. Roy Grace felt like shit. He always drank too much booze on overnight flights, in the hope it would knock him out. It did, but only for a short while and then, like this morning, it left him with a headache and a raging thirst. On top of which, he felt uncomfortably stuffed from a revolting breakfast.

If his bag came through quickly, he thought, he might just have time to go home and grab a shower and change of clothes before getting to the morning briefing. His luck was out. The plane might have come in early, but the delay at the baggage carousel wiped out that advantage, and it was 6.40 before he lugged his bag through the green customs channel and headed down to the buses for the long-term car park. Standing at the stop, in the dry but chilly morning air, he dialled Glenn Branson for an update.

His friend sounded strange. 'Roy,' he said, 'are you going to go home?'

'No, I'm coming straight in. What's new?'

The Detective Sergeant brought him up to speed, firstly with a progress report from Norman Potting in Sydney. Information on the passports held by David Nelson and Margaret Nelson had come to light during the course of the day, revealing them both to be forgeries. And Nelson had gone from his flat. Potting and Nicholl were now door-stepping all David Nelson's neighbours, in the hope of finding out more information on his lifestyle and circle of friends.

Then Branson moved on to Katherine Jennings. She was waiting for a call from Skeggs to arrange the time and location of their meeting for the handover of the stamps and her mother. Branson told him they had two surveillance units on stand-by, up to twenty people available if they decided they needed them.

'What about the firearms unit?' Grace asked.

'We don't have any intelligence that Skeggs is armed,' he replied. 'If that changes, we'll involve them.'

'Are you OK, mate?' Grace said when Branson had finished. 'You sound a little strained. Ari?'

Branson hesitated. 'Actually it's you I'm worried about.'

'Me?'

'Well, your house really.'

Grace felt a prick of alarm. 'What do you mean? Did you stay there last night?'

'Yes, I did, thanks. I appreciate it.'

Grace wondered whether his friend had broken something. His precious antique juke box, which Glenn was always fiddling with, maybe.

'It might be nothing, Roy, but when I was leaving this morning, I saw – at least I could swear I saw – Joan Major driving down your street. It wasn't fully light, so I could be mistaken.'

'Joan Major?'

'Yeah, she drives one of those rather distinct little Fiat MPV things – you don't see many of them about.'

Glenn Branson had impressive powers of observation.

If that was who he said he had seen, then almost certainly he had. Grace stepped on the bus, holding the phone to his ear. It was curious that Glenn should see the forensic archaeologist driving down his street, but hardly any big deal.

'Maybe she does a school run in the area?'

'I doubt it. She lives in Burgess Hill. Perhaps she was dropping something off to you?'

'That doesn't make any sense.'

'Perhaps something occurred to her and she wanted to see you.'

'What time did you leave?'

'About 6.45.'

'You don't pop around to someone's house for a chat at that time in the morning. You use a phone if it's urgent.'

'Yeah. Yeah, I think you would.'

Grace told him he hoped to be at the office in time for the briefing, but when he reached his car he decided that, provided the morning rush-hour traffic wasn't too bad, he would dash home first. Something he could not put a finger on was bothering him.

112

OCTOBER 2007

At 8 o'clock, when her phone finally rang, Abby had been up, dressed and ready for a good two hours. She hadn't been able to sleep properly all night, but had just lain on her hard bed, with its tiny pillow, listening to the traffic on the seafront, the occasional wail of sirens, the shouts of drunken yobs and the slamming of car doors.

She was worried out of her wits about her mother. Could she survive another night without her medication? Would the distress and the spasms bring on a heart attack or a stroke? She felt so damned helpless, and she knew that bully Ricky would be playing on that. Counting on that.

But she was well aware too that he'd seen just how devious she could be, from their time together in Melbourne and now from the events of the past few days. It wasn't going to be easy. He wasn't going to trust her an inch.

Where would he dictate that they meet? In a multistorey car park? A city park? Shoreham harbour? She tried to think where people in films met to hand over kidnap victims. Sometimes they dumped them from moving cars; or left them in a car abandoned somewhere.

Every one of her speculations ran into buffers. She didn't know, couldn't predict. But one thing she had decided, totally and utterly non-negotiable, was that she would want absolute proof, to see with her own eyes, that her mother was alive before she did anything.

Could she trust the police? What would happen if he saw them and panicked?

Weighed against that was how much she could trust him to deliver her mother back at all. If she was even still alive. He'd shown what a total, feelingless shit he was in taking an old lady and putting her through this torment.

The display said the usual *Private number calling.*

She pressed the button to answer.

113

OCTOBER 2007

Grace stared in disbelief as he drove down his street just after 8 o'clock. He recognized Joan Major's distinctive slab-shaped silver Fiat too now, parked outside his house. But it was the vehicle in the drive that astonished him the most. It was one of the Sussex Police white Scientific Support Branch vans.

Also in the street, behind Joan Major's car, was a plain brown Ford Mondeo. He knew from the number plate that it was one of the CID pool cars. What the hell was going on?

He pulled up, leaped out of his car and ran into the house. It was silent.

He called out, 'Hello? Anyone here?'

No reply.

He walked through into the kitchen to check that the automatic feeder fixed to the bowl of his goldfish, Marlon, had been working. Then he looked out of the window into the rear garden.

The sight that met his eyes defied belief.

Joan Major, and two SOCO officers he knew, were walking up his lawn. The forensic archaeologist, in the centre, was holding a long piece of electrical equipment in the shape of a canoe paddle, supported by a shoulder brace, and with a display screen of some kind in the centre.

The SOCO officer on her right was peering intently at the screen, while the one on her left wrote down something on a large pad.

Stunned, Grace unlocked the rear door and sprinted out. 'Hey! Excuse me! Joan, what on earth are you doing?'

Joan Major's face reddened with embarrassment. 'Oh, good morning, Roy. Umm. I assumed you knew we were here.'

'I had no idea. Do you want to fill me in? What is that?' He nodded at the equipment. 'What on earth is going on?'

'It's GPR,' she replied.

'GPR?'

'Ground Penetrating Radar.'

'What are you doing with it?'

Her face reddened even more. Then, as if he was having a bad dream, out of the corner of his eye he saw one of the few police officers in the CID that he really did not like. On the whole, in Grace's experience, most police officers got on with each other reasonably well. Just occasionally he had come across one whose attitude really irked him, and emerging through his garden gate at this moment was a young DC he just could not stomach. His name was Alfonso Zafferone.

A sullen, arrogant man in his late twenties, with Latino good looks and shiny, mussed-about hair, Zafferone was slickly dressed in a smart beige mackintosh over a tan suit. Although he was a sharp detective, Zafferone had a serious attitude problem and Grace had written a scathing report after his last experience working with the man.

Now Zafferone was striding across his lawn, chewing gum and holding a sheet of paper in his hand of the kind that Grace was all too familiar with.

'Good morning, Detective Superintendent. Nice to see you again.' Zafferone gave him a smarmy smile.

'You want to tell me just what is going on?'

The young DC held up the signed document. 'A search warrant,' Zafferone said.

'For my garden?'

'And the house too.' He hesitated, then added a reluctant, 'Sir.'

Now Grace was almost beside himself with rage. This was not real. No way. Absolutely no way.

'Is this some kind of a joke? Just who the fuck is responsible for this?'

Zafferone smiled, as if he was in on this too and was really enjoying his moment of power, and said, 'Detective Superintendent Pewe.'

114

OCTOBER 2007

Cassian Pewe was sitting in his office, in his shirtsleeves, reading through a policy document, when his door burst open and Roy Grace came in, his face contorted with rage. He slammed the door shut behind him, then put both hands on Pewe's desk and glared at him.

Pewe sat back and put his hands up defensively. 'Roy,' he said. 'Good morning!'

'How dare you?' Grace yelled at him. 'How fucking dare you? You wait until I've gone away and you do *this*? You fucking humiliate me in front of my neighbours and the entire force?'

'Roy, calm down, please. Let me explain—'

'Calm down? I'm not going to fucking calm down. I'm going to cut your fucking head off and use you as a hat stand.'

'Is that a threat?'

'Yes, it's a threat, you creep. Go run to Alison Vosper and ask her to blow your nose while you sit on her lap and blub your eyes out, or whatever it is you do with each other.'

'I thought with you being away – it would be less embarrassing for you.'

'I'm going to have you, Pewe. You are going to really regret this.'

'I don't appreciate the tone of your voice, Roy.'

'And I don't appreciate SOCO officers crawling all over my home with a search warrant. You fucking stop them right now.'

'I'm sorry,' Pewe said, getting a little more courageous after realizing Grace was not going to hit him. 'But following my interview with your late wife's parents, I'm not comfortable that every aspect of your wife's disappearance has been investigated as thoroughly as it should have been at the time.'

He smiled in conclusion, and Grace did not think he had ever hated anyone in all his life as much as he hated Cassian Pewe at this moment.

'Really? Just what did her parents say to you that's so new?'

'Her father had quite a bit to say.'

'Did he tell you his father was in the RAF during the war?'

'Yes, actually, he did,' Pewe said.

'Did he tell you about any of the bombing sorties his father went on?'

'In some detail. Fascinating. He sounds a character. He flew on some of the Dambusters missions. Extraordinary man.'

'Sandy's father is an extraordinary man,' Grace confirmed. 'He is a complete fantasist. His father was never in 617 Squadron – the Dambusters squadron. And he was an aircraft fitter, not a gunner. He never flew on a single mission.'

Pewe was silent for a second, looking slightly uncomfortable. Grace stormed back out, crossed the corridor and marched straight into the Chief Superintendent's office. He stood in front of Skerritt's desk until his boss had finished a call and then said, 'Jack, I need to talk to you.'

Skerritt ushered him to a chair. 'How was New York?'

'Good,' he said. 'Got some good information – I'll circulate a report. I've literally just got back.'

'Your *Operation Dingo* team seems to be making some headway. I see there's a big operation going on today.'

'Yes, there is.'

'Are you letting DI Mantle run with it, or are you taking back command?'

'I think today we're going to need everyone,' Grace said. 'It's going to depend on the geography to some extent who else we involve.'

Skerritt nodded. 'So, what did you want to talk about?'

'Detective Superintendent Pewe,' he said.

'Wasn't my choice to bring him here,' Skerritt said, giving Grace a knowing look.

'I realize that.' He was aware that Skerritt disliked the man almost as much as he did.

'So what's the problem?'

Grace told him.

When he had finished, Jack Skerritt shook his head incredulously. 'I can't believe he did this behind your back. It's one thing to have an open investigation, and that can be a healthy thing, sometimes. But I don't like the way this is being handled at all. Not one bit. How long has Sandy been missing now?'

'Getting on for nine and half years.'

Skerritt thought for a moment, then looked at his watch. 'Are you going to your briefing meeting?'

'Yes.'

'Tell you what I'll do, I'll speak to him now. Come and see me straight after your meeting.'

Grace thanked him, and Skerritt picked up the phone as he was leaving the office.

115

OCTOBER 2007

At 9.15 Abby drove the black Honda diesel off-roader she had rented last night, on Ricky's very specific instructions, up the hill towards Sussex House. Her stomach felt as if it was full of hot needles, and she was shaking.

Taking deep, steady breaths, she tried her hardest to keep calm and not let another panic attack come on. She was on the verge of one, she knew. She had that slightly disembodied feeling that was always the precursor.

It was ironic, she thought, that Southern Deposit Security was less than half a mile away from the building she was headed to now.

She pulled the car up as instructed, in front of the massive green, steel gate and put the handbrake on. Sitting on the passenger seat was the plastic groceries bag she had put her mother's medications in yesterday. Also inside it was a Jiffy bag. Her suitcase was back in her room at the hotel.

Glenn Branson appeared and gave her a cheery wave. The gate began to slide open and, as soon as there was a large enough gap, she drove through. The DS signalled for her to park in front of a row of wheelie bins, then he held the door open for her.

'You OK?' he asked.

She nodded bleakly.

He put a protective arm around her shoulder. 'You'll be fine,' he said. 'I think you are a strong lady. We'll get your mum back safely. And we'll get your stamps too. He thinks he's chosen a smart place, but he hasn't. It's dumb.'

'Why do you say that?'

Ushering her through a door into a bare stairwell, he said, 'He's chosen the place to frighten you. That's his priority, but it shouldn't be. You're frightened enough, so he doesn't need to ratchet things up. He's not thinking this through. He's not doing it the way I'd do it.'

'What if he sees any of you?' she asked, walking along a corridor, struggling to keep pace with him.

'He won't. Not unless we have to show ourselves. We'll only do that if we start to think you are in danger.'

'He *will* kill her,' she said. 'He's that spiteful. If anything goes wrong, he'd do it for the hell of it.'

'We understand that. You have the stamps?'

She lifted up the carrier bag to show him.

'Didn't want to risk leaving them in your car in a police station?' He grinned. 'Wise decision!'

116

OCTOBER 2007

Cassian Pewe was already seated at the conference table in Jack Skerritt's office when Grace returned after the briefing meeting. The two men avoided eye contact.

The Chief Superintendent gestured for Grace to sit down, then he said, 'Roy, Cassian tells me that he realizes he made an error of judgement by setting in motion what he did at your house. The team there has been instructed to leave.'

Grace shot Pewe a glance. The man was steadfastly staring at the table, like a scolded child. He did not look as if he regretted anything.

'He explained that he was doing it to help you,' Skerritt went on.

'To help me?'

'He said that he feels there is an unhealthy amount of innuendo going on behind your back, about Sandy's disappearance. That's correct, isn't it, Cassian?'

Pewe nodded reluctantly. 'Yes – er – sir.'

'He says he felt that if he could prove, one hundred per cent, that you had nothing to do with her disappearance, it would end that once and for all.'

'I've never heard any innuendo,' Grace said.

'With respect, Roy,' Pewe said, 'quite a few people think that the original investigation was a rushed job and that you had a hand in bringing it to a premature stop. They are asking why.'

'Name one of them?'

'That wouldn't be fair on them. All I'm trying to do is to revisit the evidence, using the best modern techniques and technology we have, in order to totally exonerate you.'

Grace had to bite his tongue; he could not believe the man's arrogance. But this wasn't the moment to start a slanging match. He needed to get away from here in a few minutes and into position for Abby Dawson's rendezvous, which had been set for 10.30.

'Jack, can we come back to this later? I'm not at all happy about it, but I have to get going.'

'Actually, I was thinking it might be a good idea if Cassian came with you, in your car. He could be invaluable to your team in the current situation.' He turned to Pewe. 'I'm correct, aren't I, Cassian, that you are an experienced hostage negotiator?'

'I am, yes.'

Grace could hardly believe his ears. *God help any poor sodding hostage who ends up with Pewe negotiating for him,* he thought.

'I think also it would be good for him to see how we operate down in Sussex. We clearly handle some things in a different way from the Met. Might be a good learning curve for you, Cassian, I think, to observe how one of our most experienced officers handles a major operation.' He looked at Grace and the message could not be clearer.

But Roy was in no mood for smiling.

117

OCTOBER 2007

It had been a long time since she had last come here, Abby thought, threading the car along the winding road that climbed steadily between fields of grass and vast areas of stubble. Maybe it was her heightened nerves, but the colours of the landscape seemed almost preternaturally vivid. The sky was a canopy of intense blue, with just a few tiny clouds here and there, scudding across. It felt almost as if she was wearing tinted glasses.

She gripped the steering wheel hard, feeling the gusting wind buffeting the car, trying to push it off course. She had a lump in her throat and the needles in her stomach were burning even more fiercely.

She also had a small lump on her chest. A tiny microphone, held in place by gaffer tape that was pulling uncomfortably on her skin with every movement she made. She wondered if Detective Sergeant Branson, or whichever of his colleagues were listening at the other end, could hear the deep breaths she was taking.

The DS had at first wanted her to wear an ear-piece so that she could listen to any instructions they needed to give her. However, when she told him that Ricky had picked up some previous conversations she'd had, he decided it was too risky. But they would hear her, every word. All she had to do was ask them for help and they would move in, he assured her.

She couldn't remember when she had last prayed, but she found herself praying now, suddenly, silently. *Dear God, please let Mum be OK. Please help me through this. Please, dear God.*

There was a car in front of her, driving slowly, an elderly maroon Alfa Romeo with two men inside, the passenger talking on what she presumed was his mobile phone. She followed it round a sharp left-hand bend, passing a hotel on the right, and the Cuckmere river estuary below. The brake lights of the Alfa came on, as it slowed to let a delivery van cross a narrow bridge, then it accelerated again. Now the road was climbing.

After a few more minutes she saw a road sign ahead. The brake lights on the Alfa came on once more, then its right-turn indicator began flashing.

The sign read TOWN CENTRE A259, with an arrow pointing straight on, and SEAFRONT BEACHY HEAD, with an arrow pointing right.

She followed the Alfa Romeo to the right. It continued to drive at a maddeningly slow pace, and she glanced at the car's clock and her watch. The clock was a minute slower, but she knew her watch was accurate, she had set it earlier: 10.25 a.m. Just five minutes. She was tempted to overtake, worried that she would be late.

Then her phone rang. *Private number calling.*

She answered it on the in-car speaker plugged into the cigarette lighter which the police had given her so they could hear any conversation.

'Yes?' she said.

'Where the fuck are you? You're late.'

'I'm only a few minutes away, Ricky. It's not 10.30 yet.' Then she added nervously, 'Is it?'

'I told you, she goes over the fucking edge at 10.30.'

'Ricky, please, I'm coming. I'll be there.'

'You'd fucking better.'

Suddenly, to her relief, the Alfa's left-turn signal started flashing and it pulled over into a lay-by. She increased her speed to more than she was comfortable with.

*

Inside the Alfa, Roy Grace watched the black Honda accelerate off up the winding road. Cassian Pewe, in the front passenger seat, said into his secure phone, 'Target One has just gone past. Two miles from zone.'

The voice of the local Silver commander – the senior officer running the operation – replied, 'Target Two just made contact with her. Proceed to Position Four.'

'Proceeding to Position Four,' Pewe confirmed back. He looked down at the Ordnance Survey map on his knees. 'OK,' he said to Grace. 'Move on as soon as she is out of sight.'

Grace put the car in gear. As the Honda crested a hill and vanished, he accelerated.

Pewe checked the transmit button was off, then turned to his colleague. 'Roy, you know, it is true what the Chief Super said. I was only doing it to protect you.'

'From what?' Grace said acidly.

'Innuendo is corrosive. There is nothing worse than suspicion in a police force.'

'Bullshit.'

'If that's what you believe, then I'm sorry. I don't want to fall out over this.'

'Oh, really? I don't know what your agenda is, to be frank. For some reason, you think I murdered my wife, don't you? Do you honestly think I would have buried her in my back garden? That's why you were having it scanned, wasn't it? For her remains?'

'I was having it scanned to prove she wasn't there. To end the speculation.'

'I don't think so, Cassian.'

118

OCTOBER 2007

Abby drove up the headland. To her right was open grassland, with a few clusters of bushes and one dense copse of short trees, ending in chalk cliffs and a vertical drop to the English Channel. One of the sheerest, highest and most certain drops in the whole of the British Isles. To her left, there was an almost uninterrupted view over miles of open farmland. She could see the road threading through it into the distance. The tarmac was an intense black, with crisp broken white lines down the centre. It looked as if it had all been freshly painted for her today.

Detective Sergeant Branson had told her earlier that Ricky had made a mistake choosing this location, but at this moment she could not see how. It struck her as a clever choice. From wherever he was, Ricky would be able to see anything that moved in any direction.

Maybe the detective had just said it to reassure her. And she sure as hell needed that at this moment.

She could see a building about half a mile away on her left, at almost the highest point of the headland, with what looked like a pub or hotel sign on a pole. As she got nearer she saw the red-tiled roof and flint walls. Then she could read the sign.

BEACHY HEAD HOTEL.

Drive into the car park of the Beachy Head Hotel and wait for me to contact you, were his instructions. *At exactly 10.30.*

The place looked deserted. There was a glass bus shelter with a blue and white sign in front of it, on which was written in large lettering: THE SAMARITANS. ALWAYS THERE DAY OR NIGHT, with two phone numbers beneath. Just beyond was an orange and yellow ice-cream van, which had its sales window open, and a short distance further on there was a British Telecom truck, with two men in hard hats and high-visibility jackets carrying out work on a radio mast. Two small cars were parked by the rear entrance to the hotel; she assumed these belonged to staff.

She turned left and pulled up at the far end of the car park, then switched off the engine. Moments later, her phone rang.

'Good,' Ricky said. 'Well done! Scenic route, isn't it?'

The car was rocking in the wind.

'Where are you?' she said, looking around in every direction. 'Where's my mother?'

'Where are my stamps?'

'I have them.'

'I have your mother. She's enjoying the view.'

'I want to see her.'

'I want to see the stamps.'

'Not until I know my mother is all right.'

'I'll put her on the phone.'

There was a silence. She heard the wind blowing. Then her mother's voice, as weak and quavering as a ghost's.

'Abby?'

'Mum!'

'Is that you, Abby?' Her mother started crying. 'Please, please, Abby. Please.'

'I'm coming to get you, Mum. I love you.'

'Please let me have my pills. I must have my pills. Please, Abby, why won't you let me have them?'

It hurt Abby almost too much to listen to her. Then Ricky spoke again.

'Start your engine. I'm going to stay on the line.'

She started the car.

'Accelerate, I want to hear the engine running.'

She did what he said. The diesel clattered loudly.

'Now drive out of the car park and turn right. In fifty yards you'll see a track off to the left, up to the headland itself. Turn on to it.'

She made the sharp left turn, the car lurching on the bumpy surface. The wheels spun for an instant as they lost traction on the loose gravel and mud, then they were up on the grass. Now she realized why Ricky had been so specific in instructing her to rent an off-roader. Although she did not understand why he had been so concerned it should be diesel. Fuel economy could scarcely have been something on his mind at this moment. To her right she saw a warning sign that said CLIFF EDGE.

'You see a clump of trees and bushes ahead of you?'

There was a dense copse about a hundred yards in front of her, right on a downward slope at the cliff edge. The bushes and trees had been bent by the wind.

'Yes.'

'Stop the car.'

She stopped.

'Put the handbrake on. Leave the engine running. Just keep looking. We are in here. I have the rear wheels right on the edge of the cliff. If you do anything I don't like, I'm throwing her straight back in the van and releasing the handbrake. Do you understand that?'

Abby's throat was so tight it was a struggle to get her voice out. 'Yes.'

'I didn't hear you.'

'I said, *yes.*'

She heard a roar, like wind blowing on a phone. A dull thud. Then there was movement in the copse. Ricky appeared first, in his baseball cap and beard, wearing a heavy fleece jacket. Then Abby's heart was in her mouth as she saw the tiny, frail figure of her bewildered-looking mother, still in the pink dressing gown she had been wearing when Abby had last seen her.

The wind rippled the gown, blew all her wispy grey and white hair up in the air so it trailed from her head like ribbons of cigarette smoke. She was rocking on her feet, with Ricky gripping her arm, holding her upright.

Abby stared through the windscreen, through a mist of tears. She would do anything, anything, *anything* at all, to get her mother back in her arms at this moment.

And to kill Ricky.

She wanted to floor the accelerator and drive straight at him now, smash him to pulp.

They were disappearing back into the trees. He was jerking her mother along roughly, as she half walked, half tripped into the copse. The shrubbery was closing like fog around them.

Abby gripped the door handle, almost unable to stop herself from getting out of the car and running across to them. But she hung on, scared of his threat and now even more convinced that he would kill her mother, and enjoy doing so.

Maybe, with his warped mind, he would value that even more than getting his stamps back.

Where were Detective Sergeant Branson and his team? They must be close. He had assured her they would be. They were well concealed all right, she thought. She couldn't see a soul.

Which meant, hopefully, that Ricky couldn't either.

But they were listening. They would have heard him. Heard his threat. They wouldn't rush the copse and try to grab him, would they? They couldn't risk him letting his van go over the edge.

Not for a few fucking stamps, surely?

His voice came back on the line. 'Satisfied?'

'Can I take her now, please, Ricky. I have the stamps.'

'This is what you do, Abby. Listen carefully, I'm only saying it once. OK?'

'Yes.'

'You leave your engine running and you leave your phone on like this, in the car, so I can hear the motor. You get out of the car and you leave the door wide open. You bring the stamps and you walk twenty steps towards me and then you stop. I'm going to walk towards you. I'm going to take the stamps and then I'm going to get into your car. You are going to get into the van. Your mother is in the van and she's fine. Now this is where you have to be very careful. Are you taking this in?'

'Yes.'

'By the time you get to the van I will have looked at the stamps. If I don't like what I see, I'm driving straight over to the van and I'm going to give it one hard nudge over the edge. Are we clear?'

'Yes. You will like what you see.'

'Good,' he said. 'Then we won't have a problem.'

Without wanting to move her head too much, in case he was watching her through binoculars, Abby glanced as much as she could around her. But all she saw was bare, windblown grassland, a small, curved brick structure, an observation point of some kind, containing some empty benches, and a few solitary bushes, none big enough to conceal a human. Where were Detective Sergeant Branson's people?

After a couple of minutes, she heard Ricky again. 'Get out of the car now and do what I told you.'

She pushed open the door, but it was a struggle against the wind. 'The door's not going to stay open!' she shouted back at the speaker, panicking.

'Wedge it with something.'

'With what?'

'Jesus, you stupid woman, there must be something in the car. A handbook. A rental docket. I want to see you leave that door open. I'm watching you.'

She pulled the envelope of rental documents out of the door pocket, pushed the door open and waved them in the air, so that he could see. Then she climbed out. The wind was so strong, a gust almost blew her over. It tore the door from her hand, slamming it. She yanked it open again, folded the envelope in two, making a thicker wedge, grabbed the Jiffy bag, then closed the door as far as it would go against the wedge.

Then, with the wind tearing painfully at the roots of her hair, hurting her ears, ripping at her clothes, she walked twenty very unsteady paces towards the copse, eyes darting in every direction, her mouth dry, scared stiff but burning with anger. She could still see no one. Except Ricky now striding towards her.

He held his hand out to take the bag with a grim smile

of satisfaction. 'About fucking time,' he said, snatching it greedily from her.

As he did so, with all her strength and all the pent-up venom she felt for him, she swung her right foot up as hard as she could between his legs. So hard it hurt her like hell.

119

OCTOBER 2007

Air shot out of Ricky's mouth. His eyes bulged in pain and shock as he doubled up. Then Abby slapped him across the face with so much force he fell over sideways. She launched another kick at his groin, but he grabbed her foot and twisted it sharply, agonizingly, bringing her crashing on to the wet grass.

'You fucking—'

Then he stopped as he heard the roar of an engine.

They both heard it.

In semi-disbelief, Ricky stared at the ice-cream van bumping up the track towards them. And a short distance behind it, six police officers in stab vests raced towards them from around the side of the hotel building.

Ricky scrambled to his feet. 'You bitch! We made a deal!' he screeched.

'Like the one you made with Dave?' she screamed back.

Clutching the stamps, he stumbled towards the Honda. Abby ran as fast as she could, ignoring the pain in her foot, towards the copse. Behind her she heard the roar of an engine. She glanced over her shoulder. It was the ice-cream van and she could see two men in it now. Then ahead, through the trunks and branches and leaves, she could see parts of a white van.

*

Blinded by pain and fury, Ricky threw himself into the Honda, jammed it in gear and took the handbrake off even before he had closed the door. *Teach that fucking bitch a lesson.*

He accelerated hard, picking up speed, steering straight at the copse. He didn't care if he went over the edge, too, at this moment. Just so long as the bitch's mother went. Just so long as Abby spent the rest of her fucking life regretting this.

Then a blur of colour flashed in front of him.

Ricky stamped on the brakes, locking the wheels, cursing. He jerked the steering wheel sharply to the right, desperately trying to avoid the ice-cream vehicle, which had pulled up broadside across the copse, blocking his chance of ramming the van inside. The Honda slewed round in a wide arc, its tail striking the rear bumper of the ice-cream van, tearing it off.

Then to his shock he saw two small cars that he'd also assumed belonged to staff at the hotel racing across the grass towards him, blue lights strobing behind their windscreens and radiator grilles, sirens wailing.

He floored the accelerator again, disoriented for a moment, turning, turning. One of them pulled across his path. He swerved around the back of it, dropped down a steep embankment, lurched through a ditch and up the far side, on to the firm tarmac of the road.

Then, to his dismay, he saw blue lights racing down towards him from the right.

'Fuck. Shit. Fuck. Shit.'

Totally gripped with panic, he swung the wheel left and tramped the accelerator.

*

The only door on the old rusty van which was not obstructed by branches and shrubbery was the driver's side. Abby pulled it open anxiously, carefully, heeding the warning about how close the van was to the edge.

Her nose wrinkling at the rank smell inside of faeces and tobacco and unwashed people, she called out, 'Mum? Mum?'

There was no answer. With a stab of panic, she put her foot on the step and hauled herself up on to the front seat. For a terrible moment, staring into the gloomy rear, she thought her mother was not there. All she could see was some electrical equipment, bedding and a spare wheel. It felt as cold as a fridge. The van rocked in the wind and there was a drumming resonance inside.

Then, over it, she heard a faint, timid, 'Abby? Is that you?'

They were, without doubt, the sweetest words she had ever heard in her life. 'Mum!' she cried out. 'Where are you?'

There was a faint, 'Here.' Her mother sounded surprised, as if to say, *Where else should I be?*

Then Abby craned her neck over the rear of the seat and saw her mother, rolled up in the carpet, just her head poking out, lying on the floor right behind her.

She climbed over, the van resonating as her feet struck the bare metal floor, knelt and kissed her mother's moist cheek.

'Are you OK? Are you OK, Mum? I've got your medication. I'm going to get you to hospital.'

She felt her mother's forehead. It was hot and clammy.

'You're safe now. He's gone. You're OK. There are police all around. I'll get you to hospital.'

Her mother whispered, 'I think your father was here a minute ago. He just went out.'

Abby realized she was delirious. Fever or the lack of medication or both. And she smiled through her tears.

'I love you so much, Mum,' she said. 'So much.'

'I'm OK,' her mother said. 'I'm as snug as a bug in a rug.'

*

Cassian Pewe lowered his phone for a moment and turned to Grace. 'Target Two is in Target One's car, alone. Coming back this way. Intercept if we can, safely, but there's back-up arriving behind us.'

Grace started the engine. Both men had their seat belts unfastened, which was common practice on surveillance to enable them to get out of the car quickly if need be. Having heard the report of what had been happening, now Grace thought they should put them on. But just as he reached for his, Pewe said, 'I see him.'

Grace could now see the black Honda too, a quarter of a mile away, driving fast down the twisting hill. He could hear the tyres squealing.

'We have Target Two in sight,' Pewe radioed.

The Silver commander said, 'The priority is everyone's safety. If you need to, Roy, you may have to use your vehicle in the operation.'

To Pewe's consternation, Grace suddenly swung the Alfa sideways, blocking both lanes of the narrow road. And he was on the side facing the oncoming black off-roader, he realized. The side that would take the impact if the car didn't stop.

*

Ricky clenched the wheel tight, tyres screeching again around a long, downhill left-hander bend, with nowhere to go on either side if he did come off, just steep banking. Then he lurched into a right-hander.

As he came out of it he saw a maroon Alfa Romeo sideways across the road in front of him. A blond-haired man was staring bug-eyed at him out of the window.

He stamped on the brakes, bringing the car slewing to a halt only yards from the door, and slammed the car into reverse. As he did so, he heard the wail of sirens. In the distance he could see two police Range Rovers, lights blazing, racing down a hill.

He made a three-point turn and accelerated hard, back the way he had come. In his rear-view mirror, he saw the Alfa Romeo take off after him, with the two Range Rovers closing behind it. But he was more interested in what was in front of him. Or more specifically, what was in front of the copse. Because even if the ice-cream van was still in front of it, a sharp nudge from the side would do it.

Then he would take the abandoned coach road – now just a grassed-over cart track through fields, but still a public byway – which he had found and checked out. He was certain the police would not have thought about that.

He would be all right. The bitch should never, ever have messed with him.

*

Roy Grace quickly caught up with the lumbering Honda, then sat yards from its tail. Pewe radioed that they were approaching the Beachy Head Hotel.

Suddenly, the Honda veered sharply right, off the road and up on to the grassland that separated the road from the cliff edge. Grace did the same, wincing as his beloved Alfa's suspension bottomed out. He heard and felt the grinding scrape of the exhaust striking the ground and something falling off, but he was so focused on the Honda he barely registered it.

A whole cluster of vehicles and people were ahead of them now. He saw a British Telecom truck blocking the road, with a swarm of police officers near it. Two motorcycles. Pewe turned up the volume on the radio.

A voice said, 'Target Two may be coming back for the van. It's in the copse behind the ice-cream vehicle. Cut him off. Target One is in the van with her mother.'

Pewe pointed through the windscreen. 'Roy, it's there. That's where he's heading.'

Grace could see the large, oval-shaped copse, with the brightly coloured ice-cream van parked a short distance in front of it.

Target Two was accelerating.

Grace dropped down a gear and flattened the accelerator. The Alfa shot forward, the suspension bottoming again in a dip, throwing both unrestrained men up, banging their heads on the roof.

'Sorry,' Grace said grimly, drawing level with the Honda.

On his outside now, barely inches from his door, was a flimsy-looking railing at the cliff edge. He caught a fleeting glimpse of Target Two, a heavily bearded man in a baseball cap. To his right, the railing ended suddenly, leaving shrubbery marking a completely unguarded drop now.

Grace ploughed through undergrowth, grimly hoping the shrubbery wasn't concealing an indent in the cliff they would suddenly plunge down.

He eased off the accelerator, driving level, trying to get the nose of his car just a couple of feet in front, to force the Honda further away from the edge. The copse and the ice-cream van were looming up rapidly.

As if anticipating his thoughts, Target Two swung the Honda's steering wheel to the right, banging hard into the passenger side of the Alfa. Pewe let out a shriek and the Alfa lurched perilously close to the edge.

The copse was coming even closer.

The Honda nudged them again. The heavier of the two cars, its nose well in front, it pushed them further over. They bounced crazily on some stones and uneven ground. Then it nudged them again, even closer to the edge.

'Roy!' Pewe squealed, holding on to his unfastened seat belt and sounding petrified.

They were boxed in. Grace floored the accelerator and the Alfa shot forward. The copse was now no more than two hundred yards away. He cut in front of the Honda sharply, and then, with the intention of hiding the fact that he was braking, he yanked the handbrake full on instead of pressing the brake pedal.

The effect was instant and dramatic, and not what he had expected. The tail of the Alfa broke away and the car started to slide sideways. Almost instantly, the Honda slammed into the rear wing, sending the Alfa barrel-rolling, side over side.

The force of the impact sent the Honda veering to the left, out of control, ploughing into the rear of the ice-cream van.

Grace felt himself hurtling, weightlessly, through the air. Air that was a cacophony of booming, echoing metallic noises.

He landed with a thump that winded him, jarring every bone in his body, and with a force that rolled him over several times, helplessly, as if he had been ejected from some freakish funfair ride. Then, finally, he came to a halt face down in wet grass, with his mouth jammed into mud.

For an instant he was not sure if he was alive or dead. His ears popped. There was a brief moment of silence. The wind howled. Then he heard a terrible scream, but he had no idea where it came from.

He scrambled to his feet and immediately fell over again. It was as if someone had picked up the entire headland and tilted it sideways. He stood up again, swaying giddily, surveying the scene. The bonnet of the Honda, which was lurched over at a strange angle, was embedded in the destroyed rear end of the ice-cream van. The driver of the Honda appeared to be in a daze, pushing at his door, while two police officers in stab vests were pulling on it. Smoke was coming out of the underside of the van. Several more police officers were running towards it.

Then he heard the scream again.

Where the hell was his car?

And he was suddenly filled with a terrible, sickening dread.

No! Oh, Jesus, no!

He heard the scream again.

Then again.

Coming from below the cliff-top.

He staggered to the edge, then took a sharp step back. All his life he had suffered from vertigo and the sheer drop to the sea below was more than he could look at.

'Heeeeeeeeeeeeeeeeelp!'

He dropped on to all fours and began to crawl, aware of pains all over his body. He ignored them and made it to the edge, where he found himself looking down into the underside of his car, which was tangled up in several small trees, nose into the cliff, its tail out, balanced like a diving board. Two wheels were still spinning.

The first part of this drop was a short, steeply wooded

slope. It ended in a grassy lip, about twenty feet below, and then dropped sheer for several hundred feet, down on to rocks and water. It freaked Grace out and he pulled back to where he felt safer. Then heard the scream again.

'Help me! Oh, God, help me! Please help me!'

It was Cassian Pewe, he realized. But he couldn't see the man.

Fighting back his fear, he crawled to the edge again, looked down and shouted, 'Cassian? Where are you?'

'Oh, help me. Please help me. Roy, please help me.'

Grace shot a desperate glance over his shoulder. But everyone behind him seemed occupied with the van and the Honda, which looked like it was going to go up in flames.

He peered down again.

'I'm going! Oh, for God's sake, I'm going.'

The sheer terror in the man's voice jolted him into action. Taking a deep breath, he leaned down, gripped a branch and tested it, hoping to hell it would hold. Then he swung himself over the edge. Immediately his leather shoes slid down the wet grass and his arm, holding on to the branch, jerked painfully in its socket. And he realized in that instant that the only thing stopping him from sliding all the way down the sharp slope to the lip, then straight over into oblivion, was this one branch he was holding with his right hand.

It was starting to come loose now. He could feel it pulling free.

He was truly terrified.

'Please help me! I'm going!' Pewe screamed again.

Panicking himself, Roy quickly found another branch, then, clinging on to it while the wind blasted at him, as if it was trying to prise him off the cliff, he dropped further.

Don't look down, he thought to himself.

He kicked his toe into the side of the hill and got a small, slippery purchase. Then he found another branch. He was level with the grimy, partly buckled chassis of his car now. The wheels had stopped spinning and the car was rocking like a see-saw.

'Cassian, where the hell are you?' he shouted, trying not to look down below the car.

The wind instantly ripped his words away.

Pewe's voice was muffled with terror. 'Underneath. I can see you. Please hurry!'

Suddenly, to Roy's shock, the branch he was holding on to gave way. For one terrible moment he thought he was going to tumble backwards. Frantically he lunged out for another branch and grabbed it, but it snapped. He was falling, sliding down past the car. Sliding towards the grassy lip and the sheer drop. He grabbed another branch, which was covered in sharp leaves that slid through the palm of his hand, burning it, but it was young, springy and tough. It held, almost jerking his arm off. Then he found another one with his left hand and clung to it for dear life. To his relief, it was sturdier.

He heard Pewe screaming again.

Saw a massive shadow above him. It was his car. Perched twenty feet above him, like a platform. Rocking precariously. And Pewe was suspended upside down from the passenger door, his feet entangled in the webbing of his seat belt, which was all that prevented him from falling.

Grace glanced down and immediately wished he hadn't. He was right on the edge of the sheer drop. He stared for an instant at the water pounding the rocks. Felt the deadweight pull of gravity on his arms and the savage, relentless wind tearing at him. One slip. Just one slip.

Panting, terrified, he started to kick out a toehold with his right foot. The branch in his right hand suddenly moved a fraction. He kicked harder at the wet, chalky soil and after some moments he had made a space big enough to jam his foot in and take his weight.

Pewe screamed again.

He would try to help him in a moment. But first he had to try to save his own life. He wasn't going to be of any help to either of them dead.

'Royyyyyyyyyyyyyy!'

He kicked with his left foot, digging that in too. After a short while, with both feet planted, he felt a little better, though not exactly secure.

'I'm falling. Royyyyyyyy! Oh, God, get me out of here. Please don't let me fall. Don't let me die.'

Roy craned his neck up, taking his time on every movement, until he could see Pewe's face about ten feet above him.

'Keep calm!' he called out. 'Try not to move.'

He heard a loud crack as a branch gave way. His eyes shot up and he saw the car lurch. It dropped several inches, swaying even more precariously now. Shit. The whole fucking thing was going to crash down on top of him.

Gingerly, inch by careful inch, he pulled his radio out, terrified of dropping it, and called for assistance. He was given reassurance that it was already on its way, that a rescue helicopter was being crewed up.

Jesus. That will take an age.

'Please don't let me die!' Pewe sobbed.

He looked up again, carefully studying the webbing as best he could. It appeared well tangled around his colleague's feet. The wind held the buckled passenger door open. Then he looked at the way the car was rocking.

It was too much. The branches were straining, cracking, breaking. It was a terrible sound. How much longer would they hold? When they gave, the car would toboggan on its roof down the slope, which was as steep as a ski-jump ramp, and straight over the sheer drop.

Pewe was making it worse by bending his body every few moments, trying to reach upwards, but he had no chance.

'Cassian, stop wriggling,' he yelled, his voice nearly hoarse. 'Try to keep still. I need help to lift you. I daren't do it myself. I don't want to risk dislodging the car.'

'Please don't let me die, Roy!' Pewe cried, squirming like a hooked fish.

Another fierce gust blew. Grace clung to the branches, his jacket filling with wind, pulling like a sail, making it even harder for him. For several moments, until the gust eased, he didn't dare move a muscle.

'You won't let me die, will you, Roy?' Pewe pleaded.

'You know what, Cassian?' Grace shouted back. 'I'm actually more concerned about my bloody car.'

120

OCTOBER 2007

Grace sipped some coffee. It was 8.30 on Monday morning and they had just begun the fifteenth briefing of *Operation Dingo*. He had a sticking plaster on his forehead, covering a gash which had required five stitches, blister pads on the palms of both hands, and there wasn't a bone in his body that wasn't hurting.

'Someone said you're going to be tackling Everest next, Roy,' quipped one of the DCs present.

'Yes, and Detective Superintendent Pewe's applying for a job as a circus high-wire act,' Roy replied, unable to keep the smirk off his face.

But deep down, he was still very badly shaken. And in truth there wasn't a lot to smile about. Fine, they had Chad Skeggs banged up in the custody block. Abby Dawson and her mother were safe, and by a miracle no one had been seriously injured on Friday. But that was all a sideshow. They were investigating the murder of two women and their prime suspect could be anywhere. Even if he was still in Australia, he could be using yet another completely different identity by now, and, as he had already demonstrated, new identities did not seem to be a problem for Ronnie Wilson.

There was just one ray of sunshine.

'We've had something of a result in Melbourne,' he

continued. 'I spoke to Norman earlier this morning. They've interviewed a woman today who claims to have been a close friend of Maggie Nelson, the woman we believe to be Lorraine Wilson.'

'How certain are we that Ronnie and Lorraine Wilson became David and Margaret Nelson, Roy?' Bella asked.

'Melbourne police have dug up a ton of stuff from the drivers' licensing offices, the tax office and the immigration services. It all seems to fit together. I'm getting a report faxed over, probably tonight.'

Bella made a note, then plucked a Malteser from the box in front of her.

Looking at his notes, Grace went on, 'This woman's name is Maxine Porter. Her ex-husband's a mobster, currently on trial on a whole raft of tax-evasion and money-laundering charges, and looking at a long sentence. She got dumped by him for a younger woman just over a year ago, about three months before he was arrested, so she was happy doing the woman scorned bit, and talking. According to her, David Nelson appeared on the scene round about Christmas 2001. It was Chad Skeggs who introduced him to that particular pleasant circle of friends, which seemed to include the whole of the Melbourne A-list crime fraternity. And Nelson apparently carved out a niche for himself dealing stamps with them.'

'How sweet is that?' Glenn Branson said. 'Here in England our gangsters knife and shoot each other, while in Australia they swap stamps.'

Everyone grinned.

'I don't think so,' Grace said. 'There've been thirty-seven gangland shootings in Melbourne in the past decade. It has a pretty dark underbelly, like a lot of places.'

Like Brighton and Hove actually, he thought.

'Anyhow,' he continued, 'Lorraine – sorry, I mean *Maggie Nelson* – confided in her new best friend that her husband was having an affair and she didn't know what to do. She wasn't happy in Australia, but said she and her husband had burned their bridges in the UK and couldn't go back. I think it's significant that she said it was *both* of them, not just one or the other of them.'

'When was this, Roy?' Emma-Jane Boutwood asked.

'Some time between June 2004 and April 2005. The two women talked a lot, apparently. Both of them with husbands having affairs, they had plenty in common.'

He drank some more coffee and looked down at his notes again. 'Then, in June 2005, Maggie Nelson vanished. She didn't turn up for a lunch date with Maxine Porter, and when Maxine phoned, David Nelson told her his wife had left him. Packed and gone back to England.'

'There seems to be a pattern emerging, doesn't there?' Lizzie Mantle said. 'He tells his friends in England that his first wife, Joanna, has gone off to America. Then he tells his friends in Australia that his second has gone back to England. And all their friends believed him!'

'This one didn't apparently,' Grace said.

'So why didn't she go to the police?' Bella asked. 'She must have been suspicious, surely?'

'Because in her world people don't go to the police,' Lizzie Mantle said.

'Exactly,' Grace confirmed with a wry smile at the DI. 'And the criminal fraternity over there is even more male-dominated than it is here. They're interviewing her again tomorrow, when she's going to give a list of all the Nelsons' friends and acquaintances out there.'

'That's great,' Bella said, taking another Malteser. 'But if he's legged it abroad—'

'I know,' Grace said. 'But we might find out where his favourite haunts abroad are, or if he had any hankering for some particular sunny fleshpot.'

'I've got some thoughts on that,' Glenn Branson said. 'Well, Bella and me have.'

'OK. Tell us.'

'We interviewed Skeggs quite extensively on Friday and on Saturday, and we took a statement from Abby Dawson at her mother's flat in Eastbourne yesterday morning. We also returned her stamps to her, which we recovered from Skeggs's vehicle – I took the precaution of copying them first, so we have a record. She also signed the paperwork agreeing to produce the stamps as an exhibit, if necessary, and not dispose of them.'

'Good thinking,' DI Mantle said.

'Thank you. Now, here's the thing. Bella and me don't feel we're getting the truth from Abby Dawson. We're getting what she wants us to hear. I'm not happy about her story of where she got the stamps. She's maintaining she inherited them from an aunt in Sydney by the name of – ' he flipped back through his notes, then found the page – '*Anne Jennings*. We're getting that checked out. But it doesn't tally with what Skeggs said.'

'And we know that he is a principled man who always tells the truth,' Grace said.

'I'd trust him with my last five-pound note,' Glenn said, returning the sarcasm. 'Which is probably all anyone would have left after doing business with him. He's a seriously nasty piece of work. But there's a connection to Ronnie, that's what this is all about, I'm certain.' He looked around.

Grace nodded for him to go on.

'Hugo Hegarty is certain that these are the stamps he bought for Lorraine Wilson.'

'But not so certain he'd swear on it in a court of law, is he?' Lizzie Mantle interjected.

'No, and that could be a problem down the line,' Branson replied. 'Some of the single ones have postmarks – he can't swear they are the same as the ones on the stamps he acquired for Lorraine Wilson back in 2002, because he didn't keep a record of the postmarks. Or maybe he just doesn't want to get involved.'

'Why not?' Grace questioned.

'All the dealings were done in cash. I suspect he doesn't want to raise his head above the parapet and attract the interest of the Inland Revenue, on top of the police.'

Grace nodded; that made sense. 'And how strong a claim to them does Skeggs have?'

'Skeggs was effing and blinding about Abby Dawson having stolen his stamps, saying that was the reason he took her mother, it was the only thing he could think of doing that would bring her to her senses,' Glenn Branson replied.

'He never tried just asking nicely for them back?'

Branson smiled. 'I asked him if that was the case, if he wanted to press charges against her for theft. Then he went all quiet. Surprise, surprise. Started muttering about *issues*, but he was evasive when we tried to push this line. He said he would have problems demonstrating title to them. Then at one point he blurted out that Dave Nelson had put her up to this. But we couldn't get any more out of him on that. That's why for now, despite our reservations, we've had to let Abby have the stamps back. Until there is evidence that a theft has taken place here or in Australia.'

'Very interesting he said that,' Grace commented.

'Know what I think?' Branson said. 'That there's some

kind of love triangle going on here. That's what this is about.'

'Do you want to expand on that?' Grace asked.

'I can't, not at the moment. But that's what I reckon.'

Thinking out aloud, Grace said, 'If David Nelson – Ronnie Wilson – did put her up to this, it's very significant.'

'We'll keep pressing Skeggs, but his brief's keeping him quite well bottled up,' Glenn said.

'What about putting more surveillance on her?' DC Boutwood suggested.

Grace shook his head. 'Too costly. I'm thinking that David Nelson may well have left Australia, if he has any sense. He won't risk showing his face in England. So my bet is that Abby Dawson will go to meet him somewhere. We put out an all-ports on her. If she buys an air ticket or turns up at a passport control, then we'll follow her.'

'Good thinking,' Glenn Branson said.

DI Mantle nodded. 'I agree.'

121

NOVEMBER 2007

It was one of those all too rare autumn days when England looked at its very best. Abby stared out of the window at the clear blue sky and the morning sun that was low but warm on her face.

Two floors below in the manicured gardens, a gardener was at work with some kind of outdoor vacuum cleaner, hoovering up leaves. An elderly man in a crisp mackintosh walked slowly and jerkily around the perimeter of the ornamental pond, which was stocked with koi carp, prodding the ground ahead of him with his Zimmer frame as if wary of landmines. A little white-haired lady sat on a bench on the highest part of the terraced lawns, parcelled up in a quilted coat, studying a page of the *Daily Telegraph* intently.

The Bexhill Lawns Rest Home was more expensive than the home she had originally budgeted for, but it was able to accommodate her mother right away and, hey, who was counting the cost now?

Besides, it was a joy to see her mother looking so happy here and so well. It was hard to believe that two weeks ago today, Abby had entered that van and looked down at her bewildered face sticking out of the rolled-up carpet. She seemed a new person now, with a new lease of life. As if, somehow, all she had been through had strengthened her.

Abby turned to look at her. She had the same lump in her throat that was always there when she was saying goodbye to her mother. Always scared it would be the last time she saw her.

Mary Dawson sat on the two-seater sofa in the large, well-appointed room, filling in a form in one of her competition magazines. Abby walked across, laid a hand tenderly on her shoulder and looked down.

'What are you trying to win?' she asked, her voice choked as their last, precious minutes together were ticking away. Her taxi would be here soon.

'A fortnight for two in a luxury hotel in Mauritius!'

'But Mum, you don't even have a passport!' Abby chided her good-humouredly.

'I know, dear, but you could easily get me one if I needed one, couldn't you?' She gave her daughter a strange look.

'What do you mean by that?'

Smiling like an impish child, she replied, 'You know exactly what I mean, dear.'

Abby blushed. Her mother had always been sharp as a tack. She'd never been able to hide anything from her for long, right from earliest childhood.

'Don't worry,' her mother added. 'I'm not going anywhere. There's a cash prize as an alternative.'

'I'd love you to get a passport,' Abby said, sitting on the sofa, putting an arm around her frail shoulders and kissing her on the cheek. 'I'd love you to join me.'

'Where?'

Abby shrugged. 'When I get settled somewhere.'

'And have me turn up and cramp your style?'

Abby gave a wistful laugh. 'You wouldn't ever cramp my style.'

'Your dad and I, we were never much ones for travelling. When your late aunt, Anne, moved to Sydney all those years ago, she kept telling us how wonderful it was and that we should move out there. But your dad always felt his roots were here. And mine are too. But I'm proud of you, Abby. My mother used to say that one mother could support seven children, but seven children could never support one mother. You've proved her wrong.'

Abby fought back her tears.

'I'm really proud of you. There's not much more a mother could ask of a daughter. Except maybe one thing.' She gave her a quizzical look.

'What?' Abby smiled at her, knowing what was coming. 'Babies?'

'Maybe one day. Who knows. Then you'd *have* to get a passport and come and be with me.'

Her mother looked down at her entry form again for some moments. 'No,' she said, and shook her head firmly. Then she put down her pen, took her daughter's hand with her own bony, liver-spotted fingers and squeezed it tightly.

Abby was surprised by her strength.

'Always remember one thing, Abby dear, if you ever decide to become a parent. First you give your children roots. Then you give them wings.'

122

NOVEMBER 2007

An hour and a half after leaving her mother, Abby pulled the suitcase containing almost everything she was taking with her from Brighton along the platform of Gatwick Station, and up the escalator into the arrivals area. Then she deposited it at the left-luggage baggage storage.

Carrying with her only the Jiffy bag that Detective Sergeant Branson had returned to her on Saturday, which was inside a carrier bag, and her handbag, she walked up to the easyJet ticket counter and joined a short queue. It was midday.

*

In his office, Roy Grace was reading through a wodge of faxed reports that had been sent from Australia during the past twenty-four hours by Norman Potting and Nick Nicholl. He felt a little guilty about keeping Nicholl out there so long, but the list of contacts that Lorraine Wilson's friend had given them had been too good to be ignored.

However, despite everything, they still had no positive lead on where Ronnie Wilson was.

He looked at his watch: 1.20. His lunch, which Eleanor had picked up for him from ASDA, lay on his desk in its carrier bag. A Healthy Option crayfish and rocket sandwich and an apple. He was gradually yielding, day by day, to the pressure Cleo was putting on him to improve his diet. Not that it made him feel any different. Just as he reached into the bag, his phone rang.

It was Bill Warner, who was now in charge of Gatwick Airport CID.

They were old enough friends to be able to dispense with pleasantries and the Gatwick DI cut straight to the chase.

'Roy, there's a woman you have an alert out on, Abby Dawson, also known as Katherine Jennings?'

'Yes.'

'We're pretty sure she's just checked in on an easyJet flight to Nice which leaves at 3.45. We've checked her image on our CCTV and it matches the photographs you've circulated.'

They were photographs that had been pulled off the Interview Suite CCTV cameras. Strictly speaking, under the terms of the Data Protection Act, Grace should not have used them without her consent. But he didn't care.

'Brilliant!' he said. 'Absolutely bloody brilliant!'

'What do you want us to do?'

'Just have her tracked, Bill. It's vital she doesn't know she's being followed. I want her to get on the flight, but I'm going to need some officers there with her – and some support in Nice. Can you find out if the flight's full – and if we could get two officers on? If they're full, maybe you could persuade them to bump a couple of passengers?'

'Leave it with me. I already know that the plane is only half full. I'll get on to the French police. I take it we are interested in who she might meet?'

'Spot on. Thanks, Bill. Keep me informed.'

Grace clenched his fist for joy, then he called Glenn Branson.

123

NOVEMBER 2007

'So when do I see you again? Tell me. When?'

'Soon!'

'How soon is *soon*?'

She lay on top of him, their naked skin running with perspiration from their exertions in the morning heat. His spent penis nestled in her hairs. Her small round breasts pressed into his chest and her eyes gazed into his, nut-brown eyes, filled with laughter and mischief. And hardness. For sure.

She was savyy, streetwise. She was a piece of work.

A very rich piece of work.

And she liked this goddamned humidity. This cloying heat which made him perspire constantly. She insisted on making love with the terrace doors of her house wide open and it was about a hundred fucking degrees in the room. And now she was pummelling his chest with her tiny fists.

'How soon? How soon?'

He brushed her jet-black hair away from his face and kissed her rosebud lips. She was so pretty and she had a great body. He'd come to appreciate slender Thai girls during his month holed up in Pattaya Beach, waiting for Abby to give him the signal that she was on her way.

And oh wow! He had lucked out big time with this one. Totally unexpected! Because she was everything he had fantasized about, but with a whole lot more. About twenty-five million US dollars more! Give or take a few percentage points on the Thai Baht conversion rate.

He'd met her in a stamp dealer's shop in Bangkok and just got chatting. Turned out her husband had a chain of nightclubs, which she'd inherited when he died in a scuba-diving accident – a tourist on a jet-ski had chopped his head off at the neck. She had been trying to flog his very serious stamp collection and Ronnie had given her guidance, stopped her being ripped off, got her treble what she'd originally been told they were worth.

And had been banging her once and sometimes twice a day ever since.

Which left him with a problem. Although it wasn't too big a problem. He'd already started tiring of Abby. He couldn't say exactly when that had begun to happen. Perhaps it was the way she had behaved – or *looked* – after her assignments with Ricky. Like, certainly after the first two occasions, she had really enjoyed them.

Which had made him realize what she was capable of.

A woman who had no limits. She would do anything to get rich and was, for sure, just using him as a stepping stone.

Luckily, he was one step ahead. He'd screwed up twice before. Water had not served him well. Something had gone wrong with the damned storm drain in Brighton. And who the hell could have predicted the drought continuing in Melbourne?

Fortunately there were plenty of boats for hire in Koh Samui. And they were cheap. And the South China Sea was deep.

Ten miles out and there was no chance a body was going to fetch up back on the shore. He already had the boat moored and waiting. Abby would love it. It was fuck-off stunning. And cost peanuts. Relatively. And, hey, you had to speculate to accumulate.

He kissed Phara.

'Not long at all,' he said. 'I promise.'

124

NOVEMBER 2007

Instead of following the signs for Departures when she stepped away from the easyJet check-in desk, Abby headed back into the main concourse and made her way to the toilets.

Having locked herself in a cubicle, she removed the Jiffy bag from her carrier bag, ripped it open and shook out the contents – a cellophane bag containing an assortment of stamps, some loose, some in sheets.

Most of the sheets were just replicas of the ones Ricky had wanted so badly, but several of the other sheets and individual stamps were genuine, and looked old enough to excite someone who knew nothing about philately.

She also took out the receipt from the stamp dealer South-East Philatelic, which she had visited two weeks ago. It was for one hundred and forty-two pounds. Probably more than she had needed to spend, strictly speaking, but the assortment did look impressive to the layman, and she had rightly placed Detective Sergeant Branson in that category.

She tore the stamps and the receipt into small pieces and flushed them down the toilet. Then she removed her jeans, boots and fleece jacket. She wouldn't need those where she was going. She pulled out of the carrier bag a long, blonde wig, cut and styled much how her hair used to look, and pulled it on, adjusting it a little clumsily with the help of her make-up mirror. Then she put on the sundress she had bought a couple of days ago and the cream linen jacket that went so well with it, together with a rather nice pair of white, open-toed shoes. She completed her new look with a pair of lightly tinted Marc Jacobs sunglasses.

She crammed the clothes she had discarded into the plastic bag, then went out of the cubicle, adjusted her hair in the mirror, put the Jiffy bag into a bin and checked her watch. It was 1.35. She was making good time.

Suddenly, her phone beeped with a text.

> *Can't wait to see you tomorrow. Just a few hours now. XX*

She smiled. Just a few hours. Yes, yes, yes!

She walked, with a spring in her step, back to the left-luggage area and checked out the suitcase she had deposited just over two hours ago. She wheeled it over to a corner, unlocked and opened it, then removed a bubble-wrapped Jiffy bag. Then she shoved the carrier bag with her old clothes inside, closed it and locked it.

She returned to the check-in area, found the British Airways section and walked up to a business-class desk. An extravagance, but she had decided she would celebrate the start of her new life today in the style in which she planned to continue it.

Handing her passport and ticket to the woman behind the desk, she said, 'Sarah Smith. I'm on Flight 309, connecting through to Rio de Janeiro.'

'Thank you, madam,' the woman said, and checked the details on her terminal.

She asked Abby the usual security questions and tagged

her suitcase. Then the bag jerked forward, fell over on the conveyor and disappeared from view.

'Is the flight on time?' Abby asked.

The woman looked at her screen. 'At the moment, yes, it looks fine. Leaves at 3.15. The boarding gate opens at 2.40. It will be Gate 54. You'll find the signs to the lounge after you've gone through security into the duty-free area.'

Abby thanked her, then checked her watch again. Butterflies were going bonkers in her stomach. There were still two more things she had to do, but she wanted to wait until closer to the time for both of them.

She went through into the BA lounge, helped herself to a glass of white wine to steady her nerves, craving a cigarette. But that would have to wait. She ate a couple of finger-sized sandwiches, then sat down in front of a television screen, with the news on, and went carefully through her mental checklist. She was satisfied she had not forgotten anything. But to be doubly sure she checked that her phone was set to withhold her number from anyone she rang.

Shortly after 2.40 she saw on the screen that boarding had commenced, but the flight had not yet been called in here. She walked over to a quiet section, by the entrance to the toilets, where there was no one nearby to overhear her, then dialled the number of the Incident Room that DS Branson had told her to use if she couldn't reach him on his mobile.

As the phone rang, she kept her ears pricked for the ding-dong warning that preceded any tannoy announcement, not wanting to reveal her whereabouts.

'Incident room, DC Boutwood,' a young female voice answered.

Abby disguised her voice as best she could, putting

on her best shot at an Australian accent. 'I have information for you on Ronnie Wilson,' she said. 'He will be at Koh Samui Airport, waiting to meet someone off Bangkok Airways Flight 271, which is due in at 11 a.m. local time tomorrow. Have you got that?'

'Bangkok Airways, Flight 271, Koh Samui at 11 a.m. local time tomorrow. Who is that calling, please?'

Abby hung up. She was clammy with perspiration and shaking. Shaking so much she found it hard to tap out the reply to the text she had received earlier, and had to backspace several times to correct errors before she finished. Then she read it through one more time before she sent it.

> *True love doesn't have a happy ending,*
> *because true love never ends. Letting go is*
> *one way of saying I love you. xx*

And she did love him. She loved him loads. But just not four million quid loads.

And not with this bad habit he had of killing the women who delivered money to him.

*

Sometime after take-off, she sat well back in her seat, having drunk a Bloody Mary and an extra miniature of vodka, and opened the bubble-wrapped Jiffy bag. The seat beside her was empty, so she didn't have to worry about prying eyes. She checked over her shoulder to make sure none of the cabin crew were around either, then very gently eased one of the cellophane envelopes out.

It contained a block of Penny Black stamps. She stared at Queen Victoria's stern profile. At the word POSTAGE printed in not terribly even letters. At the faded colour.

They were exquisite, but they weren't really perfect at all. As Dave had once explained, sometimes it was their imperfections that made them all the more special.

That applied to a lot of other things in life too, she thought, through her pleasant haze of booze. And besides, who wanted to be perfect?

She gazed at them again, realizing it was the first time she had ever truly looked at them properly. They really were special. Magical. She smiled at them, whispering, 'Goodbye, my little beauties. See you later.'

Then she put them carefully away.

125

NOVEMBER 2007

'Nice holiday?' Roy Grace asked.

'Very funny. I only saw the beach from the plane window,' Glenn Branson replied.

'Meant to be beautiful, Koh Samui, so I've heard.'

'It was humid as hell and pissing with rain the whole time I was there. And I got bitten on my leg by something, either a mutant mosquito or a spider. It's swollen right up – do you want to see it?'

'No, thanks all the same.'

The Detective Sergeant, sitting on a chair in front of Grace's desk, his suit and shirt looking and smelling as if he'd slept in them, shook his head, grinning. 'You're a bastard, Grace, aren't you?'

'And I can't believe you trashed my fucking record collection again. I allowed you to stay there one night. I didn't ask you to take every CD I own out of its case and leave it lying on the floor.'

Branson had the decency to look embarrassed. 'I was trying to sort it out for you. I got – shit – I'm sorry.' He swigged some coffee and stifled a yawn.

'So how's the prisoner? What time did you get in?'

Branson glanced at his watch. 'About 6.45.' He yawned. 'I reckon we've blown Sussex CID's overseas travel budget for the year in the past two weeks.'

Grace smiled. 'Did Wilson say anything?'

Branson swigged some more coffee. 'You know, inasmuch as you can say such a thing, he actually seems a nice guy.'

'Oh, sure. He's the sweetest guy you'll ever meet, right? He just has this slight problem that he prefers killing his wives to doing an honest day's work.' Grace gave his friend a look of feigned shock. 'Glenn, *you* are a nice guy. If it wasn't for all the crap in my life, maybe I'd be a nice guy too. But Ronnie Wilson, no, he's not a nice guy. He's just good at making people *think* he is.'

Branson nodded. 'Yeah. I didn't quite mean it the way I said it.'

'You need to go home, have a sleep, then shower and come back later.'

'I will. But actually he did say a lot. He was in a philosophical mood and wanted to talk. I get the feeling he's had enough of running. He's been in hiding for six years. That's why he agreed to come back with us. Although he kept going on about some Thai bird. Wanted us to let him text her.'

'Did you caution him before he started talking?'

'Yeah.'

'Good man.'

It meant that anything Ronnie Wilson said on the plane could be used in evidence in court.

'Tell you something, he's well furious with Skeggs. He wanted to be sure that, if he was going down, he took Skeggs with him.'

'Oh?'

'As much as I can figure it from what he said, it seems like Skeggs helped him when he first arrived in Australia.'

'As we thought,' Grace said.

'Yeah. At some point down the line, Ronnie Wilson acquired this parcel of stamps.'

'From his wife?'

'He went evasive on me over that.'

'I'm not surprised.'

'Anyhow, he gave them to Skeggs to sell them and Skeggs tried to screw him. He wanted ninety per cent of their value, otherwise he was threatening to shop Ronnie. But Skeggs had one weakness. He had the hots for Ronnie's bird – the one he shacked up with, he said, after his wife had, in his words, *buggered off.*'

'In the boot of a car.'

'Exactly.'

'And the bird was one Abby Dawson?'

'You're sharp this morning, Detective Superintendent.'

'I've had the benefit of a night's sleep. So Ronnie Wilson uses her as a kind of honeypot? Gets her to shag Skeggs and nick the stamps back. Am I on the right track?'

'You're on the monorail.'

'Do you think he would have killed Abby once he'd got them back?' Grace asked.

'On previous form? Undoubtedly. He's a vulture.'

'I thought you said a few moments ago that he was a nice guy.'

Branson smiled in defeat. Then suddenly he changed the subject. 'Bought a new car yet?'

'No. Fucking insurance companies. They want to invalidate my policy because I was driving in a chase. Bastards. I'm trying to sort it. Headquarters are helping me as it was on police business.' Then, changing the subject back, he said, 'So do you think Abby still has the stamps?'

'For sure.'

'Hegarty is one hundred per cent certain the stuff you photocopied is rubbish.'

'Not a scintilla of doubt.'

'I've been thinking about it a lot,' Grace said. 'That's why she kicked Skeggs in the bollocks.'

Branson frowned. 'I'm not with you.'

'The reason she kicked Skeggs when she was handing the stamps over was because she needed time. She knew she was giving him rubbish and that it would only take him a few seconds to realize that. She went for him in order to bring us into the frame. She set him up all along.'

Branson stared back at him, nodding as it slowly dawned on him. 'She's a clever bitch.'

'She is. And no one has actually reported the stamps stolen, right?'

'Right,' Branson said pensively. 'But what about the insurance companies? The ones who paid out on the compensation and the life insurance? Couldn't they have a claim on the stamps, as they were bought with their money?'

'Same problem – chain of title. Without Hegarty testifying, how are they going to prove it?'

The two detectives sat in silence for some moments. Glenn drank some more coffee, then he said, 'I heard a rumour from Steve Mackie that Pewe's applying for a transfer.'

Grace smiled. 'He is. Back to the Met. Good luck to them!'

After another pause, Glenn said, 'So, this woman, where do you think she is now?'

'You know what I think? I think she's probably lying on a tropical beach somewhere, downing a margarita and grinning her head off.'

She was.

126

NOVEMBER 2007

The margarita was one of the best she had ever drunk. It tasted sharp and strong, the barman had added just the right amount of Cointreau and had salted the rim to perfection. After a week in this hotel, he had got the hang of the way she liked it.

She loved the view from here, lying on the thick, soft mattress on the lounger on the white sand beach, staring out across the bay. And she loved this time of day – late afternoon, when the heat was less fierce and she didn't need the shade of her parasol. She put her book down for a moment, took another sip and watched the yellow paragliding boat as it powered away from the wooden jetty, across the flat water, heading out into the bay, the orange and red parachute rising into the clear sky.

She might have another swim in a few minutes. She pondered whether to go in the sea or in the hotel's vast infinity pool, which was a little cooler and more refreshing. Such tough decisions!

She thought constantly about her mother, and about Ronnie and Ricky. Despite all her anger about Ricky, and her shock about Ronnie, she couldn't help feeling just a tiny bit sorry for each of them, in different ways.

But not that sorry.

'Are you enjoying that book?' the woman on the lounger next to her asked suddenly.

Abby had noticed her earlier, asleep, with a copy of a novel she had read recently, *Restless*, lying on top of *The Hitchhiker's Guide to the Galaxy* on the small white table beside her.

'I am,' she said. 'Yes. But most of all, I'm a big Douglas Adams fan. I think I've read everything he wrote.'

'Me too!'

He was the author of one of Abby's favourite quotations, which she had come across again only recently:

> I seldom end up where I wanted to go, but almost always end up where I need to be.

Which was pretty much how she felt at this moment.

She took another sip of her drink. 'They make the world's best margaritas here,' she said.

'Maybe I should try one. I only arrived today, so I haven't sussed out what's what yet.'

'It's great. It's paradise!'

'Seems it.'

Abby smiled. 'I'm Sarah,' she said.

'Nice to meet you. I'm Sandy.'

ACKNOWLEDGEMENTS

Although the Roy Grace novels are fiction, the backgrounds in all the areas of law enforcement in which my characters exist and function are real. For help with the writing of this novel I am indebted as ever to the Sussex Police Force, and also to the NYPD and the New York City Office of the District Attorney, and to the Victoria Police, Australia.

Special thanks to the Chief Constable of Sussex Police, Martin Richards, for his kind sanction, and to Detective Chief Superintendents Kevin Moore and Graham Bartlett for generously opening so many doors for me. And a very singular thank you to former Detective Chief Superintendent Dave Gaylor, who has helped me in more ways than I can ever repay.

To single out a few other names in particular in Sussex Police who have really helped make a difference to this book (and please forgive any omissions), thank you to Chief Superintendent Peter Coll; Brian Cook, Scientific Support Branch Manager; Senior Support Officer Tony Case of the HQ Criminal Investigation Department; DCI Ian Pollard; DI William Warner; DS Patrick Sweeney; Inspector Stephen Curry; DI Jason Tingley, Ops/Intel HQ CID; Inspector Andrew Kundert; Sgt Phil Taylor, Head of the High Tech Crime Unit; Computer Crime Analyst Ray Packham of the High Tech Crime Unit; PC Paul Grzegorzek of the LST; PC James Bowes; PC Dave Curtis; Inspector Phil Clarke; Sgt Mel Doyle; PC Tony Omotoso; PC Ian Upperton; PC Andrew King; Sgt Malcolm (Choppy) Wauchope; PC Darren Balcombe; Sgt Sean McDonald; PC Danny Swietlik; PC Steve Cheesman; Ron King, Forces Controller; and Sue Heard, Press and PR Officer.

Thank you also to forensic archaeologist Lucy Sibun. And to Abigail Bradley of Cellmark Forensics; Essex Coroner Dr Peter Dean; consultant pathologist Dr Nigel Kirkham; Dr Andrew Davey; Mr Andrew Yelland, MB BS, FRCSEd, MD, FRCS; Dr Jonathan Pash; Nigel Hodge; Steve Cowling; and Christopher Gebbie. And I owe an extremely special and massive thanks to the terrific team at the Brighton and Hove Mortuary, Elsie Sweetman, Victor Sindon and Sean Didcott.

In New York a huge debt to Detective Investigator Dennis Bootle of the Rackets Bureau, Office of the District Attorney; and Detective Investigator Patrick Lanigan, Special Investigations Unit, Office of the District Attorney. In Australia a very huge thank you also to DI Lucio Rovis, Victoria Police Homicide Unit; Detective Senior Sergeant George Vickers and DS Troy Burg, Carlton Crime Investigation Unit; Detective Senior Constable Damian Jackson; Sgt Ed Pollard, Victoria Police State Coroner's Assistants Unit; Andrea Petrie of *The Age* newspaper; and my Australian linguist, Janet Vickers!

Thanks to Gordon Camping for his invaluable master classes in stamps; to Rob Kempson; to Colin Witham of HSBC; to Peter Bailey for his encyclopaedic knowledge of Brighton modern and past; to Peter Wingate-Saul, Oli Rigg, and to Phil White of the East Sussex Fire Brigade, and Dave Storey of the Nottingham Fire and Rescue Service; to Robert Frankis, who caught me out on cars again – and to Chris Webb for keeping my Mac alive despite all the abuse I give it!

Very big thanks to Anna-Lisa Lindeblad, who has been my tireless and wonderful 'unofficial' editor and commentator throughout the Roy Grace series, and to Sue Ansell, whose sharp eye for detail has saved me many an embarrassment.

Professionally I have a total dream team: the wonderful Carole Blake representing me, together with Oli Munson, and my awesome publicist, Amelia Rowland of Midas PR; and there is simply not enough space to say a proper thank you to everyone at Macmillan. Suffice it to say that it is an absolute joy to be published by them, and I totally lucked into the jackpot in having Stef Bierwerth as my editor. A huge thank you also to all of my foreign publishers. Danke! Merci! Grazie! болБшое спасиб! Gracias! Dank u! Tack! Obrigado!

As ever, Helen has been a rock, keeping me nourished with saintly patience and constant wisdom.

And lastly I have to say farewells to my deeply loved canine friends Sooty and Bertie, who have both sadly departed to the Big Boneyard in the sky, and a welcome to Oscar, who has now joined Phoebe under my desk, waiting to chew to shreds any loose pages of manuscript that should fall to the floor . . .

Peter James
Sussex, England
scary@pavilion.co.uk
www.peterjames.com

DEAD TOMORROW

Read on for an exclusive extract from the Detective Superintendent Roy Grace novel, published by Macmillan.

1

Susan hated the motorbike. She used to tell Nat bikes were lethal, that he was going to kill himself on it. That riding a motorcycle was the most dangerous thing in the world. Over and over again. Nat liked to wind her up by telling her that actually, statistically, she was wrong. That in fact the most dangerous thing you could do was go into your kitchen. It was the place where you were most likely to die.

He saw it for himself, every day of his working life as a hospital registrar. Sure, there were some bad accidents on motorbikes, but nothing in volume compared to what happened in kitchens.

People regularly electrocuted themselves sticking forks into toasters. Or died from broken necks falling off kitchen chairs. Or choked, or got food poisoning. He liked, in particular, to tell her the story of one victim who had been brought into A&E at the Royal Sussex County Hospital, where he worked – or rather, *overworked* – who had leaned into her dishwasher to unblock it, and got stabbed through the eye by a boning knife.

Bikes weren't dangerous, not even ones like his monster red Honda Fireblade (which could hit sixty miles per hour in three seconds), he liked to tell her; it was other road users that were the problem. You just had to watch out for them, that was all. And hey, his Fireblade left a damned sight smaller carbon footprint than her clapped-out Audi TT.

But she always ignored that.

The same way she ignored his moans about always having to spend Christmas Day – just five weeks away – with the *outlaws*, as he liked to call her parents. His late mother was fond of telling him that you could choose your friends but not your relatives. So damned true.

He had read somewhere that when a man marries a woman, he hopes she will stay the same forever, but when a woman marries a man, her agenda is to change him.

Well, Susan was doing that OK, using the most devastating weapon in a woman's arsenal: she was six months pregnant. And, sure, of course he was proud as hell. And ruefully aware that shortly he was going to have to get real. The Fireblade was going to have to go and be replaced by something practical. Some kind of estate car or people carrier. And, to satisfy Susan's social and environmental conscience, a sodding diesel-electrical hybrid, for God's sake!

And how much fun was that going to be?

Yawning, having arrived home at 4 a.m. and grabbed somewhere south of four hours' sleep, he sat at the kitchen table of their small cottage at Rodmell, a few miles from Brighton, staring at the news of a suicide bombing in Afghanistan on the *Good Morning* show. It was 8.11, according to the screen, and 8.09 according to his watch. And it was the dead of night according to his mental alertness. He spooned some Shreddies and diced banana into his mouth, swilled the mix down with some reconstituted orange juice and black coffee, then hurried back upstairs. He kissed Susan and patted the Bump goodbye.

'Drive carefully,' she said.

What do you think I'm going to do, drive dangerously? he thought but did not say. Instead he said, 'I love you.'

'Love you, too. Call me.'

Nat kissed her again, then went downstairs, tugged on his helmet and his leather gloves, and stepped outside into the frosty morning. Dawn was only just breaking as he wheeled the red bike out of the garage, then swung the door shut with a loud clang. Although there was a ground frost, it had not rained for several days, so there was no danger of black ice on the roads.

He looked up at the curtained window, then pressed the starter button of his beloved motorbike for the last time in his life.

2

Dr Ross Hunter was one of the few constants in Lynn Beckett's life, she thought, as she pressed his surgery bell on the panel in the porch. In fact, if she was honest with herself, she'd be hard pushed to name any other constants at all. Apart from *failure*. That was definitely a constant. She was good at failure, always had been. In fact, she was brilliant at it. She could fail for England.

Her life, in a nutshell, had been a 38-year-long trail of disasters, starting with small stuff like getting the end of her index finger chopped off by a car door when she was seven, and steadily getting bigger as life took on more gravitas. She had failed her parents as a child, failed her husband as a wife, and was now very comprehensively failing her teenage daughter as a single-parent mother.

The doctor's surgery was in a large Edwardian villa, in a quiet Hove street that had in former times been entirely residential. But now many of the grand terraced houses had long been demolished and replaced with blocks of flats. Most of those that remained, like this one, housed offices or medical practices.

She stepped into the familiar hallway, which smelled of furniture polish tinged with a faint whiff of antiseptic, saw Dr Hunter's secretary at her desk at the far end, occupied on a phone call, and slipped into the waiting room.

Nothing had changed in this large but dingy room in the fifteen or so years she had been coming here. The same water stain, vaguely in the shape of Australia, on the stuccoed ceiling, the same peeling wallpaper, the same potted rubber plant in front of the fireplace, the familiar musty smell, and the same mismatched armchairs and sofas that looked as if they had been bought, back in the annals of time, in a job lot from a house-clearance auctioneer. Even the magazines on the circular oak table in the centre, other than a current issue of *Sussex Life*, looked as if they had not been changed in years.

She glanced at an elderly couple, the man looking frail, sunk deep into an armchair with busted springs, holding a stick firmly jammed into the carpet as if trying to prevent himself from disappearing into the chair completely, and at an impatient-looking man in his thirties, in a blue Crombie coat with a velvet collar, preoccupied with his BlackBerry. There were various pamphlets on the table, one offering advice on how to give up smoking, but at this moment in time, with the state of her nerves, she could have done with advice on how to smoke *more*.

There was a fresh copy of *The Times* lying there, but she wasn't in any mood to concentrate on reading, she decided. She'd barely slept a wink since getting the phone call from Dr Hunter's secretary late yesterday afternoon, asking her to come in, first thing in the morning, on her own. And she was feeling shaky from her blood-sugar levels being too low. She had taken her medication but then had barely swallowed a mouthful of breakfast.

After perching herself on the edge of a hard, upright carver, with a tight knot of anxiety in her stomach, she rummaged in her bag and popped a couple of glucose tablets into her mouth. Why did Dr Hunter want to see her? On the occasions when she'd had previous scares, like the lump she'd found on her breast, and the time that she had become terrified that Caitlin's erratic behaviour might be a symptom of a brain tumour, Ross Hunter had simply rung her himself and given her the good news that the biopsy or the scan or the blood tests or whatever were fine, there was nothing to worry about.

She crossed her legs, then uncrossed them. Dressed smartly, she was wearing her best coat – black mid-length wool and cashmere, a January sale bargain earlier this year – a dark blue knitted top, black trousers and black suede boots. Although she would never admit it to herself, she always tried to make herself look good when she came to see the doctor. Not exactly dressed to kill, she had long ago lost the art – and the confidence – to do that, but dressed nicely, at least. Together with a good half of Dr Hunter's women patients, she had long secretly fancied him. Not that she would have ever dared attempt to make that known to him.

Since her break-up with Mal, her esteem had been on the floor. At thirty-eight she was still an attractive woman and would be a lot more attractive, several of her friends and her late sister and her brother had all told her, if she put back some of the weight she had lost. She was haggard, she knew, she could see for herself just looking in the mirror. Haggard from worrying about everything, but most of all from worrying about Caitlin.

That was nothing new. She had long ago lost count of the times she had sat anxiously in the Accident and Emergency department at the Royal Sussex County Hospital, while medics treated Caitlin. One time, at thirteen, Caitlin had her stomach pumped, having stolen a bottle of vodka from the drinks cabinet. Another time, at fourteen, she fell off a roof, stoned on hash. Then there was the horrific night she came into Lynn's bedroom at two in the morning, glassy-eyed, sweating, and so cold her teeth were chattering, announcing she had downed an Ectasy tablet given to her by some low-life in Brighton and that her head hurt.

A few months after that she'd become pregnant. Then a couple of months after the abortion, Caitlin had actually carried out one of her many threats to commit suicide after her mum had banned her from seeing her boyfriend, by downing an entire packet of paracetamol. On each occasion Dr Hunter had come to the hospital and stayed with Caitlin until he knew she was out of danger. He didn't have to do that, but that was the kind of man he was.

And now the door was opening, and he was coming in. A tall, elegant figure in a pin-striped suit, with fine posture, he had a handsome face, framed with wavy salt-and-pepper hair, and gentle, caring eyes, at this moment partially concealed by half-frame tortoiseshell glasses, giving him more the air of an academic than a medic.

'Lynn!' he said, his strong, brisk voice oddly subdued this morning. 'Come on in.'

Dr Ross Hunter had two different expressions for greeting his patients. His normal, genuinely warm, happy-to-see-you smile, was the only one Lynn had ever seen in all the years that she had been his patient. She had never before encountered his wistful, biting-of-the-lower-lip grimace. The one he kept in the closet and hated to bring out.

The one he had on his face today.

3

It was a good place for a speed trap. Commuters hurrying into Brighton who regularly drove down this stretch of the Lewes Road, just east of Coldean Lane, knew that although it was a forty mile an hour limit they could accelerate safely after the lights and not have to slow down again along the dual carriageway until they reached the speed camera, almost a mile on.

The blue, yellow and silver markings of the BMW estate car, parked in a side road and partially obscured from drivers' view by a bus shelter, came as an unwelcome early-morning surprise to most of them.

PC Tony Omotoso stood on the far side of the car, holding the laser gun, using the roof as a rest, aiming the red dot at the front number plates, which gave the best reading on any vehicle he estimated to be speeding. He clicked the trigger on the plate of a Toyota saloon. The digital readout said 44 mph. The driver had spotted them and already hit the brakes. He allowed a tolerance of ten per cent over the limit, plus two. The Toyota carried on past, its brake lights glowing. Next he sighted on the plates of a white Transit van: 43 mph. Then a black Harley Softail motorbike sped past, going way over the limit, but he wasn't able to get a fix in time.

Standing to his left, ready to jump out with his hands up the moment Tony called out, was his fellow road policing officer, PC Ian Upperton, tall and thin, in his cap and yellow high-visibility jacket. Both men were freezing.

Upperton watched the Harley. He liked them – he liked all bikes, and his ambition was to become a motorcycle officer. But Harleys were cruising bikes. His real passion was for the high-speed road-racer machines, like BMWs, Suzuki Hayabusas, Honda Fireblades. Bikes where you had to lean into bends in order to get round them, not merely turn the handlebars like a steering wheel. A red Ducati was going past now, but the rider had spotted them and slowed almost to a crawl.

But the clapped-out-looking green Fiesta coming up in the outside lane clearly had not.

'The Fiesta!' Omotoso called out. 'Fifty-two!'

PC Upperton stepped out and signalled the car over. But whether blindly or wilfully, the car shot past.

'OK, let's go. Whiskey, Four-Three-Two, Charlie Papa November.'

He jumped behind the wheel.

'Fuckers!'

'Yeah, cunts!'

'Why don't you go chasing real criminals, right?'

'Yeah, 'stead of fuckin' persecuting motorists.'

Tony Omotoso turned his head and saw two youths slouching past, one in a hoodie, the other in a shell suit with a baseball cap the wrong way round.

Because three thousand five hundred people die on the roads of England every year, against five hundred a year who are murdered, that's why, he wanted to say to them. *Because me and Tony scrape dead and broken bodies off the roads every damned day of the week, because of jerks like this asshole in the Fiesta.*

But he didn't have time. His colleague already had the blue roof spinners flashing and the siren whup-whooping. He tossed the expensive laser gun onto the back seat, climbed in the front, slammed the door, and began tugging his seat belt on, as Upperton gunned the car out into a gap in the traffic and floored the accelerator.

And now the adrenalin was kicking in as he felt the thrust of acceleration in the pit of his stomach, and his spine pressed against the rear of the seat. Oh yes, this was one of the highs of the job.

And the Automatic Numberplate Recognition video screen, mounted on the dash, was beeping at them, and showing the Fiesta's index, Whiskey, Four-Three-Two, Charlie Papa November had no tax, no insurance and was a disqualified driver.

Upperton pulled over into the outside lane, gaining fast on the Fiesta.

Then a radio call came through. '*Delta Foxtrot Four-Two.*'

Omotoso answered. 'Delta Foxtrot Four-Two yes, yes?'

The controller said, 'We have a reported serious collision. Motorcycle and car at the intersection of Coldean Lane and Ditchling Road. Can you attend?'

Shit, he thought, not wanting to let the Fiesta go. 'Yes, yes, on our way. Put out an alert for Brighton patrols. Ford Fiesta, index Whiskey, Four-Three-Two, Charlie Papa November, colour green, travelling at speed, south on Lewes Road, approaching giratory system. Suspected disqualified driver.'

Then he turned to his colleague. But Upperton, who had heard the exchange, was already braking hard, his right-turn indicator on. He swept the car round in a sharp U-turn and floored the accelerator.